Family of Women

Also by Annie Murray

Birmingham Rose

Birmingham Friends

Birmingham Blitz

Orphan on Angel Street

Poppy Day

The Narrowboat Girl

Chocolate Girls

Water Gypsies

Miss Purdy's Class

ANNIE MURRAY
Family of Women

MACMILLAN

First published 2006 by Pan Books
an imprint of Pan Macmillan Ltd
Pan Macmillan, 20 New Wharf Road, London N1 9RR
Basingstoke and Oxford
Associated companies throughout the world
www.panmacmillan.com

ISBN-13: 978-1-4050-4798-2
ISBN-10: 1-4050-4798-4

1 3 5 7 9 8 6 4 2

A CIP catalogue record for this book is available from
the British Library.

Typeset by Set Systems Ltd, Saffron Walden, Essex
Printed and bound in Great Britain by
Mackays of Chatham plc, Chatham, Kent

There are always people who give generous help in the preparation for a book. On this occasion I would like to thank the following: Lewis Jones for his time, his wide-ranging knowledge, for the tour of the Kingstanding of his childhood – and for lunch! To members of the British Polio Fellowship who pointed me in the right direction, and especially to Sisters Maria Goretti Fitzgerald and Anna O'Connor of the Sisters of Charity of St Paul the Apostle in Selly Park, Birmingham, for help and hospitality.

Part One

1926–36

Chapter One

Violet was eleven when the first of the babies came.

A scrawny, cringing stranger appeared at their door and they had to peer out past Mom to see, she was such a big woman. She and her sister Rosina, who was eight, stood by the range, listening to the whispers.

'My sister ... Might be able to manage when she's better ... A few shillings, that's all we've got ... They sent me to you ...'

On the freezing air through the door came the smoke and stink of the metal-bashing factories and the sweet sawdust from the timber yard.

Violet's mother, Bessie, was a strapping matron of thirty-four. She stood with her hands on her hips in her white, starched apron, her face hard as granite, lording it over this poor woman. Bessie was gaffer of the yard here, and she knew it. Everyone looked to Bessie Wiles, but by God you didn't want to cross her. She'd take her time to answer if she wanted.

'I might be able to,' she said at last.

After a few questions – the sick mother of the child lived round in Summer Lane – she said, 'All right. Give it 'ere,' and held out her arms.

The visitor said 'Thank you' twice over in a grovelling voice and Violet knew her mother had never seen the woman before and wondered why she had come here.

It was only when Mom turned that they saw the baby, a pale, odd-looking thing. Its head seemed too big, and was topped with a fuzz of gingery hair.

Rosina ran straight up and peered at it. 'A babby! Whose is it?'

Violet held back, wary of Bessie's beefy, slapping hands and bullying tongue, and the cat o'nine tails she kept fixed to her belt. Violet was a frail girl, coltishly thin, with pale, almost luminous skin, straggly blonde hair and sad, blue eyes.

She saw a new glow in her mother's eyes.

'It's a little wench. Miserable scrap she is – look at the size of her! The mom's been taken bad so we're looking after her. There're worse ways of earning a few bob. Don't go poking her, Rosina, you'll wake her.'

Marigold came downstairs then and joined in staring at the red-haired baby. Charlie was out playing with his pals. Marigold and Charlie were twins, two years older than Violet, but Marigold wasn't quite 'all there', was what Mom said. 'She'll never amount to much.' She said that too, as if Marigold was a stone with no feeling. Violet saw some flicker of hungry emotion in Marigold's dark eyes and she clung on at her mother's side. Marigold couldn't seem to get enough of the baby.

'You going to give 'er your titty, Mom?'

Marigold had been old enough to see her mother feed Rosina, and Mrs Cameron next door was seldom without a child hanging off her little pimple breasts.

Bessie gave a harsh laugh, her big body quivering. 'Ooh no, I'm past all that, bab, more's the pity!' Violet had once heard her saying to Mrs Cameron and Mrs Davis out in the yard that after Rosina she'd had it 'all taken away'. She said it in a low, mournful voice, with a big sigh from the depths of her. Mrs Davis said that

4

she wished *she* could bleeding well have it all taken away too, that all these babbies would be the death of her, but Bessie looked at her with tears in her eyes. It was the only time Violet had seen Mom overcome like that.

'Ooh no, Clara – my Jack – God rest him – always liked me with a big belly on me and a babby in my arms. Nothing like it.'

'You daint lose any of yours though, Bess,' Mrs Davis said. 'Bring 'em into the world and watch 'em fade away – that's when it does for you.'

With a grunt, Bessie knelt down on the rag rug on the rough brick floor, barking out orders as usual. 'Pass my shawl over, Marigold, and we'll lay her on it for a bit, have a look over her. Violet – get the kettle on.'

Violet did as she was commanded, then looked grimly down at the child. She didn't want the puny thing there. There was barely enough to go round as it was.

'Mom. How long's it got to stay? *Mom?*'

But Bessie wasn't listening.

Marigold knelt over the baby. Her black hair was chopped into a bob, chin-length, parted severely down the right side and yanked back from her face with a couple of kirby-grips. She stared and stared.

Rosina, baby of the family herself, stood twiddling her long plaits, full of questions and jack-in-the-box energy. No one could ever miss the fact that Rosina was there. Violet stayed back, feeling outside it all, seeing her mother's thick, stockinged calves and the worn heels of her shoes as she knelt over the child.

'Mom?'

'Oh, shurrup, Violet – stop keeping on!' Bessie was peeling back the rags in which the baby was wrapped.

'Don't see why we have to have it,' Violet said sulkily. 'It's ugly.'

'Not half as ugly as you were. And it's a girl, not an it.'

'What's her name?' Rosina asked.

'The woman never said.' Bessie knelt back on her haunches. 'We'll have to think of summat. What about Daisy? Marigold – there's a tanner in the jug up there – run over to Mrs Bigley's and ask her for a tin of Carnation. I'll have to feed her, soon as she wakes.'

Marigold followed her orders, as usual.

Bessie scooped the child off the floor and stood looking at her, deaf to anyone else. She started humming a little tune and carried her through to the back, with Rosina following as if the baby was a magnet. Rosy wasn't frightened of Mom.

Violet stood scowling in the front room, in her old dress that was too short, socks sagging down round her ankles. She stuck her thumb in her mouth. As usual, she felt invisible.

Chapter Two

Daisy was the first in a long line.

There was nothing official about it, not then. In the seething, over-populated slum houses of north Birmingham there was many a mother at the end of her tether, worn down by having child after child. Bessie made her name in the district.

'Take the babby round to Bessie Wiles – number two, back of sixteen in Spring Street. She'll have it off you for a bit. And her house is clean as a pin.'

She was already a tough heroine of survival in their eyes. There was Bessie, widowed at twenty-six with four to bring up, worked like a Trojan, up cleaning pubs before dawn, taking in washing, carding buttons and pins for the factories. All the energy in the world, while weaker vessels fell along the way. And everyone came to her for advice. She had the neighbourhood just where she wanted them – respectful, fearful and under her thumb.

Bessie took in the babies of mothers who died birthing them, or were taken with infections or plain worn out. She kept them until they went back to their families, or handed them over to the orphanage and was paid for her trouble.

That wasn't the first time they had had other children living in the house. Bessie had once taken in some of Mrs Davis's children. Mrs Davis, a weak, cringing woman, lived two doors away then, and life was one long struggle. They were 'three-up' houses, with two tiny bedrooms on the second floor and cockroach-infested attics, and Mrs Davis had eleven children, nine of them boys, a wastrel of a husband and her father-in-law lodged with them as well. For two years, off and on, during the Great War, Bessie had taken the two girls in every night and they slept top to toe with Violet and Rosina.

'You're golden, Bessie,' Mrs Davis frequently said, with whining gratitude. 'I don't know what I'd do without you, that I don't.'

'Oh, I know what it's like in a big family, Clara,' Bessie would say magnanimously. 'What are neighbours for, bab, if not to help?'

Violet was four when the Davis children started sleeping in her bed. They were wriggly, vexing girls, prone to itchy suppurating rashes. Violet could remember the feel of little Ethel Davis's freezing cold feet if she stretched out, and Florrie Davis wet the bed. The room always stank of wee and every morning when they woke the mattress was freezing cold and wet. She was overjoyed when the Davises did a moonlight flit to dodge the landlord and she could sleep in a dry bed again without Ethel's scratchy toenails.

Now it seemed that a whole parade of babies couldn't do without Bessie either. As fast as one was sent off to a new home a new one arrived, and at times there were as many as three at once. Bessie rose to the occasion magnificently. She got Uncle Clarence, her brother who lived with them, to build cradles out of apple boxes. She knitted coloured squares for blankets. There were always kettles of water on for cleaning out babies' bottles and Bessie was seldom without a child in her arms. All life seemed to revolve round her.

8

Marigold and Charlie were thirteen then, and Bessie made a decision. One evening as they sat over tea in the sputtering gaslight, with a baby asleep in the corner, she said, 'I've been thinking about our Marigold, Clarence. There ain't no point in her stopping on at school – 'er's never going to be one for books and learning, not the way she is. You can stop at home and give me a hand from now on, Mari.'

Marigold looked dreamily up from her plate of liver and onions, barely seeming to realize what was being said. There was a thick streak of gravy down the front of her blouse. Violet knew that Marigold didn't like school. She could just about read and write but she was slow in every way, couldn't keep up with the running about, and all the teasing from the others.

'I don't know,' Clarence said. He ruffled a hand through his receding hair as he often did when Bessie asked his opinion. He was as thin and weedy as she was big and ebullient. Even in his early thirties he seemed like an old man, sitting there in his shirtsleeves, shoulders hunched. 'We'll have the bloke keep coming round from the Board if you keep her home.'

'Oh, I'll soon see to him,' Bessie said, drawing in a fierce breath that expanded her enormous bosom even further under her black frock. 'You'd like to help with the babbies, Marigold, wouldn't you?'

'Can I stop at home an' all?' Rosina asked.

'Don't talk *stupid*,' Charlie sneered at her.

Rosy stuck her tongue out at him when Mom wasn't looking and Charlie gave her one of his stodgy looks. He was like an old man as well, Violet thought.

Clarence wiped his chin on the back of his hand. 'Whatever you think's best, Bess.' That was what he alway said in the end.

So at thirteen, Marigold stopped going to school and stayed at home and learned about looking after babies. She never said if she cared either way. In any case, Violet never heard anyone ask her.

Chapter Three

1927

'Cat's got the measles, the measles, the measles...'
Rosina was skipping ahead, dark plaits switching up and
down.

'Cat's got the measles, the measles got the cat! Oi – '
She swivelled round, landing on both feet. 'Vi – d'you
think Mom'd give us a tanner to go up the Picture
House?'

'You'll be lucky!'

Violet stared at her in amazement. Trust Rosy! She'd
never dare ask Mom for money, straight out.

'You ask – bet she won't.'

It was the end of the summer term and school was
out. Eight weeks of freedom stretching ahead, and the
day was hot as they trotted along in the blue shadow of
the houses with the heady feeling of being set free from
school routine into the wide, shapeless time of the holi-
days. Long days ahead to play out at hopscotch and tip-
cat and hide-and-seek!

Violet was excited, because you couldn't not be
excited at the end of term with all of them pouring out
of the school gates on to the street, everyone running,
shouting, cheering and tearing off home or to the park.
But there was also a sad feeling because she liked her
teacher Miss Green, who was about to leave the school.
Miss Green was plump and comforting, with curly
brown hair, and she knew Miss Green liked her and had

11

taken notice of her the way no one else had ever done, so she'd done her very best for her.

'You're my star pupil in arithmetic,' Miss Green had said a few days ago, smiling through her spectacles. 'You're working very well, Violet.'

These were words of very high praise from a teacher. Miss Green was very strict but she was fair-minded, and any words of praise coming Violet's way were rare indeed. She carried them inside her as if they were fragile birds' eggs. Clutched in her hand was the envelope containing her school report. Had Miss Green written something nice in there as well? If only she could get it out and read it, but she didn't dare – what would Mom say? She bubbled inside in anticipation.

Rosina adored the pictures. She'd sit through anything, laughing at Buster Keaton and Laurel and Hardy until she was nearly sick, riding in her seat through Westerns until people behind snapped at her to sit still, and most of all enjoying the ones with the actresses, with their big soulful eyes full of emotion and their lovely clothes like none they'd ever seen in real life. Rosina laughed, cried, trembled with them. She lived every second of it. She especially loved Lillian Gish and Mary Pickford.

They ran up the entry. Mrs Cameron was mangling clothes in the yard. The door was open as usual and they ran straight in. Charlie had beaten them home and was filling his face with a crust of bread and lard. Bessie stood, perspiring in the heat and rocking the latest orphaned infant in her arms, and the room was full of his wailing.

'Mom, Mom – can we go to the flicks?' Rosina demanded.

'I've got my report, Mom!' Violet thrust the envelope

towards her mother. She knew it was the wrong thing to do but she couldn't help herself.

'Can't you see this babby's running me ragged!' Bessie roared. 'Can't you see, you stupid wench. What's that flaming thing?' She looked at the brown envelope as if it was dirt. 'I don't want that – stick it on the mantel.'

Heart sinking, Violet did as she was told. Stupid – yes, to think Mom might want to know. Rosina carelessly put her report up there as well, then persisted with what she wanted.

'Mom, Mom – *can* we? It'll get us out from under your feet.' Rosina never gave up. If she couldn't get her way one way round she could think of half a dozen other avenues to try.

'You'd wear out rock, the way you keep on,' Bessie said crossly over the baby's screams. But she dug under her apron pocket, just near where she kept the leather cat o' nine tails which could switch stingingly across hands or legs. Instead she brought out a shilling. 'Go on then, all of you – clear off. I don't know what Clarence'll say though.'

Bessie always said this, even though Clarence never said anything of much note and she was firmly in charge and always had been.

'Come on, Vi!' Rosina cried.

Charlie and Marigold came as well and they sat in their threepenny seats through something all about the Alps, and then a Buster Keaton picture called *The Navigator*. Violet laughed along with Rosina and the others, but all the time in the back of her mind there was that envelope on the mantelpiece where things were written about her and she wanted to know what. Could she, Violet Wiles, be good at something – anything?

Had Miss Green seen something in her that no one else had?

That evening Bessie was snapping at them all, trying to feed the wretched baby and get the tea cooked. She stood by the stove in her huge flowery apron and the house stank of boiling fish. She'd obviously forgotten completely about the reports. Violet went over to the mantel and stared at them, hoping her mom would notice.

'Get to the table,' Bessie ordered.

'There's our reports – from school,' Violet said, perched on her rickety stool. 'You gunna read them?'

Bessie's face darkened. She gave a big, impatient sigh.

'Best get it over with, then.'

Violet scrambled eagerly to get them, heart thudding as her mother tore open Charlie's and looked at it. Bessie ran her eyes swiftly down the rows of brief comments from his teachers.

'Ah well, son.' She looked across at him. 'Not long now and you'll be out of there.'

Charlie and Marigold would be fourteen in October and then he'd be out to work. For Bessie it couldn't come soon enough. She had a shuddering dislike of schools and everything about them.

She picked up Violet's report and ripped it open so carelessly that she tore the paper inside. Violet sat, not eating, forgetting to breathe. What did it say?

Bessie eyed it in the same offhand manner as before, then moved on to Rosina's. Soon she dropped all the papers on the floor by her chair.

'Well, that's that. Get on with your tea. It'll be cold else.'

Violet shrank inside. She didn't want to eat smelly boiled fish. She felt sick and crushed. Course, Mom never took any notice of anything to do with school. She just thought this time she might have done well and Mom might say something. Her eyes filled with tears.

'What's up with you?' Charlie said.

'Nothing,' she whispered, and tried to swallow down the fish.

When they'd finished eating, Bessie got up and brewed a pot of tea. She plonked the bottle of sterilized milk on the table.

Violet still couldn't contain herself. She could sneak a look at the reports herself, of course, but if there was something special from Miss Green in there, she wanted to hear it, like an announcement. Wanted the others to hear it.

'Uncle Clarence – ' she whispered. 'Will you read my report?'

Clarence was sitting back, comfortable after his tea, and struggling to light his pipe.

'All right – pass 'em over,' he said indifferently. Clarence wasn't interested in anything that didn't centre on himself. Apart from two years in France in the Great War, he'd been looked after by Bessie all his life, and that suited him very well.

Violet's was on top. Clarence read, in his toneless voice, the remarks about her reading and sewing. They were ordinary enough. Violet's pulse quickened. Now he was coming to Miss Green.

' "Violet is very strong in arithmetic and geometry," ' he read. Violet sat drinking in every word. ' "It would be a waste if she did not go on to greater things." '

The sweet honey words had not had a chance to seep into her when her mother gave a great mocking guffaw.

'Who the hell wrote that load of flannel?' She continued to laugh, shaking her head, her belly quivering.

'What "greater things" is she on about, d'you think? Tea at Buckingham Palace? God, they live in another world, these people. What bloody good does she think *geometry* – ' she put on a mock-teacher voice, 'is going to be when there's a babby in her belly and no food in the pantry, eh?'

She sat shaking her head. Violet didn't hear any more of her report. She tried to hold on to Miss Green's words. *Very strong! Greater things!* But every last spark of her brief glow of pride was snuffed out by her mother's scorn.

Chapter Four

1929

Two years later the gates of school closed behind Violet for the last time.

Miss Green had long left, with her words of encouragement. Violet tried to forget her excitement over that one school report. That little opening, those thin threads of light from a dream world not her own, was long in the past now. When she received her character from school, for arithmetic it just said, 'Good.' So, good enough, but nothing special. And now it was time to start looking for work, on a rainy April morning, two days after her fourteenth birthday.

'Marigold – look after the babbies.'

Bessie was putting her hat and coat on. Violet stared at her, a terrible realization beginning to dawn.

'Where're you going, Mom?' she asked, dreading the answer.

'You needn't think I'm letting *you* loose looking for a job by yourself,' Bessie said, doing up her buttons. 'You'll say yes to anything for slave wages – or you'll end up in service, skivvying for a pittance. I'm not having that. Come on – set your hat straight, wench. No good going out like a bag of muck tied up in the middle.'

There was no point in arguing. They stepped out into the Aston drizzle. Bessie cut a forbidding, matriarchal figure, striding out of the yard in her black winter coat which only just fastened round her. She always wore her hair, raven black like Marigold's, in two plaits coiled round her head, and over these she pulled a black hat with a narrow brim which curved upwards.

'Morning, Mrs Wiles!'

'Awright Mrs Wiles – off up the shops?'

'No – I'm going to find our Violet a job.'

These greetings were repeated several times, all with deference, a few with cringing timidity. Bessie, as the gaffer of the yard, was often consulted about quarrels which broke out with so many people living cheek by jowl under the stresses of poverty; she held the 'didlum' money, the savings people put in week after week to save for Christmas or to have some money put aside for an emergency, like paying the doctor. She was respected, for her dominant toughness as much as her immense capacity for taking things on.

Walking beside her, Violet felt any vigour of her own draining away. Her mother had this effect on her. Bessie's energy seemed to flatten her, like a steamroller. Bessie lived in constant terror of the poverty of her childhood and fought it even when there was no need. She never went out without a chunk of bread pushed into her pocket.

'You never know when lightning's going to strike,' she always said.

Violet trailed along after her. Her coat sleeves were too short and one of the blue buttons was missing. Although she had tied her hair back and tried to look neat and tidy, she felt scruffy and awkward and childish. All she wanted was a decent little job she could just slip into, with a few friendly faces around her. If only Mom could let her go out and do it for herself!

They walked a way along Summer Lane. It was a

18

notorious area, famous for its poverty and gangs of violent lads. Violet looked round. She was never out at night to see what went on. Everything looked normal enough now. She could just hear sawing from one of the mills round the back. The streets were busy with people, women with small children out on their way to the shops, drays from the brewery and the Co-op, one of the horses lifting its tail to deposit dollops of manure along the street. It had barely finished when a tiny lad, no more than four years old, was in the road scooping it into a pail. Its sale to anyone who wanted fertilizer brought in handy extra pennies. Another cart passed loaded with blocks of salt, its driver yelling his way along the street.

'Right.' Bessie paused suddenly, and from the house they were standing beside a cloud of dust and dirt was flicked all over them by a broom. ''Ere!' she shouted, brushing down her coat. 'Watch where you're throwing yer muck and mess!'

'Well how was I to know you was standing out there?' came a voice from inside. 'I'm not a bleedin' mind-reader you know. Why don't yer just bugger off and stand somewhere else if you've nowt to do?'

Bessie stalked away huffily. She was out of her own little orbit and people weren't showing her the same respect.

'Down here.' Bessie led her along several streets, all tightly packed with yards of houses leading off entries and front houses with their doors flung open to let some air in and, squeezed between them all, factories and workshops. At the end of one street they came to a bigger works. 'Steel Castings', it said across the front.

Without a word to Violet, Bessie went to the door and knocked. After a wait, a swarthy man with a moustache came to the door. Violet felt herself shrink inside. She didn't like the look of the place or the man's grim expression.

'What d'you want?' he demanded.

'I want a position for my daughter. You got any vacancies?'

Violet was very embarrassed by the aggressive tone in her mother's voice, and she had an almost physical sensation of the man running his eyes over her from top to toe. To her great relief he said, 'Skinny little mare like that ain't no good to us.' And shut the door.

'Huh,' Bessie said. 'Well, bugger him.'

Oh Lor', Violet thought, full of dread, what if she ends up shooting her mouth off? Bessie had a terrible temper on her when she got going. *Mind I don't lose my temper*, was one of her warnings.

In the next street, though, they came to a factory called Vicars which made brass hinges, and this time, while Violet prepared herself for being called a skinny mare again or something worse, in fact the middle-aged man who opened up to them looked kinder. He was certainly more polite.

'Er's got a good character,' Bessie said, thrusting the School Leaving Certificate at the man, which said that Violet was reliable and capable of hard work.

The man stroked his face as if he had a beard, although he didn't.

'You're young, but we can use you,' he said. 'You can start tomorrow. Seven and six a week.' He introduced himself as Mr Riddle.

It was only then that it really dawned on Violet that when she went out to work she would be earning her own money. Seven and six! It wasn't a princely sum, not by a long way, but it was still more than she'd ever earned before. She found herself beaming at the man, and Bessie said, 'Yes, she'll take it.'

On the way home, she said, 'You needn't get any grand ideas about your wages – you'll be handing them over to me, for your keep.'

The inside of Vicars was one big workshop, with long, grimy windows all along one side, a loud, dirty, stinking place with all sorts of different machines working at once to turn out brass hinges of a whole variety of sizes. However, Violet rather liked the atmosphere, especially as the first morning she heard someone singing 'Yes, We Have No Bananas!' in a cheery voice over the racket of the machines.

Mr Riddle came to Violet that first morning and handed her an overall.

'Don't worry, love – no one's going to bite you.' He smiled at her anxious expression. 'I'll start you off over here – in at the deep end, sort of thing. You look like a sensible sort of wench and I need someone with a bit of dexterity. Lil who normally works there's been taken poorly.'

He instructed her in the use of a drilling machine, set to drilling screwholes into tiny brass hinges which one of the other girls told her were for jewellery boxes. Though it took concentration because of the size, she found the work quite straightforward and after a few mistakes she settled in well. Over the next few days she learned about all the machines, for milling, drilling and countersinking, the capstan lathes and a big stamping machine for carriage door hinges. And she also got to know the faces behind them, some friendlier than others. She was relieved to find there was a jolly-looking girl called Jo who was not much older than her. And she also identified the source of a lot of the singing – a stocky lad of eighteen with shiny black hair and a laughing, jaunty air about him, called Harry Martin.

Chapter Five

Marigold watched sparks flying from the knifegrinder's stone. Narrowing her eyes, she made the dots of light come into better focus. She didn't know she was a bit short-sighted, so it seemed normal to her that the gas lamps round the Bull Ring, the naphtha flares on the traders' stalls, even the match struck by a man close to her to light his cigarette were a soft-edged outburst of light and colour. Standing amid all the shouting as the traders vied to sell off Saturday night's cheap cuts of meat and fruit and veg, the glowing lights made her feel nice. A smile lit up her normally vacant expression.

'Want one?'

At first, she had no idea that he was talking to her. People hardly ever did talk to Marigold directly, except to give her orders. They talked round her and about her. *Marigold won't want one of them. Marigold doesn't do things like that . . .*

A few days ago she had turned sixteen. Under her old tweed coat she wore a muddy-grey frock from the pawn shop. Rosina, at eleven, wore the prettiest clothes because she had the nerve to keep on and get what she wanted. Violet was far too mousy to talk back to their mother, but at least she could save for bits and pieces with what was left of her wages. Bessie had relented and let her keep two bob a week now. But she wouldn't let Marigold go out to work. Oh no – she was needed at home. So Charlie and Violet were bringing in a wage, but not her. She never had any money to call her own. Marigold didn't complain because no one heard her if she did.

She was a frumpy sight in her old woman's clothes and flat shoes, wide as boats, her black hair chopped chin-length and kirby-gripped. Weighing her down were the carriers of meat and fruit. *Marigold'll go into town for the meat auction – she likes it.* For once Mom was right – she did like it. It was Marigold's one taste of freedom. But she didn't think for a moment that any man would bother talking to her or that her ripe, solid shape and dark brown eyes might be of interest to anyone.

'I said d'you want one?'

Marigold jumped, alarmed by the attention. He'd come close and was holding out a single cigarette. The face that looked out from under his cap was gaunt, tired-looking, but his pale eyes were friendly.

'All right.' She'd never smoked a fag before.

He leaned closer and pushed the end of the cigarette between her lips.

'Here you go.'

She saw that he opened the box of matches with one hand and then leaned down and struck the match on the ground, bringing the little flame carefully up towards her.

'Good job it ain't windy.'

She saw his left arm was missing, or part of it, and the sleeve of his jacket pinned.

Marigold was about to speak, but she breathed in a great chestful of the smoke without meaning to and coughed and retched until her eyes ran.

'First one, is it?' the man asked, grinning, once she'd stopped gagging.

Marigold nodded, gulping. She took another cautious

puff on the cigarette without breathing in. That worked better.

'What happened to your arm?' Her throat was stinging.

'Wipers, that's what "happened,"' he said sourly. She saw the muscles in his cheek clench for a moment. 'No one wants a bloody cripple working for 'em.'

'Oh,' Marigold said.

He seemed amused at her lack of pity. 'Oh? Is that all you can say?'

Marigold shrugged and puffed on the cigarette again. 'Tastes like tar,' she said.

He laughed. 'Does a bit.'

There was a pause. Sounds of the market surrounded them. The air was full of smells of smoke and cooked meat, mild ale and crushed oranges.

'Where're you going then?'

'Get a chicken,' Marigold said.

'Come on then.'

He told her his name was Tommy Kay.

'Tommy Kay,' Marigold said in wonder. 'You look quite old.'

'Old as the hills,' he teased. 'What's your name?'

'Marigold.'

She giggled with him this time, bubbly and excited. 'Violet, my sister, says it's a cow's name.'

He didn't ask her age.

Together they walked through the crowds to where a group were gathered round a chubby, red-cheeked man in a blood-smeared overall. There was a lot of pushing and jostling and shouting wisecracks. Tommy helped her buy a chicken, holding it up with laughing eyes.

'Look at the state of that – looks as if someone's sat on it!'

The chicken did look flat and dejected. Marigold giggled again. Everything seemed funny with Tommy Kay.

Tommy asked her where she lived.

'I live up Lozells. I'll walk up with you.'

Bessie always told Marigold to use a penny for the tram, but Tommy was insistent.

'No need – it ain't far. Give us one of your bags.'

'All right,' Marigold said, suddenly feeling shy and overwhelmed by the thought of walking all the way home with him. What she wanted now was to get on the tram and remember his smile, safely, like a picture from the front of those *Peg's Papers* that Mom liked Violet to read out to her, not have to go on with him. Why did he want to walk with her, daft old Marigold?

As they left the crowded Bull Ring she saw that Tommy walked with a limp. He didn't say much. Once or twice he whistled scraps of a tune she hadn't heard before.

'You're a nice girl,' he said suddenly. They were in a street with houses and factories, noise coming from the pubs.

Marigold giggled.

They crossed over a dark street and there was a factory with an alley down the side. Tommy stopped.

'Come and put your bag down a minute.' He was speaking softly suddenly. 'We'll have a rest.'

Marigold did as she was told. There was a lamp outside the front of the factory, and Tommy took her hand and pulled her into the deep shadow of the alley. Marigold thought it was a funny thing to do.

'You're nice, you are.' His voice had gone queer, low and tight. He wrapped his good arm round her and pressed her close to him.

'We're having a cuddle,' Marigold said. It was strange, but she found she liked it. It gave her an excited feeling in the bottom of her tummy. It was so dark she could barely see him, only feel him pressed against her.

Then Tommy started sucking at her lips and Marigold drew back, disgusted.

'What you doing?'

'Kissing you, silly.'

'That ain't kissing – that's dirty!'

'You never had a kiss before? I'll show you what it's like.'

The kissing was all right when she got used to it and it gave her all sorts of other feelings.

'Unbutton your coat for me,' Tommy breathed. 'And your other bits. This flaming arm – takes me an age to do buttons.'

She obeyed, not sure what was happening. It was frightening but exciting. The night wasn't too cold but she felt funny, undoing everything outside. Her large breasts lolled free under her threadbare old camisole and Tommy gave a groan of pleasure, running his hand over them. He teased up the edge of her vest and Marigold felt him reaching for her nipples.

'Ooh,' she heard herself say. Her body was flooded with feelings such as she'd never had before. She squirmed with pleasure and pressed against Tommy. It had an effect on him that she wasn't expecting. He pulled back and fumbled at his clothes.

'*Christ* . . .' He sounded angry. Marigold was confused.

'What's the matter?'

'I'm a cripple, that's what! Get your bloomers off for me – quick!'

'My *bloomers*?' She was giggling. 'What for?'

'Just get 'em off – you'll soon see . . .'

She never did see anything, in the dark, could only feel. Tommy groped at her skirt, trying to hoik it up, once she'd obediently removed her bloomers. He was panting and cursing, his breaths hot and frantic against her neck. Then she felt something jabbing at her thighs.

'Open your legs!'

There were a few moments of frustrated confusion and she heard him cursing, trying with one arm to find his way to her, to control himself. Then he was jabbing up between her legs.

'Christ!' he said again. 'Let me in . . .'

And she felt a burning and a hard thing up inside her and it ached and glowed with sensation and his jabbing in and out of her set something off in her body that started to rise and spread. It was the loveliest feeling she'd ever had and she didn't want it to stop. But it did stop, abruptly, because Tommy shoved into her very hard for the last time, gave a long grunt, and then all the urgent moving stopped and he pulled away.

'You can put your bloomers on again,' he said out of the darkness, and she fumbled to find them, confused by the warm burn of her feelings.

Tommy came up close again.

'Like that, did you, wench?'

Marigold decided she had liked it. 'Yes, ta,' she said.

'D'you come down here every Saturday?'

'I come for my mom – for the meat.'

'Well – I'll be here again.' He steered her out to the road and picked up the bag. 'How about it, Marigold?'

'All right,' she said.

She was met back home with a slap across the face.

'Where the hell've you been, you stupid good-for-nothing?' Bessie roared. 'How'm I s'posed to cook the tea if you don't bring the bleeding shopping home? Can't do the simplest thing, can you, you bonehead! Where've you been?'

'Nowhere,' Marigold's eyes were stinging from the slap. She felt wet and sore between her legs.

'Took you a bloody long time to go nowhere then,' Clarence observed. He was kneeling by the fire with his boot stuck on the end of a piece of wood, trying to fix the heel back on with weedy hammer blows. Violet and Rosina were sitting quiet, out of the way. There was no sign of Charlie. The room was full of steam and as usual a line of washing was strung across the ceiling so that they had to keep ducking under it to get around.

Marigold put the bags down wearily on the table, waiting for Mom's usual complaints about the stuff she'd bought and she didn't know why she didn't go herself. Bessie loomed over the bags of shopping.

'Is that the best you could do – look at that!' Bessie scoffed. The crushed-looking chicken hung limp in her hands. 'Looks as if a cartwheel's been over it!'

Marigold took no notice. She thought of Tommy's hands moving inside her clothes. She had a secret that was *hers*. Mom was never going to know that, however much she kept on.

Chapter Six

Violet liked working at Vicars. As the months passed she learned to operate the different kinds of machines, turning out brass hinges of all different sizes. It was very noisy and dirty, but the gaffer Mr Riddle was a quiet, fair-minded man and she found the other people friendly.

One of the girls, who had given her a cheerful smile when she arrived, was called Josephine Snell. Josephine was closer to Marigold's age than Violet's but they were the two 'babbies' of the works and ended up sticking together. Josephine had wild brown hair which she tied into a thick plait, and lively grey eyes. Her house was only round the corner from Vicars and she started asking Violet back for a bit after work sometimes.

'I can't stay long,' Violet said nervously, the first time. 'Mom'll go mad. I have to get home and help.'

'Just have a cuppa,' Josephine said. 'She won't mind that, will she?'

You don't know our mom, Violet thought, but she desperately wanted to go with Josephine. She was so happy that Jo was prepared to befriend her.

The Snells lived in a front house that opened on to the street, though in every other way it was almost identical to the one Violet lived in. What went on in that house compared to her own, though, was a revelation to Violet. She would never have taken Josephine back to her house, because of Mom.

When they got to Josephine's house, Mrs Snell was out at the front talking to a neighbour. She was a small, sweet-faced woman, and very kind.

'Mom – I've brought Vi home for a cuppa,' Josephine said.

'All right,' Mrs Snell said easily. She nodded in a friendly way at Violet. 'You the new girl at Vicars are you?'

'Yes,' Violet said shyly.

'Go in – the kettle's on, Jo. Cuppa tea'll set us up.'

As she got to know Mrs Snell, Violet found she was always doing little things to 'set herself up', a cup of tea being the chief among them. She was also a widow and had had a hard life.

Violet found herself visiting a haven of quiet, female company. She felt a pang of envy, seeing this gentle woman with her daughters and the obvious affection between them. And how peaceful and quiet their house was, not full of babies and all the washing and smells that went with them!

On the first day she had asked Josephine about the lad who was always singing. It always cheered her to hear him across the factory floor. He looked a good bit older than her and she felt rather intimidated by him.

'You mean Warbling Willie?' Josephine laughed. 'His voice is quite nice really, isn't it? That's Harry – Martin, I think his other name is. Why?' She asked coyly. 'D'you like the look of him?'

'Just wondered, that's all,' Violet said. She found she was blushing. She had barely known Jo then. Now they were better friends, Jo said, 'I reckon that Harry's taken a shine to you. He was asking about you today.'

'What? He never!' Violet really did blush then. 'You're having me on!'

To tell the truth she had barely thought about him. He seemed so much older and more superior to her – why would he even notice her?

'Ah well, you never know.' Josephine gave her a mischievous wink. 'You wait and see.'

Violet kept thinking a lot about Harry Martin after that. Was it true he had been asking about her? She deliberately didn't look in his direction or go out of her way to speak to him. She was very shy and blushed just thinking about him, knowing that she imagined talking to him, or him saying her name or giving her a look just for her with his dancing eyes.

Chapter Seven

It took months before anyone noticed, because no one ever noticed Marigold.

Her belly started to swell. She was already a large girl, in the mould of her mother, and she wore loose, shapeless clothes. But one evening Bessie came panting up into the girls' room and caught a glimpse of Marigold getting undressed in the narrow space between the beds, silhouetted in the candlelight.

'Christ Almighty!' she erupted.

Violet, who was just getting into the three-quarter size she shared with Rosina, turned to see Marigold's swollen outline in the candlelight. It had crossed her mind once or twice that Marigold was getting a bit stout. Now her belly ballooned out, forcing her camisole up.

'You filthy dirty little bitch!' Bessie loomed over her, seeming larger than ever in her fury. She grabbed the back of Marigold's vest and hauled her over to the door.

'Ow – Mom, stop it! What you doing?' Marigold whined.

'What's that when it's at 'ome?' Bessie ran her hand roughly over Marigold's belly. 'You're five or six months gone at the very least, you little hoower!' She gave Marigold a furious slap round the face.

'What you doing?' Marigold burst into tears. 'Don't hit me, Mom! Why're you hitting me?'

'I'll cowing hit you, you filthy little bugger! Whose is it?'

Violet and Rosina sat side by side, both hugging their knees. Rosina's hair hung loose down her back like a black shawl. In the gloom, Violet saw that her eyes were stretched wide with fright. Violet had a sick feeling in her stomach. What was Mom saying about Marigold? Rosina looked round desperately at her. *What does she mean? Why's Mari in trouble?* her eyes begged.

'I don't know what you're talking about,' Marigold was sobbing, knuckles in her eyes like a big, ungainly child.

'You've got a babby in your belly – that's what, and I want to know who the filth was that put it there. You've been with a man, Marigold – ' Bessie lowered her voice a bit. Violet imagined Mabel Cameron listening slyly the other side of the wall. 'Did 'e take advantage of you?'

'What d'you mean?' she wailed.

'Did someone force you, you gormless wench?' Bessie had Marigold by the shoulders and was shaking her.

'No! It was Tommy – he's my . . . We're courting!'

'Courting – you!' Bessie laughed, cruelly. 'Oh, very nice. You been out in the monkey run, picking up a fancy man, Marigold? I'd like to see that, that I would!'

'He meets me in the Bull Ring, Sat'day nights.' Marigold could never stand up for herself against the force of Bessie. Her mother could crush her to powder in seconds. 'He's my friend.'

'Is 'e going to marry you then?' Bessie demanded harshly. 'You'd better get down to the Bull Ring and see what sort of friend he turns out to be.'

With utter loathing she shoved Marigold back on to the bed. 'You filthy, disgusting little cow . . .'

Violet and Rosina sat, not moving as Bessie clumped heavily down the stairs.

'Tommy's my pal – he's nice to me.' Marigold's voice came out all muffled. She lay on her side, hugging her swollen belly, and sobbed.

Bessie put a stop to Marigold's jaunts to the Bull Ring. She wouldn't even hear of Marigold going to find Tommy Kay to see if he'd do the decent thing and marry her.

'You're staying here, where I can see you my girl. I don't want you out of my sight.'

Violet felt sorry for Marigold, but there was nothing any of them could do. Marigold was stuck, almost unmoving, at their mother's side now, handmaid to her every whim. She wasn't allowed to go out of the yard, but there was no hiding the fact of her ripe condition from the neighbours. She got bigger and bigger, had to resort to wearing dresses of Bessie's, and walked leaning backwards with a slow, lumbering gait. Bessie brazened it out with the neighbours – even managed to get some sympathy.

'Our Marigold's so simple – a man took advantage of her. My poor, innocent girl. Wicked isn't it, the things a man'll stoop to?'

When Charlie found out he looked at his twin sister with pure disgust, as if she was a bad smell under his nose. Violet wondered how Marigold felt. She didn't seem any different from usual, huge and passive, very little expression registering on her face.

Except once. One Saturday afternoon, in the heat of July, Violet went up to their bedroom to take her stockings off. It was too hot to stand them. Before she

35

had even climbed the stairs she heard Marigold's voice, and she went in to find her sister on her bed in a great big flowery dress of Bessie's. Marigold was lying on her side, her chopped black hair a line across her chin and falling over her face. She was curled forwards, her hand stroking her belly.

'. . . and you're my little babby,' Violet heard. 'It's all right, 'cause I'm your mom and we're gunna be all right . . .'

'Mari? What're you doing?' She found the sight disturbing.

But Marigold raised her head and her face was full of a shining joy Violet had never seen in her before.

'I can feel it, Vi. I was talking to him. Here –' She rolled on to her back. 'Feel him.'

The baby had pushed her body up like a steep hill. Reluctant, but fascinated, Violet put her hand on the hard drum of Marigold's belly.

'Move it around,' Marigold ordered.

After a moment, Violet felt something, a little ripple, something independent of Marigold herself, moving in there.

'Oh!' Violet said. It was alarming. She hadn't let herself think too much about how it got in there. 'It feels funny!'

Marigold beamed, cradling her arms round herself. 'It's my little babby.'

36

Chapter Eight

August 1930

'Right, Violet – I want you over here today.'

Mr Riddle led her to one of the rows of Taylor's lathes at the far end of the workshop, their belts all looping up to the pulleys high above their heads. 'You've never worked this one, have you? I'll get Harry to show you – hang on a tick.'

Violet stood by the lathe amid the bashing, stamping and drilling of the other machines, her heart beating fast. Had Mr Riddle gone to get Harry Martin? So far the most they'd ever done was exchange a simple hello. What would Harry think, having to come and help her?

Don't be so silly, she ticked herself off, even as her palms began sweating. It was a warm day, and she was all nerves. *He's just coming to work the lathe for you. It's work, that's all.*

She saw Mr Riddle coming back, and Harry's striding walk and slick black hair. His dark eyes met hers shyly for a moment, then looked away. His face looked ruddy in the heat.

'Get Violet started on here,' Mr Riddle said. 'She's a fast learner – she'll soon get the hang of it.'

'All right,' Harry said. As Mr Riddle went off, Harry gave Violet a wink which made her giggle. She was surprised to see Harry's neck turn even pinker – did she imagine it? – and he turned quickly towards the machine.

'Right – I'll show you. Come and stand here.'

Harry was an expert. Violet watched in admiration as he turned out a perfectly drilled hinge, his fingers strong and precise, his movements quick and intelligent.

'There – think you can do that?' He turned to her.

'Think so.' She was a bit nervous but wanted to prove she could. She was also a fast, accurate worker and her first attempt was quite reasonable. Harry stood leaning over, watching her concentrate. She could feel his eyes on her. Her pale hair was tied back but she had to blow a strand of it out of her eyes, and shook her head back. Suddenly he reached forward and held it back for her.

'Ta – I need a kirby-grip for that.'

'That's not bad.' He turned her hinge over in his hands. 'D'you want me to show you again just to make sure?' And he winked again, his brown eyes full of laughter. Both of them knew she didn't need showing again, she'd got it right the first time, but she wanted him to stay and he didn't want to go.

'All right. Just in case.' She smiled back, cheekily.

Harry drilled the holes in another hinge, taking his time over it. He turned to her. Violet was watching earnestly. She liked Harry's hands. They looked like hands that should be good at playing the piano, although she didn't suppose he could. He looked round into her eyes and this time he was grinning.

'D'you want me to show you once more?'

A smile spread across Violet's face. This was handsome, cheeky-faced Harry Martin, going out of his way to stay with her!

'Go on then.'

'Blimey – ain't she got the hang of it yet?' one of the other girls shouted over to them. 'You forgotten how to do it an' all, Harry?'

'If he ever knew!' someone called with a ribald laugh.

'Better be off,' Harry said. 'See you, Violet.'

'See you,' she said.

'He *likes* you,' Josephine told her as they poured out of the factory at the end of the day. The girls walked the pavement, taking their time, heads close together.

'Who?' Violet asked, blushing.

'Harry Martin – who else?' Josephine teased. 'Look at your face – like a flaming beetroot! Want to know how I know?'

'No!' Violet protested, nudging Josephine in the ribs.

'Bet you do!'

'I *don't*!' Of course Violet wanted desperately to know every detail.

Josephine kept looking at her, eyes full of fun, until Violet could stand it no longer.

'Oh, all right – tell me then.'

'Cissy told me. One of Harry's pals told her.'

'Told her what?'

'Said he thinks you're really pretty and nice and he hadn't plucked up the courage to talk to you until today when he had to.'

Violet swelled with excitement. Had Harry really been watching her, wanting to talk to her? It had taken him long enough to get round to it! She dug Josephine in the ribs again.

'You're having me on – he never said that!'

'He did – I swear to you!'

'I bet he's been out with half the works already. What about that Mary Price?'

'Well, he may've gone with her but he doesn't want to any more, so what does it matter?' They reached the corner of the street where the Snells lived. 'You coming back for a cuppa?'

Violet hesitated. Josephine never questioned why Violet didn't invite her back to their house. The Snells' was on the way home, so it would have taken Josephine out of her way, but Violet sensed that Jo knew it was more than that and never invited herself. Violet was always glad to go to Jo's house; anything, in fact, to stay away from home. Charlie was courting with a girl called Gladys and was hardly ever at home. Rosina played round at her best friend's house as much as she could to keep out of her mom's way. And Marigold stayed in the house nearly all the time, quietly, disgracefully, swelling. Violet didn't want to go home.

'Go on then,' she said. 'Just a quick one. If your mom don't mind.'

She went to bed that night with her head full of thoughts of Harry Martin's laughing brown eyes.

Chapter Nine

Violet woke in the middle of the night to the sound of Marigold crying out.

'My belly – oh, it hurts!' This was followed by a frightening groan.

Violet went next door and woke her mother.

'You can stop making that racket for a start,' Bessie ordered grimly, standing over Marigold with a candle.

Seeing Bessie in disarray, in her nightgown, her plaits hanging down, felt almost as alarming as Marigold's strange cries. Bessie was always up before them in the morning, dressed, hair coiled above her ears, ruling everything with an iron rod.

'Rosina – run round to number fifty-one and get Mrs Barker.'

Wide-eyed, Rosina scampered off to do as she was ordered.

Marigold gave another moan of pain and Bessie tutted and yanked back the sheet covering her. It was a stifling, sticky night.

'Get your bloomers off, wench. You'll not get far in those.' She stared down disgustedly at her daughter as she tried to obey. 'Well – now you know. That's what you get for being dirty.' Bessie turned to Violet. 'You'd best get off downstairs. You'll only get in the way, as usual. Get the lamp lit and stoke the range – we'll need water.'

There was a commotion as Mrs Barker arrived. Violet had the kettle on and was hurrying round in the gaslight to find cloths and rags, bowls for hot water, carbolic soap, string. She opened the door to the yard to get some air, but even outside the atmosphere was syrup thick. She started to hear little growls of thunder.

Rosina settled in the armchair which was usually reserved for Uncle Clarence, his personal throne. But he and Charlie were asleep up in the attic. Violet thought Rosina would curl up and sleep, but instead she sat perched on the edge of the seat, bolt upright, biting her nails and cringing at every howl of pain from upstairs.

'Here –' Violet gave her a cup of tea with plenty of sugar.

'Ta.' Rosina took it, with shaking hands. She looked scared, as if she was much younger than her twelve years and had woken from a bad dream.

'Will she be all right, Vi? I don't like it – it's horrible!'

'She'll be all right. That's just what happens, that's all,' Violet said, trying to sound experienced. She had never heard a birthing woman before either and it made her feel all peculiar. 'Trust Charlie to sleep through it.'

The hours crawled past. Once they heard feet on the stairs and thought it was all over, but it was Bessie demanding more tea. The thunder grew louder, cracking across the dark sky, and so did Marigold's groans. Every time she heard her Violet felt herself tighten with dread inside, and when it got louder Rosina started to cry.

'I don't like it! Why's she making them noises?' She kept putting her hands over her ears, screwing up her face.

'It'll be all right,' Violet snapped, jumping violently when there came an especially sharp crack of thunder.

'Oh God, Marigold, just hurry up and get on with it, will you!'

And then, just as Marigold's shrieks were getting louder and louder, the rain came, the sky emptying itself in a great swish of sound and coolness, and soon there was water pouring out of the broken gutters and splashing on to the grimy bricks of the yard.

'Let's go outside!' Rosina said.

They ran out in their nightdresses. In seconds Violet could feel hers clinging to her, and in the dim light from the yard lamp they could see the fast slant of the rain. She turned her face up, welcoming its coolness as it ran all over her face and neck, making her shiver as it trickled down between her small breasts to her stomach. She and Rosina were giggling and whirling round in the wet, nightdresses clinging to them. There was thunder still, but fainter, and the night's intensity was being released by the storm.

'What the hell're you doing? What's going on?'

Charlie had come down, was standing silhouetted in the doorway. They ran towards him, laughing.

'Ssh – we'll wake the neighbours,' Violet giggled.

Rosina's dark hair was like a dark, dripping cape over her shoulders. She was smiling now though.

As they stepped inside they sobered immediately. The screams from upstairs were high-pitched, horrifying.

'Mari – ' Violet said to Charlie. 'The baby.'

'Oh,' he said grumpily. 'Sounds like a pig being killed.'

Violet thought, not for the first time, that she didn't like her brother very much.

'I'll go back to bed then,' he said.

You do that, she thought. *You useless item.*

43

Soon after, there were more screams, even louder. Rosina grabbed Violet's hand and they gripped each other tight, listening, standing in their soaked night-dresses. After a crescendo of terrible cries there came a silence. Rosina's face was a mask of fear. Then came the alarmed squawk of a newborn child.

'The babby!' Rosina gasped. 'She's had it!'

'Thank God – at last.' Violet felt sick. The whole thing filled her with horror.

'Can we go and see?' Rosina was ready to run straight upstairs.

'Best wait. Mom'll only send us down.'

Some time later Bessie came down. Violet expected her to be all smiles, like she was when the orphanage babies (that was how Violet thought of them) arrived. Instead her expression was bitter hard. Violet shrank inside.

'What're you gawping at?'

'Has she had the babby?' Rosina asked.

'It's a lad, if you must know.' Bessie went to the range, looking for something to find fault with, but the kettle was full and near the boil. 'Could do with summat more than tea, I can tell you.' She didn't seem to notice the girls' sodden state.

'Can we go and see?' Rosina asked. She always dared to ask for things, not like Violet.

'No – best leave her.'

'Oh, Mom – please! We've been up all night waiting!'

Bessie wheeled round. 'I said no! Daint you hear me?'

'Why not?' Rosina persisted. 'We want to see him.'

Violet held her breath, waiting for the axe to fall. But Bessie stood, hand on hips, in silence for a moment. Then she shrugged and turned back to the range.

'Go on – go and see what happens to girls who don't keep themselves nice.'

Violet climbed the stairs behind Rosina. When they got into the room, Mrs Barker was putting all the bowls of water and red-stained cloths by the door to go down. Violet averted her eyes from the sight. She couldn't avoid the smell though, warm and bloody. It almost made her want to retch. She forced herself to stay in control and looked at her sister, propped up in the bed, hair lank with sweat and with a smile on her perspiring face.

At first she couldn't see the child because the sheet was pulled right up. When Marigold pulled it back, Violet felt another plunge of revulsion. Sucking on her sister's breast was a tiny, monkey-like baby. She could see Marigold's blue veins and the wet, slicked hair on the child's head. It all made her feel funny. Rosina didn't seem too sure either.

'You all right, Mari?'

'Told you it was a boy,' Marigold said.

Violet leaned closer and saw the tiny face, eyes and fists clenched shut, cheeks sucking in and out. There was white stuff rimed above his eyes and he smelt like cheese.

'What's his name?' Rosina asked.

Marigold looked severely at her. 'Tommy,' she said. 'He's mine.'

Chapter Ten

'Fancy walking out with me – Saturday?'

It was the next morning, and after a night with no sleep, Violet had been flagging with exhaustion until Harry found an excuse to come and see her, and whisper to her. Suddenly she was full of beans!

'He's asked me out – properly!' she told Jo during the dinner break and Jo's eyes were dancing with interest. Violet thought she'd never been so excited. First a pal like Jo, then this!

'Well, you said yes, didn't you?'

'Course I did – why wouldn't I?'

She was surprised that Harry seemed a bit in awe of her. There she was, only fifteen and he was already nineteen. But she was very flattered. Violet felt she had never had so much attention. And Harry was considered a bit of a catch in the works – a strong, good-looking lad, full of life.

That Saturday they went into town to the pictures at the Futurist. Violet had a row with Bessie before she went.

'What d'you mean you're going to the flicks?' Bessie demanded. 'No you're not – you've seen where gadding about lands you! You're going to the Bull Ring to get the meat, and let's hear no more about it!'

Violet was really fed up with spending Saturday nights traipsing back with heavy bags on the tram. She had had to take over this job once Marigold was not considered safe to be let out. For the first time, she found herself standing up to Mom.

'Why do I always have to go? Charlie never does anything – he can go tonight instead.'

'That's no job for a man.' Bessie was spooning a sloppy white gruel down one of the babies. Charlie was sitting by the door, jabbing idly at the sole of his boot with a penknife. 'You'll have to go, Vi.'

'I've told you – I'm not going!' She could hardly believe herself. 'Let that lazy sod do something to help for a change!'

'Don't talk to your mother like that!' Uncle Clarence's reedy voice piped up from his chair. 'Show her some respect!'

Violet felt as if she was going to explode.

'I'll go,' Rosy said. 'Let Violet go out.'

Bessie got up threateningly from her chair, slamming the money down on the table.

'You'll do what you're told!' She jabbed her stubby finger in Violet's face. 'And any more language like that and you'll be washing your mouth out with salt. Shift yourself – now!'

'I'll come,' Rosina whispered once Bessie had turned her back. 'I'll bring the shopping home.'

Violet was trembling with fury. She wanted to storm out, tell Mom to get someone else to be her slave for once, but she knew it was no good. She smiled at Rosina.

'Ta,' she whispered.

Snatching up her hat and the money she slammed out of the house. Rosina hurried after her. Violet was astonished at herself. She'd never gone as far as that before. But she was going out with Harry Martin. Nothing and no one was going to stop her.

'She's always on at you,' Rosina said. 'T'aint fair. Charlie *is* a lazy sod. Just 'cause he's a *boy*.'

Violet felt a warm gratitude towards her little sister for being on her side. They scurried round the Bull Ring and Jamaica Row, getting all the meat and veg, and Rosina bravely took it off her, even though she could barely carry it.

'Here – ' Violet handed her a penny for the tram – 'I owe you a favour. Thanks, sis.'

She and Harry sat through the picture at the Futurist, watching the flashing images through a fog of cigarette smoke. Harry lit up and offered her one. Violet shook her head. It was so strange, sitting here beside him. She realized she knew almost nothing about him, other than that he worked at Vicars. She kept snatching little glances at him in the darkness. Solid, she thought. He looks strong. He had a thick, strong neck and there was an urgent sense of energy about him. He was very different from her brother, who just sat about and did everything Mom told him. Harry had life in him. And she liked his wavy, dark brown hair.

After a bit, Harry slid his arm round the back of her shoulders. She didn't know what to do so she just sat still, but she liked the feel of it. It made her feel protected. She didn't turn to face him as she felt shy, but she was acutely aware of being so close to him, his muscular legs beside hers in the gloom. Later, once he'd smoked his cigarette, he reached across with his other hand and took one of hers. They sat holding hands for the rest of the time and his hand was heavy and hot.

Afterwards they stood outside, unsure what to do next. Harry looked at her from under his cap. His buoyant, joking manner which carried him round the factory was all gone for the moment and he seemed uncertain. It touched Violet to see him look shy, and gave her courage.

'Shall we walk about a bit?'

Harry nodded. 'Fancy some chips?'

Violet grinned. 'Ooh yes! My tummy's been rumbling. Did you hear it?'

Harry smiled. 'Yes.'

He bought them a newspaper bundle of chips each and they walked across town, tucking hungrily into the chips, the smell of vinegar rising off them. Harry walked quite fast, with a restless kind of energy.

'What's the rush?'

'Sorry.' He slowed down, and once more she sensed he was nervous of her.

'Where d'you live?' Violet asked, and Harry told her the name of his street, not too far from the factory. She found out he was one of five children. She told him about her family, or the bits it felt all right to tell.

'My brother's an apprentice at Simmons,' she said. Simmons was a firm of toolmakers.

'Oh – our dad used to work there!' Harry said.

'Where's he work now?'

'Here and there – ' Harry was evasive suddenly.

'What's his name? I'll ask Charlie if he knows him.'

'He won't – it was quite a while ago.' Harry seemed sorry he'd mentioned it.

They finished their chips and threw away the papers, and walking on, found themselves in the square by the Cathedral, looking up at its grand bulk in the darkness.

'You ever been in there?' Harry asked.

Violet shook her head.

'We don't go to church – only Sunday School sometimes when Mom wanted us out of the way.'

Harry said he'd never been in there either.

There was a silence as they looked up, trying to see stars, but it was too cloudy. The sky just looked like a great, featureless shadow.

'I wonder if it looks like that in Australia?' Harry said.

'Why Australia?'

'Right the other side of the world – that's where I want to be. I'm gunna go there one day. Or somewhere. Just anywhere out of here. Don't you want to see the world?'

'Yes.' She'd never thought about it, not until that moment. But to get out, away from here, from Mom ... 'I do.'

Harry slid his arm round her shoulders and she tingled at the feel of it. It made her feel excited and special. He liked her and that was a miracle! She wasn't used to anyone taking any notice of her.

'I've been looking at you,' Harry said. 'You're so pretty, you are. Thought I'd be afraid to touch you.'

Violet laughed in amazement. 'You're not, though.'

Her stomach lurched as he turned to face her. She looked up at him and his expression was very serious.

'Can I give you a kiss?'

Her eyes answered, and his face moved close to hers. With warm, vinegary lips, he gave her her first kiss.

Chapter Eleven

Marigold wasn't well after she'd had Tommy.

For days she ran a high fever and lay in bed, her breasts running with milk. The doctor had to come, and he told them to help her feed the baby.

'Trust her.' Bessie cursed her high and low. 'Always bloody trouble.'

She made Violet and Rosina help with Tommy's feeding. Bessie didn't seem to want anything to do with him or Marigold.

The two sisters were horrified at first, especially at the sight of Marigold's engorged breasts. She moaned when they latched the baby on. But soon they were fascinated by him. Violet started to see why Marigold thought he was beautiful, the way his little mouth opened at the touch of the nipple and the smell of milk. And every day he looked less like a shrivelled monkey and more like someone they knew. 'Little Tommy,' they started to call him.

The fever lasted for several days before Marigold began to get a bit better. But when Violet came home from work on the fifth day, the house was strangely quiet. She walked in to find Clarence in his usual chair with the evening paper, and Bessie in the scullery. Mabel Jones from next door was sitting at the table with her long face on and Rosina was next to her, her eyes red from crying.

'What's up with you?' Violet said, carelessly, thinking Rosy was having a blart because she hadn't got her own way about something.

'You tell her, Mom!' The rage and grief with which Rosina spat out the words halted Violet. She'd never heard Rosina speak to their mother in anything like this tone before. 'Go on – tell her!'

'Now, now,' Mabel Jones said, but she sounded rather uncertain.

Bessie came out of the scullery with a tin of flour. Her expression was hard, defiant.

'It was no good. You were all getting too bound up with him. It was never going to be any different, you know – not right from the start.'

'She *is* seventeen,' Mrs Jones put in. 'I mean I had our Michael at that age . . .'

'She may be seventeen in years,' Bessie said, thumping the flour down on the table. 'But in her head she's a child – a babby herself. The girl's not all there.'

Violet looked at Rosina, still not understanding.

Tears ran down Rosy's face again. 'D'you know what she's gone and done? She's taken Tommy away and she's given him to the orphanage!'

'You didn't?' She whispered it, disbelieving. But she saw from Bessie's defiant face that it was true.

'You can't have – he was ours! He was one of us!'

'No he wasn't!' Bessie lost her temper completely. 'He were born out of a filthy act and he was a bastard child with no father. I'm not having a bastard child brought up in my house, and that's that. You conceive in filth and you live and die in filth, that's how it is. I've done the only decent thing and I don't want to hear any more from either of you.'

Rosina had got to her feet.

52

'He wasn't yours...' She was backing away from her mother, towards the stairs. 'You think you can tell everyone what to do – but he wasn't yours. He was Mari's!'

'Any more from you, my girl, and you'll have a damn good hiding!'

Violet followed Rosina up the stairs.

'Rosy!' Outside the bedroom she pulled urgently at the back of her sister's dress. 'Does Mari know?'

Rosina turned. Her eyes were burning with grief and fury and Violet could feel her trembling.

'She knows,' she hissed, clenching her fists. 'I hate Mom. I *hate* her.'

Marigold's face was turned away and for a moment they thought she was asleep. Both of them tiptoed over to her and she moved her head and looked at them.

'Oh, Mari – your little babby!' Rosina sobbed, and she flung herself on the bed, clasping Marigold in her arms. 'Your little Tommy. How could she?'

Violet stood watching, tears running down her own cheeks. She could see no expression on Marigold's face. She was blank, as if she had been rubbed out. She said nothing. But just for a moment, feeling Rosina's warm shape pressed to hers, she lifted her hand and gently stroked her little sister's dark hair.

Chapter Twelve

Marigold's mute misery was terrible.

They could neither take it away, nor stand to see it. It was as if no one could reach her. Sometimes she just started crying and couldn't be comforted. If she did it in front of the family, Bessie sent her upstairs.

'Can't stand all that carry-on,' she said. 'Time she got used to it, that's all.'

Violet couldn't bear it. Sometimes she saw Rosina looking at their mother in a way which almost frightened her. She could imagine Rosy getting a knife and sticking it in her, the way her face went.

For Violet, Harry had changed everything. Having Jo as her friend to natter to was wonderful enough, but this was different. Although she had occasionally heard people comment on her looks, that she was pretty, she had never believed it. Now, when she saw Harry looking at her, almost drinking in the sight of her face, she began to feel pretty as well.

In the one tiny looking-glass which Bessie kept nailed to the wall near the door, she began to notice that her hair *was* a nice blonde shade, and that the eyes which looked solemnly back at her were blue and remarkably large. She did something she had never done before during her reluctant glances in the glass: she smiled at herself. A sweet though sad face smiled back, the dimple appearing in her left cheek. She brushed her straggly hair back into a loose bunch and it suited her elfin features.

'You're the prettiest girl I've ever seen,' Harry would say, and Violet drank this in, heady at experiencing more attention than she'd ever had in her life before.

She revelled in it. All the wages that she kept off Mom now went on prettifying herself: a little pot of rouge, some stockings, a blouse with a little navy tie in the neck. She didn't tell Bessie about the pay rise Vicars had given her, so now she was two shillings a week better off. Anything was better than being at home, and she basked in being wanted and admired. She never gave a thought to what she felt about Harry. He loved her, so she must love him and that was that. It was like that tiny glimpse Miss Green had given her, making her feel she could be good at something, and special, only this was so much more powerful because with Harry came a real possibility of love, of a life of her own.

And Harry was full of dreams of escape as well. His loves in life, apart from her, were the Villa ground, where he spent every Saturday he could afford when there was a match on, his mom, who Violet soon learned lived a hellish life with Harry's drunken, vicious father, and his big dream of Getting Out. As the months passed and she and Harry spent more and more time together, this was his constant refrain.

'We've got to get out of this place, Vi. I've got plans, I have. Give it a year or two and I'll be on a boat to Australia to make my fortune. I want to see our mom all right. The old man's never looked after her proper, like. I want her to live like a queen.'

Sometimes, as they were walking, arms wrapped round each other in the dark, along the back streets of

'That's nice,' she said.

'Wasting your time messing with bits of paper,' Bessie said.

But Violet hoped Marigold was feeling a bit better.

And she had a lot else on her mind. One day during that winter after Harry Martin fell in love with her, he came to work one morning with his face in a terrible state. She saw him as they clocked in.

'Oh, my word – what's happened to you?'

There was a huge shiner all across his left cheekbone and the eye was swollen and bruised so he couldn't open it.

'Nothing. I'm all right. Leave it.' He shook her off, not wanting her sympathy in front of everyone else.

'But Harry!' She was hurt.

'*Leave it* – I'll see you later.'

He stormed off in his overall to start work at the other end. During the morning she kept glancing along the noisy factory floor to see if she could see him at his lathe in the light of the long windows. Harry kept his head down and seemed to be working with almost frenzied energy. In the dinner break she kept away from him and stayed with Josephine. She and Jo usually ate their dinner together in any case. She felt upset with Harry, pushing her off like that. If that was how he was going to be, then hard luck to him!

'Sorry about this morning,' Harry said when they got outside.

Violet was with Jo. She stood waiting.

'D'you want to come home – meet my mom?'

He asked the question almost shamefacedly, looking down to avoid her eyes. Violet was immediately appeased. She knew he was trying to make it up to her. She looked at Jo.

'Go on,' Jo said. She was so easy-going. 'You go with Harry. You can come to ours tomorrow if you like.'

Walking down the road, Harry took her arm and slipped it through his. Violet didn't ask anything. She waited.

'She threw the old man out last night.' The words erupted out of him at last.

'What – you mean, for good? Is that why he hit you?'

'He came home in his usual state – only worse. Set about Mom – with the poker. Tommy and me had to stop him. Mom's told him she don't want him back – ever. He never pays a penny of the rent or nothing. It's me and the lads do that – and Marj.'

'But – where'll he go? Won't he just come back?'

Harry shrugged. 'Dunno. Last night I told him I'd kill 'im if he did.'

'You never!'

Harry turned to her, his face set and intense. 'Bloody would, an' all.'

The force of his anger filled Violet with sudden dread.

'You'd go to prison.'

'It'd bleeding well be worth it.'

'It wouldn't, Harry!' She squeezed his arm. 'You want to get away, remember, go somewhere where there're open spaces – not be locked away. Don't talk like that!'

He took a deep, shuddering breath. 'I could've – last night. Easy.' He stopped abruptly and, turning to her, took her in his arms. Violet was moved.

'You're what I need,' he said into her neck.

She held him close, stroking his back.

'Let's get wed,' he said.

She pulled back, startled, but excited. 'But I'm not even sixteen till next month!'

'Soon – next year?'

She beamed at him, and kissed his cheek, the side which wasn't all sore.

'All right. But don't let's tell anyone yet.'

Harry agreed. He released her. 'Come and see our mom.'

'She won't want visitors – not after last night.'

'It's all right. Come on.'

The Martins' house was not on a yard, but one of a row of two up, two down terraces in ill repair, identical to the hundreds of others in rows stretching all round Birmingham. Violet knew that her mother could have afforded to move from the yard into one of these now, with all their wages coming in, and it would have allowed them a bit more space, but Bessie was well established and a move would have lost her her status as yard gaffer. She was used to being the big fish in a little pond.

When Harry pushed the door open, Mrs Martin started violently. She was standing by the range in the shadowy room, having just replaced the kettle on the heat.

'Lord love us, you made me jump, bab!'

Violet saw a slender woman in her forties with a lined, anxious face and what would have been wide, brown eyes like Harry's, except that one eye was badly bruised and swollen and her top lip was thick and had been bleeding.

'S'awright, Mom.'

'I thought for a minute . . .'

Then a smile flickered across her face for a second, but she winced and her anxious expression returned.

Violet could see she was looking at a very frightened woman.

'Mom – this is Violet. Works up Vicars with me.'

'Hello,' Violet said, nervously.

Mrs Martin stared at them both for a moment, wringing her hands as if she couldn't make any sense of the situation.

'We're courting, like,' Harry told her gruffly.

'I'm all at sixes and sevens today – don't know what I'm doing. We had a bit of trouble last night . . . Don't know if he's told you. My husband . . . I don't know what's going to happen . . .' She collected herself and stepped forward. 'Nice to meet you, Violet . . . Let's . . . let's have a cup of tea . . .'

She turned back towards the range but still seemed at a loss. Violet could see she'd had a shock. She seemed nice enough anyway. But she wondered why on earth Harry had brought her here today of all days.

They drank a cup of tea together but Mrs Martin sat perched on the edge of her chair holding her cup, rocking slightly, backwards and forwards. Violet could see all the tension was affecting Harry as well.

'Oh, Harry – what if he comes back?' Mrs Martin burst out at last. 'Every time I hear footsteps . . .'

'It'll be all right. He won't.'

Mrs Martin looked stricken. 'I can't take any more . . .' Her eyes filled. 'What if he does?'

'He won't – I've told you. And if he does, I'll see to him.'

'You're a good lad. He's good, my Harry. Always was.' Mrs Martin wiped her unblemished eye on her sleeve and tried to compose herself.

'D'you like working at Vicars?' she asked Violet, calm for a moment.

'Yes – it's all right. I've never worked anywhere else, though.'

'Oh, it's nice, Vicars is. Worked there myself for a bit once.' She looked anxiously at Harry again. 'Where's he gone? Where d'you think he is?'

'I dunno. Good bloody riddance.'

Violet was glad to get out of the house. Harry walked her down to the corner. It was already dark.

'Come 'ere,' he said, before they parted. 'Are you my girl?'

'Yes,' she said. 'Course I am.'

He held her so close and tight, as if she was the most precious thing in the world, and she understood that he had wanted her to see his mom with her bruised face, for her to understand. And she knew how much he needed her.

Chapter Thirteen

1932

'I s'pose it's all right if you want to look common as muck,' Bessie said, when Violet showed her the simple frock she had found for her wedding.

She unfolded her arms and twitched at the material with her fingers.

'Could do with a good wash, I should think. You don't know where that's been.'

The dress wasn't new, but Violet felt she had had a stroke of luck finding it on the market, in with all the other frowsty old rags. It was white and scattered with tiny blue forget-me-nots and had pretty frills edging the neck and sleeves. She was delighted with it and Jo said she thought it was perfect, but of course Bessie had to spoil it, nose in the air as if it was a dirty floorcloth.

'You going to give me the money for a better one then?'

'Don't you go getting uppity, wench,' Bessie snapped. She moved away, starched apron crackling round her. 'You're not marrying the Prince of Wales. Old man Martin's a drunk and a waster and it's like father, like son – I've never seen it go different. But you make your own bed – and you lie on it.'

On an overcast May morning Violet and Harry stepped, husband and wife, out of the little Congregational church a few streets from Vicars.

Nearly all the factory had come to see them marry and shower them with rice at the door. Their wedding photograph showed Violet in her pretty dress, with orange-blossom in her hair. Rosina was not in the picture, but she was Violet's bridesmaid, with her dark-eyed looks, her long hair plaited and coiled round her head and entwined with flowers, which Josephine Snell had done for her. Rosina adored any sort of dressing-up and revelled in the attention.

'You both look lovely!' Jo said, kissing Violet outside. 'You lucky girl, you!'

The church was one which Harry's mother sometimes attended. Bessie, who never darkened the doors of any church, was not in a position to influence the situation much and she sulked. She wouldn't take much interest in the wedding, offering only sarcastic remarks.

She'd been sniffy about Harry from the moment she knew they were courting, and she'd been just the same over Charlie's Gladys, even though she was a young, red-headed harridan in the same model as herself. Charlie had certainly married his mother. Bessie's children had all been under her tight control for so long that she didn't like Violet making decisions for herself or moving out of her orbit of command. Yet weren't marriage and children all that she had insisted was a woman's place, loud and clear? Violet ignored her comments and her sulking. This was her chance to get out and away.

Bessie came to the wedding in the enormous frock she'd had made for Charlie and Gladys's wedding the autumn before, in primrose yellow, dotted with little nosegays of blue and violet, and a big straw hat. Uncle Clarence was there to give Violet away, in a dusty black suit, his balding head glistening with perspiration.

Before they stepped into the church he said, 'You quite sure about this, wench?'

'Bit late to ask me that,' she said crossly. After all, when had either of them taken any notice of anything she did, so why should he care now? Violet felt strong. She was a woman now, still at Vicars, earning as much as eighteen shillings a week on piecework if she worked overtime. And she had Harry, and Harry wanted her.

Harry's father was not at the wedding. He had shown his face a couple of times in the early days after the family had finally turned on him, then disappeared. Mrs Martin gradually relaxed, knowing he was not going to come roaring back in through the door, but she was a nervy woman who depended completely on her sons. Violet saw in her all she didn't want to be herself, and thought the woman demanded too much of Harry.

'When we're married, are you going to go and spend every evening with your mom?'

She asked it teasingly. But Harry's mother was coming to feel like an obstacle in her way, always so tired and pathetic-looking and forever whining to Harry. He seemed to be round there every spare moment. Although she tried not to feel annoyed and jealous, Violet sometimes couldn't help it.

She would have liked to live in a different area, get right away from her mother and Harry's, and from the sad spectre of Marigold. She dreaded seeing Marigold now. She was eighteen going on forty in her frumpy old dresses and with her lank greasy hair. Bessie had taken to having some of the women in the yard – and men if she could get them – round to play cards in the afternoon, holding court at the table, dishing out tea and anything stronger that was going and eating, forever eating. Lardy cakes were her favourite, and bags of sweets, barley sugar and humbugs. Marigold joined in, bracketed in with the middle-aged, one of those buzzing round her queen bee of a mother. She had no friends her own age. All she had was her pretty soapbox full of songs, all scrawled on little scraps of paper. Rosina helped her with the spelling, when she could be bothered. For the wedding Marigold had tried to dress up, and there was something even more heartbreaking about the sight of her with her badly cut hair washed and hanging dead straight, and the dress of Bessie's which had been taken in for her. Like all her clothes, it aged her and made her look shapeless and sexless like a sack of spuds.

Rosina was causing trouble now. She was thirteen but, Bessie said, very 'forward' for her age, always wanting to make her face up and nagging for clothes and wanting to be out and about. She was a precocious little miss, not like Violet. She stood up to her mother and there were frequent rows.

'You can't get married, Vi!' she said when she first heard the news. 'You'll leave me here on my own!'

All Violet really wanted was to get as far away from it all as possible.

But neither of them wanted to leave Vicars. Harry was already twenty and was champing at the bit to be able to get out and follow his dreams. But he couldn't go. Not yet.

'I want to see our mom all right first. I'll have to keep working here for now – that's all there is to it. We're young yet – there'll be plenty of time.'

Of course it made sense not to rent a place too far away. And being in the Summer Lane area meant wasting no money on tram rides to work. All the money they could put away was for Harry's dream passage to Australia.

'Let's get the lowest rent we can,' Harry said. 'There's only the two of us. We don't need much.'

So they rented a two-up house in Ormond Street, a back-to-back, on the front facing the street, with no attic. There was the downstairs room and scullery and two tiny bedrooms. For water and the toilets they had to go down the entry and into the yard. Violet looked round it, the first day they were allowed in. The place was in bad repair, great cracks up the side wall, cockroaches and silverfish all over the place. It was gloomy and stank of damp and mould.

'Oh, Harry,' she said dismally. 'It's horrible. Can't we go somewhere a bit better?'

'It'll be all right after a lick of paint!' Harry said, ever optimistic.

'But what's Mom going to say? I can't have her here!'

'It's our house – not hers!' Harry came and took her in his arms in the dismal little room and his eyes were alight with enthusiasm. 'Look – the rent's only six bob a week – think how much we can save with your wages and mine. The more rent we pay, the longer we're going to have to stay in this rat-hole!'

'I s'pose you're right.' Violet was lifted by his dream again. It just managed to raise her spirits above the sight of the stained old stone sink in the scullery and the pile of mouse droppings by the grease-encrusted gas stove. That and a lopsided shelf in the scullery were the only things in the house.

Harry was full of energy. He moved into the house two days before the wedding and spent the evenings and half the night with his big brother Tom, fixing the hinges of the front door and painting the flaking walls – pale green downstairs and white up in the bedrooms. He bought a table and chairs from a secondhand shop, and a mattress, and Violet bought some bedding and a few pans and crocks.

When they arrived back there on the evening of their wedding it looked better. Marigold had bodged a rag rug for them and Rosina had hemmed a red and white gingham tablecloth, on which were laid their white cups and saucers. Suddenly it began to look a little bit like a home.

They closed the door behind them and Violet stood still just inside.

'Listen – '

Harry stopped, frowning. 'What?'

'Peace.' In fact you could hear the murmur of voices from next door, but that was comparative peace. No Mom booming out orders and Rosina backchatting, no babies and stinking pails of napkins. Nothing but their own place.

'It's ours,' she said.

'And you're mine.' Harry turned, and she was moved by the look of pride and happiness in his face. He came and took her in his arms and his eyes were solemn.

'My wife. We're going to make it better, aren't we? Better than we've had it. Better than my father . . .' He looked vulnerable, like a little boy, and she reached up and stroked his hair.

'Course we are.'

'Up and up.'

'Yes – up and up.'

He grinned suddenly. 'Now for the best bit.' He stroked his hand over her little round breasts. She'd been very determined about not going with him before they were married. Not after Marigold. She was afraid of it. Didn't really know what 'it' consisted of except that the consequences were so frightening. And what if he went off and left her? Then where would she be? So whenever Harry had got a bit too amorous she'd pushed him off.

'Oi – don't get cheeky,' she'd say.

'No need to wait any longer,' Harry said. He took her hand and led her up the narrow, twisting staircase and both of them laughed at the sight of the bare room with nothing but the mattress on the floorboards, the sheets carefully tucked under it by Violet.

'Not exactly the Ritz, is it?' she said ruefully.

Harry pulled her down on to the mattress, kissing her hungrily.

'We've got everything we need.'

He hurriedly unbuttoned her dress and lifted it over her head, then slipped off her camisole. She looked down at his dark head, stroking his hair in wonder as his lips fastened hungrily on her breast. Later, Violet worked out that she must have caught for a baby that very first night.

Chapter Fourteen

The first week after the wedding, Bessie had said to her, 'There's no need for you to go cooking a joint on a Sunday – it's a waste of gas. Charlie and Gladys'll be round as usual. You and Harry come here with us.'

It was almost an order, not quite, but you didn't gainsay Mom. And it was quite nice, just for a bit, to be back with everyone, Marigold helping with the cooking, Rosina on about the latest picture she'd seen at the flicks, and Clarence sitting there talking about the Villa with Harry (Charlie had always supported the Albion, just to be different), and the smell of a joint of beef in the oven. Harry wasn't fussed about going, so long as he had a good dinner, and Bessie's dinners were mammoth events, with big steamed puddings.

Violet was feeling queasy that Sunday when they went, six weeks after the wedding. She found it hard to eat much and could feel Bessie noticing. They were all crammed into the little room, Bessie, Charlie, Gladys, Violet and Rosina squeezed round the table, Clarence and Harry on the sofa. Bessie always went round the table with the pans of food, breathing hard, dolloping it on to everyone's plates in huge quantities. As she came round with roast potatoes, Violet said, 'Not too much, ta – that'll do.'

It was the same with the cabbage.

Bessie sat down with a grunt in front of her heaped

plate, face red and perspiring from all the cooking. She eyed Violet.

'What's up with you?'

Violet looked down at her plate.

'Nothing.'

'You got a bun in the oven?'

The tone of her mother's voice was so grossly blunt that it cut right through Violet. Her cheeks burned red.

'Well – have you?'

Blushing, Violet looked up. 'Think I might have.'

Her mother's face changed. She sat back, seeming to swell with smug satisfaction.

'Hear that, Clarence?' She was beaming in triumph. 'Our Violet's expecting. I'm going to be a grandma. Now I really have got summat to tell everyone! 'Ere – Marigold – pass us over some more gravy will you?'

For the first time in her life, Violet felt she had done something right.

Charlie's wife Gladys, who was taking a long time to conceive a child, had to put up with Bessie's constant boasting about Violet.

'Course – she comes from poor stock, you can see by the look of her,' Bessie said.

Violet wasn't taken with Gladys, who she thought was a narrow-minded nag. All the same, she was embarrassed by Mom talking about Gladys as if she was a farmyard animal.

Violet didn't like being in the 'condition' she was in. She felt sick, and when that wore off and her belly began to swell she felt invaded, frightened and out of control. Panic-stricken, she remembered Marigold, lying there like a great bloated cow when she got big, and the

71

terrible sounds she made giving birth. Sometimes she wept with fright just thinking about it.

'I don't want to do it!' she cried to Harry one night, as they were lying in bed. 'I'm only seventeen – I don't want this yet. My life'll be over!'

'Don't talk daft.' Harry gave her a cuddle and stroked his hands over her buttocks. Her new, curving shape excited him. He started touching her and Violet sighed. She didn't want him messing with her, she wanted him to understand and reassure her. She felt very alone. Apart from his sexual excitement, she saw that he didn't really want the baby, even though he tried to pretend.

When she'd first told him was on a Sunday morning. She'd made tea and they were snuggled up in bed together, with the luxury of no work and the morning stretching ahead of them. Violet didn't feel very well, but she'd been sick and felt better for it. She lay with her head on his chest, tickling him lightly with her fingers, just below his collarbones. Close up she could see the strong black hairs curling up from his pale skin.

When she told him she was being sick because there was a baby, Harry lay still without replying. After a moment he gave a deep sigh.

'Don't!' she cried, tearfully. 'Aren't you pleased?'

There was a pause, then he turned to her, and she could tell he was making himself smile.

'Course I am. I don't s'pose it makes any difference – we can still go to Australia.'

'We'll be a family,' she said. But she felt a plunge of fear. Australia was just a name to her. All she knew of it was that it was hot and dusty, and there were kangaroos! And it was so far away. The thought was frightening. All she wanted now was safety and what was familiar.

Chapter Fifteen

'I don't know why you didn't marry your mother!'

Violet shrieked at Harry's back as he left the house once again.

There was no reply, but he slammed the door so hard that it sprang open again. Violet sighed sharply and banged it shut again.

I'm turning into a proper fishwife, she thought. She didn't like shouting like that. They seemed to be rowing so much of the time these days. And it was usually over the same thing. *But he's never here!*

'You might as well bloody live with her still! Why can't one of the others go?'

As soon as he knew about the baby, Harry seemed to spend more and more time at his mother's. Mrs Martin wasn't well; his two other brothers were married now so there was no man about the house. Harry was the dutiful son; she needed him. Violet had gone off Mrs Martin very quickly as soon as she was married. She thought she was a selfish woman who made herself constantly helpless to get her own way.

Even when he was at home, Harry never understood how she felt, that she needed comfort and reassurance. Violet turned to Jo Snell and her family. Her friendship with Jo had come to be one of the most important things in her life. She could pour her heart out to Jo, and often did.

'I expect he'll come round when the baby's born,' Jo told her. 'And if he doesn't, more fool him. You can always come and see us.'

It was marvellous to have a friend like that. But even Jo didn't know how it felt to have a baby. The one person who seemed to understand, for the first time ever, was her mother. More and more often after work she found herself slipping along Summer Lane and into Bessie's yard. Home. That's how she thought of it still, and it felt reassuringly familiar, although she lived with Harry and that was supposed to be her new home.

Suddenly though, Bessie was treating her with a new respect. Almost, though not quite, as an equal. Violet existed for her in a way she never had before and when she went round there her mother was welcoming in her aggressive way. Yesterday when she'd gone there, feeling lonely, Bessie greeted her with, 'Oh – so you've come running back again, have you? You'd better come in then. How's the babby?'

To Violet's relief, no one else was in.

'Rosy out with her pals, is she?'

Bessie scowled, banging the kettle down on the fire. 'When's she ever in, little minx. She's felt my hand a few times lately, I can tell you. There's some factory Jack hanging round her already – at her age! I've told her she'll come to a bad end. The lip she's got on her! I said to her this morning, you'll have mustard on your tongue if you carry on like that but it's like talking to the wall . . .'

Violet was surprised how little authority Bessie had over Rosina. The rest of them had always kowtowed and tiptoed round her. Rosy had always been different – now she was even more so. She was just fourteen and had started work at a button factory and according to Bessie spent as little time at home as she possibly could. Violet felt sorry for her though, left at home with Clarence and Marigold.

Bessie brewed up the tea and set it on the table. As usual, the room was as clean as a pin, plates gleaming on the shelves, the rag rug shaken out and laid back by the range. Bessie was obsessed with cleaning.

'Here – have one.' On the table were boiled sweets in a little pale blue bowl. 'Barley sugar – that'll make you feel better.'

Violet obeyed.

'You should be drinking raspberry leaf tea . . .' Bessie sat down with a grunt in the big chair by the range, smoothing her capacious apron over her lap. 'Helps with the pains . . .' She poured from the old brown teapot and spooned plenty of sugar into her cup.

Violet didn't need to say a word. Bessie sat back, holding her cup up close to her chin, her dress riding up to show inches of coloured bloomers, shoes off to ease her corns. She reminisced about her own childbearing days.

'Ooh now, you don't know what's coming to you, wench. I'll never forget Charlie and Marigold – sick as a dog I was! Just be grateful it's not twins. Jack's face when she told him there was two of 'em! Treated me like a queen he did, your father.' She gave a great sigh. 'My Jack, God rest him. Now he was a man, he was. Father of twins! He was cock of the walk!'

Violet could see her mother had felt like one of the seven wonders of the world for producing twins. It was the great event of her life. Details followed over the willow-pattern teacups about swollen legs and having 'trouble going' or, as Bessie called it, 'corkage', and piles and other gruesome delights of childbearing, until Violet felt even more sick with dread.

'Don't tell me any more,' she begged.

This made Bessie laugh, her huge body quivering. 'You'll soon find out for yourself, any road, Vi.'

'I don't know as I want to find out,' Violet said miserably.

To her surprise, her mother leaned over and patted her leg. 'Time of your life, bab – that's what it is. Makes a woman of you.'

Violet was overcome by all this sudden attention from her mother. For the first time she wasn't just the spare part, just one other girl stuck in the middle between the twins and Rosina, the pale, sickly-looking one whom no one ever noticed. Suddenly Bessie wanted her, and she was brought inside her mother's powerful orbit with a warmth and sense of approval she had never felt before and barely knew Bessie was capable of. Bessie marched her off to the doctor for a check-up, and when they went round for the big Sunday dinner which was becoming tradition, Bessie kept making mention of 'Vi's condition' and 'Vi and Harry's babby'. She knew Bessie didn't think much of Harry, but he'd given her a child and that was what mattered. Gladys was having no luck, and Marigold didn't count. At last Violet felt she counted in a way that so far none of the others did.

Chapter Sixteen

The baby was due in February. By the end of the summer Violet stopped feeling sick and began to enjoy being at work again and the fuss she received from the other women, which made her feel important. For the first time she felt like Someone. Her belly swelled and showed up quite early against her slim figure. She started to feel the baby move inside her and it aroused her curiosity as well as anxiety. Who was that in there?

But come January, it all went wrong. Violet woke in the middle of the night and knew something had happened. She had a feeling in her, not pain at first, just a sensation as if something had given way in her. Then she felt a trickle between her legs.

I've wet myself! she thought, horrified as the trickle increased to a gush and she couldn't control it. She leapt up in the pitch dark, but it was too late. She'd already soaked the mattress and more was running down her legs. It was a freezing night and the old shift she'd gone to bed in was soaked and hanging icy cold on her.

'Harry!' she whimpered. 'Wake up – I'm all wet. There's something happening!'

Harry groaned. It took her some time to rouse him and get him to light the candle.

'What the hell's the matter with you?' he asked crossly. 'Ugh – it's all wet!' he had leaned his elbow in the big, pinkish stain which had spread across the bed.

'I don't know what's going on. The babby shouldn't be coming yet, should it?' Scared, Violet started to cry. She realized that despite all Bessie's talk she had given her no real understanding of anything that would happen to her.

Harry lit the candle and, seeing there was something really wrong, came and put his arms tenderly round her. She was shivering with cold and fright.

'It's all right. Come on – get this wet thing off.'

'I don't know what's going on!' she wailed. 'I've just wet myself.' She cried out then, as a burning pain tore across her swollen belly. 'Oh, Harry, what's happening? I don't know what to do.'

She would always remember her husband tenderly for these next moments. He held her as the pain gripped her, then as it died away he said, 'Come on – lift up your arms.' He tugged the half-sodden shift over her head and, finding a dry part of it, wiped her back and legs.

'What else can you put on?'

In a drawer he found a camisole vest and a blouse and dressed her like a child.

'I'm still losing,' Violet gasped miserably, as more warm liquid seeped out down her legs. Another pain came then, sudden and violent as a crack of thunder.

'Oh God!' She clung to him groaning until it passed. 'The babby must be coming. What do we do?'

'I'd better go and get the midwife.' She could hear him trying not to panic and it made her feel stronger. 'Will you be all right?'

'Course I will. But be quick!'

Harry tore down the street like a madman and soon she heard him coming back and bounding noisily up the stairs.

'You all right?' he panted.

She was kneeling, recovering from a fresh bout of pain and nodded at him, trying to smile.

'Mrs Barker's coming. She said to get the kettle on ... Back in a tick.' And he fled downstairs again, tripping on the top step and having to right himself as he went down, stumbling and swearing. Violet managed a smile at this before the pain took her in its grip again.

'Am I having the babby?' she asked when Mrs Barker, a kind, middle-aged woman, appeared upstairs.

'Looks like it, dear.' She patted Violet's hand. 'Now don't you worry. I've seen hundreds of babbies into the world. This one's coming a bit early, but you'll be right as rain.'

The night passed in a swirl of agony. Violet lay on the mattress, which Mrs Barker covered with newspaper and then with an old sheet over the top. Violet kept hearing the paper crackling as she moved, and in between the roaring pain she was aware of Harry's voice as he ran for the things Mrs Barker requested.

As dawn broke she was becoming completely exhausted and the pain reached the point where it was unbearable, and soon the baby was born, cracking her open, then slithering into Mrs Barker's hands. There was a silence, then a tiny snuffling noise. Despite her exhaustion Violet was alert with a mother's need to hear a cry, to know it was all right.

'What's the matter?' She wanted someone to comfort her, to say things were all right.

Mrs Barker looked up, immediately trying to hide her worry. 'You've had a boy. He's beautiful, but he's a tiny little thing. We'll have to do our best to keep him warm. Let's see if he'll take any milk. You just sit up a bit, dear.'

She brought the tiny scrap of a child to Violet, wrapped up but not yet washed. Violet saw a minute face, the skin yellow, eyes tightly closed and rimed with white, the whole tiny creature pulsating like a little bird. She was frightened of him, he was so small, yet her whole being flooded with protective feelings. A little boy – *my* little boy!

'Hello, babby.' She heard the soft tenderness in her own voice.

'See if he'll suckle,' Mrs Barker ordered.

Without any ado she pulled up Violet's vest and began to massage her nipple.

'Put his mouth to you. They know what to do.'

But the little one didn't know what to do. His mouth didn't move when Violet pressed it to her breast and his eyes didn't open.

'You can do it,' she whispered.

But there was no response.

'Hand him to me,' Mrs Barker ordered. I'll wrap him up well and we'll get the fire going downstairs. It's a bitter night. We'll keep him warm till he's ready and you can get yourself a bit of shut-eye.'

Violet reluctantly handed the baby over. In a minute Mrs Barker was back.

'That husband of yours has built up a good fire – he's ever so good with him, I'll say that. Sitting holding him, he is.'

Violet smiled wanly. She was so exhausted, her pale hair plastered to her head. Mrs Barker cleaned her up and kept telling her to sleep. But she knew she would never sleep. She felt jangled and full of nerves.

But the next thing she knew, the room was filled with hard winter sunshine. Her body felt bruised and scoured out, a sodden rag between her legs and someone had just weighted the bed down, sitting beside her. It was Harry, and there were tears running down his cheeks.

'What's the matter?' She jerked upright, heart pounding.

Harry started sobbing. 'He's gone. Passed on.'

'What d'you mean?' Her teeth started to chatter. 'No!' she cried, her eyes desperately searching his face for some hope. 'No ... No – he hasn't – you're lying to me!'

But Harry's shoulders were heaving with sobs.

'He was in my arms ... He was all right ...' She could hear the shock and disbelief in his voice. 'She said to keep him warm and we was by the fire. And then he gave a bit of a shudder, like ... He wasn't breathing any more ...' He broke down and cried then, hands over his face. 'He's gone, Vi ...'

'No – he can't have! You're lying to me!' she screamed. She leapt up and ran downstairs to find him for herself.

Mrs Barker was down there and she turned. It was too late to hide the tiny form, lying on the table, wrapped in a piece of sheet.

'I'm sorry.' Mrs Barker shook her head. 'You poor young thing.'

Chapter Seventeen

They named him Bobby.

He was buried from Bessie's house, carried on the hearse of an old man who had died in Summer Lane.

Violet walked behind with Harry, and her mom and sisters and Charlie and Gladys. The day was grey and cold as stone, and Violet felt as if her heart was being torn out as she saw the hearse and the black horses with their plumes begin to move off along the row of mean, soot-grimed houses towards Witton Cemetery, carrying her little boy in the tiny white coffin.

They had had to cajole her out of the house that morning. She'd been staying over at Mom's, just for that one night. She didn't want to be with Harry – she wanted her sisters, her childhood. Harry had gone to his mother too.

Violet barely slept, lying in the old three-quarter-size bed beside Rosina. Charlie had left home, and Clarence had been very poorly over the winter with his chest and had taken to sleeping downstairs by the range. So Marigold slept in the attic and Rosina had made the room her own, with her postcards of her screen heroines, Lillian Gish and Jessie Matthews in their finery stuck to the wall above her head.

'I want my picture taken like that,' she said to Violet when they went up. 'With fur collars and feather boas and lace and silk . . .' She hugged herself at the thought.

'I've missed you, Rosy,' Violet said, miserably. 'You hardly ever come round and see me.'

'Well, you're married, aren't you?' She sat down with a bounce on the bed. 'What d'you want me for?'

It's lonely being married, she wanted to say, but didn't want to admit it.

'You could still come. Harry's not there all the time.'

'I meant to – only . . .' Rosina rolled her eyes. 'I've been busy.'

Violet smiled. Rosina seemed older than her years. She was a proper handful, bad-tempered and lippy, and although Violet sometimes admired her for it, she'd felt she didn't know her any more, or even like her, sometimes. But as they'd got into bed last night in the candlelight, Rosina stood between the two beds, her beautiful long hair loose over her shoulders, and said timidly, 'Shall I get in with you, Vi? Like we used to?'

Violet nodded, eyes filling with tears. She shifted over as Rosina blew out the candle and her slim, curving body snuggled up close to Violet. It was a comfort.

'I don't know what to say to you,' Rosina said, and Violet could hear that she was close to tears. 'I don't know what it's like. But it's so sad.'

'I want him.' Violet let go then and wept, wretchedly. 'My little boy! I just want to hold him . . .'

'Oh, Vi!' Rosina was sobbing too, and Violet remembered then how sweet she could be. Knowing her sister felt some of the pain with her was a comfort. And as she grew calmer, another thought came which had been returning to her all week as she had lain at home, aching with grief. It was the memory of that evening when Marigold found out that her mother had taken her baby and given it to the orphanage. At the time, and since, she had blocked out Marigold's great, unearthly howl of anguish. She had not understood, not then. But now she could hear it in her head. And she could feel it for herself.

'Let go of me a tick – I need to get up,' she said to Rosina.

'You gunna be sick?'

'No . . . I want to see Mari.'

She lit the candle and padded up the attic stairs to Charlie's old room. It had not changed much, still plain white and bare except for the bed and a chair. She could see Marigold's lumpen shape curled on her side in bed. Marigold hadn't said anything to her about little Bobby. She'd just silently got on with all the household tasks that were forever expected of her while everyone fussed round Violet, even Bessie, who had shown real grief over the loss of her grandson. Bessie had just taken over, and made a great to-do to the neighbours about poor Vi and all she was having to do for her.

Violet looked down at her sister, lying there with her eyes closed. No one had made any fuss about her baby going.

'Mari?' she whispered.

Marigold heaved herself resentfully on to her back and opened her eyes. Her face looked like a white, square box, framed with black hair.

Violet perched on the edge of the bed, which dipped severely in the middle. Marigold stared blankly back at her with her flinty eyes, as if she was still asleep, but with her eyes open. Tears ran down Violet's face again.

'I never said anything – at the time – about your little babby. It was terrible for you . . . I didn't know – not till now . . .' She trailed off.

Marigold's eyes narrowed for a second, into what seemed such a vicious expression that Violet's tears

84

stopped. She was chilled. But then Marigold opened her eyes again and Violet wondered if it had been the uncertain light, that she'd imagined it.

'S'all right,' Marigold said stolidly, then added matter-of-factly, 'Your babby died.'

'Yes.' The tears soon came again. 'He was so tiny . . .'

'Poor babby.' The words held no expression. There was a long silence. Violet wasn't sure what she had expected. When had it ever been easy to communicate with Marigold? She had wanted to say she understood about the baby, but hadn't she also wanted something back?

Marigold turned over again. 'I'm tired.'

'All right.' Violet got up and the bedsprings creaked slightly. 'Night, Mari.'

There was no reply.

Chapter Eighteen

1936

After Bobby, Violet had two miscarriages, the second very shortly after she knew she was expecting. It broke something in her for a time.

'I'll never be able to have a babby. There's something the matter with me!' she sobbed to Bessie, to whom she went for comfort while the griping pains still signalled the quenching of that little flame of hope that had been lit with her third pregnancy. When her body let her down again, expelling vivid red clots, it mocked her hopes so cruelly. And it was made worse by the fact that Gladys and Charlie had finally had a little boy, Norman, last year, and Josephine had married her sweetheart Percy and had a daughter with a beautiful mop of curly black hair, called Lizzie. Violet felt left behind as a wretched failure, a nobody.

She became nervy and couldn't seem to make the simplest decisions, and in her anger and sense of failure she took it out on Harry. All the things which she had put up with before, even smiled at – the way he was unpredictable and she couldn't rely on him being there, his wild, sparky energy, his refusal to be tied down – all seemed aggravating and hurtful. Now it all just felt as if he didn't care about her. He was either out with his mates or at his wretched mother's house.

'I don't know why you bothered getting married,' she raged at him sometimes, when he turned up late once again to face a congealing plate of food. 'All you want is a servant to cook your dinner.'

'Well, I'm here now, aren't I?' Often he'd come up and squeeze her round the waist, trying to win her round with teasing and kisses.

But these days she'd lost her sense of humour.

'Oh, get off – you needn't think you can get round me like that. Why don't you try coming home on time for once?'

She became a thin ghost of herself. All she could think of doing was to run home to her mom, like a child, lost in herself. She started smoking. It soothed her.

And the house was in a terrible state. The roof leaked badly over the little back bedroom and the cellar flooded, so when they went to feed the gas meter they sometimes had to wade thigh deep through sooty water. All that paint which Harry had applied so eagerly to the walls was soon discoloured and began flaking off, and the place stank of damp and mice. Violet was forever battling with infestations of bugs, but the mice were the worst. There was a constant need to place mousetraps in the scullery, and all the food like flour and sugar had to be kept in tins.

'Oh, why can't we move somewhere else, instead of festering in this bloody dump?' she would moan to Harry as she had to clean out the scullery yet again to get rid of the mouse droppings.

'We're all right,' he kept saying. 'Only a year or two now, and we'll be off . . . No point in paying more rent than we have to.'

He always seemed able to keep his spirits up, full of money-making schemes to boost their savings. His pal Goosey's dad drove a truck, and on a trip up to Stoke-on-Trent got hold of a whole load of damaged crocks. Harry and Goosey bought the job lot off him and set up with a barrow until they'd got shot of them at knock-down prices. They barely made any profit but it seemed to keep Harry happy. Christmas of 1935 Violet remembered as the 'snake' year. Harry learned from another pal how to make colourful snakes and dragons to sell as little toys. They were made out of strips of painted paper, cleverly folded back and forth again and again and attached to an empty cotton reel. When you released them and unfolded them they ran undulating along the ground, propelled by the cotton reel. For weeks the table downstairs was covered in newspaper and cheap glue and paint and Harry was begging cotton reels off the women at Vicars.

'What you up to, Harry?' they asked.

'Going to Australia!' he told them, chirpily. They humoured him.

'Oh yes, and I'm flying to the moon, darlin'!'

'You building your own aeroplane?'

Violet wondered if Harry really believed they would go. Sometimes she thought he just needed a dream to hold on to. As for her own dreams, she had none except one. A child of her own.

And then she found she was expecting again. All through the pregnancy she was frightened, on the alert for it all to go wrong. She could hardly bear to hope for better, in case the next day she started bleeding. And even if she got as far as giving birth to the baby, it might be like Bobby all over again and she would be burying it within a week. Harry did his best to be soothing.

'It's all right,' he'd murmur into her neck as she cried with worry. 'Don't worry, Vi.' And he held her so gently and kindly that she could forgive all the times they quarrelled. But most of the time she was locked into her own cold self and she knew she was gradually driving him away. After all, she knew she wasn't much of a wife to come home to. If only they could have a baby, things would be better, she just knew it. It would make everything all right.

'Look at her – she's a right bonny little thing!'

'Is she all right? Tell me she's all right!'

Violet gasped out her anxiety, now the final pangs of childbirth were over at last. Her gaze seemed to bore into the midwife, and Bessie, who had been present all through the birth.

'As healthy a babby as I've seen come into the world,' Mrs Barker said soothingly, tying the umbilical cord so she could cut it. 'Don't you fret, dear. You've had a bad time, I know, but she's your reward. A beautiful daughter for you – look!'

'She's a little peach,' Bessie said.

It was one of those rare times when gentler emotion broke through Bessie's usual bullying tones. She held up the baby, swathed in a piece of towelling, and through the blur of her own tears Violet saw a squashed, startled face, mouth beginning to open and roar. She was delicate-looking, and pale. Violet had an immediate sense of kinship with her. *She's like me*, she thought, startled. *I know her.* This, and the realization that at last she had managed to deliver a robust child, made her sob with relief and happiness.

'Let me hold her!'

'Let Mrs B. finish you off first,' Bessie said, cradling the baby in her arms. She put her face close to the little one's, crooning to it. Even though Mom was being nice,

Violet found herself brimming with rage at the sight of Bessie's huge, bulldog frame wrapping itself round *her* baby. All those babies Mom had held – four of her own and all those orphaned brats – and now she wanted to take hers as well! She couldn't stand seeing her looking into her baby's face like that as if she was the mother, taking over everything!

'Give her to me now – or I'll never let you hold her again – she's *mine!*' Violet was shrieking, tears rolling down her cheeks. She was still tightly clasping the end of the towel, hooked over the bedstead, which she'd gripped to help get through the pains.

'There's no call to carry on like that,' Mrs Barker said. 'Your mother's only helping.'

'You don't know what she's like!' Violet hardly knew what she was saying. She just felt powerless, at their mercy. 'I want my babby!'

'Here she is,' Bessie said. 'Pull yourself together, girl – no call for all that.'

She deposited the little girl in Violet's arms. Violet grew calmer and gazed at her. She had such a sweet, fine face, and when she unwrapped her from the towel, her body looked in good proportion.

'Let her feed from yer tit,' Bessie suggested, leaning over and pulling Violet's old shift away to reveal her breast, her huge frame blocking out almost all the light from the window. She went as if to latch the baby on.

'I can do it,' Violet snapped, pulling away.

'Suit yourself.' Bessie drew back, hands on her hips.

Unlike the last time, when Bobby had not had the strength even to begin feeding, the little girl latched on and began to suck.

'There you go,' Bessie said, sinking on to the chair.

The baby's suckling seemed to reach right through

Violet. Her innards contracted so strongly that she gasped.

'It doesn't half hurt!'

'You'll soon get used to it,' Mrs Barker said calmly, wringing out a rag over the white pudding basin. Bloody water ran from it over her workworn fingers.

'I want Harry to see her.'

'Bull's gone off at Mount's,' Bessie said. The 'bulls' or factory sirens had gone off one after another to signal the end of a shift. 'He'll be in soon. Time we all had a cuppa tea – more than time.'

'Joyce,' Violet whispered to the child as she suckled. 'My little babby. I'm going to call you Joyce.'

By the time Harry walked in, Mrs Barker had been paid and departed, and Violet was sitting up in bed with tea and biscuits on the chair beside her. She had Joyce cradled on one arm, would hardly let go of her for a second. Although the baby had had a good feed for one so young, Violet kept looking anxiously down at her, checking to make sure she was still breathing.

'You want to put her down for a bit and drink your tea,' Bessie said. She dwarfed the chair she was sitting on.

'No!' It was almost a snarl. 'No one's taking her off me.' Tears ran down her face and fell on Joyce's forehead. 'This time, *I'm* looking after her.'

Bessie heaped sugar into her tea. She liked three big spoonfuls. 'You'll have to put her down some time, bab,' she said complacently.

Violet stared at her with narrowed eyes. *What do you know?* she thought. *You never lost any of yours. Just keep your hands off mine.* She was startled by the violence of her feelings.

They heard Harry come in then, unaware of the surprise waiting for him. 'Anyone home?'

'Yes, son,' Bessie called, grinning. 'You'd better come up!'

Violet heard him running up the stairs two at a time. She glowed with excitement. She'd done it, at last, the thing a woman was supposed to do!

In the moment he came into the room, she saw he was afraid of what he might find, and her heart went out to him, seeing how worried he'd been, even though he hardly showed it.

'You've got a little wench,' Bessie announced.

Violet looked up at him as he came bashfully to the bedside. She felt proud, yet vulnerable, needing his approval.

'Look –' Gently she pulled back the covers and showed him the crumpled baby, sleeping so trustingly with her mouth close to Violet's nipple. 'I thought we'd call her Joyce.'

Harry leaned forward, his face intent, and very tenderly stroked the tiny creature's cheek with his finger.

'She all right?' He looked anxiously at her. His son had died in his arms and he was afraid.

'Just had a good feed,' Bessie said in the background, as Violet nodded, her eyes filling with tears again. 'Looks right as rain.'

'Joyce,' he said in wonder, and she heard the catch in his voice.

Part Two

1941–3

Chapter Nineteen

1941

Joyce was five now.

She was a thin, rather fractious child with slightly squinting grey eyes, rather like her mother in looks, with blonde, wispy hair. Soon after she was born, Bessie suggested that she look after her. At first Violet had resisted. But Harry said Violet would have to go back to work: they needed the money. Of course it made perfect sense for Bessie to look after her. Joyce would be there with her nanny and her auntie Marigold – what could be better?

So Violet handed Joyce over to Bessie and went back to Vicars.

'I'll be going back to work,' she said to Harry. 'I know I've got to – even if I'd rather stop at home and look after Joycie myself. But I won't stay a week longer in this flaming dump of a house. We've got to move.'

So now they were living only a couple of roads away from Bessie, so Violet could pop round and pick up Joyce as soon as Vicars was out. They rented another two-up two-down terrace which was not, like all the houses round there, in very good repair either, but it was a step up from the wreck of a house they had first lived in. Violet made it as nice as she could, gradually turning it into a home. She bought a remnant of pretty royal blue velvet to drape over the mantel, and Harry found a battered old dresser for them to arrange their crocks on. Violet loved that, seeing her few plates all shining and propped up in a row, the cups hanging from hooks. And Marigold came round more often now they were just round the corner and, when they first got there, she sat bodging a new peg rug for the house.

Marigold didn't have much to say, but she took to Joyce, and Violet was glad to be able to give her somewhere else to go for a bit instead of being forever at home under Bessie's thumb. She would stand and rock Joyce in her arms when she was a baby for as long as it took to get her to sleep. Marigold had reached a point in her life now where she never seemed to change. She looked roughly the same, always, with lank, shoulder-length hair, dressed in one of a couple of capacious dresses, one navy, one dark green. She never seemed to get any older or to do anything different, and lived at the beck and call of everyone else. Tucked in her pocket was always a tatty collection of paper with scraps of songs written down in her slow, looping hand. Always love songs: 'Apple Blossom Time', 'Somewhere in France with You'. Her favourite song was 'South of the Border'.

'Henry Hall made the record at the Hippodrome,' she would say solemnly. 'It's lovely, that is.'

The only times she smiled, it was usually at one of the children, but it wasn't a lively vivacious smile, more a vague uptilt of her lips, accompanied, in her eyes, by a dreamy look of affection.

'Thank goodness you're here,' Violet said to her at times, when she was most exhausted. 'I don't know how I'd manage.'

She was often worn out. Joyce had been hard work. She didn't sleep well and cried a lot, but even though it was a struggle, Violet loved the fact that she had a daughter. She could take her to see Josephine, who was soon expecting again, and little Lizzie liked being the bossy older one. And the days revolved round work and Joyce's baby needs and her mom. She had to surrender to Bessie. She knew best, Violet realized, what with all those babies she'd reared. And it was the easiest thing. Family mattered more now she had her own child, and it made her feel safe and reassured knowing there was Mom to go to, with Marigold to wheel Joyce out in the old pram every afternoon. And Harry seemed happy enough being a father. He didn't go on about Australia. Not any more. Soon after Joyce was born he came home looking excited.

'You know our bit we had put away? Well, I don't reckon we'll be needing it, so I've spent a bit of it.'

He'd bought a Norton motorcycle. Violet could see from his face how delighted he was.

'Just like a kid with a toy,' she said to Jo Snell. 'I couldn't be cross with him. I never wanted to go to Australia anyway. It's too blooming far away. What would I do in Australia without you, eh?'

When Joyce was sixteen months old, Violet took her round to the Snells one Saturday afternoon, full of excitement. She knew Jo would be there with her mom and Lizzie, as they always called in on Saturdays. The Snells' house was a home from home. Jo was heavy out front with another baby. As they sat drinking tea in their cosy back room, Violet said, 'Eh, Jo – I've got summat to tell you. I've another on the way as well.'

Josephine grinned, laying a hand on her swollen stomach.

'Must be out of our flaming heads, mustn't we?'

Linda was born in March 1938, in the small hours of

a bitterly cold night. Once again Mrs Barker was in attendance, but Bessie was not there. It was so cold, they laid a bed for her downstairs and kept the range going all night. Just as things were really getting going, the meter ran out and Harry had to go down and feed it with pennies. Violet always remembered those moments, the room suddenly drenched in darkness with only a dim glow from the range, and herself isolated in the pains of labour. Somehow it made her feel strong. A few moments later they re-lit the gas mantles and everything was back to normal, though she felt she had travelled to another world.

'This one's not like Joyce!' Mrs Barker exclaimed as Violet, groaning, pushed the baby out. 'It's got black hair!'

The child was a round-faced, black-haired little girl with Harry's stamp all over her and, as she grew older, dancing brown eyes, just like his.

'She looks like Rosina,' Bessie observed when she saw her the next day. 'She were just like that, born.'

Then her face hardened, lips twisting. For a moment she forgot that she didn't mention Rosina's name. Not any more.

She gave a bitter sigh. 'Wherever *she* is.'

Chapter Twenty

A few days before her eighteenth birthday in 1936, Rosina ran away from home.

They didn't hear from her for months after, but everyone was sure she had gone to London. She went so suddenly that she didn't even take her film pictures – Jessie Matthews and the others. Bessie ripped them off the wall in fury.

'She needn't think she's coming back here when her pockets are empty. Selfish little bitch, taking off without a word! Never gives a thought to anyone else – always been the same! Well, I wash my hands of her – she's no daughter of mine any more.'

Her rage simmered endlessly. She'd lost control of Rosina. It had been coming for years – Rosina's lippiness, her lack of fear of her mother, unlike the others.

No one had ever crossed Bessie like this before. Before her own mother had died at her own hand, she'd begged Bessie to take special care of Clarence, her precious boy. Apart from two years in France, Clarence had been with her ever since, content to be under the thumb, it seemed, rather than making a life for himself.

'He was never the same any road – not after the trenches,' Bessie always said. He did little jobs for a bit, then just as suddenly stopped and sat at home.

And she had her other three children well in her control still, circling round her like planets round the sun. But Rosina had had the temerity to break off and go spinning away on a path of her own choice and without a hint of warning. Nothing had prepared Bessie for Rosina's spirit, and the older she grew the more rebellious she became.

Violet knew Rosy had become a handful but she was too caught up in her own problems during those years to see how it was going. Rosina stayed away from home more and more, haunting the streets round the theatres – the Hippodrome and Alex in town – hungry to catch a glimpse of theatre people and life.

In the Lozells Road was a photographer's business by the name of Juggins. Rosina had heard that Alfred Juggins and his son were the official photographers for the Theatre Royal in Aston, and that actors and celebrities often frequented the place to have their portraits taken. Rosina took to hanging around the shop with some of her friends and occasionally came home radiant, full of the fact that she'd seen one of the names, great or small of the acting profession, going into the shop.

'Charlie Chaplin's been in there, when he was young!'

After she disappeared, they managed to prise out of one of the other girls the fact that Rosina had begun a passionate romance with a young actor called Michael Albie, whom she had met near Juggins photographer's. Albie was entranced by Rosina's pretty looks and vivacious personality, as well as her passionate ambition to be part of the life of theatre herself. Now, for all any of them knew, she had gone to London to be with Albie.

'She'll end up on the streets with a brat in her belly and nowhere to sleep but the gutter,' Bessie decreed, with vengeful satisfaction.

It wasn't until four months later that Rosina sent a

postcard from London, light-hearted in tone, to say that she was well and happy and not to worry. There was no address on it and she did not say what she was doing.

Bessie peered at the card, turning it over and over. It was a photograph of Buckingham Palace.

'I s'pose she thinks she's going to be living in there next.'

Violet was just relieved to hear that Rosina was all right. Running off like that felt such a daring, impossible thing to do! She could no more imagine doing that herself – even as far as London – than she could going to Australia. But Rosy had always had a spark in her. Violet felt hurt that she had not confided in her, and she missed Rosy and longed to be able to see her. But Rosina obviously didn't want to be reached.

Chapter Twenty-One

The war changed their lives.

Gas masks sat in their boxes by the door, houses were blacked out and the windows taped against blast. Air-raid shelters went up and all sorts of regulations came into force. The evenings seemed long and dark, shut in the houses, and Bessie and Clarence bought a wireless.

Groups of young men disappeared into the forces, but Vicars had gone over to making ammunition and Harry's and the others' jobs were reserved occupations. They sat out what came to be known as the 'phoney war'. It was when the raids started in the autumn of 1940, with all their fear and cruelty and destruction, that the war came up close. It was with them in the long, sleepless nights, the terrible drone of the planes overhead, thin searchlights sketching like pencils across the sky over the city, in the evil glow of fire, and mornings of dust and rubble and the stink of gas.

From August 1940 Birmingham was under frequent attack and you never knew, when dawn broke after a raid, what familiar landmark would have disappeared next. The Bull Ring was blitzed at the end of August, the Market Hall, loved by so many people as a place to meet and shop, which had seemed so permanent a part of life, was smashed to pieces. It felt as if nothing could ever be the same again. And it was this time of death and fear which started to change Violet's life.

She had settled to a small, safe existence which revolved round these few streets, with all the familiarity of their blackened bricks, smoking chimney stacks and neighbourhood characters. Life consisted of her job, her daughters and husband, and her mom.

Linda was very different from Joyce. Soft and rounded, with a sweet, fleshy face and thick black hair, she was as quiet and serious as Joyce was jumpy and jealous and easily put out. Linda had a solemn, penetrating gaze. As a toddler she would stand in front of her mother, quite close to her, and just gaze at her.

'What're you looking at?' Violet would joke, trying to make her crack her face. 'Lost your tongue? Ooh, she's making me feel quite queer staring like that! Stop it, pet! I wonder what she's thinking?'

If she was thinking anything she usually didn't have the chance to do it for much longer, as Joyce, agitated at being left out, would come up and pinch her or provoke her in some other way and make her cry.

The girls spent a lot of time with Bessie. When there were daytime raids, Violet fretted at work, in the basement of Vicars which they used as a shelter. She knew her mom took the girls under the stairs. Bessie wasn't going slumming it in any public shelter. Violet and Harry's house had a bigger coal cellar than Bessie's, so they cleaned it out and Violet went down there with the girls when it got bad. There wasn't room for all of them so Harry stayed under the stairs. It was miserable and cold in the cellar and the ceiling was very low. Violet hated it. All you wanted after that was a nice cup of tea to perk you up and sometimes the water was cut off!

'I'd rather stay in bed and take my chance with their bleeding bombs,' she complained some mornings that autumn.

But soon after, something happened that made her vow never to say such a thing again.

'Ey-up!' one of the lads winked and called to her as she clocked in for work that morning. 'Best bloody night's sleep you've ever 'ad, I s'pose?'

Violet laughed grimly. 'Slept like a babby, what d'you think?'

Like everyone else, she was exhausted. It was November 1940 and the city had been pounded night after night. The row of houses along from the works had been hit; they had scrambled into Vicars through the morning drizzle, over hosepipes and piles of timber and rubble and glass, and there was a stench of sewage. One end of the front of Vicars had been blasted. Some of the windows were out and Violet could hear the sound of glass being swept up. It was always especially unnerving when the destruction came so close.

'Trying to do to us what they've done to Coventry,' people were saying. 'Bloody kraut bastards.'

Mr Riddle looked just as worn out as everyone else. Apparently he had spent the night in the cellar of the factory.

Violet went to begin work. The engines were on, the belts turning on the lathes. She looked at her machine with some affection. They were beautiful things, she thought. Today seeing the heavy iron lathe was like seeing a steady, familiar face amid all the chaos. She looked round for Josephine, and saw with a pang of disquiet that there was no one at her machine. Jo was usually in before her, full of energy as always, calling out some clever remark like, 'Decided to have a lie-in, did you?' because she was quicker at getting up and getting her children ready.

Violet tried to tell herself that there must be a good reason – perhaps Lizzie or little Sam was poorly, or Jo was ill herself. But when an hour had passed and other people were asking, she couldn't stand worrying. She feared the worst, sick with dread.

She crossed the shop floor to find Mr Riddle. His face was pale and she could see the tired lines round his eyes.

'I can't think straight worrying about Josephine,' she said.

'Oh God – I know,' Mr Riddle said wearily. The gulf between the gaffer and everyone else on the factory floor had narrowed with all the troubles. Mr Riddle was a kind, humane man who looked out for his workers. 'It was a hell of a night last night. I've never known it as bad. Look, love – go and see. It's only up the road, isn't it?'

'Ta ever so much,' Violet said. She could tell Mr Riddle was worried too; he had a rather soft spot for Jo, who was one of his fastest workers and always cheerful.

Hanging up her overall, she hurriedly put on her coat and hat. It was still grey and drizzly outside. She thought she'd never seen such a dismal sight as that road, a great gap where five or six houses had been taken out. The end of a terrace had been destroyed; the bomb had smashed into the court behind, leaving what was usually an invisible yard of dwellings suddenly open to view in all its glorious squalor. At the end the three lavs were on full view, the door of one swinging open. The sight made Violet's heart sink. She felt sick.

'Oh God, Jo – please be all right!' she found herself muttering desperately. 'Why are you so late, you silly sod? Couldn't you have just got there on time today?'

She could hardly bear to turn into the Snells' street for fear of what she might find.

And what she saw when she did left her in no doubt. She stopped, stunned.

'Oh God above . . .!' Her hand went to her lips and her legs started to shake. She could hardly believe what was in front of her.

There were fire engines at the end of the road, and an ambulance. The right-hand section of the street, and the Snells' house, number twenty-two, was gone. There was nothing but piles of rubble, smashed sections of walls with stained strips of wallpaper clinging to them and the debris of lives – a smashed pram, a kettle, a rent book, sodden among the heaps of bricks. The mess was unbelievable. Everything was wet, and stinking and so, so sad-looking.

Numbly, Violet scrambled across the mess to one of the ARP team. He was a middle-aged man, his moustache grey with dust.

'Number twenty-two? They're my friends . . .'

Silently he waved his hand over the wreckage.

'Where was it?'

'About there.'

He shook his head. 'I'm sorry, love. This was the bit that really took it. There's no one alive in there. No chance.'

'But . . .' She couldn't take this in. 'They would've been under the stairs – Jo, her mom, the two kiddies . . .'

'They've brought them out already.' His voice was quiet and gentle, and he was shaking his head. 'All of 'em. I'm sorry. Poor souls.'

Violet stood in the road as he moved away, shoulders hunched. She was so much in shock that she didn't know how long she stood there, shaking and chilled to the bone. It was only when an ambulance turned into the street and hooted at her to move that she came to again.

It hit Violet very hard.

Days went by before she could even take it in or begin to cry over it. She had been very fond of all the Snells. They had been almost family to her. And worst of all was the loss of Jo, her best friend, whom she could tell her heart to, share all the everyday happenings of life with, and the laughter. She had always loved Jo's sunny outlook at work.

'Smile and the world smiles with you – weep and you weep alone,' Jo used to say.

But there'd be no more smiles now.

Once Violet's emotion began to release itself, she only had to look at Joyce and Linda and think about Jo's little ones and the tears would start to flow. Especially as Joyce kept asking about them.

'Why don't we see Lizzie? I want to go to Lizzie's house.'

'Lizzie doesn't live there any more,' Violet told her. 'I'm sorry, bab, but we won't be able to see Lizzie and Sam any more.'

Joyce's little face creased with displeasure. 'What about Auntie Jo?'

'Not her either.'

One day she'd have to tell them that the Germans had killed Auntie Jo and Lizzie and Sam. But not today.

Violet felt terribly lonely. 'I can't stand being at Vicars now,' she told Bessie. 'Harry says I'm being silly, that I know everyone else there. But it's not the same. It's getting me down.'

'Well – it's not the only place in the world to work,' Bessie said. 'They're all crying out for munitions workers – and the pay might be better than you're getting at Vicars.'

Violet stared at her. She realized that while she had needed to have a moan she had not seriously thought about changing her job. She wasn't good at changing things on her own, she realized. She just let things drift along and happen to her.

Chapter Twenty-Two

During that winter of the Blitz, Harry's mom fell ill. She couldn't swallow and the flesh was dropping off her.

Then one February night, in the small hours, when big flakes of snow were falling, one of Mrs Martin's neighbours came to fetch Harry. Violet listened to their footsteps dying away along the street. A train whistled in the eerie quietness. She knew her mother-in-law did not have long to live.

Before things had become really bad with his mother, Harry was walking along Summer Lane one Saturday afternoon with his pal Stan 'Goosey' Gosling. As they crossed over Asylum Road, Harry nudged Goosey and jerked his head towards a man walking away from them along the cobbled street.

'See that bloke? That's my father.'

Goosey's brow wrinkled. 'I thought your old man'd passed on?'

'Might as well've done.'

'Well, ain't you going to speak to him?'

'Ain't seen him in ten year or more. Why should I bother now?'

'I just thought . . . 'E's your dad, that's all.'

'Bugger 'im.' Harry's expression was mutinous.

But Harry dithered on the corner as his father moved away. He couldn't seem to leave it.

'You could follow – see where he goes. He don't have to see you.'

With an awkward nod, half making as if to reject the idea, then changing his mind, Harry said gruffly, 'All right. But he'd better not see.'

They dashed along Asylum Road after the man, who was almost out of sight by now. A woman pushing a pram laden with coal piled curses on them as they almost crashed into her.

'He must've been away and come back,' Harry panted. 'He can't've been round here all this time – we'd've seen him.'

Harry's father turned right into Alma Street. He stopped for a moment outside the Sheep Shears Works to talk to someone and Harry and Goosey shrank back, but then he walked almost to the far end near Six Ways, crossed over the street and disappeared up an entry.

Harry stopped, only then realizing how much his heart was pounding. Suddenly he wanted, overpoweringly, to know about his father. Where had he been? Who was he living with now? Did he ever give his family, his kids, a thought?

He gave a shrug and said indifferently, 'Oh well. Least we know where the silly sod is, any road.'

Two days after Mrs Martin had breathed her last on that silent, snowy night, Harry was standing alone by the entry in Alma Street only streets away from home. The road looked a mess, edged with filthy clods of frozen snow. For reasons he could not explain to himself, he had not mentioned to Tom and Marj, the brother and sister he was closest to, that he knew where their father was or that he was coming here.

'Right, you bugger.' His breath formed white clouds

110

on the freezing air. Harry's chest was so tight he could hardly breathe. Horrified, he realized he might cry, and had to walk up and down the road for a minute or two more to get himself under control. He braced himself, pulling his shoulders back, then strode along the entry. At the entrance, he stopped.

'*Christ.*'

He wasn't exactly used to living in luxury, but this place was among the most dreary and squalid he'd ever seen. It was small and dark, overshadowed by the back wall of a factory, and there were rubbish and filth all across it. In one corner lay a pool of stagnant water, half frozen today, and in a pile of muck round the bottom of the lamp he could see the remains of a sodden rag doll. Its grey face was turned sorrowfully towards him. There was a foul stench on the air, even in the cold. *It must pong like hell in here when it's hot*, he thought.

He stood at a loss for a moment, then a woman came out from the house behind him. She was thin and dreary-looking, not especially young, her hair roughly scraped back, and carrying a pail of ash. She stared at him with a hostile expression, pulling her black shawl round her.

'What d'yer want?'

'I'm looking for . . .' He stumbled over the words. 'For a bloke called Josiah Martin.'

'E's inside,' she said indifferently. 'Asleep – as usual.' And she walked away, the pail causing her to lean over to one side.

Harry walked into the house, as cold inside as out, as the fire was not lit. The stink of urine overpowered everything else. It was a stench he always associated with his father and he was overcome with shame. The

111

stench was coming from another bucket, by the range, which was acting as a po'.

There was a ragged chair in the corner. Harry made sense of the shape sprawled in it, taking in first the feet, toes peeping through black socks like mushrooms pushing up through soil. The right big toe was showing, the nail yellow and gnarled. His eyes followed the short legs, stocky body, bloated belly covered by a stained shirt, the buttons straining. He could see dark hairs in the spaces where the shirt was forced open.

It was as if he was avoiding the face at first because he knew what he would see. He was very like his father. When he at last forced himself to focus on the jowly, unshaven face, with its drinker's hue, the unkempt hair, once black, like his, now grizzled, it was with the horror of seeing himself as he might be twenty years on. What he might – was even destined to – become.

Memories rushed into his mind: his father when they were young, and he used to take them fishing to Edgbaston reservoir or even right out to Sutton Park. But often he'd stop, long before they wanted to leave, and go to a pub. He and Tommy and the others spent hours sitting outside pubs waiting for him to come out. There was the Christmas when Mom'd scrimped for weeks to get them all a decent meal, carried a joint of beef to the baker's to be cooked in the oven, made everything as nice as she could – and then they couldn't find him. He rolled in at five o'clock, long after they'd all finished eating, and Mom had sat crying over the dirty crocks. Eventually, though, she'd said, 'Well, sod him. You kids are my family, not him.' And for once, the only time he could ever remember, they all sat round and played cards and I-Spy and all the games they could think of that afternoon. And when Dad came home, they showed him how they were laughing and didn't need him and Mom acted as if it didn't matter if he was there or not. Harry was nine that year. And the memory of Mom's face as Dad came through the door, barely able to stand, made him want to sob like a child now, standing over him. Then he wanted to take a rock and smash his head in. He looked older. So much older.

Harry took in a deep, shuddering breath. That miserable cow of a woman would be back soon. He didn't want her around, seeing this.

'Oi – ' He shook his father's shoulder and spoke very brusquely. 'You – Josiah Martin – wake up.'

He was quite surprised how easy the man was to rouse, when you considered how deep his drunken slumber could be.

'Wha – ?' He woke abruptly, the eyes snapping open, yawning and scratching at the salt and pepper stubble on his cheek. Sitting up, he gave a loud, rasping belch. He stared round, not seeming to make sense of anything.

'D'you know who I am?' Harry said. He could feel aggression rising in him. *You're my bloody father!* he wanted to shout. *You'd better know who I am or else! Where've you been all these years, you drunken bastard?*

Josiah's bloodshot eyes turned on him. Harry could see he was having trouble focusing. His hands were shaking and his whole body seemed to quiver. His breathing, through his nose, was very loud. Narrowing his eyes, he said, 'Tommy?'

'Guess again, Dad.' He'd at least realized it was one of his sons. He and Tommy were also alike. Harry's hands, in his jacket pockets, were clenched into fists.

Josiah stared at him, at a loss.

'You one of my sons? Can't remember yer name.'

'Harry. It's Harry.'

'Oh ar. Harry.' He considered this, staring into the dead fireplace. 'Why're you 'ere?'

'Mom died. Two nights ago.'

His head tilted round. 'Elsie?'

'You can remember *her* name then.'

The savagery in his tone seemed to cut the air.

Josiah was about to speak when the woman with the ash pail came back in. Harry loathed her on sight. She walked smartly to the fireplace and slammed the pail down.

'Who's this then? What's going on?'

'I'm his son,' Harry said. 'And it's none of your cowing business what's going on.'

She was about to have a go, Harry could see, her face puckering up hatefully. He strode out of there before he punched the miserable bint in the face.

'Funeral's Friday,' he said on the way out. 'Eleven o'clock. St Mary's.'

The day of the funeral he still felt all the time as if he was going to explode. It was freezing, and wet. Couldn't have been a nastier day if it tried. The snow was all gone but there was a mizzling cold rain and the wind was bitter. He felt everything was against him.

'Put that fag out,' he snarled at Violet as they reached the church.

Smoke, smoke – all she ever bloody did these days. Like a cowing chimney.

'All right,' Violet said carefully. She dropped the stub and ground it out with her heel. His feelings softened for a moment. She was a looker all right when she took the trouble. Her hair was shoulder-length and she'd

114

curled the ends today. He could see glimpses of its gold against the black hat and coat. Her blue eyes, deep as pools, contained the sad, yearning look which had always made him feel protective towards her. She was even thinner now of course – tired-looking. Jo Snell going like that had knocked her, he knew. The sight of her moved him. He knew he loved her and wanted things to be right, but all he could feel was this tight rage and grief which blocked out everything else.

She was being gentle with him, he knew. Sorry for him because of his mom, even though he knew she could never stand the woman. She had Joycie and Linda hanging on to her skirts, all in their best clothes and bewildered by the solemn carry-on of a funeral. Little Linda looked up at him with those dark, inscrutable eyes, as if waiting for something.

'I've got to go,' he said, turning away.

He was a bearer. He had to carry his mom's coffin into the church. No good thinking about anything else. Nudging the edges of his mind all the time was the question: would Dad come? Did he care whether he did or not?

Twenty years Mom and Dad were married, he calculated as they sat in a row in the pews. The rain was still on his coat. He felt out of place in a church. It was cold and the pews were hard.

The coffin was in front of them in the aisle. He found it hard to take in that Mom was in there, that he'd never see her again. For a moment the tight feeling in him increased so that it was almost unbearable. It frightened him, the way he felt. He couldn't make sense of it. As if his whole body was about to break open.

'We brought nothing into this world and it is certain we will carry nothing out . . .'

The vicar's words passed by him, barely heard. Suddenly, though, Linda, who was standing beside him, reached up and with her little hand caught hold of the ends of his fingers. Harry looked down. The child was gazing up at him with such naked trust that he suddenly wanted to weep. He took her hand properly and squeezed it.

I'm her dad, he thought, as if he'd only realized it for the first time. He could see himself in her, the way she looked. The thought filled him with joy and fear. Whatever kind of father did he know how to be?

They were sitting and the vicar was reading: 'For a thousand years in thy sight are but as yesterday . . .'

There was a thump at the back of the church as the door opened and a bang as it closed. Harry felt the hairs stand up on the back of his head. Somehow he could not bring himself to turn round, not while they were all sitting facing the front. Whoever it was must have sat down and it was quiet again.

But within a couple of minutes, before the vicar had got to the end of the readings, they all heard it start, low at first, then louder and unmistakable; the lurching, indecipherable singing of a drunk man. A drunk man who was the husband of the woman being commended to her grave.

The eruption that had been waiting to happen inside Harry began then. He loosed Linda's hand and got up from his seat, charging down the long aisle of the church to where Josiah was sitting, slumped to one side in the back row.

'Get out!' He seized him by the lapels of his jacket and hoiked him to his feet. 'Get yourself out of here – now!'

Outside the church door, Harry had no words any

more. For the second time in his life he laid into his father, holding him pinned against the wall with one hand and punching and punching him with the other. There was no holding back on it, no reserve: all self-control was lost in the bursting floodgates of his rage and pain. Josiah made no sound except a winded 'urrgh' noise when Harry punched him hard in the stomach and he collapsed, sagging to the floor.

'Harry – don't, for God's sake, what're you doing?'

Violet was beside him.

'Don't, love – stop it! You'll kill him!'

She was pulling at his arm, trying to prevent him doing any more. Josiah lay on his side on the wet path. He was straining to breathe, after the winding he had taken from Harry's punch.

'You could've killed him!' she said. He could see the horror in her eyes but could not really take in what he might have done in his rage. 'D'you want to go to prison? Come on – we'd better sit him up.'

They managed to wedge Josiah in a sitting position against the wall. He groaned and mumbled and his face was all cut about, but Harry had done no more damage than that.

For a moment the two of them stood, stunned, in the rain. The organ was playing inside the church.

'Christ,' Harry said, his voice beginning to crack. 'Just look at him.'

'Oh, love,' Violet said.

Her eyes were full of emotion and she went to put her arms round him, but he couldn't stand her affection, her pity.

'Don't,' he said. And pushed her away.

Chapter Twenty-Three

October 1941

Violet stood by the gas stove, grimacing at the pans of butter beans and boiling fish. Harry was bound to moan. What was she supposed to do? She'd never been a good cook but now, with all the shortages and rationing, it was harder than ever.

Eyeing the clock on the mantel she wiped her hands on her apron. Saturday evening, and she was alone, as usual. She never knew when Harry would come home. Most nights he went to the pub and she didn't know what mood he'd be in when he got back. He seemed to be always frustrated and angry. With petrol in short supply, he couldn't take the bike out much now and it was under a tarpaulin out at the back. It had all got much worse since his mother died. There were still rare moments of tenderness between them, but the good times had grown fewer.

'Let's see what you've got to say.'

She switched on the wireless which stood in pride of place with its accumulator on the sideboard. Harry had come home with it a few months ago and she loved having it. He was spending more money these days – had given up on saving all the time. The wireless was company and cheered the place up no end. She missed Jo Snell and the rest of the family horribly. The ache of it never quite left her. Without Jo as a friend and with Harry hardly ever in, she was very lonely.

Making friends didn't come very easily to her. But

she tried to make things nice and keep herself looking presentable. It seemed a bit daft, the war on and everything, all those ships going down and Russian names she'd never heard before. The raids seemed to be over. There'd been warnings, of course, but not much in the way of actual raids since the really bad ones in April. But you still had to keep cheerful somehow, put a face on, a bit of lipstick and powder. She had let her hair grow over the past months, put some rollers in at night so it hung in pretty waves on her shoulders.

Humming along to the wireless, she went to the back door. The girls were playing out in the little yard in the grey light. She could see the barrage balloon – 'our' balloon, as the girls called it. A sycamore tree on the scrubby bit of ground the other side of the wall had shed its papery brown leaves over into their yard.

'Joycie! Linda – get in here for tea!'

'Mom – they'm birds, they'm flying!' Linda cried, her plump hands releasing a drifting shower of leaves into the air.

'Birds,' Violet muttered, shaking her head. That child was a proper one for seeing things a queer way.

But she smiled and leaned against the doorframe, watching them. It had been a long day, nothing but hard graft and kiddies, but it was a treat to see their cheeks rosy in the biting air, especially Linda, whose round face seemed to glow. Whenever she stopped to look at her girls she was struck by the difference in them – Joycie, five now, was thin as a twig, with her pale, wispy hair, and Linda, three, was sturdier like Harry, with his brown eyes and thick black locks. You'd never guess they were sisters. Even the way they laughed was quite different. Joyce had a high, thin giggle and Linda chuckled with a rich gurgle in her throat.

Harry stood across the table from her, and his face changed. He looked instantly sober and regretful, but behind this she could also sense an excitement. She would never forget the look on his face at that moment.

'Got summat to tell you, Vi.'

'What?' She was holding the plate of food out to him.

'Me and Goosey – we've joined up.'

'*What?*' She put the plate down with a bang. Beans spilled on to the table. 'You can't've – what d'you mean?'

'The army. We're going. The both of us.'

'But . . . You can't! You're reserved occ— Mr Riddle won't let you!'

'He's said I can. I've asked him – a few times. He was down the pub earlier on and he said, "Well, lad – I can tell you're just going to keep on and on and wear me down. If you're that restless you'll only go upsetting everyone – you'd better go with the others." '

Violet pulled out the chair and sat down, as her legs would no longer hold her.

'But – you don't have to go, do you? They want you in the factory! You mean it's what *you* want, to go off and leave us?' Her voice was starting to thicken with tears.

He came round behind her and put his hands on her shoulders; the warm feel of how he used to touch her made her weep.

'I don't want to leave *you*. That ain't it. I just . . .' He sounded completely sober now, and sad. 'You know me, Vi – I've always wanted to get out of here. I'm a silly sod, I know – itchy feet. Just want life to be . . . *bigger* than anything I've ever seen. Never thought I was going to do it, like, not now, with the kiddies and everything. But there's blokes going off and ... I don't want to be left behind.' He shrugged. 'Won't be for long, I don't s'pose.'

He sounded apprehensive, as if only now was it sinking in what he had done.

She turned to him, wiping her face. The girls were watching in silence and she didn't want to upset them.

'Oh God, Harry – why d'you have to go? I need you here – I can't do all this on my own. How'm I ever going to manage?'

'You'll manage.' He kissed the top of her head. 'You're my missis – and you're much stronger than you think.'

Chapter Twenty-Four

He left a few days later, for basic training. The night before he went, they lay together in their room with the leaking roof. It was raining and the drops fell with a metallic 'plink' into the pail underneath.

They made love with a tenderness that had been missing for a long time. She lay resting on his strong, stocky body afterwards, her cheek resting on the V of black, wiry hair on his chest. He curved his arm round her and laid his hand on her head.

'Wait for me, won't you?' he said quietly, and she could hear that he was frightened, although he wanted to go. Frightened of what was facing him, and that everything would have changed by the time he came back. 'I'll be able to think of you – in this house, the girls and everything.'

She reached up and kissed his cheek, her tears coming again. If only it was always like this – this closeness between them. For the first time in such a long time she could feel she loved him, and had a glimpse of a kind of heaven that she had always longed for. Why did it have to be snatched away now?

'I don't want you to go!'

'I'm no good to you.'

She raised her head. 'What d'you mean? Course you are!'

'Nah. Look at my old man. I'll be no better, in the long run.'

Whatever she said, that he wasn't like that, it seemed to make no difference and when he spoke like that his eyes were very sad.

He left very early the next day, when the girls were still in bed. Before he opened the door he took her in his arms once again and looked down at her.

'I just have to go. Don't really know why. But I love you. I do.'

Violet stood at the door in the dawn light, with her coat over her nightdress, and watched him walk away, past the run-down houses of the streets he had so long wanted to escape.

I'm all on my own was all Violet could think, for days. She felt desolate and frightened. What on earth am I going to do?

Out of habit, she did what she had always done. She turned to Bessie. There was no Josephine, no husband. Bessie was already looking after the girls, as well as Gladys and Charlie's two boys. It felt easier to go back to being Bessie's girl than try to do anything else for herself.

Every morning she was up early, pulling back the blackout curtains in the hope of some light to get ready by, though winter was coming fast now. She got Joyce ready for school and took both of them along Summer Lane to her mom's. Bessie made sure Joyce got to school all right and had Linda for the day. It gave Violet a soft feeling inside, seeing them playing in the yard with Colin and Norman, where she'd played out not so long ago herself. Somehow it made her feel safe, as if

125

amid all the destruction there was something that wouldn't ever change.

'Give me your ration-book,' Bessie said, soon after Harry left. 'No point in us both making tea, is there? Waste of gas. We'll all have it together.'

Violet hesitated for a moment. Wasn't this just what she had wanted to escape from? From Bessie being in charge of everything? But it was so much easier, and nice not to go home to an empty house and know no one else was going to walk in through the door that night. Charlie and Gladys took the boys every night and went home for their tea, but Violet stayed and ate with Bessie and Clarence and Marigold and the girls. Even Clarence was working more now, in munitions, and was full of importance about it.

So Violet did as Bessie told her. The more she stayed away from home, the more she could forget how alone she was.

Chapter Twenty-Five

In December they all went to the flicks together and saw the Pathé news about how the Japanese had bombed America at Pearl Harbor. It had been all every-one talked about at Vicars for the past days.

'If we've got to fight the bleeding Japs an' all, there'll be no end to it,' Clarence said. He was full of opinions these days.

However, in the Wiles family even the news of the attack on Pearl Harbor faded into insignificance com-pared with the news received a few days later. Violet had just come in, after trudging along the dark street from work.

'Look at this –' Bessie, tight-lipped, went to the mantelpiece and fetched out an envelope.

Violet stared at the looping handwriting. There was something familiar about it. Bessie watched with her arms folded. As Violet turned the envelope round, something fell out. She gasped at the photograph which lay on the table. There, after a silence of almost five years: Rosina.

'Is that Rosy?' she cried excitedly. 'Oh, my goodness, look at her! She looks like Jessie Matthews!'

Joyce and Linda ran up, attracted by the excitement, and they all pored over the picture. Rosina was dressed in a white hat with a black feather in the band, the brim upturned at the front, and a white dress bordered with black at the neck. Lacy white gloves reached almost to her elbows. Her dark hair was bobbed level with her chin and her eyebrows had been plucked to thin, elegant lines. She looked at once provocative and sweet.

'Who's that?' Joyce demanded.

'That's your auntie Rosina,' Violet said, staring at the picture, still hardly believing it. 'It *is* her, isn't it? I mean you can see it is, only I can hardly believe ... Oh, my word, look at her!' She felt a sudden surge of longing for her little sister. Marigold also stood beside them, quietly looking.

'It's her, all right,' Bessie said. Her voice was full of bitterness. Rosina had long escaped her control. Yet look at her! Violet thought. There she was, so beautiful and obviously making a go of it.

Joyce was pulling a letter from the envelope.

'Read it, Nana – read it to us!'

For a moment Violet saw a hunted expression cross her mother's bullish features.

'I ain't reading it!' The aggression was back.

'Can't you read, Nana?' Joyce laughed.

There was a terrible silence.

'Get your mother to read it. I can't be bothered with it.' And Bessie turned her back and busied herself by the range as if she couldn't care less.

'Give it here, Joycie. Ooh – ' Violet raised the blue paper to her nose. 'This paper smells nice!'

'Perfume.' Bessie tutted. 'Just like that one to drench her paper in perfume.'

There was only part of an address at the top. It just said, 'Clapham, London.'

'You might as well read it out to everyone,' Bessie ordered.

Dear Mom and everyone,

Thought it was time I dropped you a line to show you how I'm getting along. I have had a few parts lately and this is the best – running every night this month and I'm fit to drop! All going very well and I might be heading for wedding bells soon. I'll keep you posted.

Love to Violet, and Marigold and Charlie and Clarence. I'll drop by and see you all one day.

Rosina. xx

Violet looked up through her tears and to her surprise saw that Marigold's eyes had filled up as well. It was the first time she had seen her sister display any real emotion in a long time.

'Oh, Mari – It's so nice to hear from our Rosy again, isn't it? If only she'd come back. I don't half miss her!'

Marigold nodded and blew her nose.

'Little madam – if I saw her again I'd have a thing or two to say.' Bessie banged the frying pan down hard on the hob. Her body seemed to vibrate with fury.

It was maddening, of course, like Rosina always was, not giving a proper address and hardly saying anything. But she looked so pretty, so successful, and Violet ached to see her again and hear all about her life. Her own seemed suddenly so very drab and unadventurous in comparison. But Rosina wouldn't tell them where she was living or in which theatre she was playing. Was she so afraid of them coming to find her? Why? What had they done? And that hurt and made her feel rejected and angry.

'You'd think she could have let us know her address, wouldn't you?'

'Let me see it again!' Linda almost snatched the

picture from her. Her eyes seemed to drink in the sight of Rosina, but she was confused. 'Who's that lady?'

'Our auntie, stupid,' Joyce said.

Bessie shrugged angrily. 'Give it here, Linda. We'll put it away. She obviously don't want anything to do with the likes of us any more. Thinks she's far too good for us.'

But Violet noticed that she did not put the picture back in the envelope. Instead she propped it back behind the jug so you could just see Rosina peeping out from behind it, full of dark mischief.

'It's time I shook myself up a bit,' Violet decided, after they got home that night.

All evening, Joyce and Linda had been agog for stories about their mysterious auntie Rosina, whom neither of them could remember. As they walked home, feeling their way along in the darkness, Linda said, 'Is it dark where Auntie Rosina is?'

'Yes, I s'pect so,' Violet said absently. 'She's only down London.'

Yet the question didn't seem such a silly one. London, and Rosina's life, were another world to her altogether, one where she could imagine that the sun shone all the time.

Once she'd got the girls to bed, she sat downstairs, the windows blacked out. She felt restless and turned on the wireless. It was Thursday, *ITMA* day, and she distracted herself laughing at the antics of Colonel Chinstrap, Mrs Mopp and Sophie Tuckshop. But when the show was over her unquiet feelings had grown rather than quietened. She clicked the wireless off and sat there, hearing the tick of the clock and the murmuring of the McEvoys next door. She thought about Rosina, all her impatient, bounding energy.

'Oh, Rosina,' she whispered, 'you're the end, you really are.'

The sense of exasperation with her sister was still strong, but mixed with the powerful desire to see her was a deep longing of her own. Hadn't she once wanted more from life? How had she spent these years? Having her girls, it was true, but running round after Harry, appeasing his every mood, trying to keep him and his love. Had she anything left now of herself?

I'm only twenty-six, she found herself thinking. That's not that old. And Harry's gone. What's going to happen to my life? Am I just going to go to work and come back and sit here like this now, night after night? The war could go on for ever!

Turning the light off, she went upstairs and in the dark pulled back the curtain. There was not much to see except darkness and the even denser black of houses picked out by the thin moonlight. She slid the window up and stood shivering in the cold air, elbows on the sill.

What is there out there? she wondered, her thoughts wheeling like a bird. Beyond Aston, and Birmingham, way beyond to the sea, to other countries, other sights. She had never seen any of them, and knew she probably never would, but tonight she wanted to fly out over the rooftops, to spread herself into something, anything different and bigger. She stood there for a long time, the cold air stinging her face.

The image of Rosina in her finery stayed peeping out from behind Bessie's jug. Violet saw it there every day when she had tea with the girls. It seemed to haunt her.

That was when she started really to take notice of the recruitment drive for more women to staff the factories.

'Conscription for wenches now, it says 'ere,' Clarence read from the paper one evening. He showed the paper to Bessie, who looked up from her knitting to run an eye idly over the page.

'You read it – I've got my hands full.'

The government were conscripting women between the ages of twenty and thirty for war work.

'Ere – that's you, Vi,' she said.

'I'm already *doing* war work.' Violet was wiping semolina off Linda's hands.

'It says unmarried women, any road,' Clarence said. 'They ought to be doing their bit.' Though only forty-six, he was already stooped and full of ponderous statements.

'What about Marigold?' Violet said. It seemed odd no one had thought of it before.

Marigold was bent over one of her scraps of paper. The song sheets, Violet called them. Her puffy face looked across at them as if roused from a deep sleep.

'What?' she said.

But Bessie was already dismissing it. 'Don't talk daft. What use would she be? They don't want the retarded ones.'

'She could do summat,' Clarence said. 'They take all sorts now.'

But Bessie wasn't listening.

'If you take my advice, you'll go in search of better wages, Violet,' Clarence said, eyes still on the paper. 'At one of them bigger firms. Dunlop pay better'n what you're getting.'

Within days, three people had talked to her about the big works at Witton, not far away, where Kynoch's, the ICI factory, were recruiting munitions workers. And there was a smaller firm not far from Kynoch's called Midwinters, looking to recruit women to train. It felt like a sign. She had to do *something* to make life different. And Vicars had never been the same without Josephine. Every day there was a reminder of what she had lost.

By the next week she had handed in her notice at Vicars, despite the protests of Mr Riddle, and been taken on at Midwinters.

Chapter Twenty-Six

'Right, then – I'm the lucky so-and-so who's been given the job of training you lot.'

The man was tall and gangling, with a comical, thick-lipped face. He rolled his eyes in theatrical despair, looking over the six women before him, and added chirpily, 'What a shower. Old Adolf'd be shaking in his shoes at the sight of you lot.'

Of course they all giggled, and this provoked more eye-rolling and a contemptuous waggling of his head.

'Saints alive. Bunch of girls. I'm Gilbert Cook. You can call me Bert – just so long as that's the only thing you call me!'

They were standing in the yard at the back of Mid-winters, and not far away from them were two tanks in varying stages of assembly. All of them kept blowing on their hands in the freezing cold, though Gilbert Cook seemed oblivious to the arctic temperature and didn't offer any sympathy. They were all kitted out in scratchy brown boiler-suits, including Gilbert, who was so tall that the trousers dangled comically round his shins. Violet felt drab and lumpish in this get-up.

She eyed the other women. The one nearest to her was so skinny and frail she looked as if she'd snap, and had red hair and scared rabbit eyes. One was big and sullen-looking, with thick black hair and mannish hands that looked as if she might break your neck without much provocation. The third one had pretty chestnut hair and seemed rather posh and confident and the other two ... Violet had blinked the first time she looked at them. They must be identical twins! Both small and mousy and very young-looking, with thin brown hair and exactly the same pale, squinting faces.

Violet's heart sank. She was shy at making friends and none of this lot looked very promising.

Gilbert was telling them that the main works were over in Washwood Heath, making tanks – Cromwells, Valentines, Tetrarchs ...

'... but we get to finish some of 'em off. So – it now befalls me to drum into you lucky lot, the rudiments of welding ... Come on – inside. I s'pose we'll have to start somewhere.'

As they turned, almost rigid with cold, to go back inside the works, to Violet's surprise the red-haired girl came up to her and, nodding mischievously at Bert's swinging trouser legs, murmured, 'D'you think our wee man's expecting a flood?'

Violet giggled. She'd have liked to think of something clever to say in reply but nothing came to mind. The girl had a strong accent.

'We could sew a bit of gold braid round the bottom for him!' The red-haired girl was wearing bright red lipstick which clashed with her hair but the overall effect was very cheerful. 'I'm Muriel, by the way. Who're you?'

'Violet.'

'Well – nice to meet you, Violet.'

The girl's blue eyes were full of real friendliness. Violet immediately felt better.

*

135

They spent the next weeks being trained in the art of welding.

From the beginning the women seemed to fall into pairs. The twins, who were twenty-one but looked fourteen and had never been parted at any stage in their lives, were called Maureen and Doreen and seemed, as Bert put it, to be 'flaming welded together' themselves. Joan, the posh one, was from Sutton Coldfield, and she worked with the big girl, May. And Violet and Muriel worked together from the start. Muriel was from Ayr.

'My mother died last year,' Muriel told Violet the first day as they stood in the canteen at Midwinters, nursing mugs of tea with frozen hands. 'It's not been the same back home. I did nae want to leave my sister, but then they conscripted the both of us anyways. She's gone into the army, so I thought well, that's that then. I'll be on my way.'

'What about your dad?' Violet asked.

'Och no – ' Muriel said grimly. 'I was nae staying home wi' that miserable old sod. And I was only working in the tobacconist's – it was just a wee little job so I could be near my mum. Not much for the war effort that. I would have trained up there, but they did nae like Catholics.'

Violet was overcome with admiration. Here was she, after being spurred on from a distance by Rosina, thinking she was making a break in her life, and she'd only gone up the road. Muriel had come hundreds of miles – and she looked such a fragile little thing!

'Have you got somewhere to live?'

'Aye – with a lady along the way. I only got here yesterday so I don't know what it'll be like.' She shrugged. 'Who d'you live with?'

'Just my girls – my old man's in the army.'

'You're lucky then.' Muriel's lipstick lips parted in a grin to show a line of uneven teeth. 'And you're bonny too – some people have all the luck!'

The two of them quickly became friends, thrown together by the work. Both of them soon became adept at welding. Muriel had little, nimble fingers and was given intricate jobs if there were any.

'It's no different from decorating cakes when you come down to it,' she said. 'My mother used to do them to sell – she taught me.'

'If you say so,' Bert said resignedly. He had quickly come to be know as 'Bert the Flirt', because despite his quaint manner he certainly had an eye for the girls. And despite the fact she was the only married woman among the group, he had a special fancy for Violet, the prettiest of them. He seemed to spend more time hovering around her, overseeing their work, than anyone else.

'Why d'you nae go and see how the doormice are getting on?' Muriel asked sometimes when Bert was once more lurking round them. 'They've got a lot more to learn than we have.' The 'doormice' was her name for Maureen and Doreen, who did scuttle about like two little rodents.

'Exactly so – it's a pleasure to watch you ladies work,' Bert said ingratiatingly.

'More like it's a pleasure to stare at your backside in those gorgeous slacks!' Muriel muttered to Violet, and both of them got the giggles.

'I don't think I've ever worn anything that makes me feel *less* gorgeous. And what with this on an' all . . .' She pulled her welding mask down over her face with a mock seductive air. Joan, the posh girl, wouldn't wear

137

her mask at all and insisted on having a hand-held one, so as not to spoil her permanent wave.

Violet was at first puzzled, then slightly flattered by Bert's attention. He was an odd bloke, she thought, and she wasn't interested in him, but it had been a long time since Harry had paid her any compliments. She started paying more attention to her appearance, despite her jokes to Muriel about the welding masks. Since Harry left she hadn't bothered with make-up, but now she put on a touch of lipstick and powder again.

'You look pretty, Mom,' Joyce told her one day as they were getting ready in the morning. 'You've got quite a nice face really.'

Violet laughed, and heard a light-heartedness in herself that she had barely ever known before.

'Well – we all have to try and be cheerful,' she said.

Bessie took one look at her powder and lipstick and said, 'You want to go careful, my girl, going out looking like that.'

Her tone was so condemnatory, so offensive, that Violet immediately felt angry and crushed.

'What d'you mean? It's only a bit of lipstick!'

'You know what I mean. Going about painted up like a fourpenny rabbit. You want to watch yourself.'

Once again, Violet thought furiously as she went to get the bus to Witton, there was Mom going out to do her down! Going on as if wearing a bit of make-up made you into the Whore of Babylon! What the hell was the matter with her?

'Ooh, I say!' Muriel said when they clocked in together. 'Don't we look lovely today?'

'Don't you start,' Violet snapped. 'I've had my mom keeping on already this morning.'

'What – about your warpaint? But you look *gorgeous*!'

The compliment was made with such sincerity that Violet calmed down.

'Sorry. Mom just gets me worked up. She's such a bully – she has to rule everyone's life for them. Sometimes I bloody hate her!'

As she said it, she realized she'd never said that to anyone before – even to herself.

When she got home on Christmas Eve to find Harry waiting for her, it was a shock. She'd come in from Bessie's, not too late, but having no idea he was coming. Harry had lit the fire with the few remaining bits of coal and was sitting waiting.

'Dad!' Joyce and Linda ran to him.

'Hello, Joycie – 'ello, Linda.' He scooped them up and held them against his chest. 'Didn't your mother tell you I was coming?'

'I didn't know!' Violet said. It was a shock to see him. It took a minute to adjust, and then she was smiling. 'So you're home for Christmas? You never said! I mean I wondered . . .'

'I sent a wire . . .'

He put the girls down and came over to her, and she found herself pressed against his chest. He smelt of the smoky inside of a railway carriage. And it felt almost as if he was a stranger.

Chapter Twenty-Seven

Soon after Christmas, Violet asked Muriel whether she'd like to come to them for Sunday dinner. She was a bit nervous of it as Bessie was often very off-ish with strangers.

'Scottish, did you say?' Bessie demanded suspiciously, when Violet suggested the idea to her. 'I look after my own,' was one of Bessie's phrases. Anyone outside her small orbit didn't count as 'my own', and had to go out of their way to prove themselves, especially if they spoke or looked differently from her. Violet knew she'd better keep quiet about Muriel being a Catholic as well.

'She's nice, Nan,' Joyce said. 'She talks funny.'

In the event, Muriel charmed Bessie with her absolute respectfulness and sense of humour. Bessie said she was 'all right – once I can make head or tail of a word she's saying.' And Joyce and Linda loved her. With Harry gone it soon seemed the obvious thing to ask Muriel to move in as a lodger. Though Muriel put a brave face on it, Violet could tell she was finding it lonely where she was, as the one lodger of an elderly widow.

'I know it's not such a good neighbourhood as the one you're in now,' Violet said, nervous at asking. 'And I wouldn't charge you much rent. But if the girls move in with me, there's a room if you want it.'

Muriel was delighted. 'That'd be grand! We can have

a laugh – and I'll help you with your weans. Better than mouldering away where I am night after night, drowning in the smell of mothballs!'

Those months of 1942 were some of the happiest Violet had ever had. With Muriel in the house, she retrieved her ration-book from Bessie and said that they would now have their tea at home. She picked up Joyce and Linda from Spring Street while Muriel started on the cooking, and they spent cosy evenings together. Bessie sulked about this for a time, but Violet took no notice.

One of the other girls in the factory called Muriel a 'rapscallion'. She was always prepared for a laugh and a practical joke, often at the expense of long-suffering Bert. She also had an astonishing range of skills. Soon after discovering that the roof over her room in Violet's house leaked and she was going to have water dripping loudly into a bucket all night, she said, 'That's all right – I can fix it. You got a ladder?'

'Well, no,' Violet said. 'You can't do that, can you?'

'Aye,' Muriel said, without expanding on this any further.

She sweet-talked the use of a ladder off a builder's down the road and managed, from somewhere, to find several new slates for the roof. The next thing was that one Sunday morning in January, returned from Mass from which nothing short of an earthquake would keep her, Muriel was up on the roof, boiler-suit on, a green scarf holding back her hair, fixing the slates. It was drizzling lightly and the slates were dark and slippery-looking.

'I can't bear to watch,' Violet shouted as Muriel reached the top of the ladder and set off towards the

141

roof ridge on her hands and knees, holding on to the chimney stack, tools in a bag slung round her neck.

'Don't then,' Muriel called down crisply. 'Go and do something useful like making me a cup of cocoa – it's cold enough to freeze a monkey's tackle off up here.' She twizzled round for a second. 'Sorry – forgot the weans were down there!'

Joyce and Linda watched, mesmerized, eyes full of sky. A few other people started to notice, the men shaking their heads in disbelief.

'For God's sake be careful,' Violet said, heart in her mouth as Muriel's wiry figure scrambled up the roof. In a moment she was straddling the ridge, making a thumbs-up sign.

Violet was supposed to have climbed up and passed her the slates, but one of the neighbours wasn't having that and insisted on doing it himself.

'Can't 'ave two of you killing yourselves,' he muttered.

But Muriel got the job done very proficiently and was soon sliding down towards the ladder, calling out, 'Got that cocoa ready for me then?'

Poised at the top of the ladder, she looked from her bird's-eye vantage point along the street.

'Oi, oi – new neighbours, look,' she called, pointing to her left. A baker's van had drawn up outside one of the houses and Violet saw two men begin unloading bits of furniture from in the back. She didn't take too much notice, being far more interested in the moment when Muriel's feet finally touched the ground and she felt herself relax again.

'Lord – you'll be the death of me,' she said. 'Can't you stick to cake decorating?'

*

They passed the evenings talking and laughing and telling each other about their families and Muriel's exploits with 'laddies'. Men seemed to like her and she was ever baffled as to why. Violet could see why. Muriel wasn't the world's greatest beauty, but she had such a lot of life in her. Her abundant energy and good humour lifted Violet out of her usual fatalistic and gloomy turn of mind. Muriel took life at the run.

In March, Harry came home for what turned out to be embarkation leave. The notice he gave was very short.

'Look – you don't want me about if your husband's home,' Muriel said. 'Let me see if I can find a place to stay for a couple of nights.'

'No – don't talk daft,' Violet said. 'Where're you going to go? It'll be all right.'

Muriel looked very doubtful. 'Well – at least let me take Joyce and Linda in to sleep with me.' She rolled her eyes comically. 'You'll not be wanting company in the bedroom department, will ye?'

In fact, Muriel and Harry got along very well and he seemed reassured that there was another woman in the house. As they lay in bed together the night before he went, Violet realized how different it would have been had Muriel not been there. She would have been insecure and grieved at his leaving again – this time overseas. Instead, she knew, guiltily, that although she was worried about where he might be going, she barely missed him at all.

And Harry had a new light in his eye. The army suited him. He had lost the girth that too much ale and lack of much purpose in life had gradually accumulated round him. He was trim and fit, his hair clipped short. She could see he looked and felt younger.

'Well – I never thought it'd come like this – all the ideas I had about seeing the world and that.' He squeezed Violet round the waist. They were lying close and warm after lovemaking. 'I'll miss all you girls. I don't even know where we're going. The lads all think it'll be out East. Got to be really, hasn't it?'

She nodded against him, unable to imagine it. He already felt far, far away from her.

'Promise me – ' He turned over suddenly and in the dark she could feel his face close to hers, feel his breath on her face. 'You'll be here when I get back . . .' He ran out of words.

'Don't be daft.' She kissed his cheek. 'Course I will! Where d'you think I'm going to be off to?'

Chapter Twenty-Eight

March 1942

'Right, you two – up the wooden hill!'

Joyce and Linda, both ready for bed, were huddled close to the fire. It was a bitter night, the wind slamming against the windows and sucking the flames up the chimney.

'When's Muriel coming back?' Linda asked. She was very taken with Muriel.

'There's no telling,' Violet said. 'Come on – shift.'

Muriel was out with 'Dickie', a friend who she was being unusually coy about.

The girls were already upstairs when she heard knocking on the door. In the blacked-out darkness she saw a long, rather melancholy face under a cap. He was holding it on to stop the wind lifting it away.

'I . . . I live at number two . . .' He seemed distracted, or nervous. Violet recognized him – they were the family that moved in a few months back. She'd seen his wife about, a rounded, sleepy-looking woman. The man who stood in front of her was thin, and there was something gentle about him, but somehow intense at the same time.

'Thing is . . . the babby's sick – very bad. And the wife. And we've no coal. I've tried a couple of the houses, but . . . You got any to spare?'

'I've got a bit. You'd better come in a tick.' She shut the door. It was second nature now, the blackout, not letting light spill into the street.

Violet fetched the coal scuttle. She felt sorry for him.

'It's mostly slack, but there's a few bits in there. It's a bad night out.'

He took it absently, his thoughts obviously elsewhere. 'Ta. Very good of you. I'm Roy ... Keillor.'

His voice was nice, she thought. Gentle and quite well-spoken.

'How old's the babby?' she asked gently.

'Three months. Don't know if she'll last. And Iris, my wife. Cough, cough, fit to break her apart. I don't know what to do for her.' He trailed off again. She felt for him, could see how worried he was.

'What's the matter?'

'Pneumonia, the doctor says. Look – I'd best go. Very kind of you.' He tipped his cap. 'We've no fire, else, and the other kiddies're starving cold.'

'Is there anything else I can do?' Violet said, touched by this desperate picture.

He shook his head. 'No, ta. Can't do anything now but keep 'em warm.'

She watched his slim figure disappear into the dark street.

A couple of days later she learned, from other neighbours, that a tiny coffin had gone into number two. The little girl hadn't won her fight for life, but apparently Mrs Keillor was rallying. Violet felt for them.

'Brings it all back,' she said to Muriel. 'I lost my first babby – a little lad. We called him Bobby. It's the worst feeling there is, seeing 'em go like that. He died in Harry's arms.'

Muriel shook her head, her eyes filling. 'You poor wee thing. I could nae come through that, I don't think.'

'Well, there's no choice, is there? D'you think I should go round and see Mrs Keillor?'

But shyness prevented her. Later, she wondered if that might have made all the difference. In time, once Iris Keillor had recovered, Violet saw her in the street in passing and at first she made to pass the time of day. But Iris had a very shy manner. There was nothing haughty about her, she just seemed to go about in a kind of dream, although the neighbours on either side said that when you did speak to her she was always nice enough.

When Roy called the next time, Muriel was in as well.

'I've had this a while – sorry.' He held out the coal scuttle.

'Oh – ta.' Violet took it, expecting him to move away, but he just stayed, looking at her. She realized she had not said anything about the Keillors' misfortunes.

'Sorry to hear about your little girl.'

'Oh – yes –' He nodded. Again, this vagueness. Violet was starting to think that the Keillors were a pretty odd pair.

'Would you like a cup of tea?' Muriel said.

Violet could have crowned her. What on earth did she want to invite this strange man in for? They could have had a nice evening on their own!

Roy Keillor hesitated. 'Nice of you. All right.'

Muriel made tea and chatted on in her friendly way about how the two of them were welders and their work at Midwinters. Roy Keillor started to relax and he laughed at one or two things Muriel said. When he smiled, his thin face creased up and came to life. Violet thought how nice he seemed. He had laid his cap on the table beside him. He was wearing a black gaberdine which he didn't take off. Under it, Violet could just make out a maroon jersey.

'How many children've you got, you and your wife?' She sat down as Muriel brought the pot of tea over.

'Three – well, we did have. Two now. Two lads – they're twins aged three.'

There was a silence for a moment, then Muriel said, 'We've got twins at the works, haven't we, Vi? Like two peas in a pod they are – and there's no separating them. They'll both need to marry the same man!'

Roy laughed, and again Violet saw his features transformed.

'Oh – ours aren't like that. One's like me and the other's like their mother. No trouble telling them apart.'

They chatted for a while, about the families and work. Roy told them he worked at Kynoch's.

'I nearly went there,' Violet said. 'But where we are's smaller. Suits me better.'

'It is a big works,' he agreed. 'But you know – you soon settle into one section of it and get to know people. There's quite a few women now, of course.' He laughed suddenly, his face lighting again. 'Still can't get used to the idea of you two being welders!'

After he'd gone that night, Muriel said, 'He seems a nice enough fella.'

'Yes,' Violet said. She'd been sorry to see him go. There was just something about him.

Chapter Twenty-Nine

Every Sunday they went to Bessie's, pooling ration cards for whatever meal could be scratched together for them all. Everything revolved round Bessie's house. Muriel usually came along too, now Bessie had accepted her. Muriel was always polite and entertaining, but sometimes she said things which later made Violet see her family through other eyes. When they were walking home with the girls one afternoon, Muriel said, 'Why does your Marigold nae go out and get a job? She's stuck there all the time. Would she nae like to get out? She's the right age to be conscripted, isn't she?'

'She's twenty-nine this year,' Violet said.

'There you go.'

'Mom won't have it. Any road – I don't think anyone's ever asked her. It was like that when Mom took her away from school. No one ever came. It's as if no one knows she exists.'

'Well, she must have her own ration book?'

Violet frowned. 'I s'pose so.'

Another time, Muriel simply said, 'Your mother's got all of you just where she wants you, hasn't she?'

Violet was so used to things as they were that she never gave it much thought now. Bessie was still taking in the babies from time to time and she relied on Marigold's help. And where would she be without her mom? She minded Joycie and Linda – if it wasn't for that

Violet'd have to stay at home or give them to strangers to be looked after. She didn't like the idea of that, and the thought of staying at home, without all the jokes and companionship in the factory, was a very bleak thought.

She had a brief letter from Harry, written on a ship. He wasn't much of a letter writer in any case and really didn't have much to say.

'I thought he'd at least tell me where he's going,' Violet complained to Muriel.

'They're not allowed to, nitwit,' Muriel said. 'Anyway – he most likely does nae even know himself yet.'

Her married life with Harry already felt such a long time ago to Violet. She could barely even imagine it now. All those evenings spent in waiting for him, with his dinner, while he was at the pub, the loneliness of it, his outbursts of temper, were something she realized she didn't have any desire to go back to. Thinking like this made her panic. Harry was her husband! The chances were he'd be back one day and they'd have to pick up where they left off. She didn't like to think about how glum a thought this was. Life had been so much happier and more fun since Muriel had moved in. They'd enjoyed so many cosy, laughter-filled evenings with the wireless, the children safe in bed. With a shock she realized she had experienced more love and support from Muriel, certainly more *help*, than she ever had from Harry. But when the war ended ... No ... She didn't want to think about it.

She hadn't given Roy Keillor any thought either, until one evening they met him on the bus on the way home. There were always queues waiting for the buses as the firm finished work. Now the spring had come there wasn't the bitter cold wait in dark evenings, huddled there, collars turned up, and it all felt more bearable. But Muriel was impatient. She was meeting Dickie for a trip to the pictures.

'Hurry up, will ye,' she muttered as the awaited bus remained stubbornly absent.

'Got your lipstick?' Violet teased.

Bert the Flirt had been outraged earlier to find Muriel fusing a broken scarlet lipstick together with her welding torch.

'What the bleeding hell are you doing? Saints alive – I've seen it all now.'

Violet giggled. 'His face!'

Muriel had turned, lifting up her welding mask, and with lips already well coated in red advanced on Gilbert, lips pursed as if for a kiss.

'Red as a beetroot he was.' Muriel laughed. 'D'ye think he's ever been with a woman?'

'I dunno, do I? You're awful!'

The bus came swaying along the street then and they were among the last in the long queue to squeeze aboard. Muriel managed to push her way further down to the back and Violet was left standing near the front. At the last minute someone got on just as the doors were closing and a second later Violet found she was standing squeezed close to Roy Keillor.

'Oh, hello!' he said. He had evidently belted along for the bus and was panting hard.

'This is a bit of a way from Kynoch's.' She found she was blushing. He was so close to her, his left arm and hip pressed to her. When he turned to her she had the strangest feeling, as if he could see deeply into her, and she looked down in confusion, focusing on the black weave of his coat.

'I had an errand to run over here.' He was still regaining his breath.

'Oh,' she said stupidly.

'Where's your pal?'

'Along there.' She jerked her head along the bus. She could just see Muriel's arm, reaching out to hold on as the bus swayed along.

They travelled in silence for a few moments and she didn't look at him for a time, but then she said, 'How's the family? The twins and that?'

'They're all right. You've got girls, haven't you?'

'Yes – two.'

'What about your husband? In the army, is he?'

'Yes. I don't know where he is for sure. Overseas, I mean, but he was on his way somewhere last time I heard. He doesn't write much really.'

He was listening intently. But so, she realized, were a lot of the people closely packed around them on the bus. It felt an effort to speak over the noise of the engine.

Roy looked away, then back again. 'I just want to say, that night – when our babby was poorly, and Iris – you were the only one who found any coal for us.'

'Oh. Well . . . I'd been at my mom's. There was a fire there, see, so I hadn't lit ours.'

'But it was kind. You could've said you didn't have any.'

She frowned. The thought hadn't occurred to her. 'But you needed it.'

When she looked up, he was smiling gently at her.

They didn't speak for the rest of the journey, except goodbyes as they got off, but all the way she was acutely aware of his presence beside her.

*

'There's someone at the door,' Muriel called up to Violet. It was a week later and Violet was settling Linda into bed. After a moment she hissed, 'It's that Roy Keillor bloke again!'

Violet felt a jolt go through her. She thought of his eyes looking down at her on the bus. What on earth was he calling for now?

'What're you looking like that for, Mom?' Joyce said, leaning up on one elbow in bed.

'Like what?' she said crossly. 'I'm not looking like anything. Get to sleep.'

From the stairs she could hear voices, Muriel's, joking as usual, and Roy saying something softly. It struck her then how different a man he was from Harry, whose voice always carried loudly all over the house.

He was watching her as she came to the bottom of the stairs.

'Oh – ' she spoke rather abruptly, trying to cover the fact that his being there affected her in a way she was quite sure it shouldn't. 'Come for some more slack, have you?'

He smiled nervously. 'No – I er . . . Iris is getting the kiddies up to bed. I don't know why, I just . . .' He shrugged, and Violet noticed then that he was holding a thick little book with a worn leather binding.

'Tea?' Muriel asked. Behind Roy Keillor's back she gave Violet a comical smirk as if to say, *We've got a right one on our hands here!*

'Sit down – if you want,' Violet said, rather clumsily.

Roy settled himself at the table. He seemed shy.

'You'll think I'm a bit funny coming asking you this, but – do you like poetry, either of you?'

'I'm not much one for it myself,' Muriel admitted, tipping the tea grouts out. 'Cannae make head nor tail of it to tell you the truth.'

153

'Not even Robbie Burns?'

'Who?' Muriel said.

Violet, taken aback as much by the oddness of coming to ask such a question as the question itself, tried to think back to any poetry she had ever known. Bits at school of course, 'The Lady of Shalott' ... 'And through the field the road runs by To many-tower'd Camelot' – that was all she could remember. And something else about the boy on the burning deck.

'I know it's peculiar coming like this. It's just – there are things in here...' He held out the book. 'Just marvellous things. And if you don't read them at school, or afterwards ... I mean, no one talks about them – normally like, you know. I thought you might like to hear some of it?'

'All right then,' Muriel said politely. 'You carry on while I brew up.'

Violet, unsure what else to do, took a seat at the table. Roy opened the book and thumbed through.

'This is by William Wordsworth,' he said solemnly.

He began reading what turned out to be a long, long poem. Muriel filled the pot and brought cups over and dribbled milk into them and eventually, with a droll expression, she poured the tea. Glancing up at her, Violet saw the suppressed laughter in her eyes. Normally Violet would have laughed with her, but this time she found herself feeling annoyed. She liked the way Roy Keillor was reading to them, and she wanted to understand, but she had been lost almost from the beginning. It all seemed to be about meadows and birds and lambs, some of it very beautiful, she could tell, and he read it in a soft, slow rhythm. Sometimes she caught a bit of the sense of it, but then it kept slipping away from her. She listened to his gentle voice, affected by the fact that it evidently meant so much to him, but she just didn't know what he was on about.

And then in the middle of it, a few lines seemed to link up straightforwardly so that she could hear them, and she rolled along with them:

> 'Hence in a season of calm weather
> Though inland far we be,
> Our souls have sight of that immortal sea
> Which brought us hither,
> Can in a moment travel thither,
> And see the children sport upon the shore,
> And hear the mighty waters rolling evermore.'

She felt her skin prickle, as if all her hairs were standing on end, and the feeling that she had had sometimes as a child of being immense and spread out, and, as on that night looking out over the rooftops, that there was something in her that could fly and extend itself wide over the land. She felt as if in her soul she was a huge bird, or had been in another life, and the words reminded her of all that had once been and might be again that was bigger and grander than ever this life she was living now. She sat very still, feeling expanded inside herself by the words, and found that her eyes were full of tears as if for something momentous that she had lost.

A few verses later he finished reading and she had not heard much more of the poem. Just for once, she longed for Muriel not to be there. She looked up at Roy Keillor as he closed the book.

'S'pose I got a bit carried away,' he said. 'But can you see why I wanted to read it to you?'

Muriel was struggling to look polite, if not exactly impressed.

'I've never heard it before,' Violet said. 'I mean I couldn't follow it all, but . . .'

'It is long,' he agreed. 'But it's worth it.'

'Yes,' she said.

His eyes were searching her face. Violet met his gaze, and knew that no one had ever looked at her like that before and she had never looked back like that.

'Your tea's getting cold,' Muriel pointed out with just about concealed irritation.

'Oh yes.' He smiled and closed the book.

And they talked about other things.

Chapter Thirty

'Have these two weans ever seen the sea?' Muriel asked the next day as they hurried through the early morning routine.

'The sea?' Joyce piped up. 'Can we see it? I've never seen it.'

'Where is it?' Linda was four now. Violet was startled often by the life and intelligence shining out of her brown eyes, as if there was a powerful engine purring away inside her. Everything she did, even fastening her shoes, was done with intense concentration. Joyce was more vague and scatty.

'Here – eat up now.' Muriel placed a bowl of porridge on the table in front of each of them. The day didn't begin right for Muriel without porridge and she insisted on making it even though it meant getting up early to allow it time to cook. The girls were learning to like it – even salty, the way she made it – as they would have walked across hot coals for Muriel.

'The sea is round the edge of the country and we're right on the middle,' she told them. 'Where I come from in Scotland, we're only a stone's throw from the sea.'

Linda frowned. 'D'you throw stones in the sea?'

Muriel laughed, her jolly red lips parting. 'Aye, sometimes we do. One day, when the war's over, you'll have tae come up to Scotland and pay me a wee visit, won't you? Anyways – my auntie Jean married an

157

Englishman and she lives down in Brighton. What d'you think, Vi? We could make a trip?'

'I s'pose so,' Violet said. The thought had never occurred to her. She thought of the poem, the children playing along the shore, and wondered if despite all Muriel's mocking of Roy and his poems, that was what had set her off on thoughts of the sea.

'We cannae go on to the beaches now, so they say – but at least we could see the sea,' Muriel was saying, having to explain to the children that the beaches were mined and fenced off in case the Germans tried to get in.

'Are they trying to get in?' Joyce said, alarmed.

'Well, we hope not – they're not taking any chances. Vi – if we went one time when we have an early shift before a day off I'm sure Auntie Jean would put us up. You'd like her – she's my mum's sister. She and Uncle Mort have a wee bakery.'

The chance came within a couple of weeks. Auntie Jean had written back to say she'd be over the moon to see them, and if they sent a telegram to say when they were coming they'd come and meet them.

'I'll send Mort,' she wrote. 'He likes a little walk.'

It was the first time Violet had ever been out of Birmingham.

The girls were so excited they were hard to settle down in the carriage, wanting to jump about and kneel up on the seats, and Violet felt almost as frisky herself. She craned her head round as the train pulled out of her city, seeing its sooty factories and warehouses recede, its workaday yards and smoking chimneys, the barrage balloons still hanging over it like bloated guardian angels.

They all squeezed in close to the window, seeing the green expanses of spring fields and the farms and sheep and cows. Muriel kept pointing out things to them as they chugged along. The girls' excitement over the sight of a donkey or a farm dog was a cause of amusement to the middle-aged couple sharing their compartment. Violet was astonished by the orchards they saw full of pink blossom and the sheer prettiness of the countryside. She watched Linda, and at some moments, when she had seen something new, saw her face transformed in a moment of wonder, a glow which brought a lump to her throat.

At last they climbed down wearily in Brighton. It was only about nine o'clock but to Violet it felt like the middle of the night. She took the girls' hands as they walked nervously along the platform.

'Toot toot,' Joyce said, as the train let off a great sigh of steam.

Muriel carried the holdall into which they had squeezed all their clothes.

'Uncle Mort!' She raised her spare arm suddenly to wave. 'There he is!'

A short, plump man came towards them, smiling broadly.

'Well, hello there!'

As soon as she saw Uncle Mort, Violet's nerves started to subside. She could see she was going to like him. He was almost bald except for a ring of mousy hair and everything about him was plump and round:

his body, cheeks, chin. He had an old raincoat round him with the buttons done up wrong.

'Well – young Muriel!' He kissed her cheek, squeezing her hand. And this is your friend?'

'Friend – and landlady!' Muriel said.

'Very nice to see you, very nice.' He shook her hand, speaking in a deep, burring voice. 'Come on now – let's get home. Jean's on pins waiting for you.'

He led them through the dark streets, a little torch lighting their path. Soon they were in a row of terraced houses and Uncle Mort took them into one. He kept the torch on as they went indoors.

'Just follow me – up here.'

Violet knew that the couple lived over a bakery. There was a low counter on their left in the small room, and a strong, yeasty smell. They could see a light on upstairs.

'Is that you, Mort?'

The voice sounded so like Muriel's that for a moment Violet thought it was she who had spoken.

'We're all here – home and dry.'

'Bring them all up – quick!'

Violet and the girls were the last up the wooden stairs and she could hear the exclamations of 'Look at *you*!' at the top as Muriel was greeted by her aunt. Auntie Jean was in her fifties, and as round and comforting a person as her husband, with pink cheeks and her hair, still deep brown, tied back in a bun. She greeted Violet with a broad smile, then bent to speak to the children.

'I expect you little girls would like a wee piece of cake?'

Joyce and Linda nodded, wide-eyed.

Looking round fondly at Muriel, Violet was touched

160

to see that she was struggling not to cry. Auntie Jean resembled her mother very much in looks and Violet knew that for all her cheerful antics, she missed her mother and home terribly.

'I've got the kettle on – come on, sit down out here.' There was a kitchen built on to the house above the storeroom at the back. 'We have nae much room here but you're welcome to what there is!'

'We brought all our bacon rations,' Muriel said, wiping her eyes.

'Oh, you should nae have done that! Well – bacon butties in the morning for you! Here, you little ones – I hope you like a nice scone. I put a few raisins in . . .'

She offered Violet a scone, saying, 'You never said your landlady was so bonny! I was imagining some middle-aged matron!'

Violet laughed, shyly.

'Och – and you had it terrible with the bombing up there, didn't you? I should think your nerves were in shreds after that. I don't know how you all stood it.'

Jean and Mort tutted and shook their heads sympathetically.

'And you've a husband away in the forces, have ye, Violet?' Auntie Jean said.

'Yes – army. I don't know where, for certain.'

'Well, that'll be a worry too.' There was a silence. Everything looked so grim out East. It was hard not to feel pessimistic. 'Still – ' She smiled. 'We're so glad for you to come down here, both of yous, and take your minds off it all for a little while.'

They sat drinking tea with the comfortable couple. Auntie Jean asked after Muriel's father, from whom she hardly ever heard, then went on to bemoan the fact that the piers and beach were all off limits.

'These poor weans – I hope they haven't come thinking they can play on the sand?'

'They've never seen the sea before,' Muriel said.

'Have you not?' Jean looked at them in amazement.

'Well – you can see it,' Uncle Mort said, holding up his teacup. 'But you won't be able to get in it – not the way things are at present. You'll have to come back.'

'That's what I told them.' Muriel smiled at the girls.

'Come back when there's beach and ice creams!' Auntie Jean said.

'Mom! Mom!'

Violet managed to open her eyes with great difficulty. A crack of dim light was visible at the edge of the blackout curtains. She tried to think where she was. There was a strange, delicious smell.

'Mom – I want to go and see the sea!'

'Oh, Linda – what time is it? I'm sure you should be asleep.'

She realized then that the wonderful smell was of baking bread, and where she was, and that they only had one day here. Linda was right – they needed to get going!

Auntie Jean was already downstairs, in a big white apron, looking as if she had never been to bed. A row of newly baked loaves lay on the counter in the tiny shop.

'You go and have a look at the waves – it is nae far,' she said. 'And I'll have that bacon frying for when you get back.'

They walked down to the seafront in the misty morning. It felt very early. The breeze blew brisk and salty, bringing roses to their cheeks and ahead of them, grey waves heaved and shifted, breaking in a roll of frothy white.

'Is that the sea?' Linda's voice was barely more than a whisper.

'Aye – that's it. And that's the beach.' Muriel took them as close as it was possible to get. There were rolls of barbed wire stretching all along its margin. 'See – all the pebbles?'

They stared and stared. The sea sucked loudly through the stones.

'See those?' Muriel pointed at the two piers, extending out into the breakers, ghostly in the fog. 'That one's the Palace Pier – and that's the West Pier. There's lots of fun to be had on those – or there would be if it was nae for the war.'

'The war spoils everything,' Joyce grumbled.

'Aye – but we're having some fun together, aren't we?'

'We wouldn't be here if it wasn't for the war,' Violet said.

And she realized, guiltily, that she was glad.

The shop had a green and gold sign over the door saying 'Hall's Bakery'. They walked back into delicious smells, and Auntie Jean fed them on crusty white bread and the rashers of bacon. Violet knew it was one of the nicest things she'd ever tasted, and said so.

'That'll be the sea air,' Auntie Jean said, pouring dark tea from her big brown teapot. 'They say it makes everything taste better.'

Violet could already feel that the day was going to pass in a flash, and they had to be back on a late afternoon train to be at work the next morning.

They spent the hours they had walking round the town and seeing some of the grand buildings and looking in the shops, and the children played in the park and they had a dinner of fish and chips. As the day went by the mist burned off and though the breeze was cool, it was lovely and sunny. They enjoyed the town thoroughly, but all the time they kept being drawn back to the sea, sapphire blue now the sun was out, all of them fascinated by its immensity, its endless movement.

Joyce and Linda had a little bag of sweets each and they strolled along the front. There was only one sour moment, when they passed two rather smartly dressed women who spoke in loud voices, not caring who heard.

'Oh – ' one of them said, eyeing Violet and Muriel and the children. 'Must be some more of those dreadful evacuees. I rather thought we'd seen the last of them.'

'Well, we live in hope!' the other said. She turned for a moment, looking them up and down and said, '*Ghastly!*' Then the two of them went off, laughing behind their hands.

Violet saw Linda staring after them. She saw herself and her children through her eyes: down at heel, poor, not respectable.

'Oh, ignore the snooty bitches,' Muriel said, catching sight of her face. 'I'd love to see them in a welding mask!'

As the last minutes of the time they had left in Brighton went by terribly quickly, they stood looking out at the sea, the sky patched with puffy clouds. Violet found herself drifting off almost into a trance, lulled by the waves' rhythm, her thoughts stilled. How could you take in, on a day like this, all the fighting going on in the world? She was filled suddenly with a deep sense of longing. She leaned on the railing, watching the waves break and break and all she could think of was the poem that Roy Keillor had read, and over the water, like a spirit presence, she seemed to see his face.

Chapter Thirty-One

Spring was turning into summer, and often when Violet passed the Keillors' house the two little boys were playing out at the front. One was, as Roy had said, dark and delicate-featured like him, the other was round-faced and fair. At times she saw the little girl as well. Occasionally she passed him in the street, once when his wife was beside him, and they all greeted each other with a polite nod.

At this time she was trying to ignore the effect that any meeting with him had on her, the way it seemed to mean far more than it should, the excitement she felt at any chance of seeing him.

It was some time before they spoke again. She was on her way back from Bessie's. It was still light and she saw him coming along the street, an old trilby shadowing his face. As they drew closer he looked up, and she saw his expression change. He smiled and lifted his hat. Violet felt a wave of something pass through her, the way she imagined a bomb blast might feel, only on the inside.

'Hello,' he said.

'Hello.' She could feel Joyce and Linda watching them.

Then neither of them knew what to say.

'We haven't seen you,' she blurted at last, realizing at once that it was an odd thing to say and blushing.

Roy seemed embarrassed. 'After I'd been round I . . . Well, you must've both thought it funny of me – coming along like that, with the poetry book . . . I don't know why I did it.'

'I liked it. It was . . . I've never heard anything like it before. Only . . .' Everything she said seemed to be coming out wrong. 'I mean, I couldn't catch it all.'

'I don't think your friend liked it much.' He gave a chuckle and she liked the way his face looked as he did it.

'She's not very keen on poems and that, I don't think.'

He was watching her, listening to her words as if everything she said was of the utmost importance. There was another silence. Linda tugged on Violet's arm.

'It was nice, finding someone who wanted to listen,' he said.

What she wanted to say was, please, come round again, read to me again, look me in the eyes the way you do. What she said was, 'I'd better be going. Come on, girls.'

'Yes, of course,' he said, putting his hat back on. 'Sorry to hold you up.'

'No – you're not!' Why couldn't she get the right things to come out of her mouth! 'Only I've got to get these two to bed.'

As soon as they were inside the house, she said, 'Go on you two, upstairs. Get undressed – quick!'

Muriel was out. As the girls clattered up the stairs, Violet sank on to a chair. It was only then that she noticed she was trembling.

*

He came round the next Saturday night.

'I bet that's our poem man,' Muriel said, hearing the door. 'I had a feeling he'd be back.'

'Don't be daft,' Violet said, but her heart went racing. And he was on the step, with his book, holding it out to her.

'You said it was too quick – hearing it read out. I thought you might like to borrow it for a bit.'

'Oh – thank you!'

She took the book from him, excited at feeling singled out, the way she had when Miss Green had told her she was good at something all those years ago.

'D'you think his wife knows he's coming round here?' Muriel said when he'd gone. She was sitting by the window, knitting in the last of the evening light.

'Um?' Violet fingered the binding on the book. It had been in his hands. He had stroked that cover so lovingly. Her skin prickled at the thought.

'I said, dreamboat, d'you nae think his wife might find it a bit peculiar him coming round here to visit a couple of women on their own?'

'No!' Violet said. This wasn't what she wanted to hear. More than anything, she wanted him to visit. He filled her thoughts, him with his longing, soulful eyes. It was getting so that she scarcely thought of anything else. 'He didn't stay, did he? I don't think she's interested, that's all – in the things he likes.'

'Vi –' Muriel put her knitting down. 'Can you nae see he's after you? That's why he comes round here – not to read his poems. I've seen him looking at you – it's written all over his face. And it's written all over yours, too. You're going to have to be careful.'

'Oh, don't be so stupid!' Violet erupted. At that moment she hated Muriel for turning all worldly-wise on her, for pointing out these hard truths. What did she know? She was younger and wasn't even married!

'How the hell can he be after me? He's got a wife and three kids – and he's not that sort, I can tell.'

'Really?' Muriel spoke in such a flat tone of disbelief that Violet lost her patience altogether.

'Oh, for goodness sake leave me alone.' She stormed into the kitchen and picked up the kettle, shouting, 'You're worse than my flaming mother!'

She took Muriel's words to heart, even if she wouldn't admit anything to her. Was it really so obvious the effect Roy Keillor had on her? She was even more struck by Muriel's observation that Roy was sweet on her. Could that be true? Could it really?

But she tried to stamp the feelings out in herself. She just mustn't feel like this! They were both married people – Harry was off somewhere fighting a war, in danger! She ought to be ashamed of herself. And sometimes she really was ashamed of how she felt and managed to put the thought out of her mind for a while, especially if she didn't see Roy. He would have forgotten about her by now, wouldn't he? And then sometimes it all came surging back, the simple longing to see him, to look into his eyes and see him look back.

She knew, as soon as she heard the knock at the door that evening after Muriel had gone out. It was only half-past seven, and she could still hear Joyce and Linda giggling upstairs, little monkeys.

Feeling strangely calm, she opened the door. The mild June air came in and the sounds of older children playing. It was the first time, she realized, she had seen him without a coat. He wore only a waistcoat over his shirt, and a cap.

'I saw your mate walking along – thought she must be going out.'

Violet wondered who was watching. Were the neighbours peering at them, wondering if there was some arrangement between them? And why did it already feel as if there was?

'Come in,' she said quickly.

He didn't hesitate. Taking his cap off, he tucked it under his arm. Once she had shut the door she turned to him, still calm. Somehow the fact that he had come to her made it easier for her.

'Did you want your book back?' She nodded towards the black volume, stowed safely on the mantel. She had tried to read some of the poems and liked a few of them, though most she found hard to understand.

'Not if you want to keep it for a bit.' But he went and picked it up, thumbing through it as if reacquainting himself with an old friend.

There was a pause.

'I like knowing it's here.' He looked across at her.

Where does your wife think you are? She knew she should say it, but that she would not.

'The girls aren't settled yet, but they should go to sleep soon. D'you want a cup of tea? Or there's a drop in here – ' She held up Muriel's Scotch bottle. 'But it's not mine.'

'No – none of that,' he said abruptly. 'I want to keep my head.'

She avoided his eyes, but felt her heart rate quicken. *Oh God,* she thought. *What's happening to me?*

170

He stood by the table as she began to make tea, busying herself with teapot and cups.

'Sit down if you want.' She smiled across at him but kept her tone light. 'How's the family?'

'All right,' he said quickly, then in a more considered way, 'Yes – they're all right.'

'What're you going to read me today then?'

He stared at her for a moment, then with a more gentle expression said, 'I don't hold with religion, do you?'

Religion? Violet thought. Dark churches, boredom. She had barely ever been in church. Bessie had sent them to Sunday School, Sunday afternoons, to give her some peace and she'd sat through most of it in a dream. Otherwise it was funerals, the odd christening.

'No – not really,' she admitted.

' "Dover Beach" then,' he said. 'By Matthew Arnold. I didn't want to, sort of offend you, you know, if you'd been at all religious.'

'I don't know if I'll understand it.'

'You will. Some of it, anyway.'

They both sat at the table, and he started to read. She liked him reading to her, because she could look at him, at his brown eyes and thin, sensitive face. Now he had his cap off, a lock of his straight, black hair hung over his forehead. As he spoke, she saw the slight dimple in his left cheek. For three lines she was transported:

> *'The sea is calm to-night.*
> *The tide is full, the moon lies fair*
> *Upon the straits'*

The sea again! And her mind wandered and soon after she was lost, as his gentle voice moved on, too fast for her to follow the thread of meaning. Instead she just followed the musical sound, beautiful because it was his voice. She didn't know why he thought she might have been offended by it. As he finished reading she sat quietly.

'Beautiful, isn't it?' he said. 'And I think that's how it is. There is no God, at least, not of a judging sort anyway.'

Violet didn't know, not about God. All she knew was that sometimes she felt lifted, that she could circle over everything, free and high as a bird but somehow part of all of it too. And it made her grateful.

She didn't realize she was smiling.

'Violet –' His words seemed to come out under pressure. 'I can't stop thinking about you. You're all I ever think about – ever since I first saw you. I don't know what to do.'

He sounded desperate. She lowered her head, her cheeks burning hot, hearing words from him that she longed to hear, could scarcely believe she was hearing, and yet was so frightened by what they might mean.

What about your wife? She never used the woman's name, not in her head. It made her too real. *And my husband?*

Then she looked across at him and they sat, locked in each other's gaze. He stood up and came to her, taking her hand from her lap and drawing her to her feet. There was nothing she could do to resist. Nothing else mattered or seemed real. The girls could wander downstairs, but even knowing that, she could not stop herself.

'You're shaking,' he said.

'Yes,' she whispered.

He just stood looking at her, as if he could not stop.

'Will you do something? Take your hair down for me?'

She had it pinned back, quite simply, and as she began to take the hairpins out he helped her, tugging them gently and laying them on the table until her pale hair was hanging all round her cheeks. He stroked it back from her face, then put his hand on the back of her head. She felt the warmth of his palm pressing her scalp, drawing her nearer to him, and his eyes never left hers. She could see nothing but his eyes.

'What're you doing?' She tried to protest.

'I don't know.' He stopped for a moment and she saw the struggle in his face. 'You're just . . . I can't seem to see anything but you.'

'I didn't know I could feel like this,' she said, looking up at him. 'I *shouldn't* feel it, but I do . . .'

He sighed, relieved. 'It's not just me then?'

Solemnly she shook her head, and he pulled her close to him, his body slim and strange to her as her arms wrapped round him. His lips were warm and hungry on hers and she felt as if she had come home.

Chapter Thirty-Two

It was something she couldn't stop now, as if she was falling and there was nothing to break the fall. She kept going over and over that evening in her mind, the way he had held her, their kisses, that look in his eyes. When would they be able to see each other again? That was her one longing.

The week passed, somehow, in waiting.

'How're things with Dickie?' she asked Muriel, in a light, teasing voice.

'Very nice, thank you,' Muriel said coyly. She wasn't letting on much, not as she had done before with some of her boyfriends. This made Violet think this one was more serious.

By Saturday, Muriel admitted that she was going out with Dickie once again.

'You're always going out!' Joyce accused her.

Muriel laughed. 'Only once a week! Tell you what – you can have my sweetie ration – how about that?'

She didn't see Roy to let him know. Although she had the day off, he was at work. But she knew he'd come – at least to see if she was alone.

All afternoon she was aflutter with expectation.

'Mom – *Mom*! You listening?' the girls kept saying. And mostly she wasn't. In her mind she was already with him, seeing him come through the door, to be with her.

And at last he did. She'd put on her favourite frock,

pale blue, sprigged with small, dark blue flowers, and brushed out her hair. As soon as she closed the door, they were in each other's arms. Now he was here she almost felt as if her legs would give way.

'Today's been so *long*! I thought it was going to go on for ever.' She pressed him to her, loving the smell of him, the warmth of his body.

Roy made a low sound of pleasure. 'I thought I might not get here. I couldn't really believe I would!'

'Roy – what're we going to do? I feel as if everyone's watching.'

'No – course they're not.' She felt his breath on her hair. He was stroking it as they talked. 'I've thought about you – all week . . . I've never felt like this before. I can't think of anything else . . .'

It was as if he didn't hear her question. They never mentioned his wife, her husband. It was as if they were insulated together in a place that outer realities did not touch, where life's responsibilities had no meaning. This was all that mattered.

They spent their few, snatched hours talking and holding one another. It became a pattern, every time Muriel went out. There were so many risks – who might see, the children coming downstairs – but they did not care about risks. Their passion for each other was too urgent. It was some time before they made love completely and then they had not planned to. She was sitting in his lap in the big armchair. It was just dark outside, but the window was open to let in the breeze as it was a sultry night.

Roy's eyes were fixed on her as she cuddled up to him, arms round his neck. She ached to stop the time speeding by before he would have to hurry off, back down the road. The clock said just before ten.

'We're safe for about another hour.' She sighed.

Roy gently ran his finger down her cheek, then wriggled it between the buttons of her blouse. She felt him stroking the little cleft between her breasts.

She undid the top button of her blouse, but he stopped her. 'No – let me do it.'

His hands looked dark in the dusky light, especially against the white of her breasts once he had removed her little camisole. He let out an excited rush of breath.

'God, woman, you're beautiful . . .'

She had never been touched like this before. Not with this gentle attentiveness. Harry was quite rough, keen to get his own pleasure over with. Roy took his time, stroking her nipples, his pleasure found also in hers.

Without a thought she whispered, close to his neck, 'Come upstairs.'

And they crept upstairs, holding hands like children, as if unable to let go of each other, and once inside he pulled her close, enveloping her, kissing her neck, her shoulders, his body taut with desire against her. When they made love it was a revelation to her, her own excitement, because of what she felt for him, the way every part of her, her body, her feelings, responded to him all at once. She lay with him afterwards, wrapped round him, awed.

'I've never known it like that before,' she whispered, eventually.

He made a low, joyful sound.

'It's amazing, isn't it? If you do it right.'

'It's not doing it right. It's you.' She nuzzled against his neck. 'I need it to be you.'

Chapter Thirty-Three

It was such a little time they had together, those precious hours in the summer months.

Violet had never been so happy. Her gaze, uplifted by love, saw everything differently. The old street which Harry had so longed to leave, with its sooty-faced houses and chimneypots, was now the most beautiful place ever, because it was Roy's street, and the place where they loved one another. She put out of her mind the fact that it was Iris's street as well.

'You look nice,' the other girls at work said. 'What're you taking – can I have some of it?'

Violet often wondered whether Muriel guessed. If she did, she never said a word. She was in any case courting with Dickie, a jolly, freckle-faced Catholic boy from Armagh who'd come to England to work in munitions. Even so, sometimes Violet caught Muriel looking at her with her candid blue eyes in a way which made her think, *she knows*. She didn't like keeping secrets from her, but what else could she do? All that she had with Roy, the talking, his love, was the most wonderful thing she had ever known.

And then it all began to go wrong.

Her two neighbours, Mrs McEvoy and Mrs Smith, were out that morning, aprons on, kneeling by their front steps with pails of water and scrubbing-brushes. Neither of them went out to work. As Violet came out with the girls, their talk stopped abruptly and there was a silent, frosty atmosphere. Mrs McEvoy put her head down and went to work vigorously with her scrubbing-brush, but Mrs Smith stared up at her. There was a spiteful, knowing expression on her face.

'Morning,' Violet said, shooing Joyce and Linda ahead of her.

There was no reply, and when she glanced back Mrs Smith was still watching her, saying something to Mrs McEvoy.

She knew then. Whispering had begun in the neighbourhood. But she didn't want to admit it. The next evening, after dark, a note was slipped under her door. It had obviously been written in a hurry:

Dearest Vi,
    See if you can meet me tomorrow night by the bandstand in the rec. I *must* see you.
    Yours, Roy.

The time was coming when she'd have to tell Muriel. If tongues were wagging she would hear something anyway, and Violet desperately needed someone to be on her side. Already every time she stepped out of the house she felt as if everyone was watching and the street was full of prattling tongues and pointing fingers, all condemning her.

She was in such a state the next night, knowing she was out to meet Roy later, that once the girls were upstairs she poured out the whole story to Muriel, who was standing by the table, washing up. She took this outburst quietly.

'I just can't help it,' Violet sobbed. 'I love him so much . . .'

Muriel laid a cup on the table to drain and wiped her hands on her apron, looking gravely across at Violet.

'I know you do. It's always been written all over your face.'

Violet wiped her eyes, sniffing. 'Did you know he's been coming here?'

'Not for sure. I had a feeling. How did you . . . I mean what about the girls?'

'It was all right. They never saw.' She shrugged. 'What else could we do?'

Muriel came over to her and with unusual tenderness put her arms round her.

'I know. I can see. I mean, you and your husband, Harry – I could see there was not much between you. But he *is* your husband. And Roy's got a wife . . . You're heading for trouble, darlin'.'

'Has anyone said anything?'

Muriel looked away, hesitating. 'I've heard the odd whisper. You know what people are like. If he kept coming along to the house, what were they going to think? Honestly, Vi!' For a moment, her exasperation flashed out.

'We just couldn't help it. Look, he's asked me to meet him – tonight.'

'Well,' Muriel released her. Solemnly, she said. 'Go on. You'd better get going then.'

By the time she reached the foundry round the corner from the recreation ground she heard footsteps, running behind her, and he caught up with her.

Without a word, they clung to each other in the dark street.

'What's happened? You're in such a state!' She could feel it before he said a word.

He kissed her face, feverishly, as if she was the most precious thing in the world.

'Let's go to the park – if it's open. We can talk in there.'

The gate was unlocked and they slipped in, across the moonlit grass. The night park smelt lovely, of flowers, and she ached for this moment to be different, for them to be able to enjoy each other instead of being gripped by this cold fear inside her. When they reached the bandstand he took hold of her again, wrapped himself round her.

'Iris knows, doesn't she?' Violet burst out. There was no point in waiting any longer.

'I think the whole flaming neighbourhood knows.' He gave out a sigh, almost a laugh. 'Goes round like wildfire. God, Violet... How can we have been so stupid?'

'You mean –' She felt as if he had punched her. 'You wish you'd never met me?'

'*No!* God, no – you're the most... I don't know what to say. You're the woman I love. I know that. It's about the only bloody thing I do know at the moment.'

'What are you saying then?'

'We just should've been more careful.'

'But how?'

'I don't know.'

For a moment they stared intensely at each other in the darkness, then Roy broke away from her and turned his back. She stood, bereft. A dog barked, somewhere outside the park.

'I can't go on like this, Vi, I know that. Lies, trying to be in two places at once. I'd leave, honest to God I

180

would, if it was just her and me. She's all right, Iris is. She's a good sort really. But she's not you. She and I – I don't know – we've never had what we have, me and you . . . I'd leave now, for you. But there's the kids – and your girls and your husband. It's all too difficult . . . It's wrong.'

He turned to her again and she was rooted to the spot. She didn't want to hear what he was saying because it was true and therefore unbearable.

'We'll move,' he said. 'That's what Iris wants. She can't stand it any more. She can see it, see.'

'What d'you mean?' Her voice cracked.

'That I'm different. Feelings that . . . She can see what I feel about you, however much I try to hide it. It's no good.'

The last words were said with flat despair. He came to her again and drew her to him, pressing his cheek against hers. She was not crying, not yet. The tears were like a great wave, swelling deep inside her. Instead she felt shocked and cold. There was no hope now.

'I'll always love you,' she said wretchedly. 'Can't you stay near somewhere?'

'No. If I did I'd always be watching, hoping to see you somewhere, and it'd never end. I couldn't stand it.'

They held each other for a long time, silently, as if each engraving on them the feel of the other's body so it would never be forgotten.

Part Three
1950

Chapter Thirty-Five

The machine was like a long metal coffin.

Violet's hands were trembling as she reached down with a convulsive movement and stroked the blonde head, the only part of her daughter not swallowed up by the iron casing.

'Don't cry, babby – oh, don't, you'll make it worse!'

The bellows pump sucked the air from the machine again with a loud *whoosh*, and the little girl let out a sob.

'I want to come home, Mom!'

You could almost smell the child's fear.

The nurse's heart went out to the mother, with her elfin face and poor, down-at-heel look. The disease was a horror, and a scourge, and this mother was taking it especially hard. It was her first visit, you could tell by her stricken face, and of course she'd brought her other two girls, not thinking they'd not be allowed in. There was far too much risk of infection. So the two lasses had gone to wait outside, with their forlorn faces and grubby summer frocks.

'You'll be little Carol's mother? Mrs Martin?'

'Yes – ' Violet pulled her gaze away from her little girl. The nurse saw a face pinched with anxiety, with clear blue eyes and blonde hair scraped back and carelessly pinned up. Hearing a note of sympathy, her eyes filled with tears. 'I've never seen anything like this . . . It's horrible!'

'I know – it's a shock when you first see it.' To give the woman time to compose herself, she turned to smile at the child.

'D'you know why it's called an iron lung?'

She stroked a hand over the curved metal surface. There were little windows in it so you could catch a glimpse of Carol lying inside, covered with something white.

'The disease attacks the muscles, you see. Carol's lungs aren't working properly at the moment and without the machine they'd collapse. It pumps air into the chamber here and presses the breath out of her body. Then, when it sucks the air out again – d'you hear it? – her lungs get bigger and she takes in a big breath, see? Don't you Carol?'

Carol's head with its tufts of blonde hair could be seen resting on a pillow at the end of the machine. She tried to nod. There were tears running down the sides of her face into her hair. She wanted to speak, but was forced to wait for the machine to give her breath.

'Show your mother what a brave girl you are.' The nurse touched the top of the girl's head for a moment. *Don't cry*, the pressure seemed to say.

'She's the image of you, isn't she?' she said to Violet, who nodded, absently.

The nurse wondered how old the woman was. There was something so worn and sad about her.

'How long will she be in there – in that thing?' Violet kept fiddling with the bottom edge of her cardigan as if to fasten it, but the button was missing. The cardigan had once been white.

'I'm afraid I can't tell you. Not yet. It does take time though, and it depends how well her muscles come back to her. Some of the children do very well.'

'I don't understand it . . .' Violet's emotion bubbled to the surface again. 'She only had a bit of a headache. One minute she was all right . . . She said her neck was getting stiff, that was all, and then . . .' Her face contorted. 'She won't die, will she? Oh God, she can't die – she's only seven! My little babby, just look at her . . .'

'That's how it is with polio.' The nurse spoke abruptly, as if panic-stricken by Mrs Martin's emotion. She turned on her heel, flicking her white veil over her shoulder. She had other patients to attend to, after all. 'We just have to wait and see.'

Chapter Thirty-Six

'Linda? Wake up – we're coming into Birmingham.'

'All *right*. Ouch – leave us alone, will you!'

Linda shoved her sister's sharp elbow away. She wanted to push Joyce all along the aisle and off the bus in her baggy blue frock and never see her again, ever! In any case, she hadn't really been asleep. She'd sat with her eyes closed, head resting against the throbbing window, to block out Joyce and her moaning about how even when they got into town they still had to get all the way out again to the estate.

'Have we got to do this every week? It' s *miles* away and it takes up the whole day!' Joyce had bad adenoids and always sounded as if she was holding her nose when she talked.

Linda felt as if she was going to explode. There was Mom on the seat across from them, turned away as if she was looking out of the window, even though the panes were filthy dirty. *Like staring into a sandstorm.* That was what Johnny Vetch said – in the desert there were storms of sand, whirling in the air and you couldn't see out.

She knew Mom was crying and that was why she wouldn't look round. Linda gripped the edge of the seat. All that they'd seen that afternoon kept burning through her mind. That hospital, the stink of it, and glimpses of sick children before the nurse had told them to get out and they'd stood around outside, feeling lost and stupid.

When Mom came out she looked as if someone had hit her. Carol was inside a big tank thing, she said. It was called an iron lung and it stank of rubber and made big sucking sounds of the air going in and out. She said there was a little mirror by Carol so she could see a bit more of what was going on. Linda decided that *not* seeing it was worse than seeing it. Every time she thought of being inside there she felt panicky and had to take in a deep breath. She could feel sobs rising in her and she forced them down. She wanted to see Carol so badly she thought her heart would burst.

If only it was me instead! She'd give anything for Carol to be all right – anything. To see her running round again in the garden with the rabbits, or with her skipping rope, her long golden hair lifting as she jumped.

Not that polio was to blame for the cropped state Carol's hair was in. Linda's mouth twisted in fury. It was Dad who'd done that.

'I'm starving,' Joyce moaned, slouching along once they'd got off the second bus. She found something to complain about all along Bandywood Road, one of the main arteries of the Kingstanding estate where they lived. 'These shoes're pinching me rotten!'

'What d'you wear them for then?' Linda's feet were sore too, the black pumps worn wafer thin on the bottom and rubbing her toes, but *she* wasn't moaning was she? Joyce was tripping along in that stupid pair of sandals which had never fitted properly in the first place.

'Look – ' She displayed one foot. 'There's blood *pouring* down my heel!'

'Oh, shut it!

'Shurrup yourself miss bloody know-it-all!'

'Just wrap up, the pair of you,' their mother snarled exhaustedly. 'For God's sake let's just get home.'

They were walking down the row of municipal houses, doors all painted green. Theirs was number ten – the one with the garden that stood out for having nothing in it except Dad's old Norton bike, rusting away under a ragged tarpaulin amid the forest of dandelions, where it had been since he crashed it three years ago, leaving him with a deep scar on across his left cheek. Reg Bottoms next door, who grew prize-winning dahlias, took the presence of the wrecked Norton as a personal insult, which was the main reason Dad left it there.

They went along the cracked little path and Violet stopped at the front door and listened. Linda's eyes met Joyce's, all squabbles forgotten for the moment in the more momentous thought, *will our dad be in?*

He wasn't, of course, this time on a Saturday. Pubs'd be open. You could feel the house was empty. The dogs went mad when they heard the key in the lock, yowling, claws scrabbling at the kitchen door. The sour stink of parrot hit them in the hall.

'Mrs Martin!'

They were stepping inside when they heard Mrs Kaminski calling from the house the other side. The Kaminskis were Poles. They had the corner house, so the garden wrapped right round the side, and every inch of their land was covered in vegetables, potatoes right up to the front wall. Dad said they were afraid of going hungry. Mr Kaminski was a stocky, silent man who was out there almost every moment he was not at work, digging and weeding. Mrs Kaminski's face appeared over the fence, her lips a bright scarlet. She was a diminutive woman who seemed to hum with energy.

'Ze animals – again!' She hissed in warning. 'Mr Bottoms – very angry!'

'Oh . . . *no!*' Violet sagged against the doorframe.

Linda noticed how her mom never swore in front of Mrs Kaminski. She also kept the dogs well away from her because Mrs Kaminski was terrified of them. Everyone seemed to have a strange respect for the Kaminskis and she didn't really know why, but she'd heard whispers of *'After all they've been through . . .'*

'Thanks, Mrs K – girls, get out there now and catch those flaming rabbits!'

Linda and Joyce scuttled through the house, sore feet forgotten. The dogs leapt up, insane with joy when they went into the kitchen. The back of the kitchen door was all scratches from them, brown scars in the blue paint.

'Get in – now!' Violet shouted to them and all three, two brown mongrels and a beagle, shot through the house, only to be imprisoned in the front room.

'Right – get the bloody rabbits, and don't forget to shut the door.'

Linda and Joyce looked out through the back window. Over the fence they could see Mr Bottoms' head appearing and disappearing in an agitated fashion as he darted back and forth after the rabbits. Extending out of the chick-enwire run in the Martins' garden was a seam of freshly dug soil. Moonlight and Snowdrop had burrowed their way out. Again. And were running riot in Mr Bottoms' perfect garden.

'Mr Bum's going to kill us,' Linda breathed.

The two of them stared in horrified awe at Mr Bottoms' bobbing head.

'I told you to get out there!' their mom shouted along

the passage. 'Go on – before they do any more bleeding damage!'

It wasn't often the sisters were allies, but they looked fearfully into each other's eyes. 'Here goes.'

Pushing open the back door, they stepped outside as if into the line of fire. Their own garden was a half-bald patch of badly scuffed grass, pocked with holes where the rabbits had dug. The only patch of colour was the scrubby clump of marigolds Mom'd planted up in the corner by the house once in a fit of enthusiasm. Linda went to the loose bit of fence and pulled it back, wishing they could just go in and catch the rabbits without Mr Bum seeing them. If only they were invisible!

She thought he was going to explode.

'About time! Get in here and get your bloody vermin out of my—' He lunged as Moonlight shot past his ankles, then stood up, puce in the face. Mr Bottoms was a short, compact man of military trimness, with mousy hair clipped to a military length.

'Sorry, Mr Bottoms,' Joyce murmured, putting on her most syrupy voice. 'Only we've been out to the isolation hospital. Our Carol's got polio . . .'

'I don't care where you've been! Those flaming hounds of yours've been howling all the afternoon . . .'

Linda thought Mr Bottoms looked like an angry hamster, his eyes popping, and she wanted to laugh. 'And these *vermin*'ve been at my lettuce. It'll never be the same! And droppings all over the lawn. Get them *OUT!*'

Linda managed to get hold of Snowdrop first, hoiking her out of the vegetable patch, which was carefully screened off by a flourishing set of runner beans. Snow-drop was so round and greedy that she couldn't be bothered to stop eating and run away.

'About time!' Mr Bottom's spluttered again. 'Now get the other one. Filthy animals everywhere – it's a disgrace!'

Mom just couldn't seem to stop getting more animals. It was as if she was running a refugee camp.

'You naughty, naughty girl,' Linda whispered into Snowdrop's quivering ear as she continued munching.

Walking with the warm bulk of the rabbit clutched close to her, she saw Mrs Bottoms watching from the window. She was a neat, darting woman, always full of cheerful comments. Her mouth was trying to smile even now, but Linda thought her eyes looked sad in a way that didn't match. She often looked like that.

By the time Linda had deposited Snowdrop in the hutch, Joyce had managed to get Moonlight. Mr Bottoms was pacing dementedly along the other side of the fence.

'How did they do it this time?' they heard. 'Where're the little so-and-so's getting in?'

Linda and Joyce collapsed into pent-up giggles over the hutches, hands clasped over their mouths.

'I can hear you!' Mr Bottoms roared. 'And it's not funny – like a bloody menagerie, your place. A slum. No wonder you catch diseases! I'll be having words with that father of yours . . .' In a lower tone he added, 'If he's ever sober enough to take in what I'm saying.'

The fuss over the rabbits made them forget everything for a few minutes, but when they went inside they found Mom at the kitchen table, hands over her face, tears running down her wrists. There was a milk bottle next to her, and a tin of jam. Polly and Bluebell, the two blue budgies, watched silently, hunched side by side in their cage.

'I can't think of anything to cook for tea,' she sobbed. 'I just can't think what to do.'

And Linda knew Mom was crying about Carol really, and all of it got up and hit her again and she felt too sick to want any tea anyway.

Linda lay in bed. She didn't like being alone. Normally Carol was in the other bed. Joyce slept in the little room next door. It was getting dark outside and a glow of light came from downstairs where the living-room door was open. In the end they'd had mashed potato and Bisto for tea, and a bit of bread and Stork. Joyce was the only one who seemed to be hungry anyway. It didn't fill them up for long and Linda could feel her stomach rumbling again now.

She wanted to think about anything but Carol lying there in the iron lung, but that was all that flooded into her mind. If she shut her eyes she could almost hear the sound of its air pumping in and out. Tears welled under her eyelids. She was so close to Carol she could feel her feelings. It had always been the same.

How had Carol caught polio? Why her and not the others? They'd all done the same things all summer: played with the rabbits, gone to Sutton Park, gone swimming down the baths. Why Carol?

The front door opened with a clatter. Dad. Linda tensed up straight away. At least he'd got the right house. More than once he'd been so kalied he'd gone crashing into the Kaminskis' by mistake and frightened the life out of them. Poor things were easily frightened too.

The door slammed shut again.

'Vi?'

'*Ssssh*,' she heard her mother. Dad had no idea about shutting up when kids were asleep.

'What's for tea?' He gave a long belch and Linda knew there'd be that gentle snapping sound as he pulled his braces down from his scrawny shoulders. He always did that, soon as he got home. Complained they rubbed. He had to have a cushion on the chair too. He was so thin, nothing was ever comfortable.

'There's not much – I kept it warm.'

'What d'you mean, not much?' He was almost shouting now.

'Keep your voice down . . .' It was always the same. 'We've carted all the way over to the hospital – to Carol.'

'Oh – yeah. The Lad.' His tone was twisted with sarcasm. He'd got a thing about calling Carol 'The Lad' for the moment. 'How is "he", then?'

'She's bad . . .' Linda heard her mother begin to cry. There was a rattle of plates. 'It's terrible – she's in this iron lung thing. I could hardly stand to see her . . .'

'Call this my bloody tea? Potato and nowt else? What d'you think I am, an effing fairy, living on air and gravy?'

The plate hit the wall and smashed down on to the floor. 'What does a man have to do to come home to a decent plate of food of a night?'

'Earn a decent wage and not pour it down your throat, that's what!' Violet flared at him.

Linda could hear the tinkle of broken crocks as she swept up.

'It don't make any difference what I give you for your tea, does it? You're still a bloody skeleton whatever I do!'

'Don't keep on, woman! Always keeping on . . .' There was another smashing sound and Violet's voice rose to a scream.

'Stop it! Just stop it, will you? There'll be no bleeding plates left if you carry on. Coming in like the Lord God Almighty and carrying on – after the day I've had! Why can't you just eat it and shut up, coming in that time of night with your boozing and carrying on, you selfish bastard?'

'Shut up, you nagging cow!'

Linda lay, hardly breathing. She could hear Mom was crying again.

'Well, you can do without. You'll have a roast dinner tomorrow!'

'I don't *want* a roast dinner . . .' There was a crashing sound, something hitting the table. 'Not if it means going to your sodding mother's week in week out. *Christ.*'

'But we always go to Mom's. You should be grateful . . .'

'Well I'm not going to "Mom's" any more – all right? D'you think I want to sit staring at her old bloomers all afternoon? That old cow thinks she owns the whole lot of us, lock, stock and barrel!'

'Don't talk about my mother like that. You'll soon come when you want summat to eat. Everything just so long as it suits you, isn't it? Harry Martin – the one person on this earth who matters. You don't give a monkey's if your daughter's in hospital in an iron lung . . .'

'My *daughter* . . . ?' He was snarling now. Linda turned on her side under the cover, forcing her fingers into her ears. Saturday nights . . .

It hadn't always been like this. So far as Linda was concerned she'd only had a dad for four years. Before, when the war was on, Saturdays nights had been her and Mom and Joyce and Auntie Muriel when she was living with them, and it had been safe, and fun and cosy. And then the new babby came. Mom was happy then.

'I know you don't remember your dad . . .' That day the telegram had come, she'd been six years old. Carol was crawling around by then, head a mass of blonde curls, too young to understand anything. Her mother's face had been ghostly white.

'Your dad's been a brave soldier, but it says here . . . . . .' She choked on the shock of it, couldn't say it for a bit. 'He won't be coming home.' *Killed in action . . . Harry Ernest Martin.* She didn't take in that they'd got his middle name wrong, that her Harry was Harry Arthur Martin. She didn't think it was important at the time.

Mom was upset, of course, but Linda had heard her say some funny things to Muriel. 'The terrible thing is, I feel *grateful*, almost . . . He'll never need to see her . . .'

And life had gone on without him.

Then, in 1946, while they were still living in Aston, this spectre appeared at their door. A knock one evening, her mother's scream of shock.

The man on the doorstep was horrifying to see, sinister, like a puppet. He was emaciated, his head too big for his body, thin grey hair, sunken eyes, stooped over. Mom's hands went to her face and she backed away, moaning.

'Vi?'

His voice was high and reedy.

'No! No . . .!' She couldn't think of anything else to say.

'It's me, Vi, for God's sake. It's Harry.'

Someone else had got killed, not him. Harry Arthur

Martin had been a POW of the Japanese. Even now he didn't weigh much more than when he came home, and food often didn't agree with him. They said he'd been so malnourished that his body had lost the knack of absorbing it. His head had lost the knack of fending off memories and dreams, and if Mom and Dad had ever loved each other they seemed to have lost the knack of that too. Drink was his anaesthetic and on Saturday nights he took as much of it as he could manage.

Linda screwed her eyes tightly shut as the voices raged on downstairs. She thought about the gates of the grammar school, seeing them open in front of her in her mind like the gates of heaven, safe and tidy and full of promise.

Chapter Thirty-Seven

'Mom – Linda's in the lav again. Tell her to get out!'

Linda scowled, perched on the toilet seat with her copy of *Great Expectations*.

'Lin, hurry up – I need to go!'

'Linda!' she heard Mom's voice. 'Out – now!'

It had always been the same, as soon as she could read. Going to Nana's meant perching in the outside lav with her books, the one place you could get a bit of peace.

Since Nana moved, after the war, to a two-up two-down in Spring Street, they had an outside toilet not shared with anyone. It felt like *her* place, with the cobwebs and slug trails and the nail with squares of newspaper hanging, or sometimes bits of coloured tissue from round the oranges and apples begged off the greengrocer. And best of all, the rusty bolt she could pull across and shut everyone else out – especially Joyce. From there she'd travelled to other worlds in her head with comics and some of the books Johnny Vetch lent her. Most of Johnny's books were about rocks and fossils and birds, but he did once hand her a dog-eared copy of *Treasure Island*. She was completely taken up in it, scared to go to bed every night for ages after, thinking she was going to hear Blind Pew's stick tapping along Spring Street, coming to get her.

They'd left Spring Street for the estate soon after, and

now they had a bathroom inside. It was warmer, in the winter anyhow, but it just wasn't the same. She still slipped out to the outside lav in Aston when she had the chance. In any case, it got her away from Nana and the others. Of course Nana didn't like Johnny Vetch. She said he was queer in the head. And she had no time for books because she couldn't read herself. She kept that quiet out of shame. Even Mom said she'd gone all her childhood without realizing Bessie couldn't read.

'No wonder she wouldn't read my school reports,' she said.

Sundays meant dinner at Nana's house in Aston the way morning meant the sun coming up. She was famous for it in the street, the way she always had the family there every week.

'Going to Bessie's, are yer?'

'Awright Violet – off to your mom's?'

It was always the same, voices greeting them as they walked from the bus stop. Bessie hadn't moved far, and everyone knew her.

The smell of dinners wafted out to them and they could hear the wirelesses playing through open windows where curtains wafted in the breeze. The old man was standing on the corner with string tied round his jacket, Mr Baffin was tinkering with his bike a few doors along from Nana's and kids were playing out with soapbox carts and marbles.

But today there was something else.

'Where's the little 'un? Where's your Carol?'

And Linda heard her mother keep explaining with tears in her eyes about the polio and how Carol was over at the isolation hospital and everyone saying *ahh* and oh, bab, what a shame and how sorry they were, so it took quite a time to get along the road. It made Linda feel all upset again too, so she held on tight to her book and tried to block out the voices which reminded her. It seemed terrible to forget about Carol, but if she didn't her tears would come. What was happening to Carol was like an ache, always there.

It was always the same, Sundays. Same smells of cooking and Uncle Clarence with his pot of ale resting on the arm of the chair, Auntie Marigold in her baggy old frocks following orders in the kitchen, cutting up cabbage and carrots. And Uncle Charlie and Gladys came with the cousins – Norman didn't always come now he was almost sixteen, but Colin came. And once it was all cooked, Nana always commanded one of the girls to knock for old Mrs Magee who lived across the street to eat dinner with them. She'd long been a widow and Nana said no one should have to cook for one on a Sunday, it wasn't worth the gas.

The kitchen was Nana's kingdom, ruled with a rod of iron. Uncle Clarence stayed in the front doing nothing much as usual and moaning about it.

'The country's going to the dogs,' was one of his favourite moans. He didn't work any more, now the war was over.

''Allo wench!' he said lugubriously as Linda ran in ahead of Joyce. 'How's the world treating you?'

Uncle Clarence always said that as well. In fact Uncle Clarence mostly said the same sorts of things over and over again, like 'Bottoms up!' when he drank his ale, and, with a jerk of his balding head, 'You'd best ask the kitchen,' which meant Nana was in charge and what was the use of him saying anything?

'Come 'ere and give us a kiss!' Linda kissed his

stubbly cheek and he rumpled her hair, but then, his eyes mournful as a hound's, he said, 'Did you get up the hospital to see her?'

Linda nodded. 'She's in an iron lung thing. They say they don't know how long she'll be there.'

She saw something in Uncle Clarence's eyes, as if he was flinching inside and he shook his head and looked away and picked up his ale. Everyone loved Carol, even Uncle Clarence, who mainly loved his allotment. 'Poor little bugger.'

Gladys and Charlie were listening, and even Colin, who was thirteen, didn't look quite so much like a spotty sack of potatoes as usual.

'Is that them here?' Nana's voice boomed through from the kitchen.

'Our Linda's here,' Uncle Clarence called.

'What about Joyce?' Linda made a face. Joyce was always the favourite.

'She was always like that with us,' Violet told Linda once. 'Only ever had eyes for Charlie.'

'I don't care,' Linda said, shrugging. Nana was even worse now, after the grammar school.

'She'll 'ave to do then. Get in 'ere, Linda – I can't leave this pudding. Marigold – pass us that cloth!'

The kitchen was full of steam. Bessie was in the process of dropping a pudding basin, tied firmly at the top, into a pan of boiling water. It would steam away for two or three hours, to be eaten draped in custard as the dinner ran on into cups of tea and Nana's games: canasta and cribbage and ludo for the kids, and the week's sweet rations from the grown-ups, all pooled together. Nana always ate as if it was the last day there'd ever be food.

She turned, her fleshy face puce and running with

moisture. She was enormously stout now, just past her sixty-fourth birthday, but very strong-looking, hair in plaits coiled round her head. Her hair was white but it always had a yellow tinge because she smoked one cigarette end on from the last, sucking the life out of each one. She always wore big frocks in dark material, blue or black, and tight black shoes, her feet appearing small because the flesh of her ankles bulged out over them. Her voice could fill a parade ground and when she laughed it shook her whole body up to her chins. Linda had heard Dad say Nana was 'like an effing battleship and someone ought to torpedo her'.

'Don't be so rude about my mother,' Violet would shout sometimes when the beer was in and they were at it again, bicker, bicker. 'She's done a lot for us, she has – more than yours ever flaming well did. You should show some gratitude.'

'*Gratitude?* She's worse than bloody Hitler ever was!'

'There – ' Bessie settled the basin triumphantly. 'I've got a nice treacle suet in today. Linda – get over here!' She mopped her face with the corner of her huge white apron, stained all down the front with beef juices. 'Give your auntie Marigold a hand or 'er'll never get done today, this rate. 'Ow's Carol? Poor little beggar.'

Without waiting for an answer, Bessie waddled into the front room.

'Violet? How's our Carol? What've they done with her?'

'D'you want some help, Auntie?'

Linda sat across the kitchen table from Marigold, who was working on a pile of carrots. She smiled at Linda in her rather vacant way.

'You can do some of these.' Very deliberately she

wiped the blade of her knife on the floral breast of her apron and passed it to Linda. 'You be careful now.'

Marigold's hair, once liquorice black, was already fading to grey and hung limply round her collar, held back with two kirby-grips, and her fringe dipped into her eyes. Mom had told her that when Marigold and Charlie were born, Marigold came second and they hadn't got her out quick enough so her brain had been starved. Linda never really understood for years how you could starve a brain. But now Carol was having to be kept in the machine so she wasn't starved as well. Whatever exactly had happened to Marigold, she could talk to you all right and do a lot of things, but she wasn't quite like anyone else.

'Our Marigold's not the marrying sort,' Bessie had decreed for years, and no one questioned it.

Then there was Auntie Rosina, whom no one ever talked about much except to say she'd 'gone to London' before the war. If anyone even mentioned her, Nana looked fit to blow up. Auntie Rosina had wanted to go on the stage and ran off with an actor. There was that one picture she had sent, of herself all dressed up, and it stayed behind a jug on the mantelshelf. In the picture she looked very pretty and had dark eyes and hair. Gone to the bad, no doubt, Nana said.

It sometimes seemed to Linda that her mom and Charlie, despite being married and having homes of their own, were like Marigold and had never left either. They danced to Nana's tune like puppets. It was only Rosina who had ever really left.

Linda cut the end off a carrot and began to scrape off the dirt, dipping it in a bowl of water. Marigold was shelling peas, with her funny, secret smile on her face. Violet could hear the voices from the other room, Mom describing going all the way to that hospital, two bus rides away.

'I don't know how I'm going to go carting over there all the time,' she was saying.

After a moment Linda saw that Marigold had stopped doing the peas and was reaching furtively into her cleavage. With a swift movement she pulled out a little bottle full of clear liquid, took a quick swig which she swallowed with relish, then replaced the bottle with a wink at Linda.

'Don't tell on me, will you?'

'No,' Linda said, looking away, at the steam curling from the cooker over to the sink, in front of the window. There was a packet of Bird's custard on the draining board. Nana must smell the drink on Marigold's breath, but it seemed to please Marigold to think she had secrets.

'Where's little Carol?' Marigold said, as if she couldn't hear anything that was going on in the next room. When Linda explained, Marigold looked at her and said, 'Oh. Shame,' but without emotion.

They put the carrots on to boil and Nana came back in then, grunting as she hoisted the beef out of the oven with the potatoes sizzling round it and basted them.

'Vi, Gladys – set the table!' she bellowed. 'You go and get Mrs Magee,' she ordered Linda. 'You needn't think you're going to get out of doing anything.'

'I *am* doing something. It's Joyce who's sitting on her backside . . .'

'Don't you give me that lip or you'll be washing your mouth out . . .'

Linda shrugged.

Usually she had Carol to help. Mrs Magee loved Carol. Linda slipped out the back and along the entry, where the air was cool and her skin stood up in goose-pimples, until she reached the bright street. She walked into Mrs Magee's mothball-smelling house, bracing herself for the struggle.

The old lady was long and lean and sitting defiantly in her chair. She'd worked as a seamstress for years and her black clothes were old and wafer thin, but beautifully made.

'I'm not going. You can't make me.'

Her voice was high and scraped the air. She had her teeth in a teacup. They pinched her so badly that she hardly ever put them in.

'Please, Mrs Magee. It'll be all right.' Linda knew her twelve-year-old reasoning was no match for Carol's pretty charm. Carol could always persuade Mrs Magee.

'No it won't.' She clamped her knees together. Her shimmering black skirt flowed over them.

'But dinner's ready.'

'I don't care. Blasted thug of a woman. Thinks she runs the street, that she does, pushing me around, coming after my sugar ration and acting as if it's charity!'

Linda sympathized a great deal with Mrs Magee, but what could you do?

'She's just trying to be kind.' This was what they were supposed to believe.

'You can kill people with kindness,' Mrs Magee said, beginning to surrender. You could tell by the way her voice went quiet. She looked up at Linda. The whites of her eyes were bile yellow. 'I s'pose you'll be in trouble if I don't?'

Soon she was dressed in her black coat and hat to go across the road, cup of teeth in hand.

'This is the last time I'm doing this.' She said that every week.

Linda took Mrs Magee's stick of an arm so that they could shuffle across the road. The elderly lady was soon seated mutinously at the table and never took her hat off.

The afternoon passed as it always did on Sundays, with the huge meal which they ate until they were all stuffed full.

'Tummy Touching Table – that's what you want,' Bessie said, ladling out spuds.

Belly Busting Buttons, Linda thought.

When Harry had first come back, every week Bessie went on about how they had to fatten him up. She never said anything now. Even Bessie, who knew every trick there was to get around rationing, was no less defeated than the rest of them by the ravages the Japanese camps had wrought in him.

Harry ate his dinner in silence. It was Nana who held court, family her captive audience, full of her neighbours' doings, memories of Grandad Jack, her husband, who died of the influenza at the end of the Great War.

'Worshipped the ground I trod on, Jack did,' she sighed, between mouthfuls of beef. 'There's not many have a husband like I did.'

Occasionally someone else got a word in. Mrs Magee champed away resentfully with her troublesome teeth and the children listened and poured as much gravy over their potatoes as they could.

Today, though, a lot of the talk was about Carol. Linda didn't want to hear it. The others ate mainly in silence, Joyce and Colin looking sulky. Gladys nagged Charlie – 'Don't hold your knife like that, it's rude' – Charlie barely ever said a word and Harry answered in monosyllables if Nana said anything to him.

'Got enough spuds there, Harry?'

'Yes, ta.'

Afterwards, Linda took Mrs Magee back to her house – 'At last – I'm not budging next week!' – and when she got back, her dad was asleep as usual, his thin face sagging with exhaustion.

'Look at the poor bugger,' Uncle Clarence remarked.

He soon fell asleep too, the paper spread across his chest, so that the only sounds in the front room were their snores. The women went into the kitchen and talked over the first round of washing up and Violet made a pan of custard. Then Nana got her cards and boards and cribbage pegs out and they all played until it was time to put the kettle on and get the treacle pudding dished out.

'This is a good 'un, Bess – one of your best,' Uncle Clarence told her, and it was beautiful, thick and sweet and gooey with treacle, the custard not too thick or too thin.

'Very nice,' Gladys murmured. She came along with Charlie every Sunday, no question. This was what the Wileses did on Sundays and if you married one, then that was that. Bessie was the matriarch and no mistake.

Linda tried to sink into the familiar, over-fed drowsiness of Sunday afternoon with them all crowded in there together. She sat by the hearth, on the old peg rug. She knew the bright red bits in it were from a skirt she'd once had. Colin and Joyce were over in the corner, whispering. Linda wondering what they were saying. Colin never whispered to her, but she'd never found cousin Colin very interesting anyway. All he ever thought about was football. She missed the dogs, shut in at home. Nana wouldn't have animals in the house. She said they were dirty.

She tried not to think about Carol but her thoughts

kept going back to her. She was so poorly. What if she never got better? What if she died . . . ? No! Don't think about it!

She jumped up. Nana and her mom were in the kitchen, she thought, but it was quiet, and when she went through the back she saw that the door was open and they'd gone out into the yard.

Before she'd got across the kitchen she could hear Mom crying. Linda stood in the kitchen, looking out through the door. They were out there by the mangle, Nana with her arms folded, Mom wiping her eyes.

'That's why she's poorly!' she was saying. 'I can't bear it – seeing her like that, knowing she's lying there in that thing. What am I going to do? I've always tried not to show anything – not to treat her any different. It's a punishment, I know it is. But it's me should be punished, not her!'

Linda stood on her left leg, trying to balance, right leg bent up at the knee. She stood there, balanced, like a stork, listening to her mother crying outside.

Chapter Thirty-Eight

The week before Carol fell ill with polio, Harry came home drunk, on a weeknight.

'God almighty, hark at him!' Violet jumped violently as he came crashing in through the front door. The dogs all leapt up, barking frantically.

'Get away from me, stupid hounds! Violet – get 'em off me!'

The dogs were supposed to be outside at night, once the rabbits were safely stowed away.

'Why're they in the house? I've told you . . .'

'They're company – all right? Molly, Dolly – out!'

'Company – drooling bloody mongrels!'

'Well, they're better company than you ever are!'

Harry didn't mind the dogs when he was sober, was even quite fond of them. But now was a different matter because with the drink in, everything was hateful to him, himself especially.

Linda, Joyce and Carol scuttled into the hall to help Mom get Dolly, Molly and George out. George the beagle was leaping up, tongue lolling, at their dad, who was propped unsteadily against the dirty, scratched wall. His sunken eyes were glassy and he was still barely more than a skeleton draped in clothes. In the shadows his scar from the bike accident looked more pronounced than ever.

'What kind of house do I have to come home to, eh? Like a sodding zoo. Look at it!'

He pushed himself off the wall. The girls each seized hold of a dog – Carol had Molly as she was the easiest – and were dragging them by their collars towards the back door. Linda had George, who struggled mightily, his brown and white body like a ball of muscle.

They all ended up in the back room, dogs scratching at the kitchen door. There was something about Dad tonight. Linda felt her innards go all tight. It was never knowing what was going to happen, that was the worst thing.

'You aren't going to last in that job if you keep on.' Mom's voice was low and weary. 'The dairy've already warned you – they're only keeping you on . . .' She bit off the end of the sentence.

'That's it – go on!' He was holding on to the back of a chair, swaying. His voice grated out. 'They're only keeping me on 'cause what? 'Cause I'm a wreck, that's it, isn't it? "Poor old Harry, look at the state of him? Can't even shit regular like other blokes any more . . ."'

The three girls stood there, Linda pressing her shoulder against Joyce's arm, and she could feel that Carol had grabbed hold of the back of her dress and was clinging on. The fear in their eyes enraged him further.

'Go on – have a good look at the wreck!' He was trembling suddenly, as if he was freezing cold. 'Keeping me on out of pity! I'd like to've seen them . . . They didn't have to see what I . . . They've no idea – none of 'em . . .' He stuttered the words out, his face working, arms twisting at his sides as if fighting something.

'Oh, Harry –' The sadness in Violet's voice brought him to tears and he stood there gulping in front of them, hands with their bony wrists pressed to his face.

'I couldn't bear it . . . there . . . in Burma . . .' he gulped. 'And now I can't bear it here neither . . .'

213

Linda felt herself twist inside and none of them knew what to do.

Mom looked as if she was going to cry as well. She went to put her arms around him, and worst of all were the little crooning noises she made as if he were a baby, the way they had heard her doing at night when he woke screaming. Suddenly, though, he pulled his hands down and his face was contorted with rage.

'You don't know!' he screamed. 'You don't know, none of you – don't touch me, woman!'

He turned on Violet. 'Wait for me, I said. And you couldn't even . . .'

The girls all jumped as he strode over to them suddenly and grabbed Carol by her wavy blonde hair.

'Found yourself a proper man, did you?'

'Harry, don't!' Violet moaned. Her hands moved in protest, but she stood helpless.

'Ow! Dad, don't – it hurts, it hurts!' Carol shrieked. He was twisting her round by her hair, her legs pedalling to keep up. Linda felt as if every hair on her own head was being ripped as well.

'Dad – stop it!' She went to try and get him off Carol. She'd do anything for Carol. 'You're hurting her! Bloody stop it, will you!'

Harry backed away, dragging Carol with him as she sobbed and screamed and tried to get away.

'Get me the scissors, Linda, *my daughter* . . . She's the only one I can be sure about, isn't she, looking like that?'

Linda stood at a loss.

He bawled at her, 'Scissors – *now*!'

'Harry, no – leave her alone . . .' Violet tried to tackle him again but he pushed her away.

'Shut up – ' He pulled Carol even closer to the door. 'Linda – hurry up!'

Linda came back from the kitchen with the big, blunt scissors with black handles.

'Right – now then . . .' Harry was swaying slightly. He took the scissors in one hand and pulled Carol's hair all up above her head.

'For Christ's sake, what're you doing – not her hair! Leave her!' Violet was screaming now, trying to get near, to stop it. Drunk as Harry was, he kept twisting round, dragging Carol with him, fending her off.

'You know what they did with faithless fraternizing bitches, don't you? The ones who went whoring with the Krauts? Well – *my daughter* – I could cut your mother's hair off . . .' He dragged Carol by her hair again and she cried out, sobbing, hysterical with pain and fear. Linda clenched her fists; her body was so tense she felt she might snap.

'I've always fancied having a lad, though . . .' He snipped off a chunk of her hair, having to work hard with the blunt blades. The gold locks fell to the floor.

'Dad, don't!' Carol was crying. 'Stop it – don't cut my hair off . . .! Ow – you're hurting me!'

He sawed and chopped at it, hunks of it falling and Carol crying even more at the sight of it. Once the heavy length of her hair was all gone he carried on and on. The room was full of the sound of women crying. Joyce and Linda clung to each other, helpless as Dad reduced Carol's bright hair to uneven tufts all over her head. All Violet could do was hold Carol's hand.

'There you go – *lad* – ' He pushed Carol away from him and she fell into Violet's arms trembling and crying. Violet stroked her shorn head, sobbing heartbrokenly herself.

'You bastard, Harry. You pathetic, cruel bastard! Oh,

215

Chapter Thirty-Nine

Carol's illness had a strange effect on the neighbours. Or at least the women. Everyone was kinder for a start, kept asking if they needed anything.

A few days after the rabbits got into their garden, Mrs Bottoms came round to see Mom. The front door opened on her anxious face. She had on a pale blue shirtwaister, her hair was tightly curled and she held out a bunch of pink roses from the garden. Joyce and Linda stood in the shadow of the hall.

'Here, dearie, these're for you. I hope you don't think it funny of me coming round ... Only I heard your Carol had been taken poorly.'

There was a pause, then Mom stepped back. 'Come in.'

Edna Bottoms talked agitatedly as she came through the door. 'Reg said I shouldn't bother you – should mind my own business. So I thought I'd come round while he's at work. Men don't always understand these things, do they?'

'Joyce, Linda – outside. Go on.'

They scooted out to where the dogs were lying out on the strip of concrete at the back of the house, basking in the warmth. Tufts of grass spiked up through the cracks in the concrete.

Linda was wandering off to see Snowdrop when Joyce hissed, beckoning. 'Come 'ere – see what she wants!'

The kitchen window was wide open. The girls squatted under it, backs against the hot wall. Violet was making tea. There was a clink of cups and they could hear snatches of her telling Mrs Bottoms about the hospital, the iron lung, and Mrs B's concerned noises.

Joyce and Linda mimicked her, under the window. *Oh dear, oh Lord ...* They mouthed like goldfish, crossing their eyes and pulling the grievous expressions they could picture on Mrs Bottoms' face. *How terrible ... Poor little thing ... Dear oh dear ...* until they were helpless with giggles and had to move down the garden to explode into laughter, tears running down their cheeks. Linda felt a bit better after it.

'Come on – we're missing it!' Joyce dragged her back by the arm.

They squatted down again. The breeze blew the women's drifting words back and forth in snatches, but they could catch the sad, confidential tones. Mrs Bottoms was talking about a baby. She and Mr Bottoms had one son, called Frank, who was married now, but it wasn't Frank she was talking about.

'She only lived six days. Not even a week.' Mrs Bottoms was speaking in a tight, hiccoughy way. Her voice became a squeak. 'My little Daisy. She was just lying there in the cot ...' There was a long silence until they heard their mom say something: '... ever so sorry ... terrible ...'

Linda's eyes met Joyce's. They were solemn now.

'The worst of it is – it's Reg!' Words seemed to come out of Mrs Bottoms like a cork from a bottle. 'If we could talk about her, it might lay her to rest. But he won't let me. It's as if she never existed. I don't even know where they buried her – I was in that much of a state at the time. The police came. They thought ...

219

They took her away and I've never known . . . Reg said he didn't know – never asked . . . And he's not the same since the war. If I ever say anything he just says you have to forget everything. Put it behind you. But I can't . . . I try, but . . .'

When she started crying, really crying, they moved away. Linda went down on to the scrubby grass and picked up Snowdrop out of her run. She hugged the rabbit's big, robust body, stroking her cheek against the smooth white fur.

They didn't overhear when the next visitor came. Mom told Dad about it at tea, the four of them round the table, window open and a breeze blowing in.

'I met Eva up at the shops today,' Violet said.

Harry looked up, without much interest. 'Eva?'

'Kaminski. Next door.'

'Oh ar.'

'We were just going home, both of us, with the shopping and she said she'd walk with me. She asked about Carol – she was very nice as a matter of fact. Then all of a sudden she just came out with it. "You know, Peter and Alenka were not our only children." I mean, I don't always understand her – her accent and that – and I wasn't sure what she meant.'

Linda mashed her grey, boiled potato into the gravy. Glancing up, she could tell her father was listening now, elbows on the table, rubbing his hands together as if they were cold. And she could tell also that her mom was pleased he was listening, as if just for once they were talking like people who might like each other.

'What'd she say then?'

'She said they had four – another boy and girl. One was called Karol – but I think that was the boy. I didn't catch the girl's name. They were younger, she said.

Anyway, the whole family were taken off to a camp, in Russia somewhere. Nineteen-forty-one I think she said. Cutting down trees – even the kids working morning till night in the freezing cold. The boy died in the camp and then – it was a bit hard to follow – but the little girl died somewhere else, after – I think she said in *Persia*? Died in her arms, she said, in a truck they were crammed into. Nothing she could do. Couldn't even bury her. They just had to leave her.'

Her eyes filled. Everything seemed to make her cry these days. Linda felt close to tears herself.

'Terrible,' Harry said. He stared ahead of him for a moment as if seeing things none of them could see.

When they'd finished eating, the girls got down.

'Go and check the rabbits,' Mom said. They were trying not to aggravate Mr Bottoms – as much for Mrs Bottoms' sake as anything.

Harry got up from the table and put his hand on Violet's shoulder. As she was going out, Linda heard him say, 'Sorry, love. I'm sorry – about Carol. What I did – her hair. I wasn't myself.'

And she heard the half-stifled sound of her mother bursting into tears.

'She's so poorly,' she sobbed. 'I can't stand the thought of her in that horrible metal thing!'

Chapter Forty

Linda went with Violet to the hospital for visits even though she had to wait outside.

At first, Carol was very distressed and homesick.

'I want to come home,' she kept crying. 'I don't like it in here.'

Violet found it terrible to see, and made even worse by the sight of her chopped hair.

'She looks like a plucked chicken. What must those nurses think?'

She seemed glad Linda was there: someone to talk to and relieve her feelings.

The second time they visited, the two of them were utterly miserable. On the way home, Violet took her into the bomb-scarred middle of Birmingham and headed for the Bull Ring.

'D'you want a hamster?' she said suddenly.

'Ooh, yes!' Linda said. She knew Mom was trying to be nice. Carol's illness had brought out a softness in her. And it was her way of finding comfort. She collected animals the way a bird feathers its nest.

'What about Sooty?' Linda said doubtfully. He was forever bringing birds in.

'You can keep it upstairs, away from the cats. Make sure you keep the door shut.'

They went home on the bus with two tiny hamsters

in a little cage, one for Linda and one for Joyce. The man said they were sisters and wouldn't fight.

'They should behave themselves all right – like you and your sister, eh?' he added with a wink.

By the time they'd reached Kingstanding, Linda had called her hamster Goldie.

'You can't call her that – she's not one bit of gold on her,' Joyce sneered.

'Can if I want.'

Joyce called hers Loretta because she thought it was pretty.

'They all right?' Mom came up to see them in Linda's bedroom. They all knew they were trying not to think about the hospital, and Carol stuck in that machine.

The hamsters turned out not to be a good idea. Within a fortnight Linda woke up to find that Loretta had set upon Goldie in the night and killed her. She was covered in bloody gashes.

'I don't think you're supposed to put hamsters in together, are you?' Mrs Bottoms said when she heard. 'He should have told you, really.'

And quite soon after, Loretta died as well. Linda found her curled up in her bedding, cold and stiff. At the time, she thought of it as a bad omen about Carol. Fortunately, she was wrong.

'Hello, pet.' Violet bent down and kissed Carol's cheek, stroking her hair. It had grown back a little now and was like a soft, fair cap all over her head, in varying lengths. 'You all right?'

Carol gave a little nod, drinking in the sight of her mother. Her father, of course, she did not expect to see.

'I'm all right. I'm going to get better.'

223

She spoke with such certainty that Violet gave a faint smile and leaned over her, eyes filling with tears of relief, though she tried to hide it.

'Is that what the nurses say?'

'They think I'm better as well. And I told them.'

Carol's face had changed somehow since the last visit. The look of sadness and preoccupation had gone. Her eyes were bright again.

'It's going to be all right. And I'll be able to walk. He told me.'

'Who told you? Have the doctors been?'

'Yes – but it wasn't them. It was him.'

Violet's hand stilled on Carol's head and she frowned. 'Who? What're you talking about?'

'*Him*. There.' Her eyes looked up to the wall beside her. 'He comes to see me – at night mostly. And he tells me things.'

'Oh, I see – you've been having nice dreams!' Violet laughed with some relief.

'No – not when I was asleep. He's just there, when I look up. And he smiled and told me it would be all right.'

Violet frowned. 'I think I'll go and see if I can talk to one of the nurses.'

She walked off along the ward, a slim, vulnerable figure in her old skirt and cardigan, mac over her arm. She was less intimidated by the nurses now. The thin one they saw the first day often came and talked to her.

'She won't believe me,' Carol told the nurse when they came back together. 'But you do, don't you?'

'What're you talking about?' the nurse said impatiently. 'Who's this "he?"'

'I dunno. But he's there, and he talks to me.'

'She's coming on nicely now,' the nurse said, ignoring Carol. 'This week she's really made quite a stride –

everyone's pleased with her. We think she could spend some of each day out of the lung soon. And of course we're starting on the physiotherapy with her.'

Whatever had happened, there had been a definite change. When they were in Aston for dinner on the Sunday – one of the last times Harry ever came – Bessie said, 'Our Carol was looking better. Summat different about her. I'd say she was on the mend.'

That week, for the first time in ages, things felt lighthearted, as if there was hope.

When Violet said goodbye to her that day, Carol was beaming up at her, dark eyes aglow. She looked like an angel.

By the time Carol had been in the isolation hospital for just over three months, she was spending more and more time outside the iron lung. Once they were sure she could manage without it, the hospital told Violet that Carol was to be transferred to St Gerard's, the Father Hudson's Hospital at Coleshill, where she would be looked after and given more physiotherapy. Though her arms were little affected, the muscles in her legs were badly wasted and they thought it would take some time. There was also a problem with contractions in her spine. They said she might need an operation when she was older.

Violet didn't dare argue with them and took all this in quietly, but when she reached Linda outside, she burst out, 'Coleshill if you please? That's flaming miles away – it's nearly Coventry! I don't know what our mom's going to say. She'll have a fit.'

Linda wondered why Nana once again seemed to be judge and jury about every thing that happened. Surely what mattered now was getting Carol better?

Chapter Forty-One

'Ticket?'

Linda fished in her pocket for her penny and the conductor grumpily shoved a ticket at her and moved on. She made a face at him behind his back and returned to staring out of the rain-streaked window. The 29A had left the estate behind and was grinding along in the cold, wet October morning. She felt very out of sorts.

They'd been to see Carol on Saturday, right over at Father Hudson's in Coleshill. She had a proper bed now, instead of the machine, and seemed much happier. She was in a long ward with doors all along one side that could be opened to wheel the beds onto a terrace outside when it was fine. The nuns who nursed her were kind, she said. Her favourite was called Sister Cathleen. And they were doing physiotherapy every day. It was the only time her face fell, talking about that.

'It hurts ever such a lot,' she whispered to Linda with tears in her eyes. 'I don't like it.'

Sister Cathleen, who had a round, freckly face, said Carol was 'coming on grand'. But she still wasn't home and it felt such a long time since she had been, and the place was such a long way away. Nothing felt right with Carol away all the time. And Dad was drinking more. She tried to pretend to herself that that wasn't true, but she knew really it was. You never knew how he was going to be when he drank so you could never relax. All she wanted was to get out.

Yesterday she had wanted to meet her best friend Lucy Etheridge in Sutton Park, but Mom had said no.

'We're going to Nana's – you know we are.'

'But why do we have to *every* week? Can't we stay here and do something different – just for once?'

'You know we can't – she'll be expecting us!'

'Dad's not going!'

'All the more reason for you to go,' Mom snapped. She was bad-tempered all the time, living on her nerves.

'I'm fed up with going there. It's always the same and it's *boring*.'

For once she and Joyce were in agreement. 'I want to stay at home,' Joyce said.

'Enough of your bloody lip! Course we're going – no arguments.'

Violet left Dad with a ham sandwich and a plea not to go to the pub. He didn't go to the nearest pub, which sold Mitchells & Butlers beer, but walked further for his Ansells. Linda knew Mom was just trying to make herself feel better – he'd be out the door seconds after they'd gone.

Mom kept saying, 'He's getting worse. It never used to be this bad.' She looked thin and wrung out.

Linda glanced down proudly at the uniform skirt she was wearing. King Edward's Grammar School! She said it over and over again to herself like a magic spell. Even after a year the wonder of it had not worn off.

When she took the eleven-plus she was full of nerves, remembering how Joyce had said it was ever so hard. Joyce had gone without a thought to the new secondary modern school close by on the estate. Linda got part way through the test paper and wondered if it was all a mistake. If she didn't find it too difficult, did that mean she'd not understood the questions and got it all wrong? Her hands began to sweat with anxiety and her heart was banging away. She didn't have any real idea what going to the grammar school meant, it was all unknown, but there was something glowing in her, like the little pilot light in the Ascot heater in the bathroom. She *wanted* it.

And they gave her a place! It was the one time in her life when she saw she had impressed her father.

'Let her have a go,' he said. 'She's earned it.'

Mum was unsure, Nana full of scorn.

'We'll never afford the uniform,' Violet said. It was all beyond what she knew, unknown territory, and she wanted to play safe. 'And it's two buses away. No – it's better if you don't go. You'll be worse than you are already, nose always in a book. That's not real life, you know. No – it's not for people like us.'

It took Linda all her powers of persuasion – that she'd have no other clothes all year and she'd do odd jobs to get the money, she would even eat less to save the money, she'd do *anything*, if only she could go! It was Dad who stood up for her and for that she was deeply grateful.

For the last year she'd entered the portals of this other world of the grammar school, away from their scruffy house with its stinks of the animals and cabbage water and Dad throwing up – to a place where the world opened up in books and maps and pictures, the way it had that day in Johnny Vetch's house in Aston when he showed her his cases of fossils and his book about the stars and she knew it was possible for someone else like her to care about learning. At school she was in heaven, even though she never felt quite like most of the others. There were only a very few who were poor and down at heel like her. At first she'd wondered if she could ever keep up. By summer she was among the top five in her form, and though a few of the girls were snobby, they weren't all, and she had Lucy, a best friend who was prepared to stick around with her.

'If you go there,' Johnny Vetch said to her in his gentle voice, 'you'll learn things you'd never dream of in the other school. You'll be another person. It's where they separate the sheep from the goats.'

Johnny was a quiet, thin man of twenty-three. He'd gone away to college and had some sort of breakdown. He lived with his mom still and did odd jobs that didn't demand too much of him.

'He overtaxed his brain, that one,' Bessie would say. 'That's what happens. Overtaxed it. You want to be careful, my girl. You don't want to end up like Johnny Vetch. Nose in a book and no wife.' She added something else behind her hand to Mom and laughed in a way which meant it was something crude.

Be careful, was all Nana ever said. The only safe thing, so far as her grandmother was concerned, was having babies and more babies and staying at home like a fat queen bee in a hive trying to keep everyone under your thumb. Like her.

'The world's a big place,' Johnny told her one day. 'Full of interest. One day I'm going to go on a boat along the Amazon river. I've read about it. There're spiders there as big as my hand.'

The spiders made her shiver. But Johnny didn't tell her just about spiders. He told her about the birds, the snakes and butterflies in the Amazon. And the deserts across the world, full of seeds just waiting for a fall of rain so they could burst out into the brightest, most radiant flowers you could ever see. And about rocks and crystals, and the Northern Lights dancing like chiffon in the cold night, and constellations of stars. Johnny loved the blackout. You could see everything better.

One winter night before the war ended, when Johnny was still all right, he came round while Linda was at Nana's.

'Tell Linda to come outside a minute,' he said from the doorstep. 'There's something I want to show her.'

'Don't talk daft,' Nana dismissed him. 'She'll catch her death.'

But Linda was already jumping up to get her coat down off the hook. Whatever was Nana on about? She walked home every night with Mom, didn't she? It was just because Nana didn't approve of Johnny Vetch.

'Be careful...' Nana said reprovingly. 'Don't go keeping her out for long. Her mom'll be in soon.' It was getting late. But Mom sometimes was late these days.

The night was cold with the promise of ice. The air made her cheeks feel slapped. Once Nana had slammed the front door huffily, the dark closed in on them.

'Your eyes'll get used to it,' Johnny said. 'Come on.'

He took her hand and led her down the street towards his mother's house. She thought they'd go down the pitch black entry and inside, that he probably had a new book he'd ferreted out of some musty old shop somewhere. Or a new rock to show her. Linda knew people thought Johnny was strange, and that he couldn't hold down much of a job or anything. He wasn't thought of as 'normal', but she always felt safe with him. They were in tune somehow.

'Best be quick,' he said. 'This is something special. I've got the key off Mr Jacobs.'

230

Linda thought this sounded exciting. 'Where're we going?'

'Wait – you'll see.'

Two streets away was a brick church. To Linda's astonishment, Johnny led her round to the side door and unlocked it. Leading her inside, he pulled a torch from his pocket. Once more, her eyes adjusted. She could smell the place, a strange sweetness of stone and paper and wax, and as Johnny moved the weak beam of the torch around them she could make out a vast, dark space, pews stretching in lines ahead of them. It reminded her of her grandmother's funeral, when Dad had got upset and fought with that rough old man who'd turned up. The school had taken them into church once or twice, but that was all. It gave her a funny feeling, as if she had stepped into somewhere quite distinct from the street outside. She realized that Johnny knew the place very well. Perhaps he went to church every week? She didn't know.

They walked along the side aisle to the back of the church. Johnny shone the torch on a little door at the back and when he opened it she saw steps.

'You're not frightened, are you?'

'No!' It hadn't occurred to her to be afraid.

'Best thing is, if you go ahead of me, I'll shine the torch for you. I'm right behind you.'

The staircase wound round and round and the only sound was their footfalls on the stone and their breathing, and all they could see were the shadows winding round with them from Johnny's torch. At the top there was another door, and when Johnny opened it Linda felt a rush of cold air.

'This is the bell tower,' he said. 'Mind your head.'

They were in a wide, flat space, in which hung the

dark shapes of several bells. Linda would have liked to look more. They seemed so big and heavy, hanging there. But Johnny was steering her over to the side, where there was a window. Fixed over it was a mesh.

'That's to keep the birds out,' Johnny said. 'You get pigeons messing all over the bells else and it'd stink. But . . .' He struggled with something at the side of the window for a moment. 'It's loose. Look – come up this end.'

He unfastened the wire at one end and folded it back on itself so there was a space at the end for them to look out. Linda leaned against the wall, her hands on the sill, which was level with her collarbones. Johnny had to bend to look out over her head. He switched off the torch.

'You can't see much down there. We're high up, you know – above everything. If it was daytime you'd see all the houses and factories – the roofs – from up here.'

'Can we come back in the morning?'

She heard him laugh, faintly. 'One day, maybe. But look up. This must be one of the clearest nights of the year. Just for once, no clouds and you can see past all the smoke.'

She turned her gaze to the sky. Johnny was right. Apart from a few faint streaks there was nothing to obscure the arc of sky, the great sea of stars. She had never seen it like this before. The more she looked, the more of them she could make out, as if they were coming out in their tens of hundreds just for her. Silently the two of them stared into the sky's vastness and after a time she had a strange feeling, the same that she had had in the church downstairs, that she was in a special place and all that was around her was somehow alive and in communication with her, making her feel she was awash with life, but she could never have put the feelings into words. Words might have made it disappear.

'See over there – ' Johnny broke their long silence. He pointed out a shape of stars, guiding her, and eventually she could see what he was talking about. 'That's Orion, the hunter. See those three stars? Those are his belt.' He pointed out arms, legs, a sword. 'Oh – and that one's Ursa Major – the Great Bear. The Plough they call it as well.'

'Looks like a saucepan,' Linda said.

'Yes, I s'pose it does.'

He pointed out another shape which he said was a Greek lady called Cassiopeia, but she thought looked like a W on its side. She liked the pictures in the sky, but best of all she liked standing looking out in the quiet, high above everyone, in a place she'd never been before. It was some time before she noticed how cold she was.

'Best go now,' Johnny said, fixing the mesh back. 'Keep those pigeons out.'

'I like the night better than the day,' she said, and he laughed.

'Only when there's no clouds.'

When her mom asked what they'd been doing, when she finally got to Nana's, Linda said, 'Looking at the stars.' She didn't say where. Johnny didn't ask her to keep it secret, but it was *her* secret because it had been special.

'That Johnny's stupid,' Joyce said spitefully. He didn't pay Joyce much attention.

'Bats in the belfry,' Bessie said.

'He's not stupid,' Linda said crossly. 'He's clever.'

That night stayed with her; and Johnny's books and

interest in things that a lot of other people didn't seem to care about. There had to be more, she knew, than the life she saw round her. Working in factories, having babies. She couldn't have put that into words either, but the knowledge sat in her like a hunger. And going to the grammar school was part of that hunger, of answering the need for more.

Soon, Lucy got on to the bus. She was a quiet, serious girl with thick brown bunches lying neatly on her shoulders. Linda adored Lucy, but she'd never invited her round to her house. She was ashamed of the state of the place, the smell. Lucy lived in a nice villa in Sutton Coldfield with a neat front garden and clean, tidy furniture inside. She didn't have any brothers or sisters and her mom and dad were quite old and they took her to church every week. Everything about Lucy's life was gentle and calm. Linda had been to her house a few times and they were very kind to her.

'Sorry I can't really take you back to mine,' she said. 'My dad's not well. He has to have it quiet so we're not allowed to take people back.'

She didn't want home and school meeting each other anyway. At school she could be someone else, just like Johnny Vetch said.

'You done your French homework?' she asked Lucy.

'Yes. I got stuck on my arithmetic though – could you do it?'

'Most of it.'

Lucy pulled her book out, and for the rest of the journey they talked sums and lessons, heading for the hours at school, those ordered hours of timetables and routines and being sure when you will eat, in which Linda was in heaven.

Chapter Forty-Two

Rain lashed down in slanting lines. It was early in the morning, November and bitterly cold.

The men were harnessing the horses on to the floats in the Co-op Dairy, and loading them up ready for the day's delivery. The light was poor and they were cursing the cold and wet. Hot breath streamed from the horses' nostrils.

The supervisor came over. One of the carts was not being attended to.

'That Harry Martin's?' He nodded grimly at it.

'Yup,' the next man said. He rolled his eyes. 'Poor bugger.'

'We can't go on like this. Where the hell is he?'

It had been getting worse, week by week. Harry's timekeeping, the drink.

'He's here!' One of the others called, relieved.

All the men felt for Harry Martin. Who wouldn't? Christ alone knew what had got him in that state. He'd been out East in one of the Jap camps, and it was written all over him. Anyone'd need a few drinks after that. They tried to keep him going, made excuses for him. But Harry was going down the pan, they could all see it. Must have had a night of it last night.

He was shambling along, a pathetic figure, clothes hanging on him and bareheaded, no cap, even in this weather. And what was worse, he wasn't even sobered up now, his gait unsteady, lurching from side to side.

The supervisor tutted, shaking his head.

'Come on, pal,' the other bloke was saying hurriedly to Harry. 'I'll give you a hand.'

'Ta,' Harry said. He clung on to the side of the float to steady himself. His face was so thin and drawn it was pitiful to see.

'Look, Harry,' the supervisor spoke quietly, not wanting to make a song and dance about it all in front of the others. 'You've been late in every day this week. And look at the state of you! The other blokes've been covering for you, but you can't go on like this. For heaven's sake pull yourself together! I'm giving you one more chance, but after that – you're out. I'll have to let you go.'

Harry seemed to be listening but not taking in the import of what his boss was saying. A smile played around his lips. His coat hung open and they saw that his clothes were only scantily buttoned up, the top of his shirt hanging open, showing the bones in his emaciated chest. And he was soaking wet.

'Are you listening to me?' The supervisor was aggravated now. 'I'm trying my best for you, pal, but you're a bloody mess – look at the state of you! Come on – get yourself together!'

'I can't.' Harry was still smiling. His face and words didn't match.

'Come on, Harry,' the other man said, trying to shift him with briskness. 'Get to work.'

Harry was swaying, smiling, almost laughing now. 'Can't no more.'

The two other men looked uneasily at each other.

'Look – we can't go on like this. You can see that,

can't you? I'm going to have to let you go.' The supervisor felt a real heel doing it, the state the bloke was in. The last thing he needed was more punishment. 'I'm sorry, Harry.'

There was no reply. It was as if he hadn't heard.

'D'you hear what I said?' His tone was harder now. 'I'm sacking you. You're not doing your job. You'd best get off home now in any case.'

There came a dark trickle from Harry's nose, blood running down his chin, but he didn't appear to notice. Gashes of it fell on his shirt.

'Harry? You don't look any too well, mate. Go on – get yourself home.'

But Harry continued smiling and swaying from side to side. 'Can't. Can't go home.'

A moment later his legs gave way and he collapsed on the floor. His hands went over his face and he curled up on his side and lay there, his whole body trembling.

'God Almighty,' the supervisor breathed. 'This isn't just the bottle, is it? We'd best call an ambulance.'

Harry was taken to Good Hope Hospital and it was soon clear he would not be coming home for some time. He was in a state of collapse.

'It's terrible seeing him,' Violet sobbed to Bessie.

She'd taken them straight round there after visiting Harry, and sank down in Nana's kitchen amid all the napkins and the smell of milk heating in a pan. Violet had snatched up a piece of old rag which she was using for a handkerchief, and kept squeezing it into a ball in her hands.

Linda and Joyce sat at the table, pretending to play with Nana's toffee tin of old buttons.

'He's like a shell. As if he's got lost somewhere in himself and can't find the way out!'

'Terrible. Terrible thing,' Uncle Clarence kept saying over and over. For once he'd got out of his chair and was standing in the doorway, fingers hooked in his braces. 'He's never been right since them Japs.'

'I don't know what I'm going to do!' Violet said. 'What with him there and our Carol all that way away! I feel as if I'm going out of my mind with it all.'

Linda took a black coat button and ground it into a crack in the table. The button snapped in half.

'Look what you've gone and done!' Bessie roared at her. 'Can't you behave yourself for five minutes?'

Linda pushed her chair back and it scraped the floor. 'I don't want to play with the buttons!'

'Well, sit quiet and behave yourself and don't give us your lip!'

Linda would normally have taken herself off to the lavatory but today she didn't want to miss what was being said. She went and stood in the scullery, arms folded mutinously, where she could see them all, Joyce sucking up to Nana as ever, sorting buttons as if she was five years old.

Bessie poured the milk into a cup. The child she was looking after now was not far short of a year old and she was getting fed up with him. They were trouble when they got older. She only liked the young ones. She stirred a spoonful of sugar into the milk and put it in front of him.

'Ere – get that down you and pack in that blarting!'

'Where's Auntie Marigold?' Joyce asked.

Marigold was just always there, normally, like the gas stove and the table.

'We've just had a new 'un come – only a few days old. Marigold's got her in the pram.'

Linda could see her mother, sitting bolt upright, her eyes filling with tears again.

'You're going to have to pull your horns in, now you've lost your breadwinner,' Bessie decreed.

'I'll have to get a job,' Violet said flatly.

'You'll be out at work soon enough, won't you Joyce? I don't know why they keep them in till they're fifteen now, that I don't – waste of time, staying on at school for nothing. And *that one*,' Bessie interrupted, nodding her head contemptuously in Linda's direction, 'will have to stop getting big ideas – swanning off, wasting two bus fares to get to school. There's been quite enough of that carry-on. What use is all that lark going to be to her? Bad enough when you had Harry in a job, but now – well, that's the first thing can go . . .'

Linda felt the words stab her, like poisoned arrows. Her eyes narrowed with loathing towards her grand-mother.

'I don't know,' Violet was saying. 'Harry quite likes her going there . . .'

'Well, he ain't in any position to have a say, is he? He was always a fool to her – and he's not the one left to bring in the money. It's time you faced up to things. All those fares you're paying out getting to see him, and to Coleshill – it's all costing you, Vi, before you pay the rent and put a crust in their mouths.'

As if reminded, she leaned over, reaching for a finger of bread to give to the orphan child. There was a bowl of orange boiled sweets on the table and she took one for herself, untwisting the wrapper and popping it in her mouth before sitting back, arms folded across her bosom. Her skirt rode up, exposing her scarlet bloomers.

'You want to get her out of that school – all these bloody fancy ideas, and get her ready for work. She'll be no use to anyone, else . . .'

Linda looked across at her grandmother, at her broad, rough face, cheek bulging with the sweet, her battering ram of a body and bullish face, always so sure she was right about everything. The rush of rage she felt finally propelled her outside to the lav.

Between the rough brick walls she stood with her back to the stained lavatory pan, shaking, as if she was going to burst with the great, silent scream inside her. *No, no! Mom couldn't listen to that advice, wouldn't take her away . . . She couldn't . . . Wouldn't!* The thought of it was too unbearable. Clenching her fists, she banged them down on her thighs until they ached.

She stayed in there as long as possible, perched fully clothed on the edge of the toilet bowl, staring at the cobwebs across the hinges and dreading going back inside. She wouldn't say a word to anyone, not while they were still with Nana.

On the way home she could contain herself no longer. Words tumbled out.

'Mom, you won't take me away from the grammar school will you? Like Nana said? You can't, *please*. You won't, will you?'

Her mother whipped round in the road, all her own fear and tension pouring out.

'Just bloody shut up, will you? Stop going on at me! I've had enough! I don't know what I'm going to do, so just shut it till I've had time to think!'

Chapter Forty-Three

12 Bloomsbury Road,
Kingstanding
B'ham
Nov 18th, 1950

Dear Muriel,

Sorry I haven't written – have been at my wits
end lately. Harry was taken ill last week and he's in
the hospital. All the back-and-to between him and
Carol is taking it out of me and I don't know what
to do for the best.

Harry's in a very poor way. He's never been
right of course, so when he started feeling poorly we
didn't think much of it but he shouldve stayed in
bed and he kept on instead. He was taken bad at
work his lungs are bad and he's feverish and doesn't
always know me.

When I went up the hospital the first time he said
the doctors said, Do you keep birds at home? (Well
I thought he's gone barmy at first, coming out with
that.) And I said yes, we had budgies and the parrot
and they looked at one another as if to say, 'Oh,
yes, told you so.' They told him he's got some
disease you catch from birds on top of everything
else that's wrong with him that is. So I said, but the
parrot's not poorly or anything. But they said it can
be sick and not show it and I should think very hard

about getting rid of the birds as Ive got children in the house as well because you can catch it by breathing it in. I didnt like the way he talked to me as if I wear dirty or something. I suppose the dogs make a mess I might have to get rid of Silver and the budgies but the worst of it is Harry's not right at all. He can hardly do a thing for himself he's like a child and he keeps crying over the least thing. He kept hold of my hand all the time when I went the first time and kept saying, Don't go, Vi, don't leave me. He was frightened to death, I don't know where he thought he was and course I had to go home. The doctor took me aside and asked about the war and Burma and the camps and that and when I told him he said "I see." I just don't know what to do, Mu, which way to turn. I wish you lived closer.

Our Carol's still over at the hospital in Coleshill and at least she's getting better, there's no doubt. Her arms aren't too bad it's her legs. And they say her back's not right and she might have to have an operation not yet though. But I feel as if they're taking her away from me. She's fixed on one of the nuns who's looking after her she's called Sister Cathleen and I know she's very kind but it's as if they're getting their claws into her. Someone's put holy pictures by her bed and she said last week they took her to Mass and Sister Cathleen said Carol asked if she could go but I don't know if that's true. She's only young and it feels as if she's more theirs than mine now. Sometimes I feel very down.

Done nothing but moan, have I? Thanks for your card. Glad you and Dickie are getting on so well but your news came as a shock, you can imagine. Australia! Harry always wanted to go there but I don't think I'd be brave enough to start a new life. I can't say I'm glad you're going though. I miss you enough, all the way down in Brighton!

Keep in touch, won't you? Need any welding doing! Sorry if this is a bit miserable.

Best wishes, Violet. x

Chapter Forty-Four

'What're we going to do with him?'

Violet stared into the parrot's cage. 'He looks all right, doesn't he? You'd never know there was anything the matter.'

'He's shivering,' Joyce said.

Linda watched the parrot as he sat huddled up at one end of his perch. She'd thought of the name Silver after reading *Treasure Island*.

'I think he looks poorly,' she said. He had an air of misery about him.

'Don't breathe near him!' Violet said suddenly. 'Oh, I don't know! I can't give him to anyone, can I? Who's going to want a parrot with a disease?' Linda could hear tears coming in her voice.

Out at the front Mr Kaminski was working with a spade, turning over the soil in his vegetable garden. In need of another adult opinion, Violet went and asked him. Linda and Joyce stood leaning against the smelly tarpaulin covering their dad's Norton. Linda felt her head swim with tiredness. Last night Mom had been crying. It had gone on a long time.

'He is sick?' Joe Kaminski said, standing his spade up in the soil. In the winter sunlight his chiselled face was divided into planes of light and shadow. 'Then you have to . . .' He made a wringing motion with his hands.

'Ooh no – I can't do that – I just couldn't! I mean, we've had him a long time.'

Mr Kaminski shrugged. 'I do it if you want. Or you let him go. What else?'

Violet came in and shut the door with a slam. 'Fat lot of good asking him.'

Next day she decided to let Silver go. First thing, she was down there in her nightie with an old cardi over the top, the cage door open and the back room window. Silver sat stubbornly on his perch, not taking the blindest notice of this generous offer of freedom.

'He doesn't want to go,' Joyce said, eating toast.

'You don't say,' Linda retorted. They were both dressed ready for school, shivering as the frost-nipped air streamed in.

'Shut it, clever clogs.'

Violet tried moving the cage over to the window, a development that Silver looked no further impressed by.

'You'll have to get him out,' Linda suggested. 'He doesn't like the cold.'

'He's poorly. What d'you expect? How would you like to be turfed out when you've got the flu or whatever? Just hang on. Something'll happen.'

'Yeah – a wizard'll come with a spell book,' Linda said, sarcastically.

'That's enough of your lip!' Violet turned on her, wagging her finger, her eyes narrowed. 'I've had quite enough of it. You can pack in thinking you're better than the rest of us – and you needn't get ideas about staying on at that posh bloody school any longer. I'm going to tell them – after Christmas you can go to school here with Joyce like everyone else!'

It came so suddenly, like a slap.

'No!' Linda gasped. She saw Joyce looking smug.

In a fury Violet reached into the cage. Silver didn't make any protest which showed he was not well.

'Mom – Mom, you haven't said anything to them have you? You can't – don't, *please* . . .'

She was whimpering like a tiny child, so full of shock and betrayal at this attack on the one thing she held so precious.

Violet steered Silver out of the cage and hurled him out of the window. 'Go on, you silly sod – just go! Get out of my sight!'

'Mom!' It was Joyce's turn to be outraged now. 'You can't – the dogs'll get him. That's horrible!' She ran to the window. A great chorus of high-pitched barking came from the garden.

Linda could see nothing, think of nothing but the shock of her mother's words. She went to her, pulling on Violet's bony arm, her voice high and shrill.

'Mom, don't make me leave, don't, please! I'll do anything, just don't make me. I like my school – I don't want to go to Joyce's school, please, Mom, *please* . . .'

'Get off of me!' Her mother shrieked. 'Stop keeping on – you've heard what I've said so shut it, 'cause that's how things're going to be. Your dad might die and your sister's bad and all you can think of is your bloody school! I've put up with your airs and graces long enough. I said *shut up*!'

Her own nerves at breaking point, she shoved Linda violently across the room so that she staggered back and fell, hitting her head on the hard arm of the chair. The stab of pain through her temple floored her and she curled up, head down, sobbing, dimly aware of the cold, smelly lino under her and Joyce shouting somewhere in the room that Silver couldn't fly.

After a moment Linda realized she was alone, because

Mom and Joyce were outside trying to get the dogs off Silver. She raised her head and looked through her tears at the dirty floor, her arms resting on it, the woollen sleeves of her school jumper. She could still hear the dogs, wild with excitement outside. Somewhere in it all was the furious voice of Mr Bottoms demanding to know what was going on at this unearthly hour of the morning.

Linda couldn't think straight. Every nerve in her body seemed to scream NO to all that was around her: her family, the filthy chaos of her home, being taken away without any say from the one thing she really loved. She put her throbbing head down on her arms, nipped a mouthful of the sweater between her teeth and bit into it, while her body shook with helpless sobs.

Her one hope was that her mom would simply forget, or not get round to talking to the school as she didn't get round to so many things. But Mom had Nana behind her, nagging and keeping on. And Nana wanted to bring her down a peg. She always had. With despair, Linda knew that her mom was in a state and couldn't think for herself, that in the end she would always do what Nana said. No matter if Linda cried herself to sleep every night and begged and begged, Bessie's word would rule. By the end of that week Violet had been to King Edward's School and told them Linda would be leaving at the end of term.

On Saturday they all trekked over to see Carol. She had a wheelchair now and had made friends with some of the other children. Linda was so pleased that she looked better, but she could not hide her own misery. The journey over there had been silent and mutinous.

'You can't sulk for ever,' Mom said.

Sulk? Linda thought. She was too outraged to reply. Mom and Nana between them were pulling her whole world apart and Mom could call it *sulking*?

'I don't see what you're making such a fuss about,' Joyce said. 'After all, you've been to the grammar school for a bit – you can always *say* you've been there, can't you?'

Linda turned her face to the window. Joyce would never understand. The secondary modern suited her perfectly well. If you were a girl they gave you just enough to get a little job to fill in time before you got married. You weren't supposed to expect anything much.

'Oh, leave her,' her mom said. 'She'll come out of it.'

Linda's throat ached, and her body felt brittle, as if she might just break apart. She didn't answer either of them. If only she could see Johnny Vetch again. He was the one person who would have understood what it meant to have your dreams smashed. She thought of that night up on the church tower, seeing the stars, the greatness of it. But Johnny had gone away for a bit. They said he wasn't very well.

Carol was not by her own bed when they arrived. She was sitting beside a friend's bed, and Sister Cathleen wheeled her back when her visitors arrived. Carol beamed.

'Someone cut your hair?' Violet asked straight away. Now it had grown longer, it had been trimmed into a bob round her chin and it suited her. She looked very pretty.

'Sister Cathleen did it,' Carol said. She turned and beamed up at her nurse, whose freckly face smiled back very fondly at her.

'D'you like it?' Sister Cathleen said. 'Looks grand, doesn't she?'

'Yes. Thanks.' Linda heard the coldness in her mother's reply. She could tell Mom didn't trust Sister Cathleen. She didn't like Carol loving her the way she did.

'I'll leave you to have a good old chat,' Sister Cathleen said. 'She's had a grand week, though, haven't you?'

Parking the wheelchair, she moved off along the ward. Violet stared after her energetic figure for a moment.

'Sister Cathleen's been teaching me some prayers,' Carol said, as Linda and Joyce settled on her bed close to her.

'Oh, has she?' their mother said. Carol didn't hear the hostility in her voice.

'And look – she's given me some rosary beads – aren't they nice?'

From her hands dangled a set of pretty blue beads.

'She told me how to say it in Latin – it goes, *Ave Maria, gratia plena, dominus tecum . . .*'

'That's enough of that,' Violet interrupted, exasperated. 'She shouldn't be telling you all that mumbo-jumbo without asking me. Gives me the creeps, all that.'

'It's not creepy, it's nice. She says Mary is our mother and she's always with us.'

'What a load of bloody twaddle! *I'm* your mother. Aren't I good enough for you any more?'

Carol looked taken aback at the fierceness of her mother's outburst.

'Well yes, but . . .'

'Sorry, bab.' Violet stroked her hair. Linda watched. She saw the way her mother looked at Carol now. It was a peculiar thing. Carol was the one she had paid no attention to before. Now, though, it felt as if she was the only one of them Mom really cared about.

They had to tell Carol that Dad was poorly. And about Silver. Violet kept it light, so's not to upset her. Between her and Joyce they made what had happened with Silver into a funny story instead of a sad one.

'In the end, we had Mr Bum yelling over the fence on one side, and Silver was sitting there with all the dogs round and Mom lifted him up and he flapped over into the Kaminskis. I reckon he likes it in there.'

In fact, Silver had sat in the Kaminskis' garden for the rest of that day looking stunned and unwell. By the next day he had disappeared, and Linda imagined that Mr Kaminski had done what he'd suggested doing to Silver in the first place, but none of them had seen, so they all chose to believe that he had flown off into the cold blue air and found somewhere to be happy. At least that was what they wanted Carol to believe.

Linda didn't say a word all this time. Eventually Carol reached over and touched her hand.

'What's up?'

Tears came into Linda's eyes straight away. Trust Carol to be the only one to notice how upset she was!

'Mom's making me leave my school . . .' She couldn't stop the tears then. It hurt so much.

Carol's eyes widened. 'But *why*? You love it there, don't you? Mom – why?'

'It's just how it has to be,' Violet said, in a voice that said *don't argue*. 'Too much on our plates.'

'Oh.' Carol squeezed Linda's hand.

'She's making a fuss,' Joyce said. 'Can't you shut up about it now, Linda? It's getting boring.'

But Carol kept hold of her hand. 'Poor Linda,' she said, and her brown eyes were full of an understanding beyond her years.

Chapter Forty-Five

'Come on – time to go!'

Linda was up on her bed. Sunday, and time to go and catch the bus to Nana's for dinner, the way they did every week, as sure as eggs was eggs. She didn't move. Joyce was already downstairs. She heard Violet's voice, full of irritation.

'Where is that girl? Linda? Come *on*!'

Slowly, limbs heavy, she dragged herself off the bed and downstairs.

'Why d'you have to make me keep on?' Violet was hoiking the dogs into the kitchen to be shut in. She already had her coat on. She had shrunk very thin, like a dry twig, always ready to snap.

Mutinously, Linda put on her school coat and scarf. She didn't know she was going to do it, but as soon as they were out of the front door she ran for it.

'Oi – what the hell're you playing at?' Violet shrieked after her. 'Get back here!'

'No – I'm not coming!'

'What d'you mean, you're not bloody coming? Get here now, or we'll miss the bus.'

'I don't want to go to Nana's!' She stood some way off along the road, poised for flight.

'I don't care what you want – you're coming!'

'No!'

A furious Mr Bottoms erupted out of his house, newspaper in hand, practically frothing at the mouth.

'D'you think you could *possibly* conduct your family business somewhere else so the whole road doesn't have to hear it?'

'Oh, sod off,' Violet roared at him. 'Come on – we'll leave the little cow. You won't get any dinner then!'

'Don't care!' Linda yelled.

She watched her mother and sister disappear along Bloomsbury Road to get the bus. For a moment she felt bereft. It was the first weekend in December and freezing cold. Her breath was white on the air, the sun at a low angle in the sky. She didn't have a key and she'd have to be out for hours now until they all came back.

But anything was better than going to Nana's. She boiled inside every time she thought of her grandmother. It was all her fault she had to leave her school. Mom wouldn't have made her if Nana hadn't kept on. The way she made *everyone* do what *she* wanted. Like poor old Auntie Marigold. Why did everyone just do what she wanted? Why was everyone frightened of her? It was only Auntie Rosina, whose pretty, dark-eyed face stared out of the dusty photo on Nana's mantel, who gave her any hope. She'd got away, hadn't she? But where was she now?

Sunk in misery, she came to the bit of waste ground where there was an old see-saw and a couple of swings. Across the way was Mrs Nixon's house. She had a refrigerator with an extra cold compartment and she made ice cubes out of orange squash in the summer. Linda sat on one of the swings but she'd come out without a hat or gloves and the chains made her hands cold so she got off again. Her palms smelt of rust from the chains.

Soon she came to her old school, where she'd gone before King Edward's. Of course it was silent and empty. She looked over into the playground, imagining herself in it with all the others, the games of 'hot rice and cold sago', running, bouncing the ball. All the girls she'd known there went to the secondary modern except for her. Of course she still saw some of them round the estate, but there was a distance between them. She had separated herself off, going to the grammar school. And now she'd have to go back. It felt like a disgrace.

She stood listening to the echoes of shrieks and laughter, games and chants: *On the mountain stands a lady, who she is we do not know . . .*

Turning away she walked and walked to keep warm, a determined little figure, dark hair waving round her cheeks, hands pushed down into the pockets of her coat, bare legs and ankle socks. She felt defiant. Never mind the cold, and no dinner! Who cared? She'd refused to go to Nana's! It was time someone refused Nana something. She got her way over every single thing. It was Nana's fault she had to leave her school . . . At this thought she was full of rage again. *I hate her, I hate her, the bloody old cow! Just because she can't read or write!*

There was a place on the estate that Peter Kaminski had shown them, years back when he was still not above playing out. Peter was sixteen now, and an apprentice engineer. He had always been a daredevil, seemed to have no sense of danger. And he had shown them where it was. Behind a fence, tucked in out of sight, was an old Spitfire.

Linda went to the fence and peered through at the little plane standing there in the weeds, its shape unmistakable, the round-ended wings, the bits chipped off the propellors. No one seemed to know why it was there. Peter used to run round, arms out, roaring and sputtering, and they all followed and joined in, a childish squadron of Spitfires. She remembered one summer evening when they were all up here, her and Joyce, Peter and Alenka Kaminski, who was Joyce's age, with Carol laughing and straining against the straps of the pushchair as she watched them all playing. Linda used to push Carol all over the place when she was little, she never minded. And now they were having to push her again.

She hugged herself and stared at the sad, silent plane in its bed of nettles. All that cold afternoon she felt herself changing shape inside, shrinking back. No more King Edward's. No more hope of being something special. Fate hadn't chosen her for something after all. She'd go to the secondary modern and be like everyone else, leave school at fifteen, get a job. At the grammar school they talked about taking more exams, going to college or university. Another world, and it was not to be hers.

She thought about Johnny Vetch's words, 'If you go there, you'll be a different person . . .'

Her breath streamed through the fence towards the Spitfire, lying there in the citrus afternoon light. There it was, a battle hero, grounded and unseen. For a moment she felt like reaching out and stroking its wing for comfort. Instead, she picked up a big stone and hurled it, heard it thump off the rotting wing and fall to the ground.

Part Four

1953

Chapter Forty-Six

1953

'Pass me my shoes over,' Joyce ordered.

She was preening in front of the bedroom mirror in her white taffeta wedding dress, the veil a cloud of net over her shoulders. She was thoroughly enjoying the audience of her mother and sisters, who she assumed were rapt with admiration.

Without enthusiasm, Linda reached for the pair of white shoes with their two-inch stiletto heels.

Watching her, Violet was struck once more by the way that Linda was a mystery to her – quite different from the other two. She was getting tall now, curvy, with a sultry look to her, that black hair curling inwards in waves round her face. She could tell Joyce was getting on Linda's nerves – as usual. They'd heard about nothing but Danny and the wedding for months now and Linda was bored sick with it.

'God, Lin – I'm getting *married*!' Joyce gibbered. 'Can you believe it?'

'Not really,' Linda said.

'You could at least sound pleased for me.'

'I *am* pleased for you!'

'Well, you don't *sound* it.'

'You want to be careful in them.' Violet nodded towards the shoes. If you catch one of them heels in the hem you'll have a nasty tear.'

'Well, I won't, will I?' Joyce said pertly. 'I'm not that stupid, am I?'

'That's a matter of opinion,' Linda retorted.

'Oh, shut *up*.'

'Charming. Does Danny know what you're like?'

Joyce's pointy, narrowed-eyed face squinted back from the mirror, eyes filling with tears. 'You're horrible, you are! It's my wedding day and you can't even stop being a cow! You should be nice to me today!'

'Yes – cut it out, Lin,' Violet said, though half her mind was on the dogs in the garden. One of them was barking loudly and she eyed them through the window. Herself, she rather liked Danny with his stocky barrel of a body and naturally cheerful expression. Joyce had been climbing on to the back of his motorcycle in her skirts and high heels for over a year and now there were wedding bells. Joyce had struck lucky, she thought.

'You going to put your make-up on now?' Carol wanted to know. Violet and Linda had helped her upstairs and she was on the bed, watching intently. She'd been in her wheelchair since she came out of St Gerard's and was going back to hospital in the autumn, for the operation on her back which they hoped would make her able to walk properly again.

'Give me a chance!' Joyce winced as she squeezed her feet into the shoes. If there was a fashionable but viciously uncomfortable style of shoe to be had, you could guarantee Joyce would get hold of it. She looked at her meagre collection of make-up. 'D'you think blue or green'd be better?'

'Blue,' Linda said.

'Green,' Carol said.

Joyce tutted. 'Goodness *sakes*. Mom – tell them to

get out! They're getting me all mithered, fussing around me all the time!'

'Right – you two . . .' Violet was about to usher them out of the room, but Joyce, about to lose her audience, changed her mind.

'Oh, I *s'pose* they can stay,' she granted long-sufferingly. 'Only tell them to stop talking stupid.'

'No – ' Violet was firm. 'Next door, you two – you need to get changed. Quick!'

She still had her old work frock and pinner over the top and needed to get on, but she lingered for a moment, watching Joyce put on her make-up. Violet's tired features broke into a smile. There was Joyce, seventeen and with her job at Bird's, and *getting married*! Joyce really thought she'd arrived. Violet saw herself on her own wedding day, at the same age and with similar hopes. Then she thought of the wrecked, disillusioned man downstairs whom she had to go and get ready.

Heaven help you, Joycie, she thought, the smile fading. But then she and Harry had had the war, their generation sharing all that grief and trouble. It had broken Harry. But it'd be different now – had to be.

'I hope you'll be happy, Joycie,' she said gently.

Joyce turned, eyelids brushed with blue, and for a rare moment she was a soft young woman, and solemn.

'I think we will. Danny's a good 'un, Mom.'

'I know. I can see.' She put her arms round her daughter. Joyce felt to her more solid and substantial than she was herself. 'You worried?'

Joyce shook her head. 'Nah. Mind my veil . . . Is Dad . . .? Is he really going to come?'

Violet wasn't sure if this was asked with hope or dread.

'He says so. Won't hear of staying behind. He wants

to see his little girl get married. Look, I need to go and finish him, or Danny's dad'll be along before I've got him dressed.'

Let alone me, she thought, hurrying to him. Mother of the bride. It's going to be a rush job.

Harry was still in bed. She'd taken him a cup of tea earlier, and he'd drunk half and left the rest to go cold on the bedside cabinet. He lay there with his eyes closed, one arm out from under the covers, so thin in its blue-and-white-striped pyjama sleeve. He looked so settled, so still, that she wondered, as she often did, whether he had slipped away. But then she heard his breathing. It was tempting just to leave him there. She felt exhausted at the thought of getting him up.

Like having my feet buried in concrete, she thought. *That's how it feels, living like this.*

He had spent months in hospital after he broke down completely. He was better in himself now, gentler somehow, as well. But his body was never going to get any better. She knew that. And in accepting that, things had become quiet and gentler within her. Those days, after the war, when she had paced the floor day after day, weeping in anguish, were past. For a moment, in the shadowy room, she could see in his wasted features and grey hair a glimpse of the vital, energetic Harry she'd married, and the tenderness which so often saved her rose in her again. She remembered that Christmas when he and his pals had made those paper snakes to sell, paper and paint everywhere, the drive he had then to get on and get out of Birmingham.

'You silly sod,' she whispered.

Harry opened his eyes. He seemed alert, and she saw that he hadn't been asleep at all.

'What're you gawping at?'

'You, sunshine.'

'Have I got to get up now?'

'It's about time, if you don't want to be late. Sure you want to?'

'If it's the last thing I do. Give us a hand.'

She went to assist him, feeling his skeletal form straining to perform this simple movement. He groaned, already panting from the exertion, and she felt a moment of despair at the effort required to get him to the church.

'Harry . . .'

'No – don't say it. I'm going to that church.' He looked round at her. Even in the gloom she could see the sallowness of the whites of his eyes. 'I'm a useless item, but I'm not missing our Joyce getting wed.'

'All right, love, I know. Let's get you sorted out then.'

These days she surprised herself, often, by the gentleness in her voice, by her own patience. Since those months in hospital, he'd never been able to work. Not much more we can do, the doctors said. His system had taken too much. But she hadn't always been patient. Not all the way through, in those days of fear and strain. Now, though, she could see that he was moving slowly, so agonizingly slowly, towards the end of the line.

So she washed him and painstakingly shaved him, quite used to running the razor over the sharp contours of his face, and helped him dress in his old Sunday suit.

'Look like a bleeding scarecrow, don't I?' he said, but with resignation.

'You're all right,' she said, thinking, surely he doesn't imagine he's going to walk down the aisle with her? He'll never make it.

Once they reached the bottom of the stairs, his

261

breathing was so laboured you'd think he'd run a race. Violet led him to his chair by the window, and he sank into it with a groan. The ashtray on the arm was full of stubs from yesterday, and she went and tipped it in the kitchen bin.

'I'll get your porridge.' He lived mainly on porridge now. That and fags. 'Then I've got to go up and get ready.'

She cut herself a piece of bread, daubed some Stork on it and took it upstairs with a cup of tea. On the stairs she heard the girls giggling together. It was a nice feeling, them getting on for a bit, happiness in the house.

The bedroom smelt stale, with that sickly aroma of Harry. The doctor said, 'His body is slowly eating itself, Mrs Martin.' She didn't know exactly what that meant, but after hearing it, the smell repelled her more than before. She pushed the window open and smelt newly cut grass. Mr Bottoms had been out yesterday with his mower.

'Now then – get going, Vi,' she said. 'Or you'll be in that church in nothing but your girdle!'

Her dress was simple, a pretty blue and white cotton print with a white collar and sleeve edgings, and it hung flowingly over the curves of her slim figure. She'd been taking more pride in herself again now she was out at work. It was Rita, a jolly newcomer from London, who'd taken her on at the salon, just to help out at first. She could not have put into words the gratitude she felt towards Rita.

'You can sweep up and wash the brushes and that – do some washes. We'll see how you get on.'

She settled in fast. Rita, big-hearted and generous, took to her like a sister.

'You're a natural,' she said. 'I bet you could soon pick up a few basic cuts, Vi.'

And the wages, though not handsome, boosted Harry's National Assistance and Joyce's wages from Bird's.

The salon was now called 'Rita's'. Violet loved being there, after the loneliness of home and being forever surrounded by sickness. Here was a pretty, sweet-smelling female world of chat and cosseting. It wasn't just frippery haircuts, she decided. It was a way of looking after people, making them feel better, and she loved washing people's hair. They told her she had gentle hands, especially after Rita, who could be a bit vigorous on the scalp.

Rita was big and exotic-looking, with long dark hair all swept up into piled, curling styles. She'd always give Violet a cut when she needed it. She'd had her hair long and scraped back for ages, with no time or money to think of doing anything else, and it had gone lank and split at the ends. Her skin had been pasty and tired, like old congealed porridge. Rita helped her learn to take pride in herself.

'Well, this mop needs a cut all right,' Rita had said, the first time, running strands of Violet's hair through her fingers. 'Lovely colour though. It's all natural too! Oh, I'd love to be a natural blonde.' She regarded her own swarthy features in the mirror. Her dad was an Italian, she said.

'Very straight though, isn't it? No good trying to look like the Beverley sisters. You need it quite short and smooth. I'll make you look gamine, darlin'.'

'What?' Violet asked, alarmed.

'You know – boyish. Cheeky, sort of thing.'

'Well . . . if you think . . .'

'Oh, I do, love. Very definitely.'

Rita snipped the hair into a neat bob round Violet's chin.

'Ooh, those cheekbones! You're so lucky,' Rita murmured caressingly. 'A face I'd give my right arm for.'

Violet listened in astonishment. No one had told her nice things like that before. Only Harry, but such a long time ago that it felt as if she had been someone else. And Roy . . . But as soon as thoughts of him came to her mind, she slammed the door on them. No good thinking about that, his face the last time she saw him. She couldn't stand the ache it gave her inside, even after all this time.

She combed her sleek hair, stroked a dusting of blue on to her eyelids and added mascara.

'You don't look so bad, for an old 'un,' she told her reflection. 'Better than our mom looked at thirty-eight, any road.'

She had a pretty white cardigan and sandals bought specially.

'Today I'm going to my daughter's wedding,' she told herself archly, then laughed at herself. Today, no matter what other troubles there were, it was going to be good. She thought about Harry. *Please let it be all right*, she thought.

Chapter Forty-Seven

Linda had helped Carol downstairs and they were drinking Vimto in the kitchen, Carol resting in her wheelchair.

'You look *nice*, Mom,' Carol said.

A rare smile spread across Violet's face.

'Am I all right? Petticoat not showing?'

They reassured her.

'Rita's made your hair look lovely,' Linda said.

Violet was touched by this moment of warmth from her daughter. The one she now thought of as difficult, strange to her.

'And aren't you two a picture? Linda – you've done it all a treat!' Linda also had style, she saw suddenly, a knack for making things look right.

The two of them had new frocks as well, both pink. Their hair was brushed out and Linda had pinned little pink and white paper flowers at the side. They both looked so lovely: Linda with her dark looks and also smiling, for once, and Carol, oh, sometimes the way those brown eyes looked at her, those bright, soulful eyes, she almost gasped. His eyes, Roy's eyes. For an instant, just for seconds, she was awash with longing. She forced those thoughts away. She seemed to be so full of emotion today!

'Joyce still titivating?'

'She says she's not coming down because it's bad luck if anyone sees her,' Carol said.

'I'll go and see your dad,' Violet whispered. 'You stay here, eh? Let him be quiet.'

Harry was sitting in the back room, the window open on to the garden to let the smoke out. The saucer he used for an ashtray was on the arm of the chair. Outside, Molly was still barking.

'Shut up, you blasted hound!' they heard from Mr Bottoms over the fence.

'You going to be all right, love?'

'I don't know, do I?' Harry mumbled. 'For Christ's sake stop mithering me, woman.' His sweet pliability on waking had now disappeared.

With agonizing slowness he pulled himself forward in the chair, each movement costing enormous effort. Violet looked away, out of the window. Harry found any change difficult. He needed things to be the same: the daily routine, fags, *Evening Mail* and the *Daily Mirror*, music on the radio, bits of meals that he could manage, then the dogs inside later in the afternoon so he could get a walk round the garden with his stick without them jumping up at him.

'A puff of wind blows him over,' Eva Kaminski observed sometimes. Violet and Eva had become close over the years.

'He's very sick,' Eva often said. 'He looks terrible. He's not going to last for ever.' She was never one to mince her words, but she was a relief to Violet, someone who didn't pretend things were otherwise.

Violet supported Harry by the elbow and helped him haul himself up, a pathetic, gangling figure. Taking his arm, she helped him towards the door.

'All right, love? Need the lavvy again?'

'No – I'm all right. *Christ.*' He patted his pockets to make sure his packet of Capstan was in place.

A horn pipped out in the road.

'He's here, Mom!' Linda ran to the front door. The rest of the family followed, painfully slowly, Carol on her crutches now. She could manage on those for short periods. My family, Violet thought. And just look at the state of us – talk about the walking wounded!

Danny's dad, a hulking great figure, had just drawn up in his white Austin, wide face grinning out through the window.

'All right, Linda!' he called, his beefy arm resting along the edge of the open window. 'Nice day for it, eh?'

Linda nodded, smiling. It was a beautiful May day, a deep blue sky, the estate bathed in sunshine, front windows open all along the road. Bessie had said, 'You ought to have a May wedding – you can have orange-blossom. And you'll get it over with before the Coronation.' So, of course, Joyce obeyed.

'Blushing bride ready, is she?'

'Think so.'

'Don't let anyone see me!' Joyce shouted, all in a tizzy at the top of the stairs. 'It's bad luck!'

'Well, stay there and they won't, will they?' Linda called up to her.

'Tell her it's not too late – I can run her to the docks instead if she wants to get away!' Mr Rodgers joked, his barrel figure coming up the path.

Harry made a wheezing sound, his attempt at a laugh. Violet had her arm through his, which felt thin and hard as a broom handle. Between them she and Mr Rodgers helped Harry shuffle out to the car. He was all wrapped up as if it was December, scarf and all. The walk made him pant.

'All right, mate?' Mr Rodgers opened the passenger

267

door for him and helped him sink slowly on to the seat. Other men were always gentle with him, Violet saw.

'Oh – Vi –' Harry gasped before the door closed. 'Get us my cushion. Them church pews're hard as hell.'

'You girls'll be all right, won't you?' Violet said anxiously, hurrying in to get the old blue cushion from Harry's chair. Linda was outside with Carol, who was perched on the doorstep. 'Mr Rodgers'll be back for you girls, soon as he can. Don't come without Carol's crutches and for God's sake be patient with *her*.' She rolled her eyes up in the direction of the bedroom, where Joyce was shouting something about her lipstick. No one took any notice.

'It's all right, Mom,' Linda said, and Violet saw suddenly how grown-up she was. After all that sulking about school, just for today it was as if the sun had come out and she was a different girl. 'You go – we'll be all right.'

For a moment Violet felt like a child, sitting in the car, with its special smell, being waved off by the two girls, all in their pink.

'Beautiful,' she heard Harry mutter, as if he was seeing everything differently today. Even Carol. The cuckoo child, whom he was prepared to call beautiful as if she were his own. Violet's eyes filled with tears. It was one of those days when the gruelling, lonely struggle of it all was lifted into something bigger, some pattern which made sense of her life. You're a good man, Harry, she thought. I married a good man.

The church was only a mile away. Mr Rodgers chatted to Harry. Violet could see his good-natured face in the little mirror. They passed people doing their Saturday things and it seemed astonishing to Violet that to them it was such an ordinary day. Then she wondered if they all smelt of dogs and surreptitiously sniffed her sleeve. She couldn't tell. Linda said people at school complained that she stank of dogs.

When they reached the church, Harry murmured, 'There's the old battleship. What's up with her?'

'Harry!' But Violet smiled.

Bessie was standing outside, smoking, grim-faced. She and the others had come from Aston on the bus. She had on a capacious frock, mauve with white swirls on it, and a straw hat. Her expression was grim. Beside her, Marigold had on a similar dress in pale yellow, covered in pale blue polka dots, and a dark brown hat that didn't match. Violet looked at her sadly. Poor old Marigold. She wouldn't have thought of asking for anything better. For a moment she thought of Rosina. She would always have asked! You wouldn't have caught Rosina going to a wedding in a hat that didn't match her frock! She ached for Rosy for a moment, or at least the eighteen-year-old Rosina she remembered, and sighed. You felt it on days like this.

Clarence, a stooped figure beside them, had on his old Sunday suit, which he could only just do up round him, and which for some reason now seemed to be too short in the legs. The remaining wisps of his hair were combed over like strands of seaweed on a rock. Of the three of them he looked by far the most cheerful.

'We've been here close on an hour already,' Bessie complained, as soon as Violet set foot out of the car.

'Well, you knew it started at twelve,' Violet said mildly. Her mom was always at her most aggressive when out of her usual home and street. 'Why don't you go in and sit down?'

Bessie eyed the church door warily. Marigold stood, impassive as ever, though Violet could sense an excitement in her. Anything different was a treat for Marigold.

'Let's go in, Bess,' Clarence said in his quavering voice. 'My knees're killing me.'

'*You* go in then,' Bessie snapped, stubbing her cigarette out on the wall. 'And take *her* off my hands, will you?' She nodded dismissively at Marigold. '*I'm* going to see the bride arrive.'

Bessie had always liked Joyce, who did all the right things in her eyes.

Violet and Mr Rodgers helped Harry into his pew at the front of the church, settling him on his cushion.

'No sign of Tom yet?' Harry asked.

His brother, Uncle Tom, was to stand in his place, giving Joyce away.

'He'll be along. I ought to go and watch for him, see a few people,' Violet said, patting the back of her hair, agitated.

'I'll be all right.' Proud, he sat up as straight as he could. 'Leave me be, woman.'

Some of their friends and neighbours had walked over. Joe and Eva Kaminski were just coming in. Eva, dressed in bright emerald green, kissed Violet.

'This is a good day. A good day,' she pronounced, in her spiky way.

Behind them was Edna Bottoms, in a sober little navy blue outfit. She smelled sweetly of talcum powder.

'I wanted to come.' She was all flustered. 'Reg wanted to as well, only . . .'

'It's all right,' Violet said, knowing Edna was covering up for him. Imagine Reg Bottoms coming to Joyce's wedding! 'It's nice of you, love.'

She was distracted by seeing Uncle Tom arrive at last, striding up the road. The sight of him always gave her a pang. He was so like Harry! All Harry could have been in looks and physical strength.

Soon after, Mr Rodgers drew up with the three girls, Carol in the front and Linda with Joyce at the back. The few left outside all stood back to admire as Joyce climbed out of the car, full of herself, fussing over her dress and making Linda rearrange her veil. She beamed regally at everyone. Violet was aware of the special, pitying smile people gave 'little Carol' as she struggled up the steps with her crutches.

At last they were all settled inside and Joyce paraded along the aisle, Linda and Carol behind. Joyce, holding her bouquet of blossoms, tried to look solemn but couldn't contain her grin of delight.

Danny turned to greet her, looking constrained and uncomfortable in a suit, the collar too tight and cutting into his plump neck. He was very like his dad and just as jolly. Violet watched Carol anxiously, but she was managing perfectly well.

As Joyce and Danny stood in front of the vicar, waiting to make their vows, Violet couldn't contain her emotion and the tears ran down her cheeks.

'You're so young,' she'd said to Joyce. 'Just leave it for a bit. What's the rush? You're hardly old enough to know your own minds.'

'*You* got married when you were seventeen!' Joyce argued fiercely. 'And anyhow, Danny's nineteen. We're old enough to decide and you're not going to stop us. If you won't let us, we'll run away and get married somewhere else!' There was no budging her.

All Harry said was, 'She's right, Vi. She's no younger than you were.'

As she watched them standing there she was back at her own wedding day, Harry beside her as he was now, but then upright and strong, full of urgent male energy. She skipped past this painful thought. What about her own family on that day? Bessie had been approving all right. Had she married to please Bessie, or to escape her? Marigold had been there, just the same, like a sealed jar, its contents ageing in airless secrecy. And Rosina, her lovely bridesmaid. How she longed for her.

'I never knew why she took off like that,' she said sometimes. But she knew really. She was the one who got out from under Bessie.

Back in the winter they had heard from her for the first time in years. There was no special reason they could make out that prompted her to write. This time she gave an address though, in London.

Dear Mom and all of you,

    I feel I want to write to you, Christmas coming up and everything. There's too much to tell you though, to catch up over the years. We'll do it one day. I hope you're all doing well. These are my children, Clark and Vivianne. Clark's nine now and Vivianne seven. They're doing well and I wanted to show you them. Clark's really one of us, isn't he?

    Love to you all – Charlie, Vi, Marigold – I've missed you.

    Rosina.

Clark was very like her: the definite brows and the delicate, handsome features. The girl's colouring was lighter and she was round-faced and sweet-looking, with long, curling hair. With her, Violet didn't immediately feel the same sense of recognition, of affinity that she did with the boy. My nephew, she thought.

Once again the picture was propped on the mantel in Bessie's house.

'So she's remembered we exist,' Bessie said. Her tone was very hard. 'Does she think we're all going to go rushing down there now she's spawned a couple of brats?' She heaped scorn on anything to do with Rosina.

But I might, one day, Violet thought. I might see her. Rosina was her one proper sister. There was Marigold of course, but you couldn't really talk to her, her and her love songs and her closed-off life. Violet was never close to Charlie. He was always just there – Gladys, his kids, beer. You didn't get much out of him either. We're a family of women, she thought. The men are like shadows.

Light streamed in through the high windows. Violet looked at Joyce's slim back in her shiny dress. And Danny. *He* was no shadow though. He had a lot of life in him, and the two of them really did seem to love each other. When they kissed after the vows, she heard a big sigh from behind, everyone going 'Aaah', especially Bessie. Joyce turned round, blushing and looking very pleased with herself.

She's done it, Violet thought, wiping her eyes. Our Joycie – married. I might be a grandmother soon!

Joyce clung on to Danny's arm, laughing, and Violet could feel the pleasure of the moment in the people round her.

'She looks very lovely,' she heard Eva Kaminski say behind her.

Then she saw Joyce's face change, a sober enquiring expression come across it as she looked down the church, seeing something behind them all. She squinted, trying to see clearly, to make something out, and then as if uncertain, puzzled, her eyes met Violet's.

Violet turned and saw as well. Seated near the back of the church, a slim, smart figure in a large, peach-coloured hat with a sloping brim, from under which looked dark, defiant eyes. As if Violet's thoughts had winged her there.

Rosina.

Chapter Forty-Eight

Linda didn't notice Rosina until they got right outside.

Everyone was milling about, lighting cigarettes, talking and laughing like children let out of school, amid the whirl of confetti scattered by Joyce's workmates.

'Who's that?' Carol nudged her.

The woman in the peach hat and dress had collared Violet and pulled her away from the rest of the group.

Linda shrugged. But there was something about the stranger that drew her attention. She seemed familiar, yet Linda knew she didn't know her. The woman was holding Violet's upper arm as if to stop her moving away, and talking urgently. Linda saw her mother nodding in a bewildered way and then as the peach-dress woman started to pull back, Violet made a sharp movement to stop her. All this only took a few seconds and it was only then that anyone else began to notice.

'Who's that?' she heard Bessie say behind her. 'Someone come to see Violet. Looks posh. Fancy barging in in the middle of all . . .'

'That's Rosina,' Marigold's flat voice pronounced.

'Ros . . . No! Don't be so bloody silly, Marigold.'

' 'Tis. It's Rosy.'

'It's never . . . Is it?'

But the woman leaned forward, swiftly kissed Violet on the cheek and hurried away along the road on her high, white heels. She seemed almost about to break into a run. Violet stood staring after her, a hand up to her cheek.

'Vi?' Bessie shoved through the other guests to where Violet was standing by the road. Linda followed. 'Who was that? Was that Rosina?'

Violet turned. Her eyes were full of tears. 'She wanted to come. But she wouldn't stay. I wish she'd stay . . .'

'Well, what's she playing at?' Bessie erupted, red-faced. She threw down her cigarette and ground at it with her heel. 'Go after her and make her come back! Swanning in and out like that after seventeen years! Not a word to her mother. What the hell did she have to say for herself?'

'Not much . . .' Violet was weeping now, in shock and disappointment. 'I want her to be here – to see her . . .'

'Little bitch! I'd like to get her here and put her over my knee. You should've got her and made her stay. There's a few things I'd say to her, I can tell you. She always was a selfish little cow!' Bessie's raging started to filter through to everyone else and they went quiet. Joyce came hurrying over.

'Nan!' she hissed, mortified. 'Stop shouting – everyone's staring. What's going on?'

'I'll tell you what's going on. That . . . that trollop mincing off down the road there were your auntie Rosina, looking down her nose at us and then taking off as if she was royalty and too good for us. Wants a good hiding, that she does.'

God, Nana, *shut up*, Linda thought, mortified. Making all this carry-on at Joyce's wedding!

'Nan, please,' Joyce begged. 'Leave it. Everyone's staring at you.'

Bessie wheeled round to face everyone on the steps.

'Go on then – have a good look. That's it – walk away. See you down the pub, you bloody miserable lot!'

'Stop it!' Joyce wailed. 'You're spoiling my wedding. Just stop it!'

'Mom,' Violet begged, wiping her eyes. 'Don't keep on. It's no good. Rosy's gone. Don't let her spoil Joyce's wedding. Not after all this time.'

Bessie quietened and sank down on to the low wall. For a moment she looked frail. 'She's upset me, that's all, turning up like that, ungrateful little bitch.'

Everyone else, unperturbed by Bessie's outburst, was moving along the road towards the pub.

'I must go and get Harry!' Violet said, gathering her wits.

'Mom – ' Linda hurried after her, sorry for her. She felt different about everything, just today. Able to forget her own feelings. Mom never said how much she missed Rosina, but Linda could tell. 'Mr Rodgers's taken Dad home, remember? And your mascara's smudged.'

'Oh – ' Violet stopped on the steps and fished out her hanky. 'Is Carol all right? I feel all shaken up.'

'What did she say? Auntie Rosina? How did she know about the wedding?'

'I wrote to her. Just dropped her a line. It was when I wrote to Muriel telling her about Joyce, as if *she* was my sister. I just thought Rosy should know. And she'd sent her address this time. I thought she might want to know us again. And she came up all this way . . .' Violet shook her head, sadly.

They reached Carol, who was waiting by the church door. Violet laid her arm round Carol's shoulders and in that absent-minded gesture Linda saw another of those unguarded moments of devotion, of something only Carol brought out in her.

'She just said, "I wanted to come but I can't...!"'
Violet said. 'Something about not being able to face it.
It was all so quick and then she went off. It's made me
feel peculiar seeing her.'

'Mom –' Joyce came flaming up to them, all upset.
'Nana's spoilt it – she's spoilt everything!'

But Danny was close behind.

'Don't talk daft.' He put his arm round her waist and
gestured at everyone strolling off along the road. 'They
don't look bothered, do they? Come on, wench – Mrs
Rodgers! Our dad's waiting in the car.'

He squeezed her close and kissed her ear, and Joyce
softened and giggled.

'Danny! Gerroff!'

The two of them went off down the steps arm in arm
and Violet managed a smile.

'Look at them – least they're all right, anyway.'

That night, Linda couldn't sleep. She lay in bed, just
able to hear Carol's breathing in the other bed. No
Joyce next door now, of course. She and Danny were
off for a few days by the sea before moving into the
tiny flat above Mr Rodgers' garage, where Danny
worked.

There were no sounds from next door. When they
got home, after the celebrations in the pub, Dad had
been asleep in his chair, flaked out and grey in the face.
Linda noticed her mom's face alter as she saw him, that
thought that went through her head from time to time,
wondering if he was still with them, if the wedding had
been the end of him. But he woke and managed a bowl
of chicken soup.

Linda could feel Sooty, a warm, reassuring bundle

curled up by her feet. She needed comfort. Soon after they got home her monthly period had started – thank goodness not in the middle of the wedding! She lay with the thick Dr White's pad between her legs and gripes low in her belly. She felt fragile and emotional. Not that it hadn't been a good day. They'd celebrated with Joyce and Danny, and things in the family had been more or less all right. Linda felt for once that she hadn't been out on a limb, angry and misunderstood the way she normally felt these days. She knew how difficult things were for Mom, what with Dad and Carol, and she'd wanted to do her best to help. And for all that she and Joyce had never been close, she could see that she and Danny made each other happy.

But then Auntie Rosina turning up had upset Mom. Pleased her in a way too, but brought out a lot of emotion. And the wedding ceremony itself came back to her now, all the feelings that had swept over her as Joyce and Danny made their vows, then swept in triumph out of the church.

There'd been that moment as they turned, just married, Joyce's cheeks flushed pink. She looked pretty, Linda could see. The prettiest she had ever looked. But all she could feel herself was a stony sensation in her chest.

She's done it, Linda thought, she's done the right thing – the thing every woman is supposed to do. As everyone went 'Aaah', all she could see was a vision of how Joyce's life would be, mapped out in children and meals and Monday washes and hanging Danny's socks out until she was old like Nana, sighing with memories at the weddings of her grandchildren. And this ought to have seemed a happy thing, yet it made her sink inside with dread at the inevitable vision in front of her.

I don't want that, she was thinking. *I don't, I don't* ... Yet what else was there? Being old and a spinster like Marigold, or funny Miss Turpitt who lived a few houses down and talked to the starlings and pigeons in the garden as if they were her family?

And what else was there to want, anyhow? Her years at the secondary modern had brought no satisfaction. The lessons were too easy and she couldn't be bothered any more. She felt like a misfit, and became lethargic, sullen. What was the point of anything? If you stepped out of where you belonged you ended up like Johnny Vetch, in and out of the mental hospital.

The organ had started up and Carol was tugging on her arm, smiling up at her. 'Wakey, wakey,' she whispered. 'Daydreaming again!'

As they turned to walk back down the aisle to the last hymn, her father looked ashen and exhausted from the effort of it all and he didn't stand up. He was watching the couple with a haunted expression, and she saw tears running down her mom's cheeks and a soft smile on Bessie's plump face.

Outside, Linda found herself next to her grandmother and Marigold. Bessie's breathing was laboured just from walking out of the church, her lungs giving off a sound like rustling paper. Linda watched as her eyes followed Joyce and Danny, both laughing as their friends threw confetti.

'I'm s'posed to throw my flowers, aren't I?' Joyce cried. 'Come on, you lot – who's going to catch 'em?'

Bessie gave a low laugh. Soppy face, Linda thought, watching her. She was filled with a swelling sense of loathing, of panic. Look at her stupid, soppy face!

Bessie turned to her, watery-eyed.

'Well, I s'pose you're next on the list?'

And for a moment she wanted to run and run and never come back.

But lying here now, there was a weariness, a surrender, as if all her dreams were ashes and might just as well be. What did it matter? She had thought she might have a different sort of life, but she was cut out to be just like anyone else after all. This was her last term at school, and then she'd go to work in some firm or shop, meet some factory Jack, marry and settle down and that was that.

All right, she thought, her foot pressed against Sooty's warm shape. If that's what they want, they can have it.

to. The new queen had just been crowned and Coronation fever had set in all over town, infecting every street with the urge to have parties to celebrate. The occupants of Bloomsbury Road shared out the jobs – who was to set up tables, or make jelly, or ham sandwiches or cake. At least eggs were off the ration now. Violet was talking about getting chickens but hadn't done it. Sugar was still rationed though.

Grass was mowed and the gardens trimmed and watered. The Martins' garden at number 18 was still the one to disgrace the street. Even though grass was sprouting in the old bald spot where Harry's bike had stood for so long, the specimens in the front garden were not the pretty flowers of the neighbouring ones (Joe Kaminski was growing flowers between the vegetables now), but groundsel, dandelions and quitch grass.

'It looks a right mess,' Violet said, staring helplessly at it. 'I ought to clear it up . . .' But they knew she wouldn't. She was too bowed down by everything else, and didn't even know where to begin.

A week before the great event, Eva Kaminski reported that a Rumbelows van had drawn up outside and two men carried a television into the Bottoms' house. Reg Bottoms had kept mighty quiet about it though. There was another family at the far end of the road who had a television, with the tell-tale H-shaped aerial on the roof, and it was a magnet for all the kids, who they generously invited in for *The Flowerpot Men* and *Rag, Tag and Bobtail* on *Watch with Mother*, but Mr Bottoms didn't want the neighbourhood traipsing into *his* house. The little drama of the television unfolded as the week went past. Linda was home in the afternoons when her mom came in from work and Eva came trotting round to report from the front line.

'He is a selfish kind of man,' Eva pronounced with her usual energy, perched on the kitchen stool while Violet made tea and they both filled the kitchen with smoke. As usual Eva was neatly dressed, an emerald green skirt with box pleats and yellow blouse. Eva made all her own clothes and always dressed to dazzle. 'There's enough gloom in the world, without putting it in the clothes as well,' she'd say. She was tiny and tough and gristly, and wore mascara and lipstick, and had a deep, smoker's voice. 'Fancy not sharing with everyone around? It is not hurting him to share, is it? I mean I know my Joe is not a very friendly man, but he would do anything for someone who really needs it. Yes – I think Mr B. is very selfish.' She dragged emphatically on her cigarette.

In fact, on the eve of the big day, Edna Bottoms went round to the Kaminskis and asked if they'd like to come in and watch the Coronation procession on the television.

'But what about Violet?' Eva demanded. 'And her poor husband?'

As Eva reported it, Edna had gone as pink as a rosebud and said that she was very sorry, she'd like to invite everyone in, but Reg wasn't prepared to consider the Martins. They weren't his type, she said.

'So,' Eva told Violet, 'I said to her, "In that case, I say no thank you. Joe and I can listen to it on the wireless with our friends like everyone else in the street."'

Violet laughed in surprise. 'You never!' She sugared Eva's tea and handed it to her.

'Ta, baby.' Eva had never quite got the hang of the way people called each other 'bab' so she called them 'baby' instead. She took a sip of tea. 'Anyway – who

285

cares about this stupid television? We will have a nice time.'

On the morning of the Coronation when the street was full of activity – bunting flapping in the drizzle and tables arranged up and down the road and people running in and out of houses – Edna Bottoms appeared on the doorstep at number 18, hair tightly curled and her apron over a shirtwaister dress the colour of broad beans. She seemed flustered and started gabbling the moment the door opened.

'Violet – I don't know if you've heard about the television.' She was blushing again. 'I mean, Reg really can be the end. I wish we'd never bought the blasted thing, I really do, he's been so difficult about it. We've had words about it, I can tell you. See, I wanted to invite everyone in – you know, make a bit of an occasion of it, and Reg . . . Well, anyway,' she added defiantly, '*I'm* going to ask you to come and watch – that's if you want to . . . In fact I'm going to ask anyone who wants to.'

'Poor old Edna,' Violet said when she'd flapped off home again. 'She's a good sort really – it's just him. D'you want to go in, Harry?'

'No, I bloody well don't,' Harry said. Speaking made him pant. 'Sitting there looking down his nose. I'm staying here. You can go if you want.'

After a conflab with the Kaminskis they decided that the women and children would go. Linda sat at her mother's feet on the spotless green carpet in the Bottoms' house looking round her in amazement. She had never seen a room like it: the walls decorated with immaculate flowery paper, shelves of little ornaments, the chairs new and neat and not a smudge on the walls or speck of dirt anywhere. She could feel that her mom, on the sofa behind her with Carol, kept twitching her feet in discomfort. She was not going to be able to relax. In the event, Edna had invited in quite a few people; the kids squashed in on the floor and she handed them little glasses of orange pop and arrowroot biscuits. After a while Carol slithered down on to the floor as well to be with all of them. Mr Bottoms sat regally in his chair, acting as if none of them were there.

The drama opened on the fairytale world of royalty, the young Princess Elizabeth leaving Buckingham Palace in her gold coach.

Sylvia Peters appeared in her beautiful gown to report on the day.

'Oh, she does speak nicely,' Edna Bottoms said wistfully, 'Wouldn't it be marvellous to be like that?'

'Shame it's not a nicer day, isn't it?' Violet said. The overnight campers lining the edges of the Mall had woken to rain.

'She's so pretty.' Carol sighed.

Linda watched, entranced. Going to the Odeon was one thing. It was like stepping into another life, a palace of dreams in front of that giant screen, from where you emerged back into real life with a bump. But this was different – to have the screen right here in your living-room – and Edna and Reg Bottoms' living-room was already a palace of dreams compared to their house! She thought of her dad, fragile as a bird, dozing in his chair next door, dogs at his feet. And then she gave herself over to the journey of the young princess, meeting her destiny in Westminster Abbey.

Now it was all over everything felt flat, with nothing to look forward to except leaving school in two months. And then what? Joyce had got herself a job at Bird's a few months before the wedding, at Nana's urging. Bessie had worked at HP's, the sauce factory, for a couple of years – that was where she'd met Jack.

'Sets you up for life, good firm like that,' she'd told Joyce, the week she had come back triumphantly, having been taken on.

They'd had the conversation over Sunday dinner again, when Linda had reluctantly agreed to go to Nana's. Mrs Magee had died two years back so at least there was one less person who didn't want to be there.

'It's a long way to go,' Violet said. 'All the way over there – two buses.'

'That don't matter,' Bessie said. 'An early start never hurt anyone. People come from all over to work there – always have done. And what's up with you?' She finished aggressively, seeing Linda's gaze fixed burningly on her.

There was a time when she would have kept quiet, but it all hurt too much now.

'The bus fare to Handsworth for me to go to school was throwing money away – so how come it's all right her going all the way to Digbeth?'

'Don't talk daft,' Bessie scoffed, taking another large mouthful of cabbage and talking through it. 'Our Joyce'll be earning good money, not like you and your fancy books! You should never've had anything to do with that waster Johnny Vetch, that was your trouble. Load of airy-fairy nonsense – he's never been right, that one.'

Joyce was soon full of her job at Bird's. The firm was expanding. The new entrance to the Devonshire Works was opened by Roy Rogers and Trigger his horse, and Joyce got to pat Trigger's neck. She started off packing custard powder.

'It's not austerity any more,' she lectured them over tea, as if she owned the factory. 'It's the proper stuff.'

'Bully for it,' Linda said.

Joyce slammed down her knife.

'Listen to her – you never give up, do you? You still think you're above us, don't you, Miss Lah-di-Dah! I'd like to see you get a decent job when you leave school, like I have. That'll soon sort you out!'

Chapter Fifty

Linda walked into the house that afternoon, shoved the front door shut with a bang and flung down her bag. Almost immediately she heard a voice she wasn't expecting – Bessie's. It didn't improve her mood. What was Nana doing out here? She hardly ever came out to the estate.

'Hello, love,' Violet said.

They were at the kitchen table with Carol. Bessie and Violet were both smoking and there was a saucer of ash in the middle of the table next to the milk bottle. Linda felt all of it grate on her. Rage rose in her for a moment. She remembered the little china jug Lucy's mom used to pour milk into at teatime in their house. Why couldn't Mom try a bit harder? Why was the place always such a dump? Why did she have to be born into this bloody family at all? She felt them all staring at her and was about to make a bad-tempered retort when she saw an odd expression in her mother's eyes, something both wary and sorrowful.

'Cat got your tongue then?' Bessie said.

'Hello,' Linda said woodenly. She had no warmth left for her grandmother.

Carol was looking at her funny as well, she realized. They all seemed to be waiting for something.

'D'you want a cup of tea, or some squash?' Violet said, getting up. She wasn't long home herself, having picked Carol up from school on the way from Rita's salon. She looked neat and fresh in her pink dress, hair gleaming and well cut as usual. She was the cleanest thing in the place.

'Squash,' Linda said.

'Forgotten how to say please and thank you, have you?' Bessie challenged her, aggressively.

Linda ignored her.

'Here y'are – sit down love,' Violet said appeasingly. 'There's Bourbons as well ... Pass 'em over, Carol.'

Linda sat down and nibbled at the end of a biscuit. Now, suddenly, no one was looking at her. They were all staring at the blue Formica or at their cups. Something was up, it was obvious. Linda couldn't stand it any longer.

'Why're you here, Nan?'

'Well, that's nice.' Bessie sat back in her chair blowing smoke above her head. 'Can't I pay a visit if I want?'

Linda shrugged. *I only asked, you old cow*, she thought.

'Nana's brought some news,' Violet said cautiously. 'I mean, not just – you were coming anyway, weren't you? Only ...'

Linda felt her heart beat harder. What on earth had happened? Something about the atmosphere in the room was making her very uneasy.

'Something up with Uncle Clarence?' she asked. 'Or Marigold?'

She saw Carol's eyes fill with tears.

'No, t'aint that,' Bessie said.

'Let me tell her,' Violet said gently.

Linda saw her mom at her best in those moments. Whatever else she was, she was kind. It was in her eyes,

291

the way she leaned towards her as if wanting to shield her. She laid her hand on Linda's.

'Pet, it's your old friend – Johnny Vetch. He's . . . well, he's passed away.'

Linda stared at her. Johnny? Last time she'd been to Johnny he had been full of energy and excitement. Yes, too much excitement. He'd scared her a bit, the way he hadn't been able to keep still, and talked like a galloping horse.

'What was up with him?' Her throat had gone dry.

She saw Violet glance at Bessie, a dreadful knowing look.

'It's no good – I'll just have to say it. Lin – Johnny took his own life. Day before yesterday.'

Linda was about to ask how, where, but then knew she didn't want to be told. Not yet.

'Maybe it's for the best in the end,' Bessie was saying. 'He always was a queer bleeder. Square peg. I know that mother of his worried what he'd do when she'd gone. Fancy having a son like that. All that *blood*. Think how she must've felt!'

'Sssh, Mom,' Violet protested. 'Not in front of . . .' She gestured at the girls.

Linda heard Carol crying beside her and all she could think to do was to turn to her sister and take her in her arms, burying her face in her soft hair.

On Saturday she went to see Johnny's mother. She was frightened, and when she got off the bus she felt like running away again, but Mrs Vetch had always been kind to her, like Johnny was. She'd seemed grateful someone wanted to see her son. Linda walked along to the little row of terraces where the Vetches' house slotted in like one card among many in a pack, unremarkable today except for the sadness it contained. Johnny had an older sister who had long been married. He had been the only son of his widowed mother.

'Oh – hello, bab,' Mrs Vetch said, seeing her on the doorstep. She didn't look upset so much as stunned. She was a respectable, sweet-faced lady in her fifties, with a high, melodious voice. She invited Linda in and automatically made tea. They sat in her little front parlour.

'The funeral's tomorrow,' she said, as if she was talking about something far away and nothing to do with her.

She told Linda that she had come downstairs, two mornings after the Coronation, and found Johnny dead in the back room. After she'd gone to bed he had slit his wrists and thrust his hands into a washpail of hot water. She crumpled as she said it, starting to shake.

'He wasn't right. I knew it. But then he wasn't so often, was he? You remember, don't you, dear, what he was like last time you came? On and on, too wound up. I should have known. His mood used to break, like a storm. He tried something like it before – only it was such a long time ago. It was after he left the college, you know ... I think it was those mountaineers ...'

'Everest?' Linda asked. On the eve of the Coronation they'd announced that Sir Edmund Hillary and Sherpa Tensing had reached the top of Mount Everest, the world's highest peak. They'd actually achieved it on May 29th but the news was saved as an extra jewel for the British crown to add to the Coronation.

'Yes. On and on, you know what he could be like. Couldn't leave it alone. I mean it wasn't easy to be with him when he was like that. I couldn't stand it sometimes – on and on...' She trailed off sadly, eyes full of tears. 'So I went to bed early...'

As Linda walked back along the road that afternoon her body felt leaden with sorrow for Johnny. She'd loved Johnny, she knew now. The way Carol loved Sister Cathleen at St Gerard's. She loved him for the vision he had given her of a bigger world that he wanted to explore, with its deserts and jungles and his longing to take a boat up the Amazon river. She could imagine him talking about the mountains, with their white, mysterious peaks wrapped in clouds like homes of the gods. She could hear his voice, see the burning expression in his eyes as he talked about the mountaineers.

Johnny never got his trip to the Amazon basin. Maybe that was the day he knew he never would.

Chapter Fifty-One

After the Coronation, life for Linda went back to the dead-aliveness of school.

She tried not to think about what had happened to Johnny Vetch, and barely knew how the weight of it crouched inside her. All she knew was that she just couldn't be bothered. Nothing reached her, not the teachers encouraging her, saying she was a bright girl and she could do much better, nor them turning on her and telling her she was lazy. They'd given up doing either now. She'd be gone from there in two months anyway.

She let her appearance go. Her hair hung in greasy hanks round her cheeks, her shoes were always scuffed and dirty and she wore a sulky, closed expression. Everyone just left her alone, except Maureen, who placidly accepted whatever she did.

Some days she didn't go to school at all. One day, a warm, beautiful June morning, she got on a bus right to the edge of Birmingham and got off and walked into the fields and farms and spent the day wandering aimlessly. She didn't think she felt anything except the glory of having escaped from the humdrum ordinariness of the day. No one ever asked her how she felt, so she didn't find words for it. But it was her secret, running away like this, and it made her feel strong. Once in a while she did it again, not often enough to attract too much attention. She just didn't feel well sometimes, she said. Often she thought about Rosina. She'd run away too. So many times after Joyce's wedding she'd asked her mother when they were going to see Rosina. Violet would shrug and say, 'Sometime I'll get round to it,' but she never did.

That day she lay at the edge of a field of young corn, watching white clouds sliding across the deep blue. It made her feel as if she was floating, and she thought about death and heaven.

Are you there, Johnny? Her lips moved. *Can you see me?*

She saw his gentle, tormented face in front of her eyes and wondered whether he was free now. Could he circle the world and see all his deserts and jungles, see the sea creatures and stars that he'd taught her about, without all the pain he carried with him in this life?

'I wish you'd taken me with you,' she said.

She lay on her side, curled up, and cried in a way she hadn't been able to before, from deep down. After that she didn't hurt quite so much for a while, as if she had dissolved a hard stone inside.

Chapter Fifty-Two

One day she came home after school, bag slung carelessly over her shoulder, this time with Maureen Lister
tagging along beside her. Coming along Bloomsbury
Road they saw the bulky shape of someone sitting on
the doorstep of number 18.

'Who's that?' Maureen nodded at the house.

It only took a glance. It was quite unmistakably
Marigold, her swarthy features shaded by her blue hat.
She was wearing a pale pink dress dotted with little
pink roses, lace round the sleeves and bodice, like a
pretty little girl's frock made up in a very large size.
With a slight frown on her face she watched them draw
closer.

'Hello, Auntie,' Linda said. 'You can go in if you
want. Our dad's in.'

'No,' Marigold said aggressively. She didn't budge.

Close up, they could see Marigold's dress was very
grubby down the front.

'Is she all right?' Maureen whispered. She'd never
met Marigold before, but Linda wasn't worried about
her seeing. Maureen had a kind heart. She'd helped get
Carol into town at Christmas, on her crutches, so she
could see the petting zoo at Lewis's and Father
Christmas.

'Yes. Course.' To Marigold, she said gently, 'Shall we
go inside?'

Marigold lumbered to her feet. Linda saw that her eyes looked glassy as they sometimes did, and she was not very steady on her feet. All of them knew Marigold tippled, but this time she seemed quite far gone.

'Did you come on the bus?' Linda asked. There was no other way to get out to the estate but she didn't know what else to say.

'Course I bloody did,' Marigold said.

Linda took her inside and they all stood in the hall. Sally and Sooty came and rubbed themselves round Linda's legs.

'I'm gunna see the dogs,' Marigold said, indistinctly.

'Oh – all right,' Linda said, praying Mom would walk in with Carol. She showed Marigold to the back door, expecting Molly, Dolly and George to set up a great rumpus. But watching through the smeary window she saw Marigold sink down on her knees on the scrappy lawn, and the dogs, after their initial yaps of excitement, all fawned round her. After a second she realized Marigold was feeding them something out of a brown paper bag.

'She all right?' Maureen asked, peering out at Marigold.

'Yeah.' Linda turned away.

She looked in on her father. He was in his chair with his newspaper, the room blue with smoke as usual.

'Marigold's here,' she said.

Harry rolled his eyes. 'Is she? Blimey – what's brought that on? Where is she?'

'Out the back, with the dogs.'

Harry tried to move, and groaned. Linda looked out of the window.

Even though she was so used to the sight of her father, sometimes she couldn't bear to look. People asked after him sometimes. She would meet men from the dairy who'd say, 'Haven't seen old Harry in a while – I must pop in. How is he?' And she always said, 'He's all right.' She knew they didn't really want to hear the truth, how he could barely eat and that his insides were never right and that he'd break down and cry right there in the living-room. They didn't want to face this ghostly wraith of a man, or the sweet, cloying smell that hung round him. No one came near now except Uncle Tom and Joe Kaminski. Joe would come in and sit at his side, just be there. And Eva came and chatted to Mom.

'They're such good people,' Violet said in wonder sometimes. 'I don't know how we'd do without them.'

It was Joe who had finally got rid of Dad's bike, which had sat out there all this time like a promise of renewed youth. But there was to be no renewal. The tarpaulin was rotted and covered in moss, and the cycle still smashed up from the accident. Early one morning Joe took the bike away and there was nothing to see but the patch of dead grass where it had stood so long, like a wound in the corner of the garden. Later, Joe quietly handed Violet the few bob he had got for it for scrap.

'Linda?' The front door opened and Violet was calling. 'Come and give us a hand.'

She and Mom helped Carol in and Linda brought the wheelchair up the step. Maureen stood in the hall staring.

'Mom – Marigold's here.'

Her mother stopped in her tracks, on the way to the kitchen.

'*Marigold?* But she never comes out here! What the hell's she doing here?'

Linda shrugged. She heard her mom go to the kitchen and call out of the window.

'Mari? All right are you, bab? Why don't you come in and have a nice cup of tea?'

Linda helped Carol into the kitchen and Maureen followed. Marigold came in from the garden, closing the door with a great slam.

'Go easy, you'll have the glass out.' Violet eyed her sister. 'You all right, Mari?'

'Why shouldn't I be?' Marigold's tone was still aggressive.

'Sit down then – I've got the kettle on,' Violet said cautiously, reaching for the packet of Tetley. 'Linda'll find you a Rich Tea . . . That's it, sit there, love. Why've you come all the way out here then?'

''Cause I wanted to,' Marigold stated. She took off her hat, which had already been knocked to the side by the dogs. Her hair shone with grease. Linda tried not to make faces at the way Marigold smelt. She was breathing heavily through her nose. Carol and Maureen were both staring at her, fascinated.

'Everything all right with our mom?' Violet tried again.

'She's all right. Where's my tea then?'

Marigold started ravenously on the Rich Tea, crumbs dropping all down her chest. Violet brewed up a pot of tea.

'I wanted to go out,' Marigold said through a mouthful of biscuit. 'Why shouldn't I go out?'

'Course you should!' Violet smiled and sat down opposite her with the milk bottle. 'It's lovely to see you, sis. I wish you came more often. Come when you like and see the dogs – they all love to see you too.'

'She's gone, see?' Marigold said.

'Mom? Where's she gone?'

Marigold seemed to lose the thread of the conversation.

'She's gone to one of the neighbours – or the shops?' Violet prompted.

'Asleep,' Marigold said. 'Er's asleep.'

Linda saw her mother's baffled expression. She looked at the two sisters, her mom with her blonde hair, made pretty and fashionable by Rita, and Marigold's smelly locks which had never been near a hairdresser her whole life long. She found in herself, along with her sense of revulsion at Marigold's state, a sense of kinship with her, with her dirty hair and low sense of herself. That was how she felt. Sometimes she almost felt like rubbing dirt into her hair and skin to make her outside match how she felt inside.

Marigold asked a few more disconnected questions, about the dogs, and about Carol. She turned to Carol once and stroked her hand over her head, giving her a sweet smile.

'You're a pretty little thing, you are,' she said, with a genuine smile. Linda saw her features light up into someone who once might have been pretty in a handsome way.

After a while she stood up, unsteadily. 'I'm going to the bus now.'

'Linda'll come to the bus stop with you, won't you?' Violet said.

Marigold made a performance of putting her hat back on before they left. She was obviously far from sober, but seemed more mellow than when she'd arrived. Linda led her out to the warmth of the road.

They didn't speak until the corner of Bloomsbury Road. Then Linda took a chance.

'Auntie – d'you know why Auntie Rosina left the way she did?'

Marigold looked at her, seeming blank.

'You know – your sister, who was at the wedding. Then she ran off again.'

'Rosy – course I know Rosy. It was me saw her, wasn'it?' This clarity startled Linda.

'But why did she leave home – when she was so young?'

'She weren't like the rest of us,' Marigold said. 'Clever, she was.' She shook her head with apparent fondness. 'Good old Rosy. Anyway, she had a man so she left.'

Linda stood watching the bus as it rolled away with Marigold on it. She thought about Auntie Rosina. *Clever, she was . . .* Clever? Or clever to get out? She, Linda, had been told she was clever, but where had that ever got her? *She had a man . . .* The message was becoming ever clearer, from Marigold, from Bessie, from Joyce's wedding. Nothing counted, not being clever, or working hard. If you wanted to get out from where you were, what was needed was a man. And what stayed with her after Marigold had gone was the tone of deep wistfulness with which her aunt had said it.

Chapter Fifty-Three

Linda left school that summer without praise and without regret. She and Maureen walked out into the summer day and did not look back.

'That's that, then,' Linda said.

By the next week she had a job, the first one offered, for an electrical engineering works in Witton called Porteous's. It was somewhere her uncle Charlie, Marigold's twin brother, had told her about. The work meant standing in a line fixing a fiddly electronic part into power connectors for electric cables. It was repetitive, very boring and she didn't give a damn. That was what she'd been destined for all along, wasn't it? Why bother looking for anything better?

'What the hell d'you want to go there for?' her mom demanded when she came home and said where she'd been taken on. 'That's two buses – you'll have to be up at crack of dawn!'

'Well, I'm earning a wage now, so I can afford two buses, can't I?' she retorted savagely.

She was always rowing with Mom now. Everything about her always seemed to be wrong. Violet eyed her lank hair, spotty face and unkempt look, her old white shirt hanging out of her skirt, shoes all scuffed.

'I'm surprised they took you, looking like that.'

'It wasn't a fashion model they were after.'

'If you came to Rita's and had a trim – tied your hair back nicely, you'd get rid of those spots.'

'Well, I don't want to – all right? Just 'cause you've decided to pull yourself together after all these years, you don't have to keep on at me!' She slammed out of the back room and upstairs.

'Don't you talk to me like that!' Violet's voice followed her upstairs.

She knew what they'd be saying downstairs. What had got into that wench these days, cheeky bint? Needs her hide tanned (from Dad).

Not that he had the strength to do it.

Somehow, over the last weeks, Violet had ended up cooking Sunday lunches for everyone. Two weeks later she was standing in a kitchen full of the steam of cooking vegetables and the delicious aroma of roasting beef, complaining, 'Why the hell did I end up doing all this?'

''Cause Nana said so,' Carol said from behind her, sitting at the table, slicing up a lump of suet for the pudding. Carol often helped in the kitchen. She knew how to cook more things than Linda, who wasn't interested.

'And we always do what Nana says, don't we?' Linda said.

Violet turned on her. 'Don't you start off again! Nana made Sunday dinner for all of us for years on end and she's no spring chicken any more . . .' She lunged to rescue a pan that was boiling over, its water putting out the gas.

Linda looked at her through narrowed eyes. *So what're you moaning about then?* her expression said. But she didn't say anything.

Bessie, Clarence and Marigold arrived in time for lunch. As they came in, Bessie and Marigold's bulk seemed to fill the whole hall. Linda, who was taking Dad's porridge in to him, could hear Bessie giving orders.

'Hope you put the joint in early enough,' she started, loudly. 'I like a bit of beef well done, I do. Don't like to see any blood in it. Joyce coming an' all?'

'She said she was,' Violet was just saying, and then there was a rattle at the door and Linda heard Joyce and Danny being welcomed in as well. Linda's heart sank. She was hungry and wanted some lunch, but most of all she just wanted to run away.

'Here y'are, Dad –' She put the tray with the porridge on his lap. It was sprinkled with brown sugar and looked nice and creamy.

'Ta, Linda.' He shifted himself to take the tray. He looked very ill. His face was so sunken, hands skeletal. *He'll die soon*, she thought. *He can't go on like this.* He was never angry now. Petulant at times, and jumpy, but real anger required too much energy. A kind of passive gentleness had come over him, almost as if there was nothing else now that could touch him.

He often seemed dreamy, not quite with them, but now he looked up into her eyes.

'Want to stay in here with me, do you?' There was a flicker of a wink. She knew Dad had never been able to stand Bessie.

She smiled back. 'Best go back in there, hadn't I?'

But she lingered in the hall.

'Where's the other 'un?' she heard Bessie ask, roughly. She never could seem to bring herself to use Linda's name. There was the sound of cutlery being laid round the table.

'Don't talk to me about her,' Violet said. 'Got the sack, she did, this week – sent home with no pay, the lot!'

'What'd they sack her for?' Bessie demanded. 'Looking a bloody mess?'

Linda's pulse raced. She tried to bite her nails except there was nothing left above the quicks.

'No – 'ere – put them cups round – they told her she was doing it wrong all the time. I mean it was electrics. Can't have it going wrong, can you? Could be dangerous, that.'

Danny came out of the kitchen, carrying Carol in his arms as if she was a damsel in distress that he'd rescued. Carol was giggling.

'All right, Linda?' Danny said cheerfully.

Linda managed a smile back.

'Coming in, then?' he said over his shoulder.

'Waiting for our mom. I've got to help.'

'. . . she went and got another job, at least,' Violet was saying. 'In some box factory.'

'Well – let's hope that one lasts a bit longer. I can see that one being a proper rolling stone,' Bessie pronounced.

'Oh, it's just a stage she's going through. She'll find a man, settle down properly, sooner or later.' Joyce's matronly tone grated on Linda so that she wanted to scream. 'Anyway, everybody – where is Linda anyway? – I've got summat to tell you all.'

Seeing this as a moment when attention was directed away from her, Linda came and stood in the doorway. Joyce, who was looking incredibly pleased with herself, glanced at Danny as if for approval, then looked round the table to make sure she had everyone's full attention.

'I'm going to have a baby!'

306

Drowning out Violet's gasp of pleasure, Bessie gave a crude laugh. She was in the middle of lighting another cigarette.

'Well, you two didn't waste any time! Conceived in wedlock, was it? Don't want any bastards in the family, do we?' And her shoulders shook.

Joyce blushed right down her neck. 'Yes it was, Nan, as a matter of fact. What d'you take me for?'

Bessie blew out a mouthful of smoke. 'No need to get on your high horse – I was only having a joke. Good for you, wench. Make a proper woman of you, that will. There's a few I know could do with a dose of it, the way some of the girls carry on these days . . .' She eyed Linda with vicious contempt.

Linda watched Marigold, whose face was a mask. She showed no reaction to the news at all, but Bessie saw the direction of her glance.

'Yes, and she's a fine one.' Bessie spoke to Violet, but nodded her head at Marigold as if she was a wanton child. 'Playing me up good and proper. D'you know, she's started sneaking in and out, sly as anything, and I said to her, "What're you playing at, Marigold Wiles? You needn't think you can keep anything from me – I can read you like a book, I can!" And what d'you know but she's been carrying on with some bloke she met down the Crown. Old enough to be a grandfather he is! I told her, I'm not having it, so she can pack that in right away.'

'Oh but . . .' Violet protested. 'Surely he's just a friend, Marigold? I mean why shouldn't she have a friend to go out with – it's nice for her.'

'Nice be damned – it's disgusting at her age, that it is – or any age, her being the way she is. No – I've told her, I'm not having it. You don't know what she's like,

Violet, what with her drinking and carry-on. You have to keep her in sight all the time. Worn me out it has, all these years, looking out for her. Don't think you know, 'cause you don't . . .'

Violet hesitated, never up to arguing with Bessie. Marigold didn't even blink, but Linda thought she saw something in her aunt's eyes, a dark flicker, nothing more. She felt sorry for Marigold, but she was like deep mud – everything seemed to sink into her without trace. She wondered if Marigold had her usual stash of gin tucked down her bra.

Linda was about to sit down when Bessie snapped at her, 'Don't you go parking yourself. Help your mother bring the dinner in – you might as well be of some use in the family.'

As she left the room, Linda saw Carol look at her and give her a quick wink. Tears filled her eyes for a moment and in the hall she rubbed them away fiercely. She wasn't letting Nana see she ever had any effect at all.

Throughout the summer she worked at the box factory in Witton, counting flat cartons into piles of fifty to be packed. There were some kind ladies working there, but at the beginning of one week she gave in her notice on a whim and left on the Friday. She didn't tell Mom, not until she'd got a job at Wimbush's bakery, where she had to wear a neat white overall and worked amid the smell of baked bread and cakes instead of breathing in the cardboard dust in the factory. She liked working in a shop better. It was more varied, people coming in and out and chatting. She'd cleaned herself up a bit to go and ask for that job – washed her hair and tied it back.

They wouldn't want someone dirty handling their bread. And it made her feel a bit better. She quite liked the work too – cleaning down the shelves where they arranged the bread and cakes, and bagging them up and selling them, chatting to the regulars.

Mrs Richards, the middle-aged lady who employed her, was pleased with her.

'You're good at working out the change,' she said. 'Bright girl like you. Why don't you do something else? Learn to type or do accounts or something? You could get a good job, you could.'

'I might,' Linda said, without enthusiasm. 'I quite like it here though.'

'You could be a secretary, if you put your mind to it,' Mrs Richards said. 'You get a good boss in that, and you're made. My cousin Doris did that. Worked for one of the top men at . . . what d'you call it? Some place to do with pensions.' She tittered. 'See? Wouldn't have suited me – proper muddle head, me!'

Linda smiled. She liked Mrs Richards. She was kind and didn't pretend to be anything she wasn't. And she didn't mind the work. In her long days amid the bread and cakes she had time to think. She thought about Rosina. And she thought, how can I get away from home?

Chapter Fifty-Four

Carol's operation was in September.

'I wish they could tell us how long she'll be in there.' Violet was up in their room packing Carol's few possessions into a little bag. 'They never tell you anything.'

It all depended how the operation went and how quickly Carol recovered from it.

'I hate her being in there,' she said to Linda while Carol was in the bathroom. 'And she'll be under that flaming nun's thumb again.'

When they were getting ready for bed she cuddled Carol to her like a baby, tearful herself.

'My poor babby,' she said, rocking her on her lap. Carol was still very small for her age. She snuggled up, enjoying the attention, but she was in a calmer state than her mother.

'I'll be all right. I'll see Sister Cathleen and it means I'll be able to walk better when I get back.'

'You're a brave girl,' Violet said tearfully. 'Isn't she, Linda?'

Linda, sitting on her bed, nodded glumly. That was the one thing they were ever agreed on – their affection for Carol. With Carol gone for weeks, maybe even months, she was going to be the only one left! It was a horrible thought.

Soon the two of them were left alone in the half

light through the thin curtains. Carol lay very quiet and still.

'You all right?' Linda whispered.

'Yes.'

'Thought you'd fallen asleep.'

'No – ' There came another pause. 'I was praying.'

'Were you?'

'Sister Cathleen taught me. She said if you talk to God he'll always be beside you.'

Carol hadn't talked about Sister Cathleen for a while. Now she was going back into hospital, it had reminded her. No one had ever told Linda about talking to God, not in her whole life. She wasn't sure what to say.

'Don't you ever think, you having polio and that . . . That it's not fair? I mean it isn't fair, is it? You being in a wheelchair or on crutches all the time. Not like everyone else.'

'I wish I could go swimming again. They said that's where I caught it, didn't they? And to go to the park and run about. And I'll miss Joyce's babby being born when I'm away. I don't want to go . . . But I know I've got to.'

Linda was struck once more by her sister's patience. They were so different! Sometimes she burned with so much inner energy she just had to run and jump. She couldn't bear the thought of being stuck in a wheelchair, unable to run about.

'Anyway,' Carol said. 'That's why I'm having the operation, isn't it? To make me better.'

After a few moments, Carol's voice came again through the gloom.

'Lin? Will you come and get in with me? Like you used to?'

'All right.'

Carol wriggled across and Linda climbed in beside her, the bedsprings squeaking loudly. Linda lay on her back and Carol cuddled up beside her, in the crook of her arm.

'Lin?' Her voice was muffled.

'Ummm?'

'Don't get our mom too cross, will you? She doesn't mean it.'

'I don't mean to.'

'I know you don't. It's Nana, isn't it? The things she says . . .'

'I *hate* her.'

She felt Carol raise her head, could feel her looking down at her. 'Do you?'

'I don't want to stay here, not on my own.'

'You won't be – I mean, I'll be back. Course I will.'

'You'd better be.' She tickled her, and Carol squirmed. She cuddled her arms round Linda. Such a skinny little thing, she was, like a fragile kitten.

'Don't worry, sis,' Carol murmured. 'Everything'll be all right.'

The ambulance came for her the next day. Linda hugged her goodbye before she left for work, trying not to cry. Once she got on the bus she let the tears come and arrived red-eyed at the bakery.

'What's up with you, duck?' Mrs Richards asked kindly as she buttoned her overall. She was a thin, gentle little woman. 'T'ain't like you to be miserable.'

Linda almost managed to laugh at this. She felt as if she was miserable all the time!

'They've taken my sister into hospital today for her operation.'

Mrs Richards knew about Carol, and about polio. She had a niece who had been badly affected by it.

'Oh dear, you poor thing. Well – it's for the best, isn't it? Come on – we'll brew up a nice cup of tea at the back and you can choose yourself a bun. I bet you haven't thought to eat this morning, have you?'

Linda shook her head. She'd forgotten all about eating and her mom hadn't given it a thought either. She'd been in too much of a state fussing over Dad and Carol before getting out to work herself. It was lovely to be taken under Mrs Richards' motherly wing and she felt like crying all over again, but managed not to as she knew the kind woman was trying to cheer her up.

The day after Carol had her operation, Violet went over to Coleshill and Linda was left to take care of her father when she got home.

She opened a tin of chicken soup for him and carried it through on his tray to the back room. Mom had gone out and bought a standard lamp to have next to him so he could see better. It had a wide shade with a fringe along the bottom and it was the newest, brightest thing in the dingy room. Harry sat in the ring of the lamp's light, which made his sallow skin look even yellower.

'Get us a drink, will you?' he asked.

'What d'you want?'

'Pint of Ansells.' He was so breathless he could hardly speak, but he tried to smile at the joke.

She smiled wanly at him and brought a glass of water. 'I'll put the kettle on.'

'Ta, wench.'

She sat with him as he ate, so agonizingly slowly.

Linda saw as he held the spoon that the tremor in his hand seemed to get a little worse each day, so that he often cursed to himself when he got it to his mouth and there was very little soup left on it.

'D'you want me to do it, Dad?'

He looked up at her, ashamed. 'No. I can manage. It's this stuff, see,' he gasped between breaths. 'Porridge don't fall off the spoon.'

He laboured on for a few more mouthfuls.

'Go on then –' Proud, he thrust the spoon at her. 'You give us a few.'

She felt old, suddenly, as if in seconds he had become the child, she the adult. She helped him eat, holding the creamy spoonfuls of soup to his whiskery lips. He slurped loudly. After a few mouthfuls he said, 'Not so fast.' And they stopped for a rest.

He looked at her, considering her. She felt somehow as if he was really seeing her.

'Don't live like me.'

She stared at him, almost wondering if she'd imagined that he spoke.

'D'you hear?'

'Yes, Dad.'

He looked away, closing the door on a conversation that had barely begun, and left her wondering.

'I'll have a bit more now.'

She was scraping the last of the soup from the bowl when they heard the front door. Violet appeared with her coat still on, looking neat and pretty, but there were dark shadows under her eyes and she'd obviously been crying. Linda felt herself clench up inside.

'Oh – you've done his tea,' Violet stated.

'Did you see Carol? What's the matter?' She got to her feet in alarm.

Her mother came and sank into the other chair, her tears coming again.

'I saw her. They've done the operation, but they say it's not gone right. I mean, they haven't made her better ... Oh, I don't know ...' She put her head in her hands and cried, shoulders shaking.

Harry tried to say something but was overtaken by a fit of coughing.

'What d'you mean?' Linda knelt by her chair, willing her to speak. 'Isn't she going to be able to walk again?'

Violet gulped and wiped her eyes. 'They say they need to let her recover and then do it again. I mean the doctor said ... something ... about plates in her back, her spine. Curvature or summat. I don't know. I only know it's not gone right.'

'Did you see Carol? Was she all right?'

'I saw her. She was all in a plaster case thing and having to lie there – I mean, you know Carol – she was cheerful enough. The only thing she was bothered about was that that nun she's always on about ...'

'Sister Cathleen?'

'Yeah. They've sent her away – back to her nunnery place. Carol was ever so disappointed. Keeps asking for her. She doesn't like the others nearly as much.'

Linda ached for Carol. She knew how much Sister Cathleen meant to her.

'How long'll she be there then?' Harry asked.

Violet shook her head. 'Don't know. Longer than they thought. Months probably. And then so far as I can see she might be no better for it. One of the nurses kept saying to me I had to be hopeful, the next operation would make a difference. And then there'll be all that exercise and stuff for her. I just feel so bad, the thought of her lying there all that time again and nothing we can do.'

Linda lay in bed that night full of painful thoughts of Carol and how she must be feeling. Dad was coughing next door. Once or twice she heard him groan. His body was so emaciated now that moving was painful for him and even a soft mattress could chafe him to sores.

She felt utterly helpless. Her father had been sick for so long, Carol was stuck in her hospital bed, and as her mom had said, they couldn't seem to do anything about anything, ever. She willed thoughts to Carol, lying there in her bed at St Gerard's, unable to move without help. Was she awake now, saying those prayers she set so much store by?

God help her, Linda thought, and wondered if that counted as a prayer. *And Dad.* For good measure, she added, *please.*

Before she drifted off to sleep, she realized there might just be one small thing she could do.

Chapter Fifty-Five

Linda stood outside the convent walls, her heart thudding painfully.

It was an overcast, chill afternoon. The trees edging the park across the road were turning fast, their leaves adding a copper glow to the greyness. Reaching Selly Park, her nerves had increased enormously at the sight of the big, red brick convent behind its enclosing walls. It looked forbidding, like a castle. All she knew about nuns was that they wore strange robes and prayed a lot, that some were nurses, some were kind and gentle like Sister Cathleen, and others, from frightening stories she'd heard, could be anything but. It seemed so strange that Sister Cathleen with her friendly, freckly face lived in this terrifying-looking place.

For a while she walked back and forth outside the wrought-iron gates, too frightened to enter.

Well, I can't stay out here all day, she thought, and forced herself to pass under the arch into the courtyard. She felt as if she was being watched from all the many windows, and she hurried to the front door and rang the bell.

After a pause the door opened. A plain face, of an age she could not have guessed, look out enquiringly from under a black veil.

'Yes? Can I help you?' It was a melodious voice, the tone neither warm nor cold.

Linda suddenly realized she had not a thought in her head of what to say.

'Um – I've come to find Sister Cathleen,' she blurted out.

The woman's expression altered not a jot.

'I see. Well, we have more than one Sister Cathleen here. In fact we have three. Would your Sister Cathleen be an older person?'

Linda shook her head.

'Ah. Well, in that case you must be wanting Sister Cathleen Donovan or Sister Cathleen Geraghty . . .' She stood musing. 'And Sister Cathleen Geraghty has gone home to Ireland . . .'

'She's a nurse,' Linda offered. 'She was at Coleshill looking after my sister.'

'Ah,' she said again, softening a fraction. 'Well, you're lucky then, because that's Sister Cathleen Donovan and I happen to know just where she is at this very moment. You'd better come in.'

Linda found herself ushered through a dark hallway to a side room where there were a few chairs and a crucifix on the wall by the door. It was very quiet as the nun disappeared and the great building around her seemed to absorb all the noise from outside. She didn't think she had ever been anywhere so quiet.

In just a few moments the door swung silently open and she saw Sister Cathleen's round, pale face, in which the blue eyes looked very big and deep. She was wearing black now, not the white habit the nursing sisters wore, and she seemed to glide across the floor.

'Hello, dear.' She came forward with a calm, but puzzled expression. 'I hear you asked to see me?'

Linda's mouth went dry. She stood up awkwardly. Obviously Sister Cathleen didn't remember her.

'It's all right – sit down.'

Sister Cathleen sat down beside her. 'How did you know my name?' She drew back a little and examined Linda's face. 'Ah, now I've seen you before, haven't I? Would that be at St Gerard's?'

'It's my sister, Carol,' Linda blurted, feeling foolish as the tears welled in her eyes. 'You were her nurse at Coleshill. She's got polio.'

She saw Sister Cathleen's face break into a smile. 'Oh, one of our little patients, I see!'

'Carol Martin.'

'Little Carol.' She gave a little gasp. 'Oh yes, God love her! I'd not forget her. Lovely-looking girl, and she's something about her, you know. She's one of God's own and no mistake. I've not met many like her. How's she going along?'

Linda began to cry now, all her pent-up worry pouring out.

'She's back in the hospital and they've done an operation on her back and they say it hasn't worked and she's going to be there for a long time. And she thought you'd be there and she wanted to see you and you weren't there . . .'

'Oh, the poor lass . . .' Sister Cathleen looked stricken. 'The operation's not been a success? Oh, I'm sorry to hear that. Will they do it again?'

Linda nodded, wiping her eyes. 'I think so.'

'Oh dear . . .' She tutted, shaking her head. 'Such a delicate little thing as well. Now don't you be upsetting yourself, dear, I'm sure it'll be all right . . .'

'She wants you,' Linda sobbed, feeling at that moment as if the wanting was all coming from deep inside herself, not Carol. 'She wanted you to be there.'

'Oh, you poor young thing.' Sister Cathleen's eyes

were full of sympathy. 'I can see how much you feel for your sister. But at the moment I'm working here – we have a hospital of our own, in the convent. I'd like to see her, she's a special child, your Carol. But I'm not free just to go, d'you see?'

She stood up and in doing so invited Linda to stand as well.

'Send her my good wishes. Tell her to say the rosary I taught her, um? And I'll see what I can do.'

She showed Carol to the door and smiled. 'God bless you, Linda. It was brave of you to come.'

Chapter Fifty-Six

The first time he came into the bakery was late one afternoon.

He brought with him a waft of the autumn smell of smoky mist from outside as the door closed behind him, tingling the bell. Linda was wiping over shelves in the window and didn't take much notice to begin with.

'Hello, duck!' Mrs Richards' tone was very warm. 'You ain't been in for a bit, have you?'

Linda turned to see a boy not much older than herself, dressed in a baggy blue sweater and grey flannel trousers. His hair was unusually long, dark brown and tousled by the wind, his face thin, with striking grey eyes. There was an intensity about him, as if he was deep in thoughts which Mrs Richards had interrupted.

'Afternoon,' he said gruffly.

'You all right, Alan? How's your mom these days?' Mrs Richards leaned towards him, speaking as if his mother's health was in some way a secret. She gave a meaningful nod of her head. 'She having a spell in there again?'

The boy nodded abruptly, not meeting her eyes. For a moment he glanced across at Linda and she felt her pulse speed up, caught in his gaze, just for a second. 'Yep.'

'Oh, I am sorry, duck. That why you're not at

school, is it? Here – what did you want today? We've not got much left, but there's Eccles cakes . . .'

'I'll have four of them – and a white tin, please.'

His voice when he asked for the cakes was low, and well-spoken. There was something about him that intrigued Linda. As Mrs Richards fetched the bread and cakes, Linda kept taking little glances at him. The boy was tall and slim, and he stood with one arm resting on the counter, tapping his foot nervously. For a moment he looked round at Linda again and his eyes met hers with some curiosity, then he turned away and she was glad he did because she felt herself blushing at this frank look.

'Thanks, Mrs Richards.'

He handed over his coins and was gone with an impatient tug on the door.

'That's Alan,' Mrs Richards said. 'Lovely lad. Clever. Went on to the grammar school, he did. He was in here a lot at one time – last time his mother was in the . . . you know, the asylum. She suffers with her nerves. No brothers or sisters to keep him company, poor thing. There's only Alan and the father.'

Linda stared after him, seeing him for a few seconds through a patch of glass between the window shelves. She felt sorry for him. His life sounded sad and lonely, yet he did not look downcast. Instead, he had that energy about him which had drawn her to look at him. Any mention of the grammar school always hurt, though. She wanted to say to Mrs Richards, 'Did you know, I went to the grammar school as well?' But what was the use? It had only lasted a year, after all. One dreamlike year of bliss, which seemed like another life now.

The next time Alan came into the shop he was in school uniform, obviously on his way home. She didn't recognize him instantly because he'd had a haircut and was wearing a blazer. Her eyes were drawn with longing recognition to the emblem on his blazer pocket. A King Edward's boy. There were a number of King Edward's foundation schools across the city.

'Ooh, hello, Alan!' Mrs Richards greeted him.

Linda busied herself behind the counter, though her attention was fixed entirely on trying to overhear anything that was said.

He replied with a distant politeness, asking for the bread and cakes he wanted.

'Partial to an Eccles cake, your father, ain't he?' Mrs Richards said, in a conspiratorial way. Then, in almost a whisper. 'And how's your poor mother, Alan?'

'All right.' Linda saw his shrug out of the corner of her eyes. She could also see his discomfort at being questioned and wished Mrs Richards would leave him alone.

'I haven't actually seen her,' he added.

'No – course you haven't. And these things take time, don't they? Can't rush anything.'

'Could I have a couple of jam tarts as well, please?'

'Course you can, my duck – Linda, bring the young gentleman a couple of those tarts!'

Linda bagged a couple up and reached out to give them to him. She felt very self-conscious. For the first time in a long time it seemed to matter how she looked. Wearing her hair tied back in a ponytail in the shop had helped her spots clear up, but she still felt scruffy, and frumpy in the white work overall.

'Are they strawberry?' Alan asked.

'Oh yes,' Mrs Richards assured him.

'No – they're raspberry,' Linda said. 'They've got pips in.'

'Course they are,' Mrs Richards said. 'Silly me. Trust you to get it right.'

Linda saw Alan's eyes focus appraisingly on her for a moment. She tried to hold his gaze, but looked down, blushing.

'Thanks,' he said.

'This is Linda,' Mrs Richards said. Linda felt her cheeks burn even redder and she was forced to look up and meet his gaze. 'She's ever such a clever girl.'

'Hello,' Alan said. He looked about to say something else, but moved awkwardly away. Linda saw that he was embarrassed too. She was furious with Mrs Richards. Why couldn't she just keep quiet? Someone like him wasn't going to be interested in her, was he?

She tried to have nothing to do with him when he came in the next few times. But she couldn't help thinking, trying to guess. Was he one of the ones who had gone to the grammar school whose family didn't take that sort of thing for granted? She wondered what sort of house he lived in, whether he was ashamed to take people home the way she had been. Could he be in any way like her?

One afternoon he came in with another boy wearing the King Edward's uniform. Alan, however, was not dressed for school.

'All right lads?' Mrs Richards said, with the slight air she put on of greeting royalty. 'You not been to school today, Alan?'

'No.' His tone was abrupt and he looked away, putting Mrs Richards off asking him any more. Linda hovered in the background, trying not to look interested in them. In a few moments they were gone.

Seeing them made her feel miserable. She knew, somewhere in herself, she was their equal. But why would they take any notice of her, a shopgirl who lived in one of the scruffiest houses on the estate and had just left the secondary modern with no qualifications to her name?

'He doesn't have a happy life, that lad, for all he's from a good background,' Mrs Richards observed. 'His father's a doctor. They've got one of those nice houses in Handsworth Wood. Young Alan's been coming in here for years.'

Linda let this information sink in, gloomily. Not like her then. He was another Lucy after all. Someone from another kind of life. Angrily she tried to push away the fantasy that she had barely even admitted to herself, that Alan Bray might ever want to take any interest in her.

Chapter Fifty-Seven

She always went with Violet to visit Carol in St Gerard's on Sunday afternoons. Now and then Joyce would come as well, full of herself with her belly beginning to show and talking as if she was a seasoned married woman who had founts of wisdom to impart to Linda.

'Nana's made me two matinée coats,' she would rattle on. 'And Danny's mom's helping me get my layette together. You have to make sure a new babby's kept nice and warm, you know. Danny's just bought a new heater for the bedroom to make sure. He's worried about the way the windows let a draught in. Thing is, Linda, if a young babby catches just a cold it can be fatal when they're that small . . .'

But this time it was just her and Mom. It felt very peculiar. These weeks were the first time in her life she'd ever had any time with her mother on her own. At first she didn't know what to say to her.

'Remember those hamsters we bought, first time we ever went out there?' Violet said with a smile as they sat on the bus.

Linda's lips curved up for a moment. 'Didn't last long, did they?'

'You wouldn't think something so small could be so savage, would you?'

There was a silence in which she looked at Linda, at

her old navy slacks and threadbare jersey, the tired green of old dry herbs.

'Look at the *state* of you! How long've you been wearing that jumper for?'

Linda shrugged. 'Dunno.'

Violet fingered one of the loose threads. 'One pull and the whole thing'll just fall to pieces! Why d'you go about looking such a mess? Anyone'd think you did it on purpose. I mean, your hair! You know Rita'd cut it for you – *I'd* cut it for you. We'll do it when we get back. What's up with you?'

'Nothing.'

But she felt angry and tearful. Being looked at was hard. It was easier in a way to carry on feeling invisible. That way she could hold on to her angry feelings and didn't have to answer for herself. All the hurt and disappointment in her which she usually directed at her mother was hard to keep up when they were just there together, side by side on the bus, and she could see Violet's tired face. That was when she would realize Mom was just a skinny girl who'd got bigger and older but still didn't know all the answers about how to deal with her own domineering mother or what to do when she'd been saddled with almost more illness and misfortune than she could manage. And it twisted Linda's heart so she could hardly bear it.

'I'm all right,' she snapped. 'Just leave it.'

But it got worse because Violet's eyes filled with tears.

'I've not been much of a mom to you. All of you – but you especially, Linda.'

Linda didn't say anything. She wanted to smash her hand through the window of the bus and jump out and run away.

'We'll go shopping, shall we? Just you and me?'

She shrugged. 'If you want.'

'Well, if you're going to be like that . . .'

'I *said*, didn't I?' She turned sulkily away. 'If you want.'

As they walked along the ward of sick children, she could see Carol's face turned towards them, alight with excitement. She was still lying almost flat, in the plaster cast, facing the long doors at the other side which opened on to the garden. It was too cold for them to wheel the beds outside today though.

'Guess what!' she cried, almost before they'd reached the bed. Her brown eyes were full of joy. 'She came! Sister Cathleen came today – just to see me!'

Linda smiled, watching her mother kiss Carol's cheek. She could tell Mom didn't want to hear about Sister Cathleen.

'She came specially for me! She said you'd been to the convent to find her Lin – '

Violet's head snapped round, astonished. 'Did you?'

Linda nodded, smiling at Carol's delight.

'When the hell did you do that?'

'A while ago – when she first came back.'

'Well, blow me – you're a dark one.'

'They said she could come over – her superior nun said. And she came and took me to the chapel to Mass . . .'

'Oh, *did* she?' Violet said, folding her arms tightly. 'So that's what she was after!'

'Mom!' Linda protested. Why did she have to be jealous when Sister Cathleen had such a kind heart?

'Well, how did you do that when you're flat on your back?'

'They've got these special beds in the chapel – sort of stretchers. They lie you on them at the front and you can see the priest and everything. And Sister Cathleen sat on one of the chairs behind me. Oh, and it's so pretty in there. They say I can go again next week if I want.'

'I brought you some comics,' Violet said, and out of her bag she fished *Girls' Crystal, Beano, Girl* and a little book of *Amazing Stories*. 'That keep you going for a bit?'

Carol beamed. 'Thanks, Mom. Least I've got my hands free – not like before.'

Linda thought of Mom's description of the iron lung with a shudder.

'Here's some sweets for you.' Secretively, as if it might not be allowed, Violet slipped some mints and Cadbury's Fruit and Nut on to the bed. Sweets had been off the ration for months now, so they could treat her.

Carol seemed very happy. Once more Linda was humbled by her sister's patience. She liked the girl in the next bed very much, she said. Her name was Bernice and she had had polio as well. Her mother was a lovely-looking, dark-haired woman who had smiled at them as they walked past.

'Guess what – Mr Bum's got a new car,' Linda told her. 'It's parked out the front and he has fifty fits every time we go anywhere near it.'

'I don't know what he thinks we're going to do to it,' Violet said indignantly.

'He'll be out there carrying on if a bird messes on it,' Linda giggled.

'Linda!' Violet hissed, but she looked reassured to see her laughing.

'How's my dad?' Carol asked.

For a second Linda saw a strange register of emotion in her mother's face, as if someone had probed a hidden scar.

'Harry? Not very good, is he, Linda? He's not been out for days now. Says he just hasn't got the strength. I mean the doctor's been in and that – a few times . . .' She stopped herself pouring out all her worries. This was not the place. She could do that to Rita, about how she didn't know how Harry kept going at all, the way he was, and Rita would say, 'He's a strong man with a strong will, love, that's what it is.' But she shouldn't burden Carol with it. 'I s'pect he'll pick up – he always does,' she finished, brightly.

They left Carol at the end of their visit, delighted with her comics. As they left the ward and turned to wave, Violet suddenly said, 'I don't know what I did to deserve her, that I don't.'

Chapter Fifty-Eight

It was closing time, a week later.

Mrs Richards told Linda she could go and get the early bus. It was already dusk, and quite foggy, when she closed the shop door behind her. Everything seemed sunk in grey except for the red lights on the back of cars, and she liked their scarlet glow, slightly fuzzy in the moist air.

'Hello!'

She was a good way along the road when the voice called out. Her thoughts were on whether she'd make the bus, and wishing she had some gloves, because the sleeves of her skimpy gaberdine were too long to pull down over her hands. She was hungry, and it was cold and raw out there, but at least it wasn't wet. She had bits of cardboard in both her shoes to cover holes in the soles.

'Hello – Linda, is it?'

Alan came hurrying up behind her and she stopped, cheeks burning in confusion. At least he wouldn't be able to see – it was too dark. Why on earth was he coming after her? He was huddled up in a duffel coat and scarf and under one arm was what looked like his usual parcel of bread and cake. He smiled at her in the gloom. She smiled back.

'She said you'd gone, so I thought . . . I don't know . . .' He laughed. He was talking quickly, obviously nervous.

'I thought it'd be nice to talk to you, but when *she's* there you can never get a word in, can you?'

Linda liked the way he spoke. His voice was deep and smooth. 'No. She's all right though.'

'Yes, I know. I didn't mean she wasn't. D'you live far?'

'I have to get the bus.' She found she didn't want to tell him where she lived. 'It's quite far.'

'Well . . .' He seemed at a loss. 'Would you like . . . I mean, if you're not in a hurry we could try and find a tearoom, or if you like you could come back to my house? It's only down there and – there'll be no one else. My father won't be in.' He waved the bag. 'I've got Battenberg!'

'What – me?' she said stupidly.

He laughed. 'Yes – you! Only if you'd like, though.'

'But . . .' She couldn't think of a but. There was no Carol at home. Mum got in before she did these days and there was nothing at all to get back for. No homework – nothing.

'Yes, all right,' she said, not quite believing she was saying it, and added, 'please.' And thought afterwards she should have said thank you, not please, but it was too late now.

Why have you invited me? she wanted to ask. *You must know all sorts of interesting girls.* Then she told herself off for being silly. He'd only asked her for a cup of tea. Perhaps he even felt sorry for her, seeing how boring things looked in the shop? Or maybe he was the sort of boy who was always asking girls home for tea?

They walked side by side along the road. The shops were shutting up as they passed. Alan's walk was bouncing, energetic, as if he was full of barely curbed energy and she was having to walk abnormally fast to keep up. His nervousness gave her courage.

'D'you do all the shopping then?' She nodded at the parcel under his arm.

'Well, no. We have a woman in to help a bit. We muddle along, you know.'

'Yes.' She did know, exactly. 'Sounds like our house.'

'Oh – does it?'

He was quiet again for a moment. She liked him for not questioning her too much, for just letting things be.

'You been at school today then?' she asked. She wanted to ask him how old he was, but if she asked too many things he'd think she was nosy.

'No.' There was an awkward silence. 'As a matter of fact, they've kicked me out.' He swung his foot at a lump of something dark on the pavement and sent it skittering. It was a beer bottle. With venom, he added, 'Bastards.'

She gasped. 'What – the grammar school?'

Alan nodded. 'Doesn't matter,' he said quickly. But she could hear that it did. Somehow it made her spirits lift. Someone else who'd had it taken away! Someone who would know how it felt!

'But *why*?'

He reached out and touched her arm for a minute, steering her.

'We need to cross here...' He released her again. 'School? I was never there anyway. Hardly ever, anyhow. What's the point – all that algebra and Latin ... Bores me to death. Won't be of any use to me, not where I'm going.'

For a moment rage flickered in her. All that algebra, and Latin and music and history – all the things she craved, that he had been given and seemed not to care about!

'Well, where're *you* going then?' *What makes you so blooming special?*, she wanted to add.

'America. I'm going to write for the movies. It's the only thing for me. I just know that's what I'm meant to do. D'you like them? Movies – the flicks, I mean?'

'Yes. I go to the Odeon sometimes.'

'I go as often as I possibly can. I'd live in the cinema if I could! D'you like Westerns?'

She looked at him, saw the intense set of his face. 'Well – a bit,' she fibbed.

'They're my life. They're just – *it*!' He made an emphatic gesture with his arm. It all takes you off somewhere else. Away from it all. Oh, that silver screen! I've written two scripts already. When I leave school, I mean, *properly* ... the old man thinks he can talk them into taking me back, saying I've been playing the wag because of my mother and everything ... But when it's over, I'm going to go to America.'

'How d'you know?'

'I just *have* to. My father goes there sometimes. He's a scientist – works in laboratories in Massachusetts.' He talked about his father's interest in a bored, offhand tone. 'I've never been, but one day I shall. I have a penfriend, the son of one of his colleagues. We're the same age – he's called Stanley...' He stopped and indicated that they should cross another road. They were in a nice area, the houses getting bigger, timber-framed, with tidy front gardens. 'Nearly there ... Stanley tells me all about the movies that we haven't seen over here yet. They're *mad* about the silver screen over there! Have you seen *High Noon*?'

'No.'

'It's the *best*. Absolute best I've ever seen. Stanley got hold of a poster for me – had it sent back with Dad last time he was over there.'

'Oh. That's nice.' She felt stupid, not able to think of anything to say. She didn't mind Westerns but they all seemed pretty much the same to her, all galloping about on horses and shooting. She liked the quieter bits when there were women in them too.

'Mrs Richards said your father was a doctor.'

'The old man? He is – but not of medicine. He's an industrial chemist. Researches things for various firms. Dunlop – I know he's worked for them in the past. It's all very useful apparently. He lives and breathes it but I'm not really interested. Shame for him really – only son and I'm not much good at science. Can't possibly follow in his footsteps.'

'What do you like?'

'Oh – history, English literature, French – that sort of thing. Music. I'm more like my mother, I suppose.'

Linda didn't like to ask any more questions about Alan's mother. A moment later he led her up the path to one of the houses.

It was very dark and Alan felt round inside the door for the light switch.

'Dad won't be back until goodness knows when – there!'

He snapped the light on and Linda found she was in a spacious hall. There was a deep red carpet with hectic squiggles of yellow on it. Opposite the door stood a coat-rack with various old jackets and macintoshes flung over it, and beside it a small table with a telephone. Around this there were chaotic piles of paper and notebooks. As well as a broken umbrella and some wellington boots near the stairs, there were more

335

bundles of papers stacked in one corner. Under the front window, next to the door, was a little bookcase crammed with paperback volumes.

Linda was a little comforted by the mess. It was different from the down-at-heel, squalid, doggy mess of her own home, but it wasn't all immaculate like Lucy's house. At least he didn't live in a perfect palace of a place, even if it was big.

Alan took his coat off and threw it on to the coat-stand, from where it slithered off on to the floor again. Underneath he had on a sea-blue jumper, very large and baggy, and the sleeves hung down partly covering his hands. Linda watched, wondering what his mother was like and what was the matter with her. He stood at a loss for a moment, as if he'd forgotten why he had asked her to come with him.

'Oh yes – let's get some water on for tea!'

The kitchen, at the back of the house, was much tidier. There was a table in the middle with a teapot waiting on it and there was an air of cleanliness and order.

'Mrs P. sorts out the kitchen for us,' Alan said, putting the kettle on the gas. 'She seems to feel it's worth keeping the kitchen under control. I think she's given up with various other parts of the house.'

He looked across at Linda, who was standing by the table, and grinned suddenly. This lit up his face in such an extraordinary way that she felt herself lurch inside. He had high, prominent cheekbones, his pale face taper-ing to a quite pointed chin, and his normal expression was rather sombre. The smile, however, brought out his vivid, deep grey eyes. His teeth were even, and quite large. She liked his smile.

'Fancy some cake?'

'Yes please.'

'I don't think there's much else . . . There might be some Rich Tea . . .' He shook the biscuit tin hopefully but it gave off only silence.

'Cake'd be nice.' She felt so shy and awkward. It was as if she needed opening up to tell him things, say things, but she didn't know where to begin. She just knew that they were the same in some way, and that was why she felt drawn to him.

He cut the cake on the table and, as an afterthought, produced two pale green sideplates. She watched him, saw the way his hair curled a little, just behind his ears. He interested her, not like most boys, whom she found dull. But she still couldn't think of anything to say.

'There – ' He handed her a cup of weak tea. 'I suppose we'd better stay here and have this. Sit down.'

She nibbled the sweet marzipan round the cake, feeling tongue-tied and self-conscious. She stared down at the table-top, its pitted wooden surface, surprised at how old and rough it was.

'I expect you're wondering about my mother. Everyone does, and they don't like to say anything.' He was talking rather fast, almost gabbling, stirring a lot of sugar into the tea. 'No one likes to talk about things like that. She's been in and out of the hospital for years. I can't remember a time when she wasn't. She goes mad, you see,' he said candidly. 'Some of the time she's all right and gives piano lessons. And then . . .' He shrugged. 'She really can't help it. She says she's sorry and everything. It just comes over her.'

'Oh dear,' Linda said, helplessly.

There was a pause.

'Must be lonely. Being here on your own so much.'

'I'm used to it.'

'My dad's poorly,' she offered. 'And my sister.'

His thin face turned to her and she felt the force of his gaze. 'What's the matter with them?'

'Dad's just ... never well. Hasn't been really since the war. He was in a Jap camp. And my sister, Carol – she had polio. She's in hospital now, having an operation on her back – she'll be there months.'

'Gosh,' Alan said. 'That sounds terrible.' He looked closely at her for a moment. 'There's something about you. I mean – I don't know how to say this without being rude, but you don't look quite right in the bakery.' Still gazing at her, he said, 'You're *so* pretty.'

'Aren't pretty girls allowed to work in bakeries?' she quipped. But her face was pink again, with mixed delight and confusion. He'd seen something in her, he had, despite her down-at-heel shoes and cheap clothes! 'Thing is – a lot of things have gone wrong in our family. Sickness, and that. I was at the grammar school too – the girls' one in Handsworth. Only I had to leave – family reasons really.'

'Oh, I see.' Somehow she had expected light to dawn in his face, for this to be important, a big statement, as it was for her. Oh – that explains it! she wanted to hear. I thought there was something different about you, something special. As if there were two versions of her, the one that had gone to King Edward's, the real her, whom everyone else had forgotten, and the other disappointed one who went to the secondary modern, the mask behind which she was forced to live now. She desperately wanted someone to recognize the first version of her and for a second she thought he had. But he just said it matter-of-factly, as if it didn't matter.

'So you were just there for a bit then.' As if it was as easy as that. It would have been for him. He'd just go back to the grammar school – of course he would.

'Yes.' No one but her knew her sinking heart. 'Maybe.'

He drained his teacup and pushed the chair back.

'Come on up – I'll show you my room.'

She followed his long legs as he bounced upstairs, and had a brief impression of the upstairs landing, flowery curtains at the window, more of the crimson carpet and a very straight-backed chair standing between two doorways, but otherwise bare.

His room was not bare – anything but. It was not very large, and the bed, chest of drawers, desk, chairs and bookshelves took up much of the space. But there were the books and papers and clutter of Meccano and tools, several replica guns and piles of clothes strewn on the bed and floor. Most eye-catching in all the mess was the big poster dominating the wall above the bed. It was all in a harsh brown and bright yellow, dominated by Gary Cooper's face looking out over his gun.

'"Gary Cooper's *High Noon*,"' she read.

'Fantastic, isn't it?' Alan even slid into an American accent. '"The man who was too proud to run." See – ' His English accent returned. 'That's the great thing about knowing Stanley. He sent it me all the way over in a big cardboard tube. It's my most precious possession. He says he may be able to get me some more – *Red River, Shane, Rio Grande, She Wears a Yellow Ribbon* ... Any of them! I want them all!'

As soon as he started on the pictures an almost quivering excitement came over him. He sank down on the bed and went off into a description of all his favourite scenes from *High Noon*. She sat beside him and listened, feeling proud that he wanted to tell her all this. Something about him touched her, so passionate, so alone here in this house with his enthusiasms. She noticed how thin his wrists were, as if they could so easily snap. After a time, he stopped.

'Gets me going,' he said, glancing shyly at her. 'Sorry. There's not usually anyone to talk to, you see.'

'That's OK. It's interesting.'

'You're very nice,' he said, looking at her properly. 'You really are. D'you know, I kept coming in to buy extra bread! You've got a lovely face – it's so kind and friendly-looking.'

Linda giggled. 'Don't be silly!' She would have liked to say how much she liked his face, and about how much he moved her, but didn't know where to begin without sounding daft.

'No – I'm not. It's true. I don't know any other girls, you see. No sisters – well, or brothers either. And school's all boys.'

'D'you think they'll take you back?'

'Oh, I don't know. Maybe.' He sounded weary suddenly, and rather wretched. 'I just can't keep my mind on anything.'

'Because of your mom?'

'Maybe.' He shrugged it off, not meeting her eyes.

'Don't you want to go back?'

'The old man wants me to.' What did he think of his father, she wondered? When he spoke about him it sounded as if he loathed him.

'But you – don't *you* want to?'

He looked down, said sulkily, 'Yes – s'pose so.'

Suddenly, after all his talk, things seemed to come to a standstill and neither of them could think of anything to say.

'I'd better go,' she said. 'I've got to get all the way home.'

'Where's that?'

'Kingstanding.'

'Blimey – miles away!' He jumped up. 'Why didn't you say?'

He walked her back to the bus stop and waited with her. She felt his loneliness, which linked hands with her own and drew her to him.

'Will you come again?' he asked, as the bus swayed into view. 'I mean, meet me?'

She smiled, full of happiness suddenly.

'Yes – course. If you want.'

Chapter Fifty-Nine

Even before she got out of bed Violet could tell it was foggy outside. The estate was still almost out in the country, and the thick, waterlogged air curled up from the fields and along the streets in a grey pall.

The clock said ten past seven – time to get moving. She didn't want to get out of bed. It was cold, and Harry was settled, still asleep. The nights were so disturbed that broken sleep had become a way of life to her, and she was tired to her bones, aching to lie and sink back into the warm darkness. She thought of Carol in her bed in the hospital, as she did every morning. Her poor little lamb.

'Come on – out you get,' she said to herself. Her old pink nightdress was covered in bobbly bits and one of the cuffs was torn. 'Proper glamour puss, you,' she muttered to herself, hurriedly pushing her feet into her shoes and pulling a cardigan on in the chilly room.

She slipped next door and to her surprise found Linda was already out of bed.

'Blimey – what's come over *you*?' she teased, in a low voice.

'Dunno. I just woke up early.'

Linda was half naked, standing shyly with her back to Violet. She probably needed to start wearing a bra, Violet realized. They still hadn't been shopping. For a moment she studied her daughter's shapely back, the long dark hair falling in waves down it. *She's lovely*, she thought. *When did she suddenly get so lovely, almost a grown-up woman like that?*

'Want a cup of tea?'

'All right. Yes.'

There was something different about that girl suddenly, Violet thought as she went downstairs. Linda, her mystery child. She was still a mardy little madam at times, but something had shifted in her. She wasn't so *heavy* in herself. In fact she seemed almost happy.

The cats were circling her legs in the hall, miaowing as if they hadn't been fed for a month.

'All right, all right . . .'

As she opened the kitchen door the smell of the dogs hit her, overpowering. The three of them leapt up, full of excitement and she shushed them, wrinkling her nose and hurried to open the back door.

'Go on – get out. You stink! And don't go making a racket.'

They tore out into the milky air like children dismissed from school. Violet left the door open to air the room and grimaced at the floor, all muck and dog hairs. Would there be time to mop it before work?

She stood by the stove as the kettle boiled, hugging herself. Linda had even agreed to let Violet trim her hair. A smile came to her lips. Amid all the struggle of her life, the best thing to come out of it lately was Rita. She adored going into work every day, getting out of the house, the edge of glamour it gave to life, the chatter and companionship. And Rita was warmth and generosity itself.

'I don't know how you do it, Vi, love,' she was forever saying. 'Keeping going the way you do with all your problems. I think you're marvellous. I've only got

343

my Micky to deal with and that's quite enough, I can tell you!'

No one had ever told Violet she was marvellous before.

Rita seemed prepared to teach Violet everything she knew. Although they were about the same age, Rita mothered her and she revelled in it. She was learning how to cut in different styles, how to do a permanent wave and set hair in curlers.

'Ooh, you do learn fast,' Rita would say admiringly. 'You'll put me out of business, you will!'

But they laughed, both knowing that was the very last thing Violet wanted to do.

She didn't want anything about her work to change – she loved it exactly as it was. It was much better when Rita said, 'You're my right-hand woman, that's what you are.' She liked being someone's right hand: it wouldn't have felt right being in charge.

By the time she'd poured three cups of tea, Linda was already dressed and downstairs, hair tied back ready for work. Violet looked her up and down. Her skirt, blouse and jumper were all pretty long in the tooth, but she seemed to be dressing with more care.

'You look nice, bab.'

'Mom – can I get something new to wear?'

'I promised you, didn't I? How about we go for a bit of a shop – late Saturday after I've finished? Rita'd let me go early.'

Linda's eye wandered, as if she had other plans in mind. 'Maybe,' she said guardedly. 'Or I could go by myself . . .'

'Suit yourself.' Feeling let down, Violet headed off upstairs. Why was it she never seemed able to do anything right for that girl, even when she was doing her best?

Putting the cups down on the sill in the bedroom, she drew the curtains. It still felt as if she was trying to stare out through muslin, everything shrouded and indistinct. She rubbed a layer of mist off the damp window but that only made a small difference.

'Proper peasouper,' she said.

It seemed a shame to wake Harry, but she had to make sure he had something to eat and drink before she left. She'd pop back at dinnertime, of course. Rita was quite all right about it. Harry wasn't getting up every day now. One morning, only two or three weeks back, he'd looked at her from his bed with a defeated expression and said, 'I don't want to have to make the effort today, Vi. Just let me lie here for a bit.'

That frightened her. It seemed to bring the inevitable closer. Up until then he had fought on, battling his declining body and frail mind.

She heard the hooves of the horse pulling the milk float outside, the man calling 'Milko!' and it pierced her with sadness. He used to be out there, early mornings. He used to . . . But it was no good letting her mind run down the road of the things Harry used to be able to do.

'I've brought your tea,' she said, more brusquely than she meant to. It was a way of trying to keep her emotion at bay. 'Harry – time to wake up, love – I've got to go soon.'

She carried the cup over and perched on the edge of the bed, leaning over to switch on the little lamp between the beds. They hadn't shared a bed since he came out of the hospital.

'It's not fair on you,' he'd said ashamedly. 'I don't

345

want you to have to put up with it.' She tried to argue, just a little, but he was adamant.

'No – don't, wench. I'm done for. I'm horrible. Just sleep across the room from me so I can see you.'

'Harry?' His stony, deep-sleeping face brought out her tenderness. 'Your tea, love.'

She reached for his hand, felt its stiffness, and it was then she knew. Her pulse picked up speed. She heard the blood thump in her ears.

'Harry!' She touched his face, shook him, but it made no difference to the cold statue he had become. 'Harry – love! Wake up!' She didn't realize she was screaming.

'Mom?' Linda came running upstairs. 'What's happened?'

Violet was backing away from the bed, both hands to her face. She was trembling all over.

'He's . . . your dad . . . I think he's . . .'

Linda went to her father, hesitating for a moment as if too scared to touch. Then she leaned down and laid her fingers on his neck, feeling for a pulse.

How does she know how to do that? Violet thought.

As if she'd spoken aloud, Linda said, 'You can see it moving, the vein in his neck. Like a heartbeat.' She turned, eyes wide. 'It's not beating any more.'

'Oh God,' Violet whispered.

You could see now that he wasn't there any more. His body had been vacated, life's current lost. His face was even more sunken, the last sparks of him flickering off into the darkness of night while they were sleeping. They both stood staring for a few moments, too shocked to move. Then Linda took a step towards her and they were in each other's arms. They didn't say anything. Violet stroked Linda's back. Her daughter smelled of Lifebuoy, and her curving shape in Violet's arms felt a great reassurance. After a moment, they stood apart. Linda had tears in her eyes.

'Poor Dad.'

Violet shook her head, too full to speak. 'Tell you what. Go and put the kettle on again.'

She didn't know why she said it, except that she wanted to give Linda something to do, and before calling the doctor, and telling Joyce and her mother, before all the busyness of death, she wanted to be alone with him, with his body, to know more fully than she could so far that he was gone.

Linda nodded, somehow understanding, and went downstairs. Her footsteps sounded sad.

With tentative movements Violet pulled back the bedclothes covering Harry. She thought there might be something to dread, smells, that he had soiled himself in passing as people did, she knew, but there was nothing but the cold that now seemed to hang about his skeleton body in the dark blue pyjamas. He had worn little but pyjamas these last weeks. Maybe it had been obvious that the end was coming, but somehow life just went on and she couldn't let herself think about it.

She laid her hand on his chest, on the protruding bones, a hard ache in her throat. His shoulders, ribs, chest, were nothing but jutting bones. She was so used to him, to washing, dressing him – not lovemaking, that had ceased a good while back – yet today she saw it all afresh.

'What the hell did they do to you?' she whispered. And everything in her began to ache and tears ran down her cheeks. And following came the realization that he had never told her, never felt able to talk to her. The years in Burma were something he could not voice, not to her, perhaps not to anyone, and this seemed the most heartbreaking thing of all. Had he been able to tell Joe Kaminski? Joe, who had also seen horrors in Poland untold to anyone around him?

For one second, half closing her eyes, she made him once more into the robust young man she had married, but he was too altered and the picture slipped away. So long ago now, before the war, before . . . Roy Keillor's face rose in her mind and she pushed the memory away, fraught as it was with guilt and longing. No good thinking back to the things you could have changed. That Roy and she . . . No – don't think. Nothing could be changed now, not one second of it.

Wearily she leant down to rest on her husband's body, moving her head to find any softness in him, and the only yielding place she could come to rest was on the concave drum of his belly. She put her arms round his wasted frame as if comforting a child.

'I'm sorry,' she whispered. 'I'm so sorry.'

Why she was saying those words she wasn't sure. It seemed the only thing that brought together everything she meant. And she thought of the night their little son Bobby was born, when Harry tenderly undressed her out of her soaked nightie in between her labour pains.

I loved him then, she thought, as her tears began to come. And holding him now, she knew she loved him today as well, and that despite it all, she had done her duty to him. Sitting up, she stroked her palm over his stubbly cheek, then rested it on his forehead.

'It's all right, love, you can stop struggling now. You can have some peace.'

Chapter Sixty

It was the sweetest, most exciting feeling.

Alan had burst into Linda's life, filling her with love and happiness and hope like a shower of rainbows. After that first day, walking home, she had felt like dancing along the pavement from the bus stop. She liked him and he wanted to see her again and he had told her he thought she was pretty. *Her!* Scruffy little Linda Martin, *pretty*! And the way he looked at her moved something in her, and he was lonely and unhappy and she was drawn in by him immediately. When would she see him again?

He was lovely to her when her dad died. The burial at Witton cemetery felt unreal to her. She couldn't seem to take in what was happening. The family were there, of course, except Carol. Joyce sobbed uncontrollably through the whole thing.

'I can't seem to stop,' she kept saying afterwards. 'I think it's because I'm expecting.'

Eva and Joe Kaminski came of course and, to their astonishment, so did Reg and Edna Bottoms.

'Another old soldier,' Mr Bottoms murmured. 'Just wanted to pay my respects.'

Mom looked exhausted, and so thin, with dark crescents under her eyes.

'I've looked after him all this time,' she said as they got ready that morning, just the two of them at home.

'And it's been a burden, I can't say it hasn't. But now –
I feel lost.'

Linda wanted Carol. At least she could look after
Carol so that she didn't have to think about herself.
Joyce had Danny to comfort her and everyone was
saying what a shame it was, losing her father with a
baby on the way. Bessie was there, of course, with
Marigold and Clarence, and Charlie and Gladys, but
Linda didn't expect anything from any of them. Otherwise it was just her and Mom. The family seemed to be
disappearing. She couldn't take in for a while afterwards
that Dad had really died, that he was gone for good. He
had been fading for so long to a poignant whisper: now
silence. It was only when Mom started rearranging
things, cleaning the room, bringing the table back in
from the front to where it really belonged, taking his
chair out, tears running down her face as she did so,
that it began to sink in.

'We'll burn this.' She looked down at the stained
chair with his blue cushion on it, cigarette burns along
the arms. 'No good to anyone, is it? I can't stand to see
it.'

Somehow it was arranged that Joe Kaminski would
deal with it. A few days later Linda saw him outside
going at it with an axe.

The house felt empty. Mom kept saying she didn't
know what to do with herself.

'You all right, Linda?' she kept saying. 'You thinking
about that boy? Why don't you bring him home to
meet me?'

She'd had to tell Mom about Alan. A bit about
him anyway, that that was where she went sometimes
after work. And was she thinking about him? Of
course she was. She scarcely ever thought about any-

thing else! He occupied her imagination, his pale face, expressive hands, his words, something she examined over and over again. Each time she thought of him, the intense, yet vulnerable way he looked at her, it made her heart lurch. But she wanted to keep him to herself.

When she went to Alan's house he was almost always alone. She had met his father, Dr Bray. He was a large, imposing man, almost bald, with a residual ring of fuzzy brown hair and little half-moon glasses through which he peered at her. Though he always wore a suit he was not a smart man, but had a rather dusty, sagging air about him which Linda supposed was partly because his wife wasn't there to do something about it. He also smoked a pipe and always smelt of tobacco.

She went there a few days after the funeral. Sometimes Alan came to the shop to meet her but that day she had walked there by herself, expecting to find him alone in the big house as he so often was. But it was Dr Bray who answered the door.

'Ah – hello. Come in.' He spoke impatiently through his pipe, which trailed smoke as he stood back to let her in. She didn't like the way he looked her up and down. Despite his brusque way of talking, his sludgy eyes seemed to linger on her for too long.

'Alan!' Dr Bray took his pipe out of his mouth and called upstairs. 'Your friend's here!'

She heard Alan's footsteps on the landing, then he appeared at the top of the stairs.

'Hello – why don't you come up?'

'That's not very polite,' Dr Bray said. 'Why don't you come down and welcome your guest, Alan?'

It came over as false the way he said it, trying too hard, like trying to force a rusty piece of old machinery.

Alan didn't say anything. He stared stonily down at his father. Linda went up to him.

'Sorry,' Alan said, as they went into his room. 'He came home early.'

'S'all right.'

He leaned forwards and kissed her shyly on the cheek. 'Thank God you're here.'

He was always so pleased to see her. His need of her thrilled her the way nothing ever had before. Very quickly she had begun to feel in conspiracy with Alan: the two of them against the adults with all their messy difficulties, against the world. It felt as if he was all she needed.

He closed the door and went to his cupboard, bringing out his packet of Silk Cut, and held it out to her.

'Ta.' She took one nonchalantly and they shared a match. The first couple of times she'd smoked with him she'd coughed and found it a bit strong, but she'd got used to it now.

'Won't he smell it?'

'He doesn't care what I do, so long as I don't bother him.'

Alan put his head back and blew smoke at the ceiling. But he slid the window open before coming to sit by her on the bed. They ended up in their usual position, leaning against the wall, Alan's arm round her waist. She cuddled up to him. Nothing else mattered when she was with him.

Alan always spoke about his father in tones of complete contempt. He didn't talk much about his mother, though Linda had shyly tried asking, but she knew Alan blamed his father for her being ill. He'd only talked about it once. They were down in the kitchen at the table, smoking then as well.

'Course, *he* wouldn't notice what state she was in,' he once said savagely. 'Not till it was too late, anyway.'

His mother had been all right, he said, until she got married and had a baby.

'So it's my fault too, I s'pose.' He said it as if it was a joke.

'How can it be your fault? You were a baby!'

'Oh, I dunno.'

He stubbed out the cigarette fiercely into a saucer. Then he wouldn't talk about it any more.

Today there was a heaviness about him, a mood of melancholy. They sat in his room without the light on. It was nearly Christmas and the daylight was almost gone for the day. Outside was cold and damp.

'What've you been doing?' she asked. All his days must be so long and boring, she thought, without school, or a job. Dr Bray had talked the school into taking Alan back – after Christmas they said, as the term was almost over now. 'I s'pose they think they're giving me time to stew,' he'd said sarcastically. 'Appreciate what I'm missing.'

'Nothing much. Playing a bit . . .' He indicated the guitar propped against his desk. 'Reading. Thinking.'

'How's your mom?'

'Dunno. I'm going to see her on Sunday.'

'Oh.' She wasn't sure what to say. 'That's nice.'

'Yes, a trip to the asylum's always rather jolly.' He blew out another swirl of smoke. 'Sorry – I didn't mean it. Not to you.' He looked at her. 'How's your sister?'

'They say she's getting better but it takes ages. But she's all right. That's the weird thing about Carol. She's happier than anyone. You could come with us one day – come and see her.'

She had taken herself by surprise, inviting him. She'd

353

never invited him home yet, although it would be all right now – there was only Mom. In a way she wanted to, but in another she wanted him to be her secret. She didn't want the family's comments. Mom'd be bad enough, but imagine Joyce – and Nana! No, she wanted to keep Alan all to herself.

'Yes – I could,' he said. He sounded unsure, but pleased. He took another drag on the cigarette.

'Let your hair down – will you?'

She kept her hair clean now and enjoyed the feel of it swinging in a high ponytail. Alan liked to stroke it so she pulled the ribbon out and it fell in dark, glossy waves over her shoulders.

Alan sat up and stubbed out his cigarette. Eyes fixed on her face, he took her head in both hands, stroking her hair.

Chapter Sixty-One

On the Saturday afternoons when she wasn't working, they mooched about in town.

Sometimes they went to the pictures, but Alan wasn't really interested if it wasn't a Western.

Birmingham was a building site, still recovering from the war, everyone managing their shopping round the mess, the banging noises and scaffolding. They sat in a coffee bar at the top of the High Street, where there were other people their age, and felt grown up.

Alan could be very funny when he wasn't being gloomy. He had a biting sense of humour, keeping up a running commentary on the people walking past outside – 'My God, look at that coat. D'you think someone should tell her? It'd be a public service wouldn't it?' And the faces he pulled were very funny. It felt good being with him, made her feel properly alive, as if she'd woken from the long uninspired doze she'd been in ever since Mom and Nana made her leave her beloved school.

He bought a pair of denim jeans, like the Americans wore, and Linda saved up wages to buy a pair as well, which she wore with a big black sloppy jumper. She wore her hair long and loose, trailing down her cheeks, when she wasn't in the bakery. Alan said he liked her with her hair down. And she managed to pick up a secondhand duffel coat. She felt excited about how she and Alan dressed and talked. It was different from most people. Almost all of the girls she knew dressed exactly like their mothers. It meant something, being different. They were the young ones, making the future. Violet didn't seem to see it that way.

'It's not very flattering, is it?' she said, looking at Linda's new outfit. 'I thought you were going to go shopping with me – get a nice new skirt?'

'Well, I like it,' Linda snapped. 'I don't just have to wear what you want, do I?' *I've done quite enough of what you want already*, she wanted to add.

The other thing about Alan was that he talked about ideas. He liked philosophy. He talked about something called existentialism which he said was about getting past all the 'tosh' all the adults talked about, with their establishment values, their religion and politics.

'We have to carve out the way for ourselves – with the choices we make,' he said to her earnestly, as they sat at a little table and sipped dark, strong coffee. 'Not be trapped in systems made by other people.'

Linda listened to him, feeling ready to go off pop. It was exciting enough sitting here with him, the taste of coffee and tobacco in her mouth, feeling all grown up and sophisticated. But now she could feel her mind expanding as well, the way she longed for it to do. If she'd carried on at the grammar school, wouldn't she have been able to have ideas like this, instead of finding them out from him by chance? But then, wasn't it romantic discussing them in a coffee bar with your boyfriend instead of with a load of girls in a classroom? At last here was someone who felt what she felt!

'Everyone's stuck, aren't they?' she said passionately, nodding out of the window at the Saturday afternoon shoppers trailing past in the Birmingham drizzle. 'I mean look at them – you're born, you work in a factory, have loads of kids, get old and fat and boss everyone else around to make them do exactly what you've done, and then you die!'

She spoke with such vehemence that Alan stared at her and then burst out laughing.

'What?' She blushed. 'What's so funny? It may not be like that for you, but that's what it's like for me, what I'll be stuck in if I let myself.'

'Can't imagine you getting fat.' He was grinning.

Linda stared at him, completely enraged by the laughter in his eyes. She was startled by the force of her anger. He'd missed the whole meaning of what she'd said! How could he reply in such a shallow way when she was laying out all her feelings in front of him? She took a fierce drag on her cigarette and blew the smoke in his face.

'No. Well – it's different for you, isn't it? You can just go back to school!' She was on the verge of tears suddenly. 'It's all there for you, if you want it.'

He was startled by the force of her emotion. 'Hey – what's up?'

'You just don't get it, do you? And I thought you would.'

Holding back the tears made her throat hurt. Wasn't there anyone who would understand how she felt, locked inside herself with this enormous hunger to escape?

She was quiet after that, couldn't find words. Alan finished his cigarette. He looked uncertain.

'Shall we go then?'

Linda followed, mute. As they walked back to the bus stop she didn't say a word and he knew he had offended her. It was the first time they kissed, properly, that afternoon. They went back to Handsworth Wood, to his house, almost in silence. She felt as if there was a well of sadness building inside her that needed release, and suddenly, on the smoky, upstairs deck of the bus, for no reason she could name, tears began to run down her cheeks.

'Hey –' Alan sounded alarmed for a moment, then shyly slipped his arm round her shoulders.

She put her hands over her face and had a quick cry and all the time was aware of the warmth of his arm round her, the woolly smell of his duffel coat. After, she dried her eyes and looked out of the smudgy window, because something had altered. There were strong, charged feelings between them and she didn't know what to do.

Upstairs in his room, Alan stood in front of her, eyes anxious.

'Sorry. I don't know what to say.'

'S'all right.' She looked at the floor, miserable.

He came to her then, and put his arms round her, but in a way that also felt as if he was a child and needed her and they clung together. After a moment he drew his head back and looked into her eyes. She scarcely knew what a kiss was, except something that happened in the pictures, but Alan was moving his face closer to hers and she found herself responding. The feel of his lips on hers was new and strange at first. His lips were warm and soft. They kissed shyly, then more passion-ately, pulling each other closer, and it was all new, his warm tongue between her lips, his hands stroking her back until she was floating amid all these sensations.

He drew back and looked at her again.

'I love you.'

This caught her so unawares that she giggled. Alan looked hurt.

'I mean it!'

'Sorry.' She managed to straighten her face. 'D'you really?'

He nodded. 'I need you, Linda. I do.'

It seemed a big thing to say, like stepping out somewhere new, but she said it anyway. 'I love you too.'

He pulled her close again and she rested her head against his shoulder and closed her eyes. He was all that made sense in a lot of confusion.

'We don't need anyone else, do we?' he said. 'Just you and me.'

The next time she saw him was a couple of days before Christmas. As soon as he let her into the house, she could feel how low his mood was. He was alone and there were no signs of any Christmas preparations. She and Mom had at least put some streamers up together and planned presents for Carol and Joyce and Danny. In fact Mom was gradually doing the house up, bit by bit. She seemed to be full of energy. She'd painted the back room and put new lino down on the floor and was starting to clean up the kitchen, with Joe Kaminski's help. Alan's house, though, was dark and cheerless.

'What's up?' she asked.

'Nothing much.' His voice was surly as he led her upstairs.

'You look like a wet weekend.'

'Thanks.' There was so much aggression in his voice she felt quelled.

'Alan?' She faced him across the room.

'It's just . . .' He sat on the edge of the bed, elbows resting on his knees, chin in his hands. 'They thought my mother might be out for Christmas. But she's worse, they say. She's not coming.'

Linda sank down beside him. 'So – is it just you and your dad?'

Alan nodded. 'S'pose you've got all your family.'

'Umm,' she agreed. She'd been dreading it – Christmas dinner with Nana moaning about Marigold, and Clarence coughing and hawking and the first one without Dad. But compared to Alan's Christmas it suddenly all seemed quite cheerful. There was Carol to go and see for a start, and they'd get together with Eva and Joe Kaminski and there were cards arriving – one had come from Australia, from Mom's friend Muriel, that morning.

'Wish I could be with you though,' she said. 'That's all I want – to be with you.'

He put his arms round her and rested his head on her shoulder.

'My girl,' he murmured. He kissed her cheek. 'Come to America with me?'

She was startled.

'When?'

'When I've finished school. I could work – you could go back to school there. It's all easier over there.'

She turned to face him, eyes alight. Everything seemed to open up full of hope. 'D'you really mean it?'

'I'm going to write movies, I told you. I want you with me.'

'I'll come with you!' she cried. 'I'd go anywhere with you.'

Part Five
1954

Chapter Sixty-Two

The clock on the mantel struck with a mellow-sounding 'bong!'

Marigold sat in the chair by the fire, which was usually sacrosant. It was Bessie's chair. But now Marigold was basking rebelliously in it. She also had her coat on, belted tightly round her, and a new hat she'd bought from the pawn shop, blue like her coat, a soft wool circle nipped in at the sides to fit round her head, her black hair sticking out below.

She smiled at the clock.

'Tick tick,' she said.

She was waiting to make sure there was no more noise from upstairs. Bessie and Clarence had gone up to bed as they always did when the clock struck ten. Wireless off, cup of cocoa, regular as clockwork.

'Get up to bed now,' Bessie bossed her, struggling to her feet, wincing at the pain. Her feet were no good now. She had rheumatism and bunions, bandages round her stout, ulcerated legs, and she couldn't walk far. Once she was upstairs there was no getting her down in a hurry. How long before she couldn't get upstairs? But this was not a question Marigold was interested in. Every day was Mom's legs and Clarence's wheezy chest, her at everyone's beck and call. Now, though, she had only one thing on her mind.

She got up with a little grunt, patting the bottle in

her coat pocket. Gordon's gin – her favourite. Clarence saved a bit of his pension money every week, kept it in a sock under his mattress.

'What're you hanging on to that for, you silly old sod?' Bessie would ask. 'Your own bloody funeral?'

And Clarence would nod in an enigmatic way, as if he had immense plans no one else was to know about. He never remembered how much was in there, which was a lucky thing for Marigold, who extracted a small amount from his stash each week, to make sure she could always get more gin. The rest she took from Bessie's jam jar of coins in the pantry. Why not? Bessie never noticed, not like she would have done years ago. Too taken up with her aches and pains these days.

Marigold went to the window and pulled back the curtain. It was snowing outside, flakes seeping down into the street where they disappeared into dark gullies of shadow. It was only by the lamp you could see a thin layer accumulating on the pavement. She giggled at the sight, excited as a little girl. And she had her new hat. She patted it proudly. Time to go.

'Dirty girl, dirty girl,' she whispered, going to the door. She snickered as she opened it. 'Dirty girl's going out, and sod you.'

She could hardly contain her laughter: it was bursting out of her as she stood on the step she'd scrubbed that morning, and would scrub tomorrow morning and every day of her remaining life, it seemed. Scrub, scrub. Rub-a-dub. What was that song? *I'm gonna wash that man right outa my hair* ... Mary Martin, *South Pacific*. She hadn't written that one down yet. Tomorrow she'd do it, with her pencil and pad. But wash him out? Her Fred – oh no! Mom thought she'd washed him out, but Marigold was cleverer than they knew.

She set out along the dark street with her little bag over her arm, her steps silent on the cushion of snow. It was that cold, flat time after Christmas. Christmas Day they'd sat in Violet's house, nice and clean now, for a beef dinner and there were decorations and a big pudding. Violet looked nice too, Linda hardly saying anything, Joyce there with her belly all out. Marigold kept looking at it, Joyce's heavy belly. Full, like a pod.

'Two months to go!' Joyce said. 'I can't believe I'm going to be a mom!'

'And I can't believe I'm going to be a nan!' Violet smiled. She was looking nice. Pretty, with her hair and that. Good old Vi.

Joyce's belly made Marigold feel funny. She didn't like it. All she wanted was to stick something in it and make it go down. But she couldn't stop staring at it either.

Babby ... new, sticky babby between Joycie's leggies, her scrawny white thighs ...

And while they were eating beef and potatoes and trimmings, Mom said in that voice she used, 'Marigold had herself a fancy man – did I say before?' She laughed, belly wobbling, forkful of cabbage. Then her voice changed and turned hard, contemptuous. 'Huh! I soon put a stop to that, I can tell you. Bloody disgusting – and at her age!'

That's what she thought, anyway! Ha, ha, that's what she thought, the old cow!

The lights of the pub beckoned her. She felt warm inside.

'That you, Marigold?'

'Yes – it's me.' She giggled again, seeing Fred's burly shape come out of the pub door.

'Took your time! Just got time for a quick 'un before closing.'

He was big, Fred, fat and red-faced, owned a butcher's shop. 'How's my girl, eh?'

'All right,' she laughed.

'Quick drink –' Fred laid his hand on her left buttock as he steered her through the door. 'Then we can get down to business!'

She was welcomed into the den of the pub. It wasn't far off closing time now, the air heavy with ale and smoke, the sawdust sodden underfoot, spittoon holding a murky liquid with a thin froth on top.

'Your usual?' Fred asked.

He brought her half of stout and another brown ale for himself. The old piano was quiet now, no more music, but a couple of Fred's pals were there and they all welcomed her.

'Here y'are Marigold – she let you out, has she? Come and sit here, bab!'

Marigold felt like a queen. She had never had friends before, not like this. She didn't need to say anything. She sat in her hat and coat, snowflakes melting on her shoulders, enraptured simply to be there, amid the desultory conversation of half-soaked men, out of home, away from Bessie, with the promise of ... She looked at Fred and he winked at her.

'Drink up, old girl!'

She was draining her glass as the bell rang for closing time and they all had to mill out into the white street. The flakes were bigger now.

'Won't last long, I don't suppose,' one of the men said, squinting up at the dark sky. 'Too bloody wet.'

They said their goodbyes and Fred immediately put

his arm round her. With his free hand he reached round and gave her breast a squeeze.

'Let's be off, wench.'

Fred was a bachelor who lived in two rooms a street away fom the pub. Marigold went back regularly with Fred and shared his bed, nice for both of them, until it was time to creep back into her mom's house.

She liked Fred, and he liked her, but there was no ceremony about it. As soon as they were through the door into his spartan man's abode, his hands were under her coat, reaching for her breasts. Marigold took her coat and hat off and got ready to luxuriate in a man's attention.

'Just a minute, girl . . .' He went fumbling into the bedroom and she heard him relieving himself noisily into the chamber-pot. He didn't bother to button up when he came out.

'That's better. Let's be having you then.'

Soon they were on Fred's unmade bed with its wrinkly grey blankets, only half undressed. He rucked Marigold's dress up, yanked her bloomers off, fumbling at himself.

'That's it,' he grunted contentedly, steering himself into her. 'Into the harbour – that's my girl!'

Marigold snickered, then moaned as he jerked back and forth, fired with her own pleasure. This was a bit of all right. She always got what she wanted as well, whoosh, like a firework all down there. Nothing like it.

'You're a fine wench, Marigold,' Fred said, kissing her affectionately when they'd finished. 'Glad I found you, that I am.'

'You're all floppy,' she giggled, eyeing his flagging manhood.

'That I am . . .' He yawned and teased at her nipple under her blouse. 'Till the next time, anyway – eh?'

Half an hour later she left Fred snoring and crept back home. No one was stirring. Nearly half past twelve and Mom and Clarence none the wiser, once again. She took a swig of the gin as a congratulatory nightcap and lit a candle to get upstairs.

The boards creaked on the upper landing. She stopped for a moment, but heard her own loud breathing, nothing else.

Something made her go into her mother's room. A sense of triumph, of wanting to crow. Creeping over to Bessie's bed she stood over her. Bessie was on her back, her thickened face tilted to one side, mouth half open and snoring, oblivious to the fact she was being watched.

Marigold held the candle high and stood, looking down at her.

Chapter Sixty-Three

Joyce's baby was born in Good Hope Hospital on a February day as the clouds sprinkled sleet upon the sodden streets. There was more falling later that evening when Linda got home.

'Where've you *been*?' Violet was in the hall the moment the door opened.

'Out.' Linda pushed the hood back and peered out at her mother between long curtains of hair.

'She's had it! Joyce – they've had a little lad! Danny came round earlier to tell us and he drove me over to the hospital to see her! He's ever so bonny – just like Danny. He's got footballer's legs!'

Linda peeled off her damp coat, a smile coming over her face at the thought of a baby looking like Danny, with little football boots on. And it had distracted Mom from noticing how late she was. It was nearly ten o'clock.

'Let's have a drink . . .'

Violet led her through to the kitchen and put the kettle on in a celebratory way.

'Joyce's doing marvellously. They told her she's a natural mom – gave birth easy and that. She's very pleased with herself.'

Yes, Linda could imagine. But she leaned up against the side in the kitchen, full of a sense of wonder.

'Our Joycie a mom!' Violet said. She couldn't seem

to stop smiling. 'Don't seem five minutes since I was having her!'

'You're a nan.'

Violet looked solemn for a moment, then giggled. 'Blimey – I am, aren't I? God – it makes you think!'

Linda walked over to the flat on the Sunday morning. They'd been to see Carol the afternoon before and she was very excited about the baby. The nuns said Carol was doing exceptionally well and might be able to come home the next month. She'd finished the scarf she had knitted for Linda, a brown and yellow striped creation with a few missed stitches and wonky bits, but Linda loved it. It looked scruffy and in keeping with her look.

'Goes with my coat,' she smiled, indicating her mole-coloured duffel coat.

Carol beamed. 'It's cold out. I wanted it to keep you warm.'

The wool was a bit itchy, but the scarf was cosy to wear. She had it on, her hood up in the rain, as she walked round the Kingstanding circle and turned off towards Danny's dad's garage and the flat which was up a staircase at the back. Danny let her in, face dark with stubble and still in his pyjamas.

'Oh – it's you.' He sounded a bit bewildered. 'What time is it?'

'Dunno. 'Bout ten.'

'Little 'un's been on the go all flaming night. I've lost my bearings.' But he grinned good-naturedly. 'He can't half blart when he gets going!'

'Who is it?' Joyce called. She didn't need to raise her voice too much. The flat was small – one bedroom plus a boxroom, a living-room, and tiny kitchen and bathroom.

'It's your sister.' Danny was lighting the gas.

'Come on in then, Linda,' Joyce called regally. 'You'll have to take us as you find us. That's how it is with a babby in the house.'

Linda went into the bedroom, most of which was occupied by a double bed. There was an oil heater in the corner and they'd got quite a fug up, bedroom stuffiness mixed with paraffin and an animal, milky smell. It was so warm, Linda took off the coat and scarf and put them on the floor behind the door on what seemed to be a pile of laundry. Joyce was sitting propped against a couple of pillows, in a nightgown with frills at the neck. Her hair was long and loose and there was something different about her, as if she, like the baby, had been under water for a long time and the water had washed her features looser in some way.

'Here he is!'

In her arms was a bundle of blanket, at the top of which Linda could just see a crown of fuzzy dark hair. Joyce sat him up and the bundle gave out a sneeze.

'Ooh – bless you!' Joyce giggled.

Linda heard a tone in her sister's voice that she had never heard before, a wholehearted tenderness towards something outside herself. She was humbled by it.

Sitting on the edge of the bed, she leaned forward and Joyce laid the baby across her arms. He was more solid than she had been expecting, with a swarthy complexion and strongly carved features, almost like a grown man already. His eyes opened a slit to show cloudy grey pebbles. He was the first baby she'd seen close up in a very long time and she was astonished. And it was Joyce who had produced this miracle of a creature!

'God, Joyce – he's lovely, isn't he?'

Joyce beamed, gratified by her sister's genuine enthusiasm.

'He's the most beautiful babby *ever*,' she pronounced.

'I mean – where did he *come* from?' she stuttered.

'In my belly, stupid!' Joyce laughed.

'No – but I mean – I *know* that ... But it's ... I mean it feels as if he's come from space – just arrived on a flying saucer or something!'

'You been watching too much *Quatermass*?' Joyce laughed.

'Fat chance. Mr Bum won't let us near that television again!'

'D'you want a cuppa tea, Lin?' Danny called from the kitchen. They could hear him clinking cups and spoons.

'Yes, ta! Here – I'd forgotten. I bought something for him.' She reached for her coat.

Danny came in then, with a mug for each of them.

'Ta, love,' Joyce said comfortably, taking the tea.

From her coat pocket Linda took out a beautiful pair of bootees she'd seen in a shop window, wrapped in white tissue.

'*Ah* –' Joyce seemed genuinely touched. 'Aren't they pretty? That was nice of you. Thanks. Look, Danny.'

Danny nodded. 'Ta. Very nice.'

He came and perched wearily on the other side of the bed with his own mug of tea and leaned forward to look adoringly at his son.

'Ya cheeky little bugger! You're going to have to learn to sleep a bit better'n this!'

'We thought we'd call him Charles – you know, after the prince. And then –' Joyce looked to Danny for approval, 'Harry. For Dad. Only we're not sure yet...'

'Eh, Charlie, what d'you reckon?' Danny leaned over to tickle his son's nose.

'Careful – you'll spill your tea all over him!' Joyce chided.

'No I won't – don't talk daft.'

Linda shifted the little boy in her arms so they could all see him properly.

'Charles Harry Rodgers,' she said. And she drew him close and kissed his bulging cheek, surprised at the affection she felt for him already.

She left Joyce, Danny and the baby resolved to go and see them as often as she could. She was so caught up with Alan that the visit to Joyce's had been a surprise, like emerging from a darkened room. Alan was almost all she thought about, and every spare moment they had, they were together. He had become the centre of her life.

Alan had gone back to school after Christmas and she would see him after work, but soon after the baby arrived she went round there one afternoon to find him in a strangely excited state.

'Well – guess what,' he said after letting her in. She could smell drink on him and his eyes didn't look right.

'What?' she asked, uneasily.

'They've just chucked me out again.' He flung the information casually over his shoulder as they went upstairs.

She was shocked. 'Why?'

'Oh – not turning up . . .'

'But I thought you had been . . . haven't you?'

Alan flung himself down on the bed, and looked up

contemptuously at the ceiling. Beside him, Gary Cooper stared out enigmatically over his gun.

'Not much. And it wasn't just that. I had a skinful.'

She knew he was drinking, but hadn't realized it was that bad. He didn't drink much with her.

'What – just today?' She slid her coat off and flung it on the chair.

'Today, yesterday, last week . . .'

'Oh, Al . . .' She sank down beside him on the unmade bed and took his hand. He shook her off at first, then his hand reached for hers and he looked up at her, hungry for reassurance.

'Why d'you do it?'

He didn't reply.

'You've really torn it now, haven't you?'

'Come here.' He pulled her closer and she lay down in his arms. She reached up and kissed him and she could taste the booze on him.

'What're you going to do? What'll your dad say? He'll be livid!'

She felt Alan shrug. 'Let him. Who cares?'

'But you can't just stay at home.'

'I'll get a job. Hey –' He released her suddenly and leapt up. 'I got a letter from Stanley today – there's this new movie he's seen . . .'

He fished about on his desk for the blue airmail letter and sat down beside her. In Stanley's small, painstaking handwriting were pages of description of a film called *Hot Blood*. Alan ran his eyes over the page, though he already seemed to know the gist of it off by heart.

'It's about a gang of motorcyclists called the Black Rebels and the leader's called Johnny Strabler . . .'

'Sshh – you don't have to shout . . .'

'They ride in and take over this town in California.

Stanley says it's the most fantastic film, it's like nothing else! Everyone's talking about it and the establishment types think it's a Commie movie.'

As usual, when he started on the subject of 'movies' his voice was taking on an American twang.

'I hope they blasted well hurry up and show it over here.' He turned to her, as if a thought had just occurred to him. 'That's what I'm going to do. Get Dad to buy me a bike.'

Linda sat up, laughing in disbelief. 'You must be joking! After you've just been expelled from school, *again*!'

'I can use it to get to work.'

'Well, where are you going to work?'

'I dunno.' He sat down again and put his arms round her, kissing her passionately. 'We can get out of here – ride off together.'

And again she found herself caught up in his dreams, which in some way spoke to hers.

Chapter Sixty-Four

Within a fortnight, Mrs Bray was sent home from the mental hospital for a trial period.

When Linda went round one afternoon she was startled to find all the family there.

'My mother's here,' Alan said at the door. His face looked different, as if something had loosened in him.

'You mean – they've let her out?'

'Yes – she came yesterday.'

Linda started to back away. She was muffled up in Carol's woolly scarf, speaking through it. 'I'll go home . . . You don't want me there . . '

'I do – please!' Alan seized her wrist. 'Come on – she likes a bit of company and I've told her about you. I want you to meet her.'

Linda was very nervous. She didn't know what she expected Mrs Dorothea Bray to be like, but the idea of the 'asylum' struck fear and dread into everyone. She'd seen Nana shudder at the very mention of it.

To her surprise, she could hear dance music coming from the living-room at the back of the house. There was a radio in there, Linda knew, but Alan led her to the kitchen. Standing by the table was a slim, black-haired woman with Alan's wide grey eyes. Linda had an impression of someone neatly dressed, in a calf-length skirt, pale blouse and a long black cardigan. Her hair was parted in the middle and taken back in a rough bunch at the back. What was startling was how young she appeared, almost girlish.

For a moment her face was blank and then, mechanically, as if having to recall how to do it, she smiled.

'Hello. You must be Linda?'

Her voice was soft, well-spoken. Linda had to remind herself to free her chin from behind the scarf. She unwound it and took it off.

'Hello,' she said, feeling very shy and at a loss.

'What a nice name,' Mrs Bray suddenly spoke very fast. 'Did you know Linda means "pretty" in Spanish? I expect you did.'

'No.' That was the truth of course. 'I didn't.'

'Well – it's very nice to meet you. I'm glad you're a friend for Alan because his father works so hard and my poor boy is alone so much with me being ... ill.' She leant forward distractedly and picked up the tin of tea from the table. 'You know I've been away?'

Linda nodded.

'They did something to my head, you see, and now I'm back.'

Linda could feel Alan's discomfort reaching her, almost smell it. He seemed younger suddenly, now his mother was here.

'I can't always ... manage, you see.' Dorothea Bray smiled brightly. 'Would you like some tea? I can make tea now, Alan.'

'Thanks – that'd be nice,' Linda said.

As Mrs Bray turned to light the gas with slow deliberation, she whispered to Alan, 'Where's your daddy?'

Alan rolled his eyes upwards. 'I think he's working.'

It seemed to Linda very odd and unkind of Dr Bray to be up in his study when his wife had only just got home. But she was relieved he wasn't here. He was so stiff and hard to talk to.

'You sit down, both of you,' Mrs Bray said. 'Let me make you tea. I haven't made tea for a long time.' She stood as if thinking for a moment, then said, 'You see, they did something to my brain – to try and make me better. Everything takes me a long time . . .'

She was so transparently open, like someone whose skin has been removed, that Linda was disarmed and felt sorry and somehow tender towards her. She began to relax, and saw that she was helping Alan to do the same.

'That's all right,' she said. 'You take your time. There's no need to hurry, is there?'

'No.' Mrs Bray gave a sudden little laugh. 'No, of course you're quite right. No reason to hurry at all.'

Watching her prepare the tea was agonizing. She laid out four cups and saucers with the slow deliberation of a child.

'Sugar . . .' she murmured, and opened the cupboard to stand staring for an age, while Linda and Alan could both see it right in front of her but thought they had better let her find it for herself. The same rigmarole went on with the refrigerator.

Just as she had found the milk and was closing the door triumphantly, Dr Bray's voice came booming from the upstairs landing.

'Isn't that tea ready *yet*, Dorothea?'

The effect was terrible to see. Linda thought Mrs Bray was going to drop the milk bottle, which she had finally identified in the fridge, and she only just managed to steer it to the table. Her eyes were terribly frightened and she was all of a quiver, almost to pieces. Linda was appalled.

'Y-yes, Arn . . . Arnold. Just a moment, please!'

Alan got up abruptly from his chair.

'No – Alan, don't!' Mrs Bray protested, but he was already out in the hall. They heard him say something low and emphatic and he came back with his cheeks red.

'Oh dear – I'm so slow,' Mrs Bray said. 'He does hate things to be slow.'

'Why's he like that?' Alan erupted suddenly. 'Why does he always have to be like that?' His voice was tearful. 'How are you supposed to get better?'

'Don't, Alan . . .' Mrs Bray was weeping herself now. She was trembling all over and she went to Alan and took him in her arms, cradling his head. 'Oh, my boy, my lovely boy . . .'

Linda watched, her insides knotting tighter and tighter. It was like it had been when Dad was ill and you didn't know how he was going to react to anything, that sense of fear and dread at what might happen. She knew it was one of the things that bound her and Alan together. Poor Mrs Bray! And poor Alan! He was crying now, his sobs sounding too deep and manly for his slim body. Behind them the kettle boiled and boiled, filling the room with steam.

'Why don't you leave him? Get away from him – he makes you ill. You wouldn't be like that if it wasn't for him!'

'Don't say that, darling!' She pulled him from her and took his face between her shaking hands. 'That's not true. I would. I truly think I would be. It's how I am and it's very hard for Daddy.' She managed a brave smile. 'And where would I go? Who would want a person straight out of the madhouse – eh?'

She chucked his chin, trying to be brave, to lighten things. She seemed suddenly more self-possessed.

Linda got up, shakily, and removed the kettle from the gas.

'Oh dear, yes – look at all this smoke . . . no, steam, that's it – steam. Like a Turkish bath!' Mrs Bray said. 'Thank you, Linda! What a way to welcome your lovely, pretty friend. Come on now, darling.' She poured water into the teapot. 'We must look on the bright side – umm? I'm home now. Now you take your father his tea to keep him happy. I don't suppose he'll want to come and drink it with us.'

They sat together drinking tea, with a plate of biscuits, and Mrs Bray talked about some of the other inmates in the hospital in Winson Green.

'Some of them are really very nice,' she said. 'One does make friends – even in the oddest of places. But still – ' she braced her shoulders. 'I mustn't linger . . . I must be here now . . . Look after my boy . . . I've not been much good.'

She patted Alan's shoulder and, looking at Linda, she gave a terrible, sad smile.

'You'll help me look after him, won't you?'

Chapter Sixty-Five

Three weeks later they came to take Mrs Bray away again.

Linda didn't realize at first.

Alan was outside when she arrived that Sunday morning. It was March, sunny, but still very cold, the air whirling white with their breath, but he was outside without even a jacket on, squatting down on the front path by a very smart silver and black motorcycle. He was polishing the front mudguard, frowning sternly.

'Blimey! Is that yours?'

'BSA Star Twin. Smashing, isn't it?' He stood up, his expression lightening a little. 'Got her yesterday. I've been out a couple of times already.'

Linda thought of her dad's old Norton, rotting away in the front garden all those years. Poor Dad. For a second she had a glimpse of the younger father she could barely remember.

'Is it new?' It appeared to be in perfect condition.

'Nearly. Dad got it off someone in Sutton. Said he had a shed out the back with a whole load of them. The bloke collected them and tinkered about with them, but he hardly ever rode them.'

'So – did he buy it for you? Just 'cause you asked him?'

Alan shrugged. 'He's got enough money. I can

381

always get money out of him. He's stopped going on about school, now he knows I'm not going to get to university like he did, he doesn't care a damn what I do.'

She watched his face carefully, seeing how much he cared underneath all his pretence not to.

'What about your Mum?'

Avoiding looking at her, he rubbed his cloth along the line of the handlebars, then circled it over the BSA trademark.

Linda bent down and looked quizzically into his face but he looked away.

'She's not here.'

She tried to make sense of this.

'She went bonkers again,' he said harshly. 'They came for her – yesterday.'

'Oh, Al!' Mrs Bray had seemed distracted, it was true, and odd, but she hadn't realized it was that bad. 'What happened?'

He ignored her. 'So – d'you want a ride, or not?'

Once he'd wheeled the bike out to the road, they both climbed on and it started up with an impressive roar.

'Get your feet up!' he shouted, and they sped off along the road. Immediately she could tell he was in charge of the thing, seemed naturally to know how to handle it, and she relaxed, arms wrapped round him, the cold wind rasping against her face, making her eyes sting, but she didn't care because even on the staid roads of Handsworth Wood it felt like freedom and she just wanted to ride and ride. She let out a cry of excitement and heard Alan laugh. They didn't go far, not this time. It was so cold, and by the time they got back her cheeks were raw and stinging.

When they jolted to a standstill outside the house again, she laughed, exhilarated.

'That's the *best* thing I've ever done!'

'Told you, didn't I?' He took the bike in on to the path and started polishing it all over again. 'Now we can really go places.'

As the spring came, the bike was like their magic carpet.

They went to Sutton Park and beyond, out into the countryside, whenever they could get away, and it felt to Linda as if everything about her life that was sad and limited and frustrating blew away as Alan rode faster and faster along the country lanes with her whooping, excitedly behind him, and the wind tore through her hair, seeming to wash her mind clean.

One Sunday he said, 'You've got to let me meet your mother. It's not fair if I never see your family.'

Linda hesitated. There was something about bringing together this dream world of Alan with home that she didn't like. His home was not a happy place, that was true, but that was his, not hers. She could manage it with him, give him comfort. But taking him home to hers felt difficult.

'We'd have to go on a Sunday,' she said. 'She's at the hair salon every other day.'

'Let's go now then.'

They whizzed out to Kingstanding. On the way, Alan pulled up abruptly by the Maryvale Orphanage to stroke the pet donkey which grazed outside and was a friend for the children. She had never thought of him as loving animals before.

'Never been allowed them,' he said. 'Mum couldn't cope – not with anything else.'

Linda looked into the donkey's wise brown eyes. 'Carol would love this.'

'When's she coming home?'

'Soon. They say in the next month or two.'

Alan rubbed the donkey's face. 'Must be nice – having other people. Brothers and sisters I mean.'

'Sometimes.' Linda laughed. 'It's better with Joyce now she lives somewhere else though. She doesn't half get on my nerves if I have too much of her!'

It felt grand somehow, riding into the estate on the bike. Along Bandywood Road, she suddenly spotted Maureen Lister, whom she barely ever ran into these days, and waved, yelling, 'Hello, Maureen!' as they streaked past. Maureen got the message almost too late and Linda saw her gawping in wonder.

When they pulled up to the door in Bloomsbury Road the dogs started barking frantically. They heard Violet ticking them off, shutting them out the back, and then she appeared, in her apron. She'd been in the middle of cleaning.

'What the hell's all the racket about? Oh – it's you. Nice of you to put in an appearance,' she said to Linda. *You're never here*, she was forever saying. *For all I know you could be lying in a ditch somewhere. I mean you never know . . .*

'Hello, Mrs Martin,' Alan said. Linda heard how polite he was, how he could put that on when he wanted. Somehow she felt proud of him, although she was anxious about him being here. She became aware just how desperately the front door needed a new coat of paint.

'Brought you out of hiding then, finally, has she?' Violet said. 'I was beginning to think she was making you up.' But her tone was friendly.

'Can we come in?' Linda said, trying not to sound irritated. She didn't know what it was with Mom these days. Sometimes she felt really sympathetic to her, what with being a widow after all that had happened to Dad and Carol being in hospital and everything. At other times it was as if devilment rose in her and she couldn't stand anything about home and her mom and all she could think of were rude, bad-tempered things to say.

'Course you can. Aren't you going to introduce me first?'

'This is Alan,' Linda said, grumpily.

'Come on in, Alan,' Violet said. 'I'll put the kettle on, shall I? We've got some cake over from yesterday, haven't we, Lin? We've always got cake, with her working at Wimbush's.'

She turned and smiled at them and Linda saw her suddenly. *Mom's pretty*, she thought. Maybe she always had been and she'd never noticed. She was certainly more relaxed and happy-looking than she had ever known her.

'Where d'you work, Alan?'

'Nowhere.' A hunted look came over Alan's face. 'Not at the moment.'

'Oh well – ' Violet put a plate of sponge slices on the table. 'Never mind, love – you'll find something soon. Plenty of jobs about if you're ready to knuckle down, aren't there?'

'Well – yes,' Alan said. And Linda saw him relax. At home he felt a failure, but Violet accepted him just as he was.

She watched him getting on with her mother. He asked her about Carol and her job and then if he could see the dogs.

'Oh – you don't mind if I let them in again then?'

385

Violet was delighted. 'Some people don't like them – Mr Bottoms next door doesn't, does he, Lin? If you're all right with them, I'll bring them in.'

Alan loved the dogs and made a big fuss of them.

'They like you,' Violet said. 'They can tell when someone really takes to them, can't they, Lin?'

Once Alan had ridden away that afternoon, though, Violet said, 'Seems a nice enough boy. Bit posh for you, though, isn't he?'

Without answering, Linda left the room and slammed the door. *Trust Mom to want to drag me down as usual!* she thought, thumping up the stairs. She'd keep Alan well away from here, she decided. They were better off without anyone telling them what to do and who to be – just the two of them.

The next Sunday was a bright day and they rode right out to the countryside and sat out of the breeze behind a blackthorn hedge, looking across a sloping field where tiny shoots of green were sprouting like hair. Clouds came and went across the sky.

'Smoke?' He held out a packet to her.

Linda took one and enjoyed the trail of it on the fresh air. They were huddled, side by side. She fished out ham sandwiches and they munched in silence for a time, alternating with puffs on the cigarettes.

'Here – ' Out of his bag he pulled a bottle of Bell's whisky.

Linda wrinkled her nose. 'Don't like it much. Got anything else?'

'No – go on. It's Dad's. It was in the cupboard in his office.'

'Won't he want it?'

'Probably. He'll just have to get some more, won't he? Get out on his footsies and buy some for himself.'

She unscrewed the bottle and took a swig, gasping as it burned down.

'It's horrible!'

'You get used to it.' He drank himself, grimaced, then wiped his mouth.

'D'you know what?' He was full of indignation suddenly. 'The damn film censors...' He swigged again.

She pushed her fingers through the dropped stitches in Carol's scarf. The smell of the damp earth rose up between her knees. 'What're you on about?'

'That movie – the one Stanley told me about? It was *Hot Blood* – the one about the bikers; Marlon Brando...? They've renamed it *The Wild One*. But they've banned it – they aren't bloody well going to show it over here! The mealy-mouthed reactionary bigots in this pathetic small-minded country won't let us see it because it's too *controversial* for us. As if we're kids and can't make our own minds up! God, I was *dying* to see that. I was looking forward to it. Stanley's got a leather jacket – like the guys in the movie!'

'Stanley seems to get everything,' she remarked. She got a bit tired of hearing about Stanley. He was older than Alan, and already a college student.

'That's what comes of living in the US of A. It's another world from here. Everything here is so *staid* and tired and unexciting.'

'Mom says it's because of the war. Austerity.'

'It's not just that – it's the way we are. I don't want to be British. I don't want to be *me*!'

He flung himself over on his side, impatiently, as if trying to escape from his own skin. He was still holding the bottle and she could hear his voice getting louder, the way it did when he drank. She reached over and took it from him, standing it down beside a big thistle.

Suddenly he leaned over and kissed her on the lips. She wrapped her arms round him. At least when he kissed her he stopped being angry. She saw the tender side of him then, and he moved her. She loved him so much, the feelings seemed to fill her whole body.

Chapter Sixty-Six

A row of bright red tulips along the garden fence swayed in the spring breeze.

Violet stood by the sink, looking out.

'I planted you,' she whispered.

They were the first thing she had ever planted. Now and then there had been marigolds and pansies which she'd bought ready-grown to try and brighten up their patch of garden, but these tulips she had put in as dull, dry bulbs and now look at them!

She held her cup of tea clasped in both hands, and could feel the steam warming her chin. Today was special: she had taken the day off – 'Of course you've got to be at home, darlin'!' Rita said – because it was the day Carol was coming back from St Gerard's.

Linda had only just left for work, the door slamming shut to leave the house with this strange miracle of quietness. The cold tap was slowly dripping and she tightened the faucet to shut it up. She could dimly hear sounds from next door – the Kaminskis must have their radio on.

Out beyond the tulips, at the bottom of the garden, was a freshly dug patch with a little wooden cross on top made from slivers of the broken fence. This was Dolly's grave, one of the two old mongrel sisters, who had died last week. Violet's eyes filled with tears looking at it. Linda and Alan had buried her, taking turns with the spade, Joe Kaminski occasionally peering over the fence, baffled by such sentimentality. Violet knew she wouldn't get any more dogs. They still had the cats, and Snowdrop, and the budgies. Before she had craved animals, had gathered them round her for comfort. Everything was different now.

She had watched Linda and Alan burying Dolly. Sweet together, they were: Lin, with her long hair all round her face, both of them out there in those sloppy clothes they seemed to want to wear. One moment they had their arms wrapped round each other, the next they were down there scraping at the earth like little kiddies digging on the beach . . . She couldn't believe she already had one daughter married with a babby – and now it looked as if Linda was heading the same way. Linda of all people! But it was the natural way of things, wasn't it? She'd worried about Lin when she was younger, knocking about with that queer bloke Johnny Vetch, and all that business about the grammar school. It was as if her girl had taken off into a foreign country where Violet couldn't speak the language. Lin had been angry for a bit of, course, when she had to leave, but it had been for the best, hadn't it?

Only gets you into trouble, pushing out into water that's too deep, Violet thought. Best stick with your own and what you know. When it came to marriage – well, that she *did* know something about! What good ever came of kicking over the traces? For a moment she thought uneasily of Rosina, her agitated departure from Joyce's wedding in those fancy clothes. She should do something about her, get in touch. But there'd been so much else to get through, no time, no energy left. And who was Rosina now? The truth was, she wasn't sure she could face it.

For a moment she pictured the future, with her still living here in this house she was now licking into shape, month by month, room by room. She felt proud of it now – she'd done a lot of it by herself, with odd bits of help from Joe Kaminski and Danny. There were things left to do, of course, like the garden and their mess of a front door. But she'd made a real home of it. The girls would live nearby with their husbands, grandkids over at the weekend, her cooking, queen bee at the middle of her family. She smiled, in the direction of the tulips. It had all been such a struggle – making ends meet – where would she have been some weeks without the Divi stamps from the Co-op? But at last she felt on top of things a bit, could feel she was the driver in her life instead of always riding pillion on events and letting them happen to her.

Not like Muriel and Dickie, upping sticks and going all the way to Australia! They'd had Christmas on the beach! She did wish Muriel hadn't gone so far away. Sometimes she ached to see her, with her crisp Scottish accent and her jokes, to talk over old times. But the two of them sounded happy, that was the main thing – even if they hadn't managed to have any kids of their own.

I must write to her, she thought. Finishing her tea, she put the cup in the sink and sat down at the table. It felt like the first time she had sat down for twenty years and she smiled at this thought. God, there'd been some hard times! Considering that, she wasn't in bad nick, was she? She looked down at herself, trim in her blouse and skirt and stockings. And Rita had done wonders with her hair. In fact she felt better than she'd ever done in her life before.

Sitting back in her chair, she looked round the room, dwelling on familiar objects in a way she never normally had time to. This kitchen was a luxury compared to anything Bessie had ever had. She could have had it by now, of course, if she hadn't been too stubborn to move. Everything looked beautiful today, the sink with its wooden drainers, pans on the stove, handles all pointing the same way, the colander, sieve, potato masher, big metal spoon all hanging from hooks beside the sink, her life, with its mundane tools for feeding them all day by day. And on this day there would be a feeling of rightness, of gathering everything in, because, after almost seven months, Carol was coming home. Roy's Carol.

A bar of weak sunlight slanted across the floor and she watched it lazily, allowing herself to dream. How much had she ever really got to know Roy? Did he love that wife of his? He had seemed to, and loved his children, of course. His life had gone on, somewhere, children growing up, he getting older, and all she had of him were those pictures, frozen in her mind, of those ecstatic days when they had loved each other during the war. Real life wasn't like that, she reminded herself. Things change. Roy and his wife would be a middle-aged couple living out their life somewhere . . .

'And I,' she said, pushing herself up from the table, 'had better get on with it, not sit drooling here.'

But even now, at the thought of his lips on hers, a pang went through her almost as deep as the day he left.

They came with Carol soon after midday. Violet heard sounds outside and opened the door to see her getting carefully out of a car, not an ambulance this time. Her hair was long now, a gold blaze over her shoulders.

'Hello, Mom!'

And Carol walked, beaming, towards her carrying a little cloth bag. Violet saw that the limp was still quite bad. Her left leg was slightly withered, and though St Gerard's had done everything they could on her spine, her leg was not likely to get better than this. But Carol was delighted.

'It's lovely – I can walk properly!' That first time she had paraded up and down the ward to show them. One of the nurses clapped.

Violet still felt a mother's sadness at any disfigurement to her child, but of course it was true – she was walking, and without even a stick or a caliper! Her life could be much more normal now. Violet's eyes filled. Carol could have died, she could have been crippled for life, but here she was, walking up the path, almost right as rain.

Once they stepped inside, Violet took her girl in her arms.

'Hello, babby – ' She lifted Carol off the floor. She was eleven now, but still a little scrap of a thing. 'Oh, you're home at last.' She closed her eyes, feeling Carol's arms gripped round her convulsively.

'We've done up Joyce's room for you to have,' Violet told her excitedly. 'Linda chose the colour for you – it's ever so pretty.'

Violet showed her the new bedroom, pink walls and curtains, a teddy waiting for her on the bed. Sooty was asleep on there curled up as well. Then she wanted to see the rest of the animals and Violet made her a sandwich.

Carol was quiet at first, then talked in a constant stream, all about her friends at St Gerard's, Bernice and the others, the daily routine, what they'd be doing now. When she'd finished her sandwich she limped over to fetch the cloth bag. It was made of faded green velvet.

'That's nice,' Violet said. 'Who gave you that?'

'Sister Maria,' Carol said. She sat down at the table and from the bag pulled out a black book with a worn leather cover. Violet was startled for a moment. It looked almost like that poetry book that Roy had brought to show her!

'What's that, pet?'

'Sister Cathleen sent it over for me.' Carol hugged it for a moment as if it was a doll. 'She came to see me on Sunday because they told her I was going home, and she said it was hers. It's called a Missal – ' She flicked through the delicate pages. 'It has all the readings in that they do at Mass every day.'

'Oh,' Violet said. She felt resentful. Why give a child something like that? It seemed most peculiar – and why on earth was Carol so pleased with it? Thank heavens they were out of there and had seen the last of that meddling Sister Cathleen!

'I'm going to read the readings with them,' Carol said.

'I've got some chocolate biscuits,' Violet said. 'D'you want one?'

'Umm – yes please!'

'And shall we have a game of Ludo?'

Carol beamed. 'Yes, OK. When's Linda coming home?'

'She'll be in – soon as she's finished work.'

It was so lovely to have her back and Violet spent the afternoon close by her, wanting nothing else but to drink in her presence, and trying to understand that Carol had been away for a very long time and that she was full up with chatter about the day-to-day rhythms of the hospital because she had known nothing else.

When it was nearly dark, they were sitting together

in the back room and heard noises at the front. Carol gasped.

'Linda!'

A moment later, Linda appeared. Violet saw the two sisters' eyes meet and the joyful smile which spread over Linda's face.

Chapter Sixty-Seven

They were laughing. Linda had never heard Alan laugh that much before.

They were not laughing about anything in particular: it was the drinking that made all the difference, cider this time, a big bottle of it standing half empty in the bright summer grass by Alan's head.

'God – it's flaming strong!'

Linda started tittering after only a few mouthfuls. The stuff licked its way down into her stomach, and in no time she felt floaty and blurred in the head as if all she could ever do was lie in that spot for ever, unable to move.

'What the hell's that made of?'

'Apples,' Alan told her, taking another huge swig.

'No – it's never!' She giggled.

''Tis!'

The field started to swerve around her.

'I think I'm going to have to lie down!'

All she could see was the sky like a blue saucer, smell the heavy scent of cow parsley, waving close to their heads. Behind them, the bike was propped against the gate. Just for once she'd taken the denim jeans off as it was hot and put on a checked frock, and fronds of grass tickled the backs of her legs.

The more they laughed, the more they set each other off.

'You sound like a girl!' She laughed even more, hearing him.

'No I don't!'

'You do . . .'

He drank some more, wiping his mouth on his bare arm, then lay down beside her and they held hands.

'It's like standing waiting for the bus,' he said.

'What?'

'If you tipped us up, so's we were standing up. You're standing next to me . . .' His voice was slurred. 'Christ – it *is* strong, that stuff . . .'

He raised his arm and pointed two fingers at the sky.

'Bang . . . Bang!'

Then he pedalled his legs in the air. 'Roger Bannister! Four-minute mile!'

Laughter seemed to come out of Linda without her asking it.

'Stanley's going to get me a picture – Marlon Brando on his bike. *The Wild One.*'

He leaned over and kissed her on the lips. It was then he told her about the job.

He'd hung about for a few weeks in the spring, never seeming to get round to doing anything but tinker with the bike and go to the pictures. Linda liked him coming and meeting her from work, and Mrs Richards was always ever so pleased to see him.

'He is a nice lad,' she said frequently to Linda. 'You are lucky – you hold on to him, duck.'

Course, Mrs Richards could think about nothing but wedding bells and babies either. Linda didn't know why she felt stifled any time anyone talked like that. Even Carol had asked her if she was going to marry Alan. Carol said she hoped so because she liked him.

In May he'd announced he'd got himself a job, in a

foundry near the middle of town. At the time, they'd quarrelled about it.

'What d'you want to do that for?' she said. 'You can do something better than that, surely?'

Alan became suddenly hostile. 'What d'you mean, *better*? What – you think you're above an ordinary working-class job, do you?'

'No, but you could get a better job – in an office or a shop or something.'

'Maybe I don't want that kind of job – and anyway, what are you doing, eh? Are you going to stand there with Mrs R selling buns for the rest of your life?'

That stung. She didn't want to talk about her limiting of herself – she wanted to criticize him for doing the same instead!

'I dunno,' she snapped. 'But I'm not you, am I? I don't have a dad who works in a university ... You could do better.'

'Well, maybe I don't *want* to. Maybe I don't think it's worth the bother. I don't want to be like him.' The anger in his voice went so deep that she was silenced by it.

So he went to work in the foundry. She could never get much out of him about it. Of course he didn't come and meet her out of Wimbush's any more, and he seemed tired by it. Otherwise, if she asked he just said, 'It's not too bad. It'll do.'

Now, he said, 'I've finished – at the foundry.' He was looking down at her, his face quite near hers, and she saw a flicker of something in his eyes, a strange, closed look. His eyes already had the glazed look that drink gave them.

''Bout time you gave that up,' she teased.

'I didn't give it up – they sacked me.'

'Alan!' she half sat up. 'Why?'

Offhandedly he said, 'Didn't get there on time. Didn't always turn up.'

'I thought you wanted to do that job!'

'Nah. It's a bore.' He lay back, reaching for his fags in his pocket and lit up. 'I've started writing a script.'

'What did your dad say?'

'Nothing much.' He handed her a lit cigarette. 'Usual sort of lecture . . . got to learn to knuckle down, bow to authority . . . the British Empire didn't get built by this sort of attitude . . . rolling stones gather no moss . . . blah, blah, blah . . .' He hurled the match away into the grass. 'He's covered in so much bloody moss he can't see out.'

There was silence.

'Did you hear me?' It was a shout, almost. 'I'm writing a script.'

'Yes – I heard you.'

He rolled over, aggressively. 'D'you love me?'

'Yes, I love you.' But suddenly she was afraid.

They lay smoking and staring up at the sky. Linda felt the harsh smoke in her throat, the breeze on her face, and a floaty feeling as if they were not attached to the earth but on a raft, floating on a wide, empty sea, all alone, just the two of them. And the raft seemed to spin faster and faster and she wanted to put her hand out to stop it. She had no idea where they were floating off to, the two of them. None at all.

Chapter Sixty-Eight

Bessie and Clarence were in their chairs either side of the range.

Bessie never sat down, of course, not an actual 'sit down' like some idle old bag of bones with nothing better to do. When she did sit she was always about something – darning, knitting. She had a great-grandchild to knit for now of course, a boy, no less, and little Charlie was going to have nothing less than the best.

The half-knitted matinée coat in pale blue wool lay on the stool next to her chair. *I'll get going in a minute*, she thought. Opposite her Clarence was asleep, head tilted back, snoring. So he wouldn't be checking up on her. *That's it, Bess – you have a rest.* That would have made her pick up her knitting right quick. She wasn't having anyone thinking she was slowing down, starting to grow barnacles, oh no.

The back door was ajar to let the breeze through but she fanned her face with her hand. She was perspiring heavily. It was too hot! She could never remember a day as hot before. Flies circled round the ceiling, stubbornly dodging the curl of flypaper hanging from the light cord. They were after the waste bucket in the kitchen. She thought about going to tip it outside. Later would do. No need to move now.

It was the heat, that was what. That was why she couldn't seem to get going today. It made her dead tired, with a heaviness she'd never felt before except in the last month before a baby. A moment of deep longing went through her and she sighed. Those were the days all right. Her and Jack, babbies coming. The only really good time of her life, that was the truth, like a picture with a shining gold frame. And twins! Boy and a girl all in one! She'd felt like one of the seven wonders of the world, all the fuss from everyone when Charlie and Marigold arrived.

Marigold. Her mouth twisted bitterly at the thought of her slow, lumbering daughter with her sly ways. Out gadding somewhere, no doubt. Bloody disgrace she was, a woman of forty, stinking of booze and out round the pubs the way she was, like a bitch on heat. Thought she had secrets, didn't she? Thought her mother didn't know she pinched money off her, when Bessie could read her like a book, the silly little cow, with all her carry-on. She should say something – course she should. Kept putting it off. Her mind slid away from the thought, from the look she saw sometimes in Marigold's eyes that made her keep her lip buttoned. It was only a few bob she made off with, after all. Easier to keep the peace now.

Any road – I wash my hands of her, Bessie thought. I've done more than a mother should have to, over the years, that I have. Not just for her either.

She rested her head back in the chair. It was so seldom that she just sat. Her hands were resting on the arms of the chair. She stared at them for a moment, misshapen, puffy-knuckled. They weren't her hands, were they? *Old woman's hands.* Then down at her wide lap, capacious flowery frock falling in a curve between her thighs, at her old woman's feet, all swollen, the ankles bulging out of her sloppy old shoes. Better than

401

being scrawny, though. Quite enough of that as a child. Years she'd spent, thin as a broom-handle.

'You're not bad for sixty-two, Bess,' she whispered. 'Better nick than *him*.'

After all, if she didn't give herself a puff up, who would? Sixty-two years she'd lived in this area, Aston born and bred, worked like a dray horse all her life, brought up four kiddies by herself and fostered scores of other women's brats. *Fostered*, they called it now – had to find a posh name for everything these days. In her day you just took them in out of pity and did your best. And a fat lot of thanks anyone had ever given her when you came down to it. Oh, there was the odd remark, and the money, of course. But not real *gratitude*, not what she really felt she was owed for all those nights she'd turned out of bed for a screaming brat and the mess and nappies everywhere. No real credit for the way she'd managed everything. *They owe me*, she thought, her mouth twisting bitterly again. *This neighbourhood owes me.* Not that anyone cared. No one cared about anything these days. You had to make sure you thanked yourself – no one else would.

She eyed Clarence malevolently. His face was parchment pale, cheeks sunken and his hair was almost gone now, except for a few strands which clung across his bald pate like the last survivors in a shipwreck. Looking over him she saw the white shirt, clammy-looking and stained with food, his skinny old shanks in shiny black trousers and his mouth hanging open like a bird waiting to be fed.

That's all he's done all his bloody life – wait for me to feed him.

Like the rest of the family, she decided, rage swelling in her. Take, take, take. Violet with her fancy ways now and her frippery little job mucking with women's hair. Thought she was too good for them now, she did, and that Linda, like something the cat dragged in. Serve her right, miss smartypants. Never did to get above yourself, did it – grammar-school airs and graces. She'd never seen it come to anything that a bit of hard collar couldn't do just as well.

As for Carol – well, who was the father of that one, eh? So it served them right really. Polio – Vi knew it was her punishment.

Behold I was brought forth in iniquity, and in sin did my mother conceive me . . . The words jumped into her mind, startling her. Where did she know that from? Somewhere way back – Sunday School? Any road, Joyce was the only one with any sense, getting on with life the way it should be. Like Charlie and Gladys – they'd done it right, never been any trouble.

Not like Rosina. Her picture and the two letters were still gathering dust on the mantel. Bessie never looked at them – not to take out and really look at. The letters were no good to her – she couldn't make head nor tail of them. But Rosina's face was there, always present behind the jug. She'd catch sight of a dark eye or the shoulder of her frock as she moved about the room. The scene at Joyce's wedding replayed in her mind. Rosina's glamorous get-up, her nervous, haunted expression and then her taking off along the street without even a glance at her mother, holding that hat on with her skinny arm, the ungrateful, scheming little bitch . . . Bessie realized her heart was beating so hard she had to push herself up in the chair and take in some deep breaths.

Oh, I mustn't think about it . . . I don't feel right today, that I don't . . .

403

If only there was someone to make her a nice cup of tea. That'd sort her out.

'Clarence?' It came out in a hoarse whisper. 'Clarence? Oh, wake up, you deaf old bastard you. You useless, stinking old bag of bones, you're no use to anyone, are you? Saddled with you all my bloody life . . .'

Rage engulfed her like a wave and she had to sit and concentrate on breathing until she felt a fraction calmer. All right, she'd have to make her own tea then. There'd been no one to help all her life – she wasn't going to cave in now.

As she got the things together to make tea she realized her hands were shaking. The teaspoon clattered on the saucer. She steadied herself, holding on to the edge of the sink as the kettle heated. That stinking waste bucket! The stench of it seemed overwhelming. Sweat was running down her face.

She didn't remember walking into the front room, sitting back down in her chair. A blackness spread through her head. When Clarence woke up, the kettle had boiled dry.

Chapter Sixty-Nine

'Get on.'

Alan yanked the bike away from the wall outside the pub.

It was a few nights later and they had been drinking with two of his old school friends. The two of them had been on at Alan. What was he playing at? Why didn't he pull himself together and get a proper job? Alan had lost his temper and stormed out, Linda following through the press of bodies, into the sultry evening.

He was trembling with fury.

'I said get on!'

'Alan!' But she obeyed.

Before mounting the bike himself he reached into his bag and took out a bottle, swigging from it.

'Al – be careful.' Fear slithered like worms inside her. He was more angry and unpredictable than she had ever seen him.

He mounted and started up the engine, revving it furiously. Luckily she held on tight to him, because he shot off very fast along the road.

Frightened, Linda shouted out, not knowing if he could hear her. It made no difference so she pressed her cheek to his thin back in his leather jacket and held on tight as they roared along the Birmingham roads, taking corners very fast so that her stomach lurched with dread, and he headed north. She only had on a thin cardigan, with her jeans and short-sleeved blouse, and the air felt much cooler as they tore along, but she was sheltered by him. She closed her eyes, fighting the fear. The bike swerved from side to side, leaning right over as they went round corners very fast. There was nothing she could do except cling on and wait until it was over.

Finally, right out in the country he took them up a hill and stopped by a gate. Linda peeled herself shakily off the bike.

'God, Al!' she raged at him. 'You scared me. You go too fast!'

'Don't be daft. I know what I'm doing. Come here.'

He took her in his arms and kissed her hard on the lips, then drew back, and she could see him looking intently at her in the darkness.

'D'you love me?' he said.

'Course I do.'

'No, I mean really – do you?'

The intensity of the question took her aback. She did love him, didn't she? She tried to quell in her the sense of unease that was growing. The voices of his friends had come back to her as she clung to him on the bike. *What the hell are you doing? You're messing up your life!* And she was angry and insulted by them because she knew they thought she was part of the mess, that she was beneath Alan. But her anger left her and she felt very tender towards him again.

'I do love you.' She kissed his cheek, tears in her eyes. 'I *really* love you. But you scare me sometimes.'

'I don't mean to. Look – let's go up there.' He nodded at the gate, behind which the field sloped up a little further, topped by a small clump of trees.

They climbed over and walked up in silence, holding

hands. They had to leave the edge of the field and walk through the wheat to get to the top. They could hear it swishing against their legs. Once they reached the top, they sat in front of the trees. The moon was coming up, half full, and its light showed the pale wheat falling away in front of them and the darkness of the lower-lying ground beyond. You could just make out more trees at the far edge of the field, the warm night air mingled with the smell of wheat.

'Those two, in the pub – were they your best mates at school?'

'Yeah – I s'pose they were.' Alan tore off a head of wheat and fiddled with it. 'Not sure I see eye to eye with them now though. They seem – I dunno – as if we don't care about the same things. Don't speak the same language any more.'

Linda thought of Lucy Etheridge from the grammar school and how hard it would have been to keep that friendship up once she left.

Into her silence, he said, 'I've got you, though.'

She smiled, though there was a moment of unease at the island the two of them seemed to have become, dark sea all round, no boats in sight.

'Haven't I?'

'Yes – ' She took his hand again, but he pulled away and put her arm round her shoulders instead, pulling her close.

'My Linda – God, I don't know what I'd do without you.'

He rested his head against hers for a moment.

'Look – ' she pointed – 'Stars.'

It was as if they suddenly became aware of them, as if they all came out at once.

'I knew this bloke when I was a kid, called Johnny

Vetch. He took me up a church tower to look at the stars.'

'Why?' Alan sounded puzzled.

'He was just like that. It was in the war, when it was all dark. Johnny saw things different from everyone else. He was nice – to me, anyhow. But he killed himself.'

'How?'

'Cut his wrists.'

'God. Why did he do it?'

'I don't know.' She wanted to cry suddenly and had to swallow hard. 'Everyone said he wasn't right in the head. But he was nice. He knew a lot about things.'

After a moment, Alan said, 'I don't want to be like my father.'

'I don't want to be like my mother.'

'Your mum's nice!'

'Yes. But I don't want to be like her.'

'I just want to get away.' Alan stared up at the sky, the great distance of it. 'Be somewhere else. Be some*one* else.'

Lowering his head, he said, 'I'm so glad I met you.' He kissed her and, passionately, she kissed him back.

She hadn't given any thought to how far it might go that night. Neither of them had. They lay back at the edge of the wheat, flattening a swathe of it like a bed and clinging to each other. They had done very little before except kiss, but now neither of them was completely sober and she felt his hand slip under her blouse.

He hesitated. Neither of them knew what to do. 'Can I?' he said.

She nodded, wide-eyed, not knowing exactly what she had said yes to.

She had a moment of panic at the newness of what was happening, his warm fingers on her skin, and then nothing mattered but the sensations of his hands and their lips, which carried them through the unbuttoning and sliding off of jeans and their skin against one another's until she could feel him between her legs, pushing into her, and though she barely understood what was happening she didn't want to stop him. She wanted the feelings, and what would happen next. As he lay still on top of her afterwards, her arms and legs round his back, she felt awed, a bit afraid, almost unaware of what had happened. Alan made a small sound of contentment, and she kissed his cheek, stroking his back. Their faces were close together, his breath on her neck.

'You scared me,' she whispered. 'Don't scare me, Al. On the bike. You were going too fast.'

'Sorry,' he murmured. 'Didn't mean to. You're everything . . . The whole world to me . . .'

She could hear that he was sleepy, overcome by the drink. He slid off her and they lay close. She held his slim body as they slept, naked on their bed of wheat.

She had never seen her mom so angry.

'Get in here.'

Violet opened the door to leave for work as Linda crept up to the house after Alan had dropped her off. Once the door was shut, she got the full force of her mother's ire.

'Where the bleeding hell've you *been*? Out all night without a word, you selfish little cow – I thought . . .' Violet raked her hand through her hair, which for once did not look immaculate.

'You thought I was dead in a ditch,' Linda mocked sarcastically. She'd felt a bit sorry on the way home, until Mom started on her. Now she just felt fed up.

'Well, I don't need to ask who you've been with, but God knows what you've been up to! I'm glad your sister's at school so she doesn't have to see you coming in with the bloody milk. You look as if you've slept in a field!'

'I have slept in a field, if you really want to know.'

'Oh yes – slept and what else – eh? All I can say is you're running out of control – as if I haven't got enough on my plate, with your nan having a turn . . . I'll have words with you later, young lady – you're making me late for work. Go on – out of my way . . .'

Violet yanked the front door open furiously.

'What's wrong with Nana?' Linda asked.

'I don't know – she had some sort of blackout. Marigold came over last night – not that you care 'cause you weren't even here. I've got to go over after work.'

Violet flurried out of the door, then turned, eyes narrowed, and as an afterthought hissed, 'You just better not have been up to anything – that's all.'

Chapter Seventy

Bessie was smiling.

Violet stood by the range, looking at her mother's sagging body sprawled wantonly in the chair. She felt a sense of discomfort, disgust even. And shame, because she wanted to feel kinder. But Bessie was not a kind woman. She was strong and in charge, or she was as nothing, Violet saw suddenly. Like a candle with no wick.

Marigold sat silently by the table, watching. She had a pencil in her hand, although there was no paper on the table.

'She won't stay in bed.' Clarence's stooped frame hovered behind her. Violet's nose wrinkled at the smell of him. His voice was high and quavering and if you heard it without seeing him it would have been hard to tell if it was that of a man or a woman.

'I said to her, Bess, you stay in bed today after a turn like that, but she wouldn't have it. I said I'd make her a cuppa tea and she did let me, and I took it up . . .'

'What happened?' Violet interrupted.

Clarence sucked his gums for a moment. 'Well, I helped her sit up in bed, and . . .'

'No – *yesterday.*'

'Oh!' Clarence stood wavering, supported by his stick. 'Well, I woke up, see, and there were these noises – the kettle . . . And Bess was – well, much like she is now only there was summat different. I mean, I can't say really. I tried to wake her and she wouldn't come round . . .'

'The doctor's been, then?'

Clarence nodded hard. 'Oh ar – well if it wasn't for Mrs Jenkins calling in – I mean, she got the doctor. Marigold weren't here, you see . . .'

'What did he say?'

Clarence stared back at her with his rheumy eyes. Violet was seized with a longing to shake him by the shoulders.

'Well . . . He daint say much really. 'Cept she'd had a turn, our Bess . . .'

Violet tutted. 'Well, that wasn't anything we didn't know, was it?'

'She'd come to herself again, more or less, by then. Said her head was hurting—'

Bessie's eyes opened then, so suddenly that Violet jumped. But she did look dazed for a moment. She leaned forward muzzily in the chair, looking up at Violet.

'What're you doing here?'

'I came to see you. They said you had a turn.'

Bessie stared up at her so blankly that for a moment Violet wondered if she had really lost her mind. She put one hand to her forehead and rubbed it.

'Oh ar,' she admitted vaguely. 'I came over a bit dizzy.' She began to rally, to take charge. 'That's all though. As if my head went a bit numb. No need for a fuss. Marigold – put the kettle on.'

Silently, Marigold obeyed.

'The doctor just said to rest a bit and see.'

Violet went into the scullery where Marigold was lighting the gas.

'I wasn't here,' Marigold whispered emphatically, as if she'd been accused of a robbery.

'I know, Clarence said. You all right, Mari?'

Marigold nodded, and Violet saw that she did really look all right. Violet smiled at her, then got the cups down from the shelf.

There seemed nothing much to be done. Mr Bottoms had given her the impression that all this was an emergency, but now she was here, her mother just seemed a bit off colour and there was nothing she could do. She drank her tea with them and set off home again.

On the bus though, like a delayed reaction, emotions set in. She hardly ever went to the Aston house now. Life was too busy and, she realized, she had been avoiding it. But going back there, as soon as she walked into that house, so full of her mother's overweening presence, she shrank inside into a younger, more timid version of herself, who felt unsure and invisible, fit only to be pushed around.

Habit, that's what it was. It had always been like that with Bessie. She had to take up all the room. She could make you feel like nothing, as if you didn't exist.

I've changed, Violet thought. It came as a revelation, because she had not seen it before. All that had happened, Harry, Carol, everything, had made her stronger. And now there was Rita, her ebullient kindness. *You go off early, Vi, if your mum's been taken poorly. Course you must.*

All those years she'd been almost afraid to breathe without her mom to tell her what was what. But not now. She didn't need all that now. She inhaled the hot, smelly air in the bus, lost in her own thoughts, which were suddenly full of satisfaction.

I'm me now, she thought, smiling to herself. Really me.

Chapter Seventy-One

Linda stood at the back door, looking out at the sun-browned grass.

Carol and two little friends, all in little pastel frocks, were playing with Snowdrop. The two dogs were stretched out fast asleep by the back wall. Linda sat down on the step and stroked their hot, smooth fur. Next door, Mr Bottoms was hammering something, *chink, chink,* in his little lean-to at the bottom of the garden.

Linda poked at the frayed hole in the knee of her jeans. She hardly wore anything else now, when she wasn't at work, even in this heat. Her hair had grown very long, falling most of the way to her waist, and she wore it loose today.

She smiled wistfully at the sight of the three girls crouched over the fat old rabbit. Being little like Carol seemed such a long time ago. Now she was sixteen it felt as if parts of her life were spinning too fast, out of her control, and for a moment she wanted to run backwards into childhood again. It was as if she was locked into the separate world she and Alan had made, and couldn't get out.

'You coming to see Snowy?' Carol called to her.

'Nah. Going out in a minute.'

Carol's face fell. 'You going out, *again*?'

Linda didn't answer. She felt guilty. Of course she

loved spending time with Carol, but she had to do other things as well. Carol was in with all her little friends, and Mom took her out to those polio things – the society where they all met sometimes and had nice parties. Carol had made some pals there as well.

'Is Alan coming again?'

'Yeah. In a minute.'

The three girls stared at her for a moment, then turned away and continued chattering.

Linda sighed. Alan couldn't come earlier because he'd been to see his mother. Since that one last visit home, she hadn't been allowed out at all. Alan went about once a month now and she knew how much it affected him. She found herself at once full of tenderness for him, yet also dreading what mood he would be in. That was the trouble with Alan – he was so much pain and pleasure all rolled into one and she couldn't make out which she felt most.

Another twinge of panic went through her. All week she'd been so worried, trying to put it out of her mind. She couldn't believe now what had happened that night last week. That she'd actually gone all the way with Alan! Afterwards it had seemed like a dream. She'd barely known what was going on at the time, not to start with, all hazy from the drink. How could she have! She'd lost her virginity at sixteen! Didn't that make her cheap and dirty? A blush rose up her cheeks thinking about it, and about how it had felt. They'd got carried away, that was all, or Alan had. It had been over so quickly . . .

But what if . . .? What Mom had said – about babies? This was what was really making her panic. Surely there wouldn't have been time for anything to . . . well, have *happened*? With a feeling of despair she realized she knew nothing about any of it. And there was no one

415

she could ask, was there? Certainly not Mom – God, no! Even if she asked the most innocent-sounding question Mom'd be off, carrying on. Joyce was the only one who had given her any clue.

She'd gone round there a couple of days ago. Little Charlie was six months old now, a real bruiser of a kid who looked just like Danny. Joyce was besotted with him, but she was also tired and bored and a good deal fatter than she had been before she had him. She looked pale and exhausted and was wearing a shapeless pink frock.

'He's everything to me,' she said, pushing her unbrushed hair out of her eyes. 'But I don't half wish I was back at Bird's sometimes. I'm just stuck in all day long – Danny's hardly ever here.'

Linda thought she looked a mess. She didn't understand what it was like to be Joyce, she just knew it was the last thing she wanted. As Joyce brewed up some tea, Linda perched on a stool in their tiny kitchen and tried to steer the conversation round so she could ask what she needed to. As it turned out it was easy, because Joyce turned and with desperation in her eyes said, 'I had a scare last week. Thought I'd caught again.'

'What d'you mean?'

'You know – thought I was going to have another one. I mean, it's too soon – we need to wait a bit.'

'Oh.' She didn't know anything about how you might choose to have or not have a baby. 'So . . .' She spoke casually, trying not to sound too interested. 'How d'you know you're not?'

Joyce gave a mirthless laugh. 'If you come on. You know – your monthly. Turned up yesterday. I've never been so pleased to see that, I can tell you!'

Linda digested this quietly and with great relief. So

all she had to do was wait and see if her monthly visitor turned up and she'd know she was all right. She'd been so afraid she'd have to tell someone, or even go and see the doctor! She calculated when she might be due – not until next week. And she wouldn't say anything to Alan. She just needed to make sure they didn't do anything again. Even so, she felt deeply ashamed. What if anyone found out?

A sound brought her out of her thoughts, the bike revving outside.

''Bye, Carol – see you later!'

Alan lined the bike up alongside the kerb, his slight figure dressed in jeans and leather jacket. His face looked tense, the jaw clenched.

'You'd better not be late!' Violet's face appeared at an upstairs window as Linda hurried down the path, pulling her cardi on. 'I want you back by nine o'clock, miss – at the latest!'

'Oh, Mom!'

'Nine or nothing,' Violet said adamantly to her upturned face. 'I'm not sitting here wondering where you are all bloody evening! All right, Alan? Bring her back on time, won't you?'

Alan raised a hand in salute, though he didn't smile. ''Llo,' he said gruffly.

'Hello. How's your mom?'

'All right. Same really. Let's go, eh?'

She swung her leg over the saddle and soon they were speeding north out of the estate, up past Pheasey and out into the country. Linda was filled with the usual sense of elation, the two of them like king and queen of the world, the rushing air, like flying away from everything, the sun, hanging between zenith and evening, hot on their faces.

'Where're we going?' she yelled.

He shouted something back that sounded like 'Anywhere', but she couldn't hear. Now he had the bike he always seemed to want to get right out of town, to the middle of nowhere. Fancies himself as the Lone Ranger, she thought. Only he wants me there too. *Needs* me, as he kept saying. She hugged her arms tighter round him.

He had his canvas bag resting on his thigh, the strap across his back. She slid her hand down and felt the hard bottle shape inside, and was immediately uneasy. The bike swerved and she quickly held on tight round his waist again. That fear again, like it had been with Dad. *Don't let him drink too much . . . Please don't let him.*

Chapter Seventy-Two

They passed the last of the sprawling new estates and headed into the countryside. It was such a beautiful afternoon, wheat and barley ripe and gold in fields stretching away from the road and tucked around green hills and clumps of dark trees. She saw that they were back close to where they had been last week, and soon Alan stopped and they found a beautiful sloping spot, where they left the bike tucked in by the hedge and walked a bit further up.

Alan took her hand and it felt nice, that they belonged together, just the two of them.

'Did your dad go with you today?' she asked as they found a place to be.

'Nope.' Alan swung the bag round and lifted the strap over his head. He put it in his lap and uneasily she saw him take out the bottle. For a moment she thought it was a bottle of water, then read the label: Vodka, this time.

'He's not here,' Alan said, unscrewing the cap. He spoke in a tight voice, as if he was keeping angry emotion under control. 'He's in America.' He took a swig from the bottle.

'*America?*'

'Some institute in Boston. He's working with Dr Rutenburg – Stanley's dad. He wouldn't take me with him, the mean old sod. Said I didn't deserve a free trip at his expense after all the trouble I've caused. That I need to knuckle down and stick it out with my job.' He gave a harsh laugh. 'In a sweet shop!' That was the latest thing.

'Maybe next time he goes . . .'

She felt so angry for him. There he was, alone in the house with just that housekeeper coming in. Dr Bray acted as if he didn't even have a son! Even her own father had paid a bit more attention to them all. Once he was sick, anyway, and couldn't drink. She thought of him staggering to Joyce's wedding, looking like a ghost. Dr Bray probably wouldn't even notice if Alan got married.

'He won't ever take me,' Alan said flatly. 'He just won't – I know it.'

He swigged at the bottle, drinking as if it was water. Linda didn't want to see. She stared down between her knees. There were ants, a tobacco-brown line of them.

'Your mom,' she said gently. 'Did you tell her your dad was away?'

There was a long silence. Alan twitched one knee up and down. Tersely, he said, 'No. It wasn't much of a conversation.'

She dared to touch his arm. 'Why not?'

'She just – what she was saying. It didn't make any sense. And her face . . .' Suddenly he was struggling not to cry, his face working. 'I've never seen her as bad. I don't think she'll ever get better . . .'

'Oh, surely she will!' Linda said, because she didn't know what else to say.

'What do you know?' he snarled. 'It won't happen just because you say so!'

'I know . . . sorry . . . I didn't mean it like that.'

After a minute he rubbed his arm across his face and said, 'Sorry.' Anxiously he turned to her. 'I love you.'

'Love you too.'

In the hedge, close behind them, were flowering nettles. She picked one, thinking of Lucy Etheridge who had told her the stems of the flowers taste sweet, like honey. There had been some in Lucy's garden.

She plucked the pale flowers and sucked.

'Here – try,' she said to Alan.

He put the ends of two in his mouth.

'Can't taste anything. Too much of this.' He patted the bottle and drank again. She wanted to tell him to stop, but didn't dare.

'Want some?' He held it out to her. She shook her head.

'Have you finished your script yet?'

'No.'

Something in the way he said it stopped her asking any more. She wanted to talk about being out here last week, about what had happened and how it mustn't happen again, but his mood was so low and he felt so distant from her that she didn't dare.

After a moment he put the bottle down and put his arms round her, lips searching for hers. He kissed her hard, desperately. Sometimes she almost felt he was trying to suck the life out of her. His arms were tight round her and they tumbled back, lying there wrapped round each other.

'Don't ever leave me, will you?' He stared deep into her. He had 'drink eyes' already, glazed, too intense.

'Not if I can help it,' she said. But she felt helpless suddenly, and frightened. Whatever he needed from her it felt too much. She loved him so much that it was an ache inside her, but now, when he was like this, she just wanted to get up and run away from him.

They slept for a time, in each other's arms. When Linda woke and stiffly sat up, the sun had sunk to orange, a last half-circle of it disappearing as if into the fields in the far distance. The sky was turning a mauvish blue. Alan was still asleep. She picked up the bottle, holding it up in the dim light. He had drunk a good half of it and she could tell by his breathing that he was very deeply asleep. He looked as if he might stay that way for hours. She looked at his sleeping face, feeling like a mother looking down at a baby. Even Mrs Bray had asked her to look after him.

Then she panicked. What time was it? She was really going to get it from Mom if she wasn't back on time tonight! Alan had a watch and she leaned over him to look at it. A quarter past eight. They'd better get going.

'Al – Al!' She tugged at him, shook him, wondering in panic for a moment if he was actually unconscious and she wouldn't be able to rouse him. Eventually he opened his eyes and stared ahead as if he was blind, then up at the pale sky, not seeming able to focus. How were they going to get back with him in this state?

'Alan – come on. It's getting on for half past eight.'

His eyes rested on her and to her relief he seemed more alert.

'How long've I been asleep?' he asked, muzzily.

'I dunno – an hour? Maybe more. But we need to go.'

Alan sat up and reached for the bottle again.

'No!' She tried to snatch it but he pulled it out of her grasp. 'Don't have any more, for God's sake!'

'Need a drink.'

There was something lost about him, as if he had let

422

go and fallen from a great height and was now lying crushed with nothing else to lose.

He drank, then got up, staggering.

'Come on then.'

She didn't feel too well herself, especially once they were walking. Everything seemed distant and her head hurt, a hard ache in her left temple, and she was queasy. The thought of the ride ahead was dreadful. *I don't feel safe*, she thought hazily. But how else was she going to get home from the middle of nowhere?

He started off slowly. It was going to be all right, she decided, relaxing, her cheek pressed to his back. He was talking, but she couldn't hear him. He started to pick up speed, and she could feel he was flinging out words with a violence which vibrated right through him.

'What?' she yelled. 'I can't hear you!'

He didn't turn or say anything to her. Then she realized he was cursing and swearing, she could feel the force of the words, and knew he was in a world of his own and she might just as well not have been there. She was really frightened then.

'Al – slow down!'

Instead they were picking up more speed, the bike going full throttle so that it began to judder, the light of the lamp jerking in the dusk.

'Al – for God's sake – you'll kill us!'

She was tugging at him, her legs gripping so tightly to the saddle she felt as if the bones in her groins would crack.

'Al, please – you're scaring me!' She started sobbing, hitting at his back, but he didn't seem to hear whatever she did, and her cries cut out to a terrified gasp as the bike bumped into a hole in the road and he only just managed to keep it upright.

'Stop . . .!' She hated him suddenly for making her so afraid, just wanting to get off and be anywhere but on this hellish machine where she had no control and he didn't seem to care about her at all. But there was no getting off, as they swung along the curved road up a hill, the night air beating against them and hedges, trees, gateways flashing past in a blur. She closed her eyes and buried her face against his back, crying to deaf ears for him to stop.

She felt, rather than saw, the bike reach the brow of the hill, and with a lurch inside her she knew that on the downhill it would go even faster. There was a bump at the top which left her stomach hanging sickeningly somewhere in the air, and then she felt them pick up speed even more, rushing downwards, ever faster, terrifying.

At the point when Alan lost control of the bike, she felt it at once. All she saw, opening her eyes, was the blur of faint outlines and darkness, but she felt the bike veer and hit the verge and a cry come out of her mouth and then she was wrenched away from Alan, being flung through the air, her arms and legs heavy, out of their element, then falling until the hard ground slammed into her from below.

Chapter Seventy-Three

'You can see him now – just for a few minutes.'

The nurse led her along the ward to a bed where Alan was lying with his eyes closed.

'He's very drowsy,' she whispered. 'I doubt you'll get much out of him.'

It was a shock. They'd told Linda what his injuries were, but the right side of his face was so bruised and swollen she could barely recognize him. There was something under the bedclothes, holding the weight of them off his legs, and above the line of the sheet she could see bandages round his left shoulder, up into his neck.

'He's in a mess,' the nurse added disapprovingly. 'He's broken both legs, there are at least three cracked ribs and he's dislocated his shoulder. He's lucky it's not worse.'

Linda sat on the chair by the bed, nursing her left arm in its sling. She had got away with scratches and bruises and a broken wrist, on which she had landed after being flung high away from the bike as it crashed. Alan had evidently clung tightly to it and gone down with it, he and the bike cartwheeling over together, and Alan ending up with it on top of him.

The ward was full of evening bustle, but she was oblivious to it. Her arm ached inside the cast and her head was throbbing. She had to move about very cautiously. Of course, they'd drunk a lot last night. When she came to, lying on the lumpy surface of the field, it had been pitch dark. All she could hear were night sounds: an owl, a car in the far distance, and her own heart. She was sure she'd heard that, thumping like a drum. She could remember lying there in the dark, gradually feeling colder. Nothing hurt, not until later. She was numb. Her head was all foggy, and although she thought about getting up, she never could seem to make her limbs move to do it. Vaguely, as if it was a dream, she wondered where Alan was. After a time she fell asleep, half waking on and off through the night, cold, but sinking back into unconsciousness again.

All she knew next was that it was dawn, and misty and she was wet. When she opened her eyes, everything seemed white – the sky and air – except for the black trousers of the man standing over her, accompanied by the hot breath of a brown dog.

'Hello?' the man was saying. 'Miss – can you hear me?'

It seemed a queer question.

'Yes,' she said impatiently. 'Course I can.'

'You've had an accident – you and your friend. You look in better nick than he does.'

His car was parked by the road and he went and called an ambulance. All day she had been in Good Hope Hospital, getting patched up, sleeping. Her hands and face were scratched and she felt bruised all over. They said the police would tell her mother what had happened. And Alan's father. But of course, she remembered, Alan's father wasn't going to be back for two more days.

She was about to lean forward and speak to Alan,

but stopped herself. She wanted to let him sleep – he'd be more hung-over than her – but it was more than that. She wanted to look, to *see* him, while he was not looking back at her. Last night, on the bike, he had cancelled her out as if she wasn't even there. He hadn't cared about her fear. It had cut something off in her.

He looked fragile, that was her first thought. Such a skinny boy and so defenceless lying there. A wave of tenderness went through her, wanting to stroke his forehead, his dark hair, to comfort him, but she still held back. Mixed with her tenderness was a great sense of weariness. There were so many thoughts she had not allowed herself while she was with Alan. About him, and even more about herself. She had felt wanted, honoured, by the way he clung to her, needed her help, her love, to heal him. But all that had happened was him sinking, drinking more and more. She could never truly help, never be enough. Something caved in in her as she stared at him under the bald light of the ward. All his dreams were his escape from pain, but he would never finish a script for a film, never go and work in America. Would he ever be able to make something of his life, or just spiral down into the hurt of it, taking her with him? And hadn't she taken shelter in him, used him as a reason to limit herself? It had felt so right, so exciting to begin with. Now all she could feel was the hurt and hopelessness of it.

If you stay with him, it will always be the same. It was almost as if she heard a voice whisper it. *Save yourself.*

Tears welled in her eyes. It felt like a door opening on to light, from the darkness in which Alan lived. Only lately had she noticed how dark it really was. And though her guilt and sorrow were overwhelming, so was her sense of relief.

'Oh, Al, it's no good – I can't stay. I can't do this any more. I've got to get out.'

She spoke the words aloud, but he couldn't hear her.

Chapter Seventy-Four

'What's up, Lin?'

She heard Carol come limping into the room and felt her sit next to her on the edge of the bed. She lay on her bed, facing the wall, crying. She couldn't seem to stop crying.

'Mom says d'you want a cup of tea?'

Linda nodded. 'OK.'

She wiped her face and turned to sit up, wincing. Carol went to the door for a moment and called down to Violet.

'I'll bring it up,' Violet said.

That made Linda cry again. It was something to do with feeling looked after, and the way she knew that Mom would have been furious, the night before last, when she didn't come home, and then her shock when the policeman appeared and told her there'd been an accident. Mom had come up to the hospital. When she saw Linda with only the sling on her arm and no other damage, she put her arms round her and wept.

'I thought something much worse had happened. God, girl, don't ever do that to me again. That boy deserves a good hiding . . .'

She spent money on a taxi, of all things, to get them home. Linda had never been in a taxi before.

And since then, there had been such a feeling of gentleness in the house, of the preciousness of her being alive. When they were children, Linda realized, Mom had been so full of worries, looking after Dad and Carol, she hadn't had much left for anyone else. She'd had so little attention for them. It wouldn't go on like this, Linda knew, this special feeling, but it was something while it did.

That morning, when Linda woke, she'd also come on with her period. At the sight of the rusty blood she sat in the toilet and burst into tears. It was only then she realized how much she had been worrying, deep down, that she might be expecting a baby, even though the thought didn't seem real. Now there was a gripey but reassuring ache in her belly.

'Is your wrist hurting?' Carol asked.

'A bit. Aches.' Linda looked at the plaster cast. It still felt an alien thing on her. 'You've had much worse though.'

'I got used to it,' Carol said.

They sat in silence. Linda wiped her eyes. The window was open and a warm breeze blew at the flimsy curtain and they could hear some kids playing out at the front. They didn't need to talk. Carol just sat with her. She could always do that, sit with you, very still, just being there. She looked at Linda and smiled her dimply smile.

'Must be nice, not being in that chair any more,' Linda said.

Carol nodded. 'I can go down the park on my own.' She picked up the old rag doll on Linda's bed. 'Poor old Polly. She needs new eyes.'

They heard Violet coming up the stairs.

'Here you go. Brought you a couple of bits of toast.'

The toast smelt delicious, real butter melting across it. Linda's eyes filled with tears again. 'Ta.'

'You feeling bad?' Violet asked anxiously. 'D'you think you had a bad bang on the head?'

'No. I'm all right.'

'You'll want to go and see Alan, I s'pose?' Violet asked.

Linda didn't reply.

'You can't go back to work yet,' Violet said. 'We'll have to let her know.'

For two days Linda stayed around the house, happy to withdraw, just to be there with Carol and the dogs while Mom was at work. And she knew she ought to go and see Alan, but didn't feel well or strong enough. If she went back she might never be able to leave him. She tried not to think about him, lying there alone. One afternoon she took a couple of towels and lay out drowsily on the grass. For a time she stared at Snow-drop in her run, at her confined rabbit life, her quick breaths and staring red eyes.

'Don't you want to get out?' she said to her.

Snowdrop stared back impassively at her. She never bothered to try and escape now, not like when she was young.

During those days, Linda started thinking again about Rosina. All she had ever seen were those pictures she had sent out of her long silence, and that glimpse of her at Joyce's wedding, so nervous-looking, so afraid of facing them all, it seemed. When her mother came home that evening, she said, 'Are you ever going to go and see Auntie Rosina?'

Violet sat down wearily. Lighting a cigarette, she took a drag and blew smoke at the ceiling.

'Oh, I dunno. Sometimes I think I will, and then I think: well, she could've come to see us, couldn't she? Properly, like, instead of how she was at the wedding.

I mean Rosy and me, we got on all right, as kids, you know – rubbed along. But she's made it clear she didn't want us.'

She drew on the cigarette again and frowned. Linda noticed how lined her forehead had become.

'Rosy was never like that – not stuck up. I dunno what happened to her.'

'Was she being stuck up? I thought she looked scared.'

'Well, what's she got to be scared of?' Violet said impatiently. 'We're only her flaming family, aren't we?'

Linda could see her mother was not going to tackle this.

But there was something about Rosina that tugged at her, goaded her on. It was the unknown, the enigmatic glimpses of her, and something about a sense of kinship with her, that Linda felt instinctively. They looked alike, it was true, but it was something more than that. Something of her spirit.

By the time she went back to work – something else she had to change, she realized – she had decided that whether Mom wanted to or not, she had to go and find Rosina.

Chapter Seventy-Five

'Are you quite sure Bernice is coming?' Violet said anxiously as they sat on the bus. 'I'm not sure I want to go if they're not going to be there.'

'She'll come,' Carol assured her serenely. 'You know she said she wouldn't miss it for anything.'

Violet was chewing the side of her finger. 'Well, I hope so.'

She was dressed in her best frock – white with pink roses on – and white shoes. She was really pleased with the dress. It was the prettiest she had ever had and flattered her slim figure. And she had treated herself to the little white bag which lay in her lap. Rita was paying her generously, and was talking about them being partners in the business. *You've got flair, love*, she told Violet. *And it'd take the pressure off me.*

'The other people are nice too.' Carol looked up at her. Violet was always taken aback by her daughter's trust in others. It was a precious thing, she decided. And she was getting better with people herself now, coming out of herself, with having to talk to customers in the salon.

They were on their way – a two-bus journey to Edgbaston – to an August Bank Holiday garden fête held by the Infantile Paralysis Fellowship. They'd been to a couple of their other fundraising socials. Carol loved going, because she saw old friends and there was the immediate understanding that the polios shared, even though some were much worse affected than others.

It was a fine day, although you could already feel the wane of summer in the way the light fell. The leaves had lost the fresh, expectant look of spring. As they walked from the bus stop to the imposing Edgbaston house, Violet plucked nervously at the edges of her white cardigan and ran a hand over her hair. She looked approvingly at Carol in her yellow sundress and little pumps, her gold hair in waves down her back. *My girl,* she thought. *That's my little girl.*

For a moment they stood uncertainly outside the house, in the shade of a tree. Then Violet heard a voice call, 'Come for the fête, dear? Do come in!'

There was a side gate to the garden and a tall woman in a hat was waiting to show people in.

'Here we are – you're very welcome. Hello, dear!' she finished, cheerily, to Carol. '*Don't* you look pretty!'

The garden was a long oblong, surrounded by a wall along which were climbing roses and hollyhocks, and they could smell flowers as soon as they walked in. All across the grass were stalls, run by women in cheerful frocks, and children, some in wheelchairs, others on crutches or with calipers on their legs, others their siblings, running about whole-limbed and unimpeded. A woman hurried past carrying a big metal teapot, smiling anxiously. Violet would have liked to see the garden with no people in it. It would be a sleepy place, she decided, full of the sound of bees.

'Come on, Mom – let's look at the stalls!'

Carol had half a crown's spending money which was burning a hole in her pocket. Feeling shy and uncertain herself, Violet was glad of Carol's self-assurance and followed her as she limped fast across the grass, eagerly in search of the white elephant stall and tombola. She was on home territory here with other polios.

Amid the bric-a-brac of old vases, a chipped teapot and embroidered napkins, she found a little china dog with soulful black eyes.

'Oh, Mom – can I get it?' She was almost jumping with enthusiasm. 'I'll give it to Lin – it'll cheer her up!'

The woman running the stall was elderly, with grey hair in a bun, and she laughed at Carol's excitement.

'It's very nice, dear, isn't it? I think you could have that for tuppence. Does that sound fair?'

Carol nodded and handed over one of her sixpences. Looking up again she cried, 'Oh, look – there's Bernice!' and took off with the little dog in her hand.

Violet rolled her eyes and accepted the change for her.

'She's not one of the polios?' the woman asked, with gentle tactfulness.

'She is,' Violet said. 'See how she's limping – it left her with one shortened leg.'

'Goodness though – you'd hardly know, would you? She's been lucky.' Her face clouded. 'My little niece wasn't so lucky, unfortunately.'

'Oh dear . . .' Violet said.

'Died within a few days with it.' She shook her head. 'Terrible disease. A scourge.' Her face cleared. 'Go on – you get after her. She's lovely.'

Bernice was still in a wheelchair, awaiting more operations at St Gerard's. She and Carol were nattering away while Mrs Miller, her mother, a slim woman with long dark hair, stood watching with a smile.

'Hello, Violet – lovely to see you. And what a wonderfully pretty dress!'

Violet had been very intimidated by Bernice's mother when she first met her in the hospital. She was a rather well-spoken, confident lady and Violet felt silent and awkward beside her, as if she had nothing to say. But they had had their daughters in common, and the terrible, long-lasting worry of polio, and all that had dissolved some of the social lines between them.

'Hello, Rachel – how is she?'

'They say she's doing well. She's due to go back in in two months.'

Rachel Miller smiled, though her eyes wore a wistful expression. She had a wide mouth, her face sensuous, with high cheekbones. 'It would be so nice if it was all over. I'm sure I get in more of a state about it than she does.'

Bernice and Carol were giggling and the two women smiled at the sight.

'I know,' Violet said. 'Carol's so calm. Just sort of takes what comes. I wish I could.'

They talked for a little longer and Rachel said, 'Come and see us, will you? We're not so far from you. Bernice would be so pleased.' She took a little oblong of blue paper from her bag and wrote down her address. 'May I take yours? Just in case we're in the area?'

'Oh – you'd be welcome to come,' Violet said, feeling remiss. She wasn't used to visitors, except Eva from next door. She jotted down her address in Rachel Miller's diary.

'Mom – Mom, look!' Carol was hopping with excitement. 'It's Sister Cathleen!'

In the distance Violet caught sight of a thin figure in black. For a moment she thought Carol had got it wrong, then realized that the nurses only wore white in the hospital. Carol had already darted away, dodging round the tables.

'I'd better go and say hello,' Violet said. 'I'm never sure what to say to her though, really.'

Rachel rolled her eyes sympathetically. 'She's very kind though. Don't forget – you're welcome any time. We're nearly always at home and I'd love the company too.'

Violet peered through the crowd, trying to see Carol, past a lady dipping her hand into a deep basket full of cloakroom tickets for a tombola, and the Guess the Weight of the Cake stall. The garden was getting quite crowded now.

A woman with two maroon velvet coathangers in her hand passed, saying, 'Don't forget there's tea and cake for everyone on the terrace, will you?'

Violet was more than ready for a cup of tea. She hesitated. Carol would be all right of course. She was quite happy. She caught a glimpse of her in the distance, being embraced by Sister Cathleen, her face alight with happiness. With the pang that she always had when she saw how much Carol loved this woman, she turned away, annoyed with herself for being jealous. She should be glad, after all. She turned towards the house, where, on the paving slabs at the front, there were chairs, and tables laid with teacups. She'd go and have a quiet sit-down with a cup of tea.

All she caught sight of in that instant was a tall man, just beside her, half turned away and helping a boy in a wheelchair to spin the dial on a game at one of the tables. It was his hands she noticed. There was a stab of recognition, as if by her body more than her mind. One hand guided the boy's as he could barely reach up high enough. The sight of his long fingers rooted her to the spot.

After a second she dared to turn her head, tremblingly afraid of him looking round and seeing her before she could be sure who it was, and how she might react.

That look left her in no doubt. The thin, gentle set of his face, the dark eyes, looking down at his son, the long, thin back. It could be no one but Roy Keillor. In those seconds she told herself to breathe, to move, to do something other than just stand there before he turned round. But she kept wanting to look at his hands, remembering his touch, which filled her with the kind of longing she had not felt in a long time.

'Excuse me – ' Someone wanted to come past and she was forced to step even closer to him.

'Sorry,' she said, and he looked round to acknowledge the remark, glancing at her, and away.

'Not to worry,' he said.

Deflated, she started to move past, and realized she was shaking. Tea, that was what was needed. But all she could think was that he hadn't recognized her, hadn't known her, instantly the way she knew him!

Before she reached the terrace, though, he caught her up, beside a flowerbed, full of bright blooms.

'Violet?'

He had hurried over without the wheelchair.

They looked at each other for a few seconds. He had spoken softly, his voice not giving anything away. Suddenly she was coldly calm. There seemed no other way to be. There was nothing to expect.

'Your son,' she said. 'You've left him.'

'He's having another game. The lady's helping him.'

There were more seconds of silence, full of the

impossibility of beginning. She thought of his face that day they'd said goodbye, before she even knew she was carrying his child. How could they begin on this here?

'How are you?' He moved his shoulders in a way which acknowledged the lameness of the question.

'All right, thanks. What about you? The family?' She was finding it hard to look him in the eyes. Back then, she had looked so deeply.

'Yes. All right. Well – except for Philip.' He nodded back in the direction of his son. 'They both caught it, the twins. John had it much worse – he died of it after a few days. And Philip – well, they're working on him.'

'Oh, how awful,' Violet said. She could really look at him then.

'Yes – what with that and us losing one before, well . . .' The sentence petered out, implying something, but she was not quite sure what.

'Are you still living in Aston?' he asked.

'No. We moved out to Kingstanding – years ago, you know, after the war.'

The conversation felt so awkward, it was excruciating. She longed to be alone with him properly, to let go and talk.

Roy frowned suddenly. 'Why are you here? One of your two didn't catch polio, did they?'

The next couple of seconds seemed to stretch endlessly, as if her heart had stopped. She longed with every fibre of her to tell him about Carol, but she was so frightened by it. Eleven years had gone by – why did she need to tell him now?

'It's my youngest.' Carefully, she looked into his face. 'She's just over there. She's eleven.'

'Oh.' He nodded, and she could see her words had not registered. He had not worked it out.

There was more silence, the moment growing so awkward that he was starting to say, 'Well – I'd better go and get Philip. Nice to see you, Violet. You look . . . well, you look very nice.'

And they said goodbye and he turned back towards his son.

Violet went and got a cup of tea and sank down on one of the chairs by the wall, praying that no one would come and talk to her. She needed time to recover. There was both relief and a devastating sense of let-down at the same time. What else could she have expected, after all? But seeing him brought back all the feelings of those years, the only time she had had such feelings, as if he was burned into her in a way no one else could be.

'Ah – here she is now!'

To her disquiet she heard Sister Cathleen's cheerful voice, and she and Carol came up, Carol radiant and holding her hand.

'Hello, Mrs Martin – how are you?'

Violet stood up, trying to keep a grip on her dainty cup and saucer.

'I'm all right,' she said. Why was it that this nun always made her feel so awkward?

Sister Cathleen's pale face beamed down at Carol. 'Isn't this one looking a picture? Marvellous, isn't it?'

Violet smiled. 'Yes – she's going along well.'

'I should say she is! Quite the little miracle. Well I hope we shan't be seeing you back at St Gerard's again – not for treatment, anyways. Though it's always a treat to see you Carol, if you want to come to St Paul's . . . You take every care of yourself now, dear.'

She embraced Carol once more and said her good-byes. Carol stared adoringly after her.

'D'you want a drink?' Violet asked, brusquely. 'There are cakes, as well.'

Carol settled beside her with some home-made lemon in a glass and an angel cake, its little wings stuck on with butter icing.

'Why don't you make these, Mom? They're nice.'

Violet laughed. 'I'm not much of a cook. Perhaps we'll give it a try?' She put her cup down. 'D'you want to stay much longer? We ought to be . . .'

The rest of the sentence was snatched from her when she saw Roy again, coming towards them, pushing his son in the wheelchair. There was no sign of his wife with him. He saw her notice him and there was no point pretending she hadn't. He came towards her. Philip, the remaining twin, must have been about fourteen, she realized, though he seemed small for his age. As well as his legs he had one arm badly affected by polio.

'Hello again,' Roy said, and was obviously going to keep walking past. But then she saw him notice Carol. Everyone noticed Carol because she was so pretty, but this was different. She saw him stop and look, and Carol looked back in her usual open, inquiring way. Violet saw him take in her deep brown eyes, his eyes, looking back at him, and she saw the realization breaking over his face.

Part Six

1954

Chapter Seventy-Six

September

'All change please, all change!'

Linda walked along the platform at Euston Station. A lady in her carriage had taken her under her wing and explained about the Underground and what to do after that, very carefully, as if she was speaking to a class of six-year-olds.

But it wasn't just finding her way that she was nervous about.

She hadn't exactly planned to come today. She'd been secretly saving up the money for her ticket. This Saturday she knew Carol was out at a friend's house for the day and Mom was working, then going to Aston to see Nana. Bessie still wasn't right after her funny turn. The day was fine, and the only thing to do, it seemed, was dress in a skirt and blouse – she wanted to look not too scruffy and she didn't have anything very smart to wear – and go get on a train to London. She had to dare herself. It felt as if she was going to the other side of the world.

She had been determined to post the letter on the way. She stood by a postbox in town for minutes, after getting off the Kingstanding bus, trying to make herself push it through the slot. But the letter, with its Handsworth Wood address, was still in her bag. How could she just tell Alan that she couldn't see him any more? It seemed very brutal, especially when he was so injured.

She had not even been to see him because she was afraid that if she did, at the sight of him she would cave in and be dragged back into his strange, sad world and never escape again. And she knew now that she had to escape from that. But she felt terribly guilty.

'Dear Alan,' she had written last night, sitting up in bed, once Carol was asleep. At least it was her left arm in plaster, or she wouldn't have been able to write at all. She stared at the cast along her forearm for a moment. *He could have killed me . . .*

'I'm sorry for not coming to the hospital.' After that she sat for an age. How could she explain? *I don't think I can be with you – you make me feel sad and stuck and you're not good for me. With you I can see no real future.* How to say that to him? There wasn't a kind way to tell the truth. All she could say was, 'I don't think we can see each other any more. I'm very sorry. With best wishes from Linda.'

That was the note she put in the envelope. And she despised herself for it and that was why she couldn't bring herself to hand it over to the letterbox, to be free of this constant ache of dread and sadness because something had to be finished but it hurt too much to do it. As a result, the ache was still there, mixed with her nervousness at being alone in London, and looking for Rosina.

To Violet's surprise she had offered to go and call in on her grandmother in the week, to see how she was.

'This is a surprise,' Bessie greeted her, voice heavy with sarcasm. 'Bit like royalty showing up, ain't it, Marigold? What're *you* after?'

Marigold was knitting. She looked up at Linda in silence, but her treacly eyes held a twinkle and Linda sensed she was pleased to see her. She had a cup of tea with them – Marigold's with a drop of extra which she sneaked in behind Bessie's back – and put up with Nana's jibes about her clothes, her job, about anything at all that she could think to criticize. In the meantime she also managed to slip Rosina's letter out from behind the jug and into the scullery for long enough to memorize her address. She noticed that her grandmother really did look ill: puffy round the face, beads of sweat on her forehead and somehow simply changed, as if something had given way inside her. Not that it had sweetened her up in the process, Linda thought sourly as she left the house. It'd take more than a funny turn to do that. But she'd put up with it long enough to get what she needed. The address! She said it over and over in her mind and wrote it down as soon as she got home: Rosina Croft, 3a Brewer Street, London W1.

The lady on the train had frowned at the sight of the address. 'Are you sure that's where you want to go, dear?' She had an A-Z map book and, on a piece of writing paper, drew her a plan of how to get to Rosina's address from the Tube. On the Underground train Linda stared at the little map, hardly able to believe that soon the lines on the powder-blue paper would turn into real streets and she would be walking along them, moving closer to Rosina.

Until now she had two pictures of Rosina to hold on to. One was the pretty young woman in her stage costume whose face stared brazenly out of the picture she had sent to the family; the other was that glimpse of her peach-satin-clad figure retreating from the church at Joyce's wedding. These two images conveyed glamour, daring and mystery. The streets Linda found herself walking in search of her spelled something more ambiguous.

The country's on its knees . . . Uncle Clarence's whining words came back to her. Of course she was used to it in Brum, all the bombsites, mess and grime, all those years of Stafford Cripps, austerity and rationing, only just ending. And then came the building sites, the sense of old things giving way to new, but in the end always seeming workaday, functional, not glamorous at all. She had thought London would be different, even though they had the worst Blitz of all, that it would be cleaned up, smart and exciting. But she found herself in gloomy, seedy streets between run-down buildings strewn with rubbish and poky-looking cafés and bars. There was a life in it, it was true, people coming and going, neon signs outside clubs and theatres, and most passers-by in the street seemed to be speaking a whole array of languages she couldn't understand. She felt suddenly very young and overawed and out of place.

She stopped on a street corner and looked at the teacher lady's map to get her bearings. One more street and then she had to turn right . . .

'You working?' It was a gruff whisper in her ear and she jumped.

Behind her was a stringy-looking man in a singlet. He was not very old but his skin was deeply tanned, his face leathery and lined as if from screwing his face up against the sun and his chin covered in stubble. He stared at her suggestively.

'What?' Her heart was beating fast in shock at his sudden appearance.

'I said, are you *working*, love?' There was an edge of threat in his voice.

'No.' She shook her head vigorously.

'Fair enough,' he snapped, and walked off. She saw he had a limp. Linda looked round, hoping no one else had been close enough to hear. She didn't know for sure what he meant but she could guess. She felt dirty. Could he see she wasn't a virgin? Could people tell, somehow?

She scurried on and round the corner. Thank goodness she was nearly there!

Chapter Seventy-Seven

Standing outside number 3, from where Rosina had written her only letter in years to Bessie, Linda felt more and more nervous and foolish.

The house had a tall, forbidding frontage of red bricks darkened by soot. Linda was torn between her longing to get off the streets and fear that Rosina might not be there or would laugh in her face and turn her away. What if she told her to get lost? She'd have to go straight back to the station and go home.

There were four buttons. Two had names beside them, but the space next to number three was blank. She rang it anyway.

There was a long silence. She thought about ringing again, but then came faint sounds from inside of someone in heels clacking downstairs. After a moment she saw a movement through the clear spaces in the glass, and caught her breath. The door opened just wide enough for a woman to look out. She had dyed blonde hair, darker at the roots and scraped back into a pony-tail, and her eyelids were laden with blue tints and mascara. She was obviously poised to slam the door shut again.

'Yes? Who're you?'

'I'm ...' Linda lost courage. 'I thought I'd got the right house but ... I'm looking for my auntie. Her name's Rosina.'

'Oh?' The woman looked taken aback, though some of her hostility faded away. She opened the door wider, letting out a strong, musty smell. Linda saw that she was dressed in a bright blue frock which barely reached down below her knees and high-heeled white shoes. She stared at Linda again for a moment, but in a different way from before, as if she had to calculate what to say.

'Does she live here?'

'She's not here – not at present,' the woman said. 'I mean, well, Rosy does live here. This is where ... I mean ...' She seemed oddly confused. 'Only she's not here at the moment, see. She's ...'

'I've come all the way from Birmingham to see her,' Linda said, desperately. 'I saved up for the ticket and everything and if I don't see her I don't know when I'd be able to come again.'

The woman was still staring at her in that odd way. Then she said abruptly, 'Look – hang on a tick.' She disappeared into the house and came back a moment later with keys, closing the door behind her. On the doorstep she pulled out a powder compact from her bag and used the mirror to apply deep red lip-stick.

'Can't go out without my face on, can I?' Rubbing her lips together, she clipped the compact shut. 'Come on, love. I'll take you.' She beckoned to Linda to follow her along the street. 'It's not far. Only, you're very young, see, only a nipper, aren't you? I know Rosy doesn't have much to do with her family. Not surprising really.' Casually she added, 'I don't know if you know anything about her?'

'Well, no.' Linda felt more and more bemused and nervous, although the woman was behaving in a more friendly way now and she could see she was quite nice really. 'She's my mom's sister, that's all.'

'Well, you're in for a shock, love, I'd better tell you that now.' The woman laughed. 'I can hear you're from the same neck of the woods anyhow. Rosy still speaks like a Brummy even after all these years! My name's Irene, by the way. Reeny, I go by, though. Tried to get 'em to call me Irene – sounds better, don't you think? But I'm Reeny whether I like it or not – it's stuck to me. What's yours?'

'Linda.'

'That short for *Be*-linda?'

'No.'

'Oh – just wondered. S'pretty, anyhow.'

Linda had barely noticed where they were going, she was listening so intently to Irene, who took nervous little drags on her cigarette as she minced along on her heels.

'Now – Rosy's place is where we've just been. Her flat, I mean. She's got it nice up there – you can't tell from outside. But she don't get home till midday usually. I live with her, see, look after Vivianne and Clarkie – least when they're home from school. Almost like my own, those two. Not that she doesn't pay me well – she's a good 'un, Rosy is. We've been through some times, me and her – always stick together, see?'

Linda didn't see – not at all.

'Working the way she does, she has to be a bit careful – who she lets on to and that. Bit of a double life, but she manages. Ever such nice schools she's got those kids in. Clarkie's away boarding now. A real gentleman he's going to turn out. But all I'm saying is, she might be a bit put out to see you, just at first. You'll have to promise not to let on – to look out for her – OK? Then she'll be all right.'

Linda nodded, feeling even more worried.

'Whose wedding was it she went up for?' Irene asked curiously. 'Not yours, was it – you look too young?'

'My sister, Joyce.'

'Oh yeah, Joyce. Poor old Rosy – she got cold feet. Wanted to be there but she said she couldn't face it all in the end.'

After a time they turned left, and there was another line of very tall red-brick houses, rather wider than the ones in the last street.

'We're down the end here,' Irene said. 'Rosy's Palace, they call it – dirty old sods.' She gave a throaty chuckle. At the far end of the street, the last house, though not the smartest, still had an imposing air about it. All the windows were shrouded with curtains and blinds.

'Come on – round the back,' Irene said. She was clearly at home in the place.

Up some steps at the back, she rang the bell beside a black door, and after a pause it was opened by another young woman, also with long blonde hair.

'All right, Pol? Rosy up and about?' There was a noise from inside, voices on a radio. Then Irene lowered her voice and looking warily upwards, hissed, 'Is *he* about?'

'Nah. Not yet, thank Christ. But he'll soon come swanning down, no doubt. Rosy's in the kitchen doing him some breakfast. Who's this then?'

'Her niece. Name's Linda.'

'Oh,' the woman said, blankly. 'Well – I s'pose that's all right.'

Linda didn't understand the next part of the conversation.

'Is Rosy . . . down?'

Polly eyed Linda, and nodded. 'Yeah. Well – pretty much.'

Suddenly, Irene reached round and took Linda's hand, in such a naturally motherly way that Linda was touched.

'Right, love – come on.'

They went along a tiled passage that smelt of cigarettes mixed with a sweet, cloying smell, and frying bacon. Linda suddenly realized she was ravenously hungry. She'd had a bit of toast before she set out, which now felt like several days before. Irene took her into the kitchen. It was almost all too quick then, as if Linda was suddenly unprepared for the sight of a woman standing at the stove with her back to them, in a long, peach-coloured robe, a woman who was both shorter and more fleshed out than she expected. Her dark hair was lifted into a bunch and she was smoking and jiggling the handle of a frying pan with the other hand.

'Rosy!'

The first impression of her aunt's face, the brown eyes, strong eyebrows, still pretty, mischievous features was unmistakable, yet she was plumper in the face and older and she had a worn look, dark smudges under her eyes. She took the cigarette out of her mouth and frowned, though more with puzzlement than annoyance.

'Who's this, Reeny – brought me a new recruit?'

Irene laughed. '*No!* Chrissakes, Rosy – this girl's come to see you all the way from Birmingham. Says you're her auntie. I couldn't turn her away, could I?'

She really did have Rosina's attention then.

'Here –' she jerked her head towards the pan of bacon. 'Finish this off for his nibs will you? He wants a couple of eggs thrown in as well.'

She stubbed out her cigarette on a saucer then came over, slowly, and Linda could feel she was being sized up.

'My God,' she said. 'Now – which one are you? You one of Charlie's?'

What a long time Rosina had been gone, Linda realized. She wasn't even sure who was who in her own family! Close up, her presence had a strong impact, fleshly, feminine, and perfumed.

'No – I'm Linda – I'm Violet's second girl. Joyce's sister.'

'Course you are!' Rosina put a hand over her mouth and to Linda's astonishment, she saw her aunt's eyes fill with tears. 'Oh – Reeny, get me a hanky, will you? I feel all ... Oh blimey, look at me!' And the tears ran down her face. She came close and leaned to kiss Linda's cheek, wetting it with her tears. 'Aren't you pretty, darlin'? How old're you then?'

'Sixteen,' Linda said. She suddenly felt like crying herself.

'She's the image of you, Rosy – I could see that straight away,' Irene said, flipping the bacon over, then going in search of a hanky and handing Rosina a square of checked cotton.

Rosina wiped her eyes and seemed at a loss for a moment. Someone else came in and asked her something about towels and she replied as if she had barely heard the question.

'Did you come all the way down today?'

Linda nodded.

'What – just to look for me?'

'Yes.' She felt foolish.

'Why? I mean ...' She laughed suddenly, good-naturedly. 'Well, you're a one, aren't you? You might not've found me! Little thing like you let loose in the big city.'

'Bit like you then, Rosy,' Irene reminded her. She

tipped the bacon unceremoniously on to a plate. 'Does *he* want fried bread an' all?'

'Yes – anything . . .' Rosina seemed to gather her thoughts finally. Almost formally, she said, 'Look, Reeny – I want to spend some time with my niece. Get Barbs to hold the fort, will you? She'll have to clear it with him. But this is family and it doesn't happen every day. All right, Linda? Give me a few minutes to get my glad rags on.'

Chapter Seventy-Eight

Linda sat in the kitchen sipping a strong cup of tea.

'Rosy won't be long, lovey,' Irene said, sinking down on to a stool with her cup. The plateful of food for 'him' had been despatched upstairs. Linda wanted to ask who 'he' was, but didn't dare. She was glad of the tea, and realized she had been almost faint from hunger.

Irene kicked off her shoes and rubbed her left foot. 'Bloody kill me, they do. Look nice though, don't they?'

She chatted about Rosina's children. Linda still had the picture in her mind of the two young faces in the picture tucked behind the jug on Bessie's mantel, but of course Clark was barely a couple of years younger than herself and Vivianne was twelve.

'Little beauty she's turning out to be,' Irene said. 'Course, she's a handful at times. Stormy, that's our Vivianne. Little madam. But clever – all she's learning at that school, sewing and that. Beautiful at it, she is. Rosy's got them at good schools out in the country. She couldn't have them round here – not with the business. Shame you won't meet them. Clarkie's a darlin' – soft as butter and always has been. He's a clever one and all. She's got high hopes for her kids, Rosy has.'

Linda felt intimidated by the thought of Rosina's children and their posh schools. How did Rosina afford it? she wondered. She had no clear idea of what Rosina did or of her life. She just felt overwhelmed and confused, sitting in this stark, high-ceilinged kitchen.

Sooner than she expected, Rosina appeared, clad in an apricot-coloured frock and with her hair brushed and smoothed back into a stylish knot. Her heart-shaped face was made up, lipstick and powder, and she looked very pretty.

'Here she is – quick-change artist.'

'Is he taken care of?' she asked anxiously, rolling her eyes to the ceiling.

'I'll ask Pol to tell him where you are. You go on out, girl, and sod him.'

Rosina smiled faintly. 'Ready Linda?'

'I'll get back now then, Rosy.' Irene pushed her feet, wincing, back into the shoes. 'You two have a nice time!'

'Bet you've never been to town before, have you?' Rosina said as they stepped back out into the street.

'No,' Linda agreed. She had a floaty, unreal feeling now, as if this was all a dream.

'You all right, bab? You look a bit peaky. I s'pect you could do with a square meal inside you. Come on – I'll treat you.'

She felt safer now, walking out there with Rosina, who knew the way. And she had liked her as soon as they met. They went back to the main street and Rosina stopped her, amid all the traffic and the great looming buildings and lights.

'This is Piccadilly Circus,' she said.

'Down there's the Houses of Parliament – and Nelson's Column. Anyway –' She took Linda's arm and looped her own through it. 'We'll go and see my friend Mario.'

They took another turn, along a narrow street half

458

blocked by stalls selling fruit and veg and a churning collection of people of different colours. It was all very lively and noisy. They squeezed their way through and reached a place with a big white sign saying, 'Soho Café Restaurant – Food Served All Day'. Inside was a long room lined with bronzy tiles and yellow Formica-topped tables arranged all along one wall, opposite the serving counter. Most of the tables were full, a cacophony of voices speaking various languages rising above the red lightshades on the tables, faces reflected in the mirrors all along the walls. Amid all the noise, a radio was playing as well. The man behind the counter, black-haired, with mischievous brown eyes, greeted Rosy immediately. 'How're you this fine day – eh, Miss Rosy?'

'Not so bad.' Rosina spoke quietly, as if not wanting to attract anyone's attention, but she smiled fondly at the man. 'This is Linda – my niece. She's come down to see me, all the way from Birmingham, and she needs the biggest meal you can make her – OK?'

'Birmingham, eh?' Mario gave a little bow. 'That's a long walk! What you want – eggs, bacon, chips?'

Linda nodded avidly. 'Ooh yes!'

'Coming up – what you want, Rosy?'

'Tell you what – I'll have the same. Celebrate! I'm all in, I tell you.'

'Sit – sit . . .' He waved towards the tables.

'We'll go down the end.' Rosina led her to the furthest table, down in the corner. 'Have a bit of peace,' she said, and indicated to Linda to take the seat facing back up the café. 'You can't hear yourself think in here sometimes.'

Linda liked the place. She'd hardly ever eaten out in a café or restaurant anywhere and this one felt exciting, with its swivelling chairs and colourful décor. In the middle was a coat-stand, a trilby hat stuck on one of the arms, tilted at an angle. As they sat down the tune on the radio reminded her, with a pang, of Alan.

'Sometimes they have a skiffle band in here,' Rosina said, lighting a cigarette. 'You know, with the washboards and that. I s'pect they'll roll in later.'

She sat back and looked very directly at Linda, turning the little tin ashtray round and round on the table. Linda blushed at this frank appraisal.

'You look like your dad,' Rosina observed. 'How is he? Looked very bad at the wedding.'

'He died – last year,' Linda said.

Rosina's face changed. 'Oh God – poor thing. Poor old Vi.'

There was a pause.

'How is she?'

'All right.'

'Good. Really all right, you mean?'

'I think so. She works in a hairdresser's, with Rita – she's the owner. Mom likes it. She's good at it.'

She hadn't realized that until she said it, but she saw that it was true.

Rosina laughed. 'Good old Vi. Time she had a life of her own. She was like a bleeding shadow at home with our mom. Hardly dared to breathe. None of us did.' Her tone was very bitter. She took a drag on her cigarette and looked at Linda sharply, weighing her up. For a moment Linda saw a steely hardness in her aunt's eyes.

'How's Marigold, poor cow?'

Linda shrugged. 'All right. The same. She's got a boyfriend, and Nana doesn't like it.'

Rosina burst out laughing, a chesty, smoker's laugh.

'I bet she doesn't! Christ alive – good old Mari. She must be gone forty now, ain't she? And what about Charlie? he still with that harridan Gladys?'

'Yes.' Linda couldn't think of much to say about him. 'He's all right. Norm's getting married in a while.'

'Little Norm! He was just a babby when I left.' She sighed, flicking the cigarette at the ashtray. 'Fancy that.'

She asked about Joyce and Carol, and Linda told her about Joyce and Danny's baby and Carol's polio and her operations and Rosina listened, looking alternately pleased and interested and wistful.

'Poor old Vi – she's had a plateful, she really has.' Then more quietly, as if broaching something difficult, 'And how's . . . Bess?'

'Nana? Poorly. She had a bit of a turn, a while back.'

Rosina digested this. Quietly, she said, 'And is she still the same?'

Their eyes met. 'Yes,' Linda said bitterly. 'She is.'

Without either of them having to say more, there was understanding. Linda didn't know why Rosina had run away all those years ago, nor anything much of her life now, but she sensed that they were in some way the same, that there was something they both needed. It was an exciting feeling. It gave her butterflies in her stomach.

They became aware of a thin man approaching the table. Rosina seemed to recognize him. Before she could stop him he unwrapped a piece of cloth he had taken from his pocket and showed something to Rosy. Linda couldn't see what it was but she could see the panic on Rosina's face.

'No,' she said sharply. 'Not now. Get lost, Pete.'

Suddenly her aunt was strange to her again. What

was going on? But the moment was interrupted by Mario swooping towards them with two plates of food.

'Here we are, ladies! Here you – clear off and leave these ladies alone!'

The thin man melted away. When Linda turned, she couldn't see him anywhere.

'Rosy . . .' Mario tutted at her. 'You gotta look after yourself better.' No more was said, but Linda saw, in the looks they gave each other, his affection and reproachful care for her.

'Thanks, Mario. That'll keep us going all right!'

He had cooked them a feast: rashers of bacon, two fried eggs each with perfect, gleaming yolks, sausage, fried bread and chips piled along the side. From under his arm, magician-like, he produced a bottle of ketchup. 'You want tea?'

'Yes – oh ta, Mario.' Rosina laughed. 'He's good to me, he is.' She smiled at Linda.

'You ladies got to keep your strength up!' He stepped back with a flourish. '*Buon appetito!* Tea coming up!'

'He's golden,' Rosina said as he strode off again. 'He's been like a brother to me – no funny business, nothing like that. Got a wife and four kiddies and he's good as gold. I'd trust him with my life, and there's not many you can say that about round here. Eh – tuck in, girl!'

Mario soon produced large mugs of tea, and as Linda ate, ravenously, she started to feel better. More colour came into Rosina's cheeks as well, and after a short time they ate more slowly, talking between mouthfuls. Rosina did nearly all the talking.

'Do they . . . I mean, back home . . . Do they ever say anything about me?'

'Mom wanted you to stay – after the wedding. They wanted to know why you ran away again.'

'I lost my bottle that day. Lost it bad.' She hesitated, kept looking at Linda as if unsure how much to say.

'Do they know you're here today? Did your mom send you?'

'No. I just came.'

'Where d'you get the fare?'

'I'm at work. It's my money.'

'You're at work! Blimey, yes, I s'pose you are! So you just took it into your head . . .?'

Linda looked up at her and nodded. There was another moment of unspoken understanding.

Rosina leaned forward, elbows on the table, lighting another cigarette. 'You want to know about me – is that it?'

Linda nodded slowly.

'Will you tell them?'

'Dunno. Not if you don't want.'

Rosina laughed suddenly. 'You've got a mind of your own all right, haven't you?' She sat back again, blowing smoke away at the ceiling. 'All right. I'll tell you. I've never told anyone – not the full thing. 'Cept Irene of course – she knows most of it. But you – ' she jabbed the cigarette in Linda's direction. 'You're a bit like me. Dunno how I know. I can just feel it. There's some in our family can't see over the wall and all they ever do's sit on their hands. That's Charlie, for a start, and Vi. God knows with Marigold. Probably she'd've been different, given the chance. And there's those of us who get up higher and can see over and we want something of what's over there. That's me – and that's you, Linda, isn't it?'

Goose-pimples came up all over Linda's skin. She

was filled with emotion suddenly, as if she wanted to cry. Someone could see her, see what she was like! But all she could do was nod again.

'Well, who I am's nothing to be proud of, believe you me. But you pays your money and takes your choice and this is me. OK?'

Chapter Seventy-Nine

'I s'pose you want to know why I left? I dunno – look at you. You're only a kid yourself. I shouldn't be telling you all this – but you want me to, don't you? Seems a whole lifetime ago now. I don't even remember you being born. '38? Yes, I was long gone by then. I remember Joycie arriving. Vi'd had all her problems with babies. I s'pose that's why I wanted to come for the wedding. And 'cause Vi'd written to me. She never has otherwise. S'pose she's had too much else going on.

'They probably told you I went off with an actor. Michael Albie was his name. I met him in my days hanging round the photographers and the stage doors at the Hip and the Alex. I was mad about Michael. Never felt the same way about anyone after him . . . All right, Mario? Yes, another cuppa'd be lovely. We'll be here for a bit yet, ta, love.

'See, I left Brum with Michael because I wanted more – I wanted life and the stage and I was in love with him. And I couldn't stand any more of our mom. There was no room for anyone in that house except for her and what she wanted. Sometimes you could hardly bloody breathe, and all them babbies and that carry-on. Always had to be queen bee, Mom did, never mind who she walked all over. I mean what she did to poor old Marigold. That was an evil, wicked thing she did. Don't s'pose you know all about that, though? No, I thought not. You'd've been too young . . . But you're just the age now that she was. See, this'll shock you, but Marigold had a child herself. A little boy. He was born at home – I'll never forget that night. It frightened me at the time, hearing it. But I can see him now. Beautiful, he was. But our mom upped and took him straight to some orphanage. Never would say where. She might as well have thrown him out with the rubbish, the attitude she had. Not a by your leave to Mari – she never had a say in anything. Christ, Linda, I can feel myself boiling inside even now, thinking about it. God knows who the father was – she was a poor old thing, Mari. But she loved that babby – you could see.

'Thing was, when I left Brum I was carrying Michael's child . . . oh, I'm going to get all weepy now . . . I mean I wanted to go anyway, but if our mom had known . . . I'd never have had a say either. And I loved Michael, wanted nothing else but to be with him. I'd only just found out and his stint at the Alex was ending and he was coming back to London. He wasn't poor, Michael wasn't. He was much older than me – gone thirty already and he had money from his family, not like a lot of the stage crowd, all living on a shoestring. He had a little flat – not so very far from here in fact. Anyway, when we got down here he started on me. If I wanted to be in the theatre it was no good thinking about carrying on with the child. He didn't want it, of course. Most of 'em don't – that's what I've found. They're not like us, Linda, men, that's one thing for sure.

'I gave in in the end. Course, I was frightened. I was only seventeen when we left, turned eighteen in the December. Michael took me to this woman . . . It makes me go cold now . . . Thing about it was how ordinary it

466

all was. It was her flat, up some dark stairs, and her kitchen, a washing-up bowl and that. On her kitchen table in this flat. I s'pose that's where her kids ate their tea. She had a great big bottle of antiseptic stuff. It hurt, Linda. Hurt so much I fainted . . . Phoo – makes me go all hot and cold to think of it. Michael had to get a cab to take me home and I wasn't right for weeks after. When I got better he started on me to look for work and I wanted to, of course, although I'd lost a lot of weight and was a bit too skinny. But he helped and I got a couple of parts – stand-ins in chorus lines. I can sing, see, as well. I've got a half nice voice, even now. And then he left me. Locked me out of the flat one night and he was going off to work up north some-where. Never said where. I was left with only what I had to stand up in. We'd only been together six months, altogether. That night, I slept in Hyde Park. Sounds bad, doesn't it? At the time all I could think about was Michael. Broke my heart, he did. I didn't care about sleeping on a bench in the park, only that he'd left me and I couldn't understand why.

'I was quite presentable still and I managed to get a job the next day. That was a miracle then. Jobs were hard to find and I didn't have a reference, but it was this woman, see, Mavis her name was, ran an eating joint off the Tottenham Court Road. I dunno if I reminded her of her daughter, or what, but I was bloody lucky is all I can say. She said I was pretty and that was good in a waitress as long as I could do the work. She worked me hard and tried to patch up my heart. Course, any time I could I was round the theatres, trying to get something else. I did get one little speaking part. That was the picture I sent you. I think my face's always been my fortune because I knew next to nothing. They said I had the right look and it was a play called *The Garnet Ring*. I had two appearances in it. I don't think it was much of a play but I can still remember the lines now! The first time I went on I had to say, "Mr Fellows, I do wish you could arrange to conduct your private business elsewhere . . ." Well, you can imagine what that was all about – yes, it was funny. And then later I had to say, "It's no good, I'm going to hand in my notice. Never have I had the misfortune to put up with conditions like these before!"

'Anyway, things went on like this for quite a while – can't say exactly how long. I had a few fellers come and go of course. Nothing serious. I was still in a mess after Michael. And then I met Johnny – just before the war. Hot and lovely it was, that summer. Johnny was an actor and he was no better off than me. Both of us had our rooms in seedy lodgings. But he was so handsome, Johnny was. Dark and *sleek* somehow, with thick wavy hair and sort of little boy looks. His eyes were blue as anything. China blue. He bowled me over. He was going to get somewhere with acting, I thought. With looks like that how could he not? He was quite young, see, not like Michael. He was only a couple of years older than me. I didn't want him to know how things had been. That I'd begun . . . a child, and that. I was very careful, held off from anything much in the love department. Very prim and proper I was – you should've seen me!

'Course, soon as the war broke out there was trouble – they closed the theatres and that, for a bit. But there were shows put on – Johnny got me into a few things. Bloody frightening it all was then – all those gas warnings, air raid sirens . . . I hated them public shelters. Stank to high heaven and you never knew who you were going to be with. Anyway – the thing was, I couldn't last out with Johnny. The Virgin Mary bit, I mean. By the time the Luftwaffe were hammering the guts out of us every night I was expecting again. Couldn't believe it – I mean I thought we'd been careful, you know, taken precautions. I'm one of them only has to look at a man, I reckon . . . Sorry, bab, keep forgetting your age. You seem older, you know, Linda. Well, you've guessed it – first hint of a babby on the way and Johnny was off. I mean I didn't tell him straight away, not after Michael. I thought, bide your time, Rosy, see how the land lies. I tried to get out of him whether he wanted to marry me. But you can't hide a babby for ever and I wasn't *doing away* with it . . . Sorry, I have to whisper that. I wasn't doing that again. It does summat to you, however much you don't want to keep the baby.

'Any road, Johnny guessed, in the end, saw my little belly swelling. "So now you know," I said. "And what're we going to do about it?"

'"I dunno," he said. "It's not me that's having a baby, is it?" Just like that. Couldn't care less. So I knew he'd be off and I took off first. Found a new room. He'd have come back for his bit of fun otherwise and I wasn't having that. I don't know what you must think of me – you're keeping very quiet. But it gets worse, Linda. I told you, if you've come to find someone to model your life on, you're barking up the wrong tree with your auntie Rosy.

'Any road – the best thing happened then. I'd finished working at Mavis's place a while back and I was in another joint in Soho. Course it was a bit different here then – not so many coloureds for a start – and the war was on. That's where I met Reeny. Irene Bartlett.

Best thing that ever happened to me – apart from my kids. Irene's bloke had joined up, gone in the army, and that was the best thing ever happened to her, an' all. Proper toe-rag he was. Joined up almost before Neville Chamberlain had finished telling us there was a war on, and good riddance, she said. He came back at the end, you know – but not to her. Had some bit of stuff somewhere. Reeny had her boy, Kevin. He was six then, and she had her mum up the road. We always hit it off, Reeny and me, and she was golden to me. Like a sister – always had been. "Don't you worry, Rosy," she used to say. "Us women'll stick together and sod 'em."

'And we did. Not half we did. She asked me to move in with her and Kev and we had some laughs. It was a godsend. But of course neither of us had any money. She was getting by doing a bit of waitressing while her mom was in with Kev. And I was all right till Clarkie arrived. Reeny was there with me, and her mom – one night when there was no bloody air raid for once! Had him easy, I did. I mean it hurts like hell, screamed my head off and that, but I mean it came natural to me. And Clarkie was big and healthy and – oh! Light of my life he is – and Vivianne. But that was later.

'Things got hard then, see, 'cause Reeny's mom took sick. It was so quick – she just wasted away in front of our eyes and by the time Clark was six months I carried him to her funeral. Poor Reeny. She always said, if she hadn't've had me she'd have gone off her head. Anyway, this is where things took a turn, as you might say. Reeny was working in the day, and I worked at night, doing what I knew best. See I'm blushing even now. When I'm here, the life I live – well, it's just how it is, day by day. I've got used to it, see? D'you understand what I'm saying, Linda? What it is I do to earn my

bread? Course, it's not *me* doing it any more. Never –
not now. I've got my girls and I treat them well. Come
and work at Rosy's and you're as safe as you're likely
to be – not on the streets, fair's fair ... You do know
what I'm talking about now, don't you? But I couldn't
come out to face you all, let you see what I was, not all
at once. I've got a nice little flat, kids at good schools –
that's all I want anyone to see, but it ain't the whole of
me, see?

'I'm getting out of order now. There was a lot more
road to walk before I got to this bit. Reeny and I kept
each other going. She had her little house, kids upstairs,
and I used the front room, nights, took the punters back
there. The daytimes were another world – all kids and
Reeny and me playing happy families and Kev at school.
Clean, and nice.

'And then I met Humphrey ... I'm running out of
fags. This is my last one – I'll have to nip out and get
some more ... Anyway, this bit I'm ashamed of. It's
different when it comes to friendship, see. I let Reeny
down. Let her down bad. She forgave me, but that
doesn't make it any better. Humphrey was this posh
geezer. Not like the others. I never took old Hump
back to Reeny's. Hump had money – *real* money. He
had a wife and couple of kids. He was some top-notch
city type – worked high up in a bank. Reserved occu-
pation and all that and plenty of lolly to splash about.
Only he had a taste for ... well, let's call it lower life
than what he was used to. Wanted his nose in the gutter
– it gave him a thrill. I met him when I was working the
corner and he came and started the chat-up bit. Ugly
sod he was really – one of them with a round face, looks
about twelve years old still, all chin and no cheekbones.

'"I can take you somewhere nicer than this," he said,

471

all posh. "How much for the evening?" Well, I thought I'd up the score so I said "Ten quid" – well, what I really said was, "That'll be ten pounds to you, sir," trying to speak posh for him.

'He took me back to his place – over in Kensington. Lovely little flat, top of one of them big houses on a square, all trees in the middle. It became a fixture – every Tuesday night, all night. God knows where wifey thought he was, I never asked, poor cow. Or perhaps she didn't care. Thing was, Hump was fond of me. Sort of fell for me, in his way. Dunno if that sort can fall in love, exactly. Public school, sent away when he was four and all that. Always looked as if his shirt-button was done up too tight at the top – even when he was starkers!

'I met him – when was it now – sometime in 1941. I know it was pretty cold the night he came up to me and he had a nice little electric fire in the flat. I'd never seen such a nice one. And he asked me to move in there. "I want to think of you here, even when I'm not here. You won't be given any trouble – I've an arrangement with the landlady."

'"I can't," I said to him. "I've got a boy, not a year old."

'"Well," he says, "I don't mind that – so long as he's not there when I'm there. Thing about me is, Rosy, I don't like competition. I like to have my woman all to myself."

'And to my shame I went. I mean you should have seen the place! Me living in Kensington, all posh! Me and Clarkie, except for the times Hump was there – and that wasn't all that many – and Reeny had him then. I thought I'd arrived. I'd left Reeny, pretty much – after all she'd done for me. Told her it was an investment for the future. Course I kept meaning to go back and see her more often, but it was a treat, living it up in Kensington. I felt like a lady and didn't want to think about what else I was. Not until I got lonely, anyway. Humphrey was hardly ever there and when he was, he wasn't much company, not really.

'We kept it up all through the summer. He kept saying, "I'll come and take you out for a day. We'll take a boat on the river." I liked the idea of that – even with him. I mean he wasn't that bad – quite easy to please really. Course he never did, though – take me out in a boat, I mean.

'Anyway, you've guessed – he was Vivianne's father. He got me up the duff. I told him, soon as I knew, and waited for him to run. I s'pose I just wanted to get it over with. That was men. I never expected anything of them – not by then. The soft bit of me that expected had all dried up with Michael. Everything hurts more when you're young. Course, he did run, but my God, Linda, he was all right, really, Hump was. He cried, you know, when I told him, went on about how he couldn't understand his children – they had two already – and he was a hopeless father and husband, unfaithful and no good to anyone and now he wasn't going to stay with me either. I mean I ended up feeling quite sorry for him, poor bloke. He seemed as if he was locked in a box and couldn't get out and I thought well, at least I'm not as bad as that.

'I went back to Reeny and asked her to forgive me. She was all right, she understood, she said. She'd've done the same. She wouldn't, though. She's more loyalty than that.

'Thing was, though . . . Old Hump waved me good-bye as if he'd never have another thing to do with me.

Oh well, posh bastard, I thought. That's how it goes, and you've had your fun, Rosy. Then one night I'm back at my post on the corner and back he comes, hat pulled down over his face.

'"I want you to know,"' he says, and he sounded quite tearful. Made me feel really sorry for him. 'That you've been a real light in my life, Rosy. You're all the things I'm not – courageous, strong, amusing. And I don't want you to remember me as a . . . as a complete cad . . ." was what he said, I think! "So I want you to have this."

'He gave me this envelope and kissed me on the cheek and off he went.

'Well, business wasn't looking good that night anyway and I went back to Reeny's and opened the envelope. And what d'you think was inside? There was a note, saying, *You'll need to set yourself up. This is for you and the child. With love from H.* He'd written me a cheque for *five grand*! Yes – well, I gasped even louder than that at the time! Reeny and me toasted him with champagne all that week, I can tell you.

'But I've got a good head for money, when I've got hold of any. I wasn't going to fritter it away. This was my main chance and I took it.

'First thing I did was buy us a house, number twenty, the one you've just seen. The flat didn't come till later. But Reeny and me and the kids had a bigger home and I ran my little business from downstairs. Vivianne was born in 1942 and that put me out of action for a bit, but Reeny was working – regular work, I mean, in a shop – and we managed. I bought the flat after the war. The kids were old enough then to notice what was going on around them and I wasn't having that. I can remember the day the war ended, everyone dancing and the tugs blowing their hooters along the river, V for victory! And dear old Winnie up there on the balcony with the Royals – we were there, Reeny and me. We took the kids. And as we stood there and everyone was drunk with happiness, I thought, I'm going to make a future for my kids. Whatever it takes, it doesn't matter about me, but they've got to have something better. Oh dear – where's my hanky? Soppy old thing aren't I, really? See, they don't know what I do, to this day. They go off with their little boaters on to their nice school and life's sunny and happy. Their dad was killed in the war, that's all they know. Their mum works for a firm and she often has to work late. But there's Reeny, you see. She's like a second mom to them, always has been. Happy as Larry they are, trips out and about, me all dressed up and coming along to the do's at school.

'They don't even know about Richie. He's my bloke – and he doesn't know about them. Proper Jekyll and Hyde, me, ain't I? Richie's not the sort I want round my kids. He's a love really, deep down, only he's got a temper and he's not the family sort. I just like to have a man about – for me and for the house, just in case, you know. I don't love him – nothing like that. I'm past all that. He's my night life, if you like. Only – I dunno. Coming to Brum, seeing you all, I was frightened. I admit it. I didn't want things brought together. Didn't want to admit that the left hand doesn't know what the right's doing. Yes – you're right, Linda. Sooner or later Clarkie and Viv are going to ask more questions . . . and honest to God, I don't know how I'm going to answer them.'

Chapter Eighty

They sat in Mario's café all afternoon.

'I don't want to take you back to the house,' Rosina said. 'You shouldn't be in a place like that – not a kid your age. Next time, you come home, properly, when Clarkie and Vivianne are here. You're cousins, after all!'

Later on she slipped out to buy more cigarettes and on the way back in joked with Mario and asked him for 'a nice bun or something', and he brought toasted teacakes to them, with butter and jam. Linda had barely digested the huge dinner, but she tucked in anyway, while Rosina continued to smoke endlessly, one cigarette after another. The whole afternoon passed for Linda as if bathed in light. She was overwhelmed by Rosina, shocked and impressed by what she had seen in her of steeliness and tears. And the feeling that she had always known her, not just the familiar dark eyes from Bessie's picture, but that she had always known that she would be like this, that she would feel familiar.

'What d'you do with yourself?' Rosina asked, sitting back and drinking yet more tea.

'I've got a job – in a bakery.'

Rosina stared shrewdly at her.

'Any boyfriends?'

Linda moved a blob of butter round with her knife on one half of the teacake. 'Sort of.'

'What d'you mean, sort of?'

She found herself spilling it all out, Alan, the accident.

'That what's wrong with your arm?'

Linda nodded. 'I was all right. It was him got the worst of it.'

'Serves him flaming well right, by the sound of it. It's no good, love – if he drags you down, ditch him. It won't get any better. What does your mom say?'

'Nothing much. She likes him.'

Rosina watched her for a moment, and Linda blushed.

'What're you going to do?'

'What d'you mean?'

'I mean, with yourself? Don't you want more than working in a bakery for ever more?'

Linda met her gaze, hungrily. '*Yes.*'

Rosina leaned forwards and looked closely at her. 'You could go far, girl, d'you know that?'

'Like you?'

'I think you are like me – in a way. Only, Linda love – don't be like me, eh? What am I when you come down to it? The madam of a whorehouse with two bastard children who she can't look in the eye and admit what she does, and who can't face her own family. God knows, sometimes I ache to see someone else who's flesh and blood. Maybe I'll get up the courage again one day. But don't be like me – be more than me.'

They left the Soho Café after Rosina had exchanged more fond banter with Mario while paying the bill.

'You're the best bolthole in town!' she told him.

'Eh – that's what they say about your place, Rosy!' he joked.

'You'll need to get back or Vi'll be doing her nut,' Rosina said. 'I'll walk you to the Tube, all right? But you come down again, girl – I'll pay your fare. That ain't a problem. Will you?'

'Yes.' Linda felt a smile break across her face. 'Course I will.'

Before Linda disappeared into the Underground, Rosina hugged her tight, and when she let go, Linda saw the tears in her eyes.

'Will you tell them, at home – about me?'

'D'you want me to?'

Rosina put her head to one side. 'No – best not. Not all of it. I don't want you lying – just hold a bit back, eh? One day I'll have to get out of all this – and then it won't matter any more anyway. Take care, love.'

And she turned, and walked away amid the crowds in Piccadilly, curvaceously attractive in her bright dress, and resolute, yet somehow the more vulnerable for it.

As Linda watched her, she caught sight of a postbox across on the corner of the street. She found a moment of resolution of her own. Making her way across the road, she took out the envelope, *Mister Alan Bray . . .* on the address, and glanced at it for a second. The feelings Alan brought out in her rose up again – the longing and sympathy, the sense of hopelessness. *I do love you,* she thought. *But I can't stay. I need to live – properly.* She slipped the letter into the box. For a moment she felt stricken, then elated.

'Bye, bye,' she said.

Chapter Eighty-One

'Cold today, isn't it?' Violet said loudly. She was doing a wash and set for old Mrs Busby and had to speak up or the lady didn't hear a word. 'Feels like winter already, doesn't it?'

'Don't say that,' Rita said, pushing a trolley of rollers, pins and combs past her. As usual she had on the highest pair of heels you could find, in a bright shade of green to match her skirt. 'Gets you down thinking about it. One of these days I'm going to go and live somewhere where it's always hot and sunny.'

'Nice to have dreams!' Violet quipped, rolling a section of the lady's thin hair round a fat roller.

The girl Rita now employed to clear up and do some of the washes was sweeping up bits of hair round her feet. Violet stepped aside for her, feeling a sense of satisfaction. Not long ago that had been her job, salon skivvy, before Rita had made her a kind of apprentice, and now they were partners in their own little business! She eased her shoulders back, standing straighter in a gesture of quiet pride. For the first time in her life she was getting somewhere, being someone for herself!

'Cuppa tea, Vi?'

'Ooh, yes please – I couldn't half do with one. D'you want me to do it?'

'Nah – you're in the middle of Mrs Busby. I'll get it.'

Rita disappeared out the back and as she did so

479

Violet saw a familiar figure hurry past. Like everything else outside, she was stained yellow by the protective film hanging behind the windows to mute the sunlight. They looked out on a surreal, yellow world.

It was Joyce, with Charlie on her hip. She seemed flustered and pushed her way in through the door. Violet twisted round, still pushing pins through Mrs Busby's roller. Joyce looked pale, sickly. She had announced a couple of weeks back that she was pregnant and she wasn't feeling very well with this one and was none too pleased about the fact.

'Hello, babby – Charlie boy! What're you two doing here?'

'It's Nana,' Joyce panted. 'Danny's just had Clarence on the telephone – from the phone box. Nana's had another bad turn … Marigold's with her but … He said I should get you.'

'Well, how bad is she?' Violet, immediately tense, snapped out the words.

'I dunno, do I? And there's no need to take it out on me, I only came to tell you!' Joyce was almost in tears.

'Oh, for goodness sake,' Violet said. 'I didn't mean it like that.' She left Mrs Busby and went to kiss Charlie's squashy cheeks. 'Sorry, Joycie – don't get in a state. It's only that I'm in the middle of – you know, everything.'

'What's up? Oh – hello, Joyce!' Rita walked in with two mugs of tea. 'Ooh, look at him – you going to let me have a hold today?'

'It's my mom,' Violet explained.

'Well, you go – I can manage,' Rita said. She had taken Charlie's little hand. There was something so inviting about him, everyone wanted to touch him. 'Poor old duck – no good her being there on her own, is it?'

'I'll finish Mrs Busby . . .'
'Don't be daft – I can do her. Go on – scarper!'

On the bus over to Aston, Violet looked out at the grey sprawl under a heavy grey sky and felt her spirits sink low. In the background of her mind was the nag of worry about her mother, but she couldn't do anything until she got there and saw what was what. She'd deal with it then.

She knew the reason for her low spirits. After all, most things were going well. She loved her job, Carol was well and thriving and happy at school, and Linda was like a changed person. Quite a bombshell that, coming home saying she'd been to London – to Rosina! She had some nerve, Violet had to hand it to her!

Whatever had happened, a few days after Linda came home she announced she was going to start at night-school, learn all sorts, shorthand, typing, accounts – maybe even a language if she could. She was full of it!

'I want a better job,' she said. 'I can't stay doing what I'm doing for ever, can I?'

And that Alan lad seemed to have disappeared off the scene. Violet was half sorry about this – he'd seemed rather nice and obviously wasn't short of a bob or two, with that bike and everything, even if he did dress like a tramp.

As for the business about Rosina, she still felt stirred up about that.

'You should go and see her, Mom,' Linda said. 'I think she misses the family.'

'Why doesn't she come and see us – we're all up here, it's only her down there, all on her own. Is she all right? She's not in trouble?'

'No. She's all right.'

Linda had been quite cagey about Rosina, just said they'd sat and talked a lot and Rosina had told her about her children. Violet knew perfectly well she wasn't getting the full story.

What had kept her from contact with Rosina all these years? All her own troubles, the war, Harry, Carol, had all loaded down on her so there was no room to see out. And something else about Rosina herself: the distance she had created between them by taking off, accentuating a distance that had always been there somehow, the way it was with Linda, because they were so opposite to her. They were bold, hungry, they saw things very differently. *They've got guts*, Violet thought. Not like me – I've always been a stop-at-home. Not much about me really. That was how she had always felt, except for that brief, glittering time with Roy, Roy who had seen something in her . . .

And that was the source of the pain she felt now. For all these years she had turned her back on the memory of those months during the war, tried to see it as a time when she had been unfaithful, wicked, and that Carol's illness had been sent to punish her. How much more so, she thought, knowing what had happened to Roy and Iris's twins. A double curse! They had paid all right, both of them. Didn't that show how wrong they'd been? It was the war – all sorts of things happened, a chaos which sent people flying in all directions like skittles. And when peace came you had to settle back to what you knew, to the real commitment of your life. And she had done, hadn't she? She'd been a faithful, caring wife to Harry in sickness and in health – sickness especially. She had done her duty.

When she'd seen Roy she had not let herself feel

482

anything much – not at the time. It had all been too quick. Once she was alone, the reaction set in. She sat in the back room, smoking to try and calm herself, shaking. Eventually, out of the deep ache, the tears came. Roy, after all this time, those eyes, hands . . . and all the questions she wanted to ask, things she wanted to say – *This beautiful girl is your daughter . . . Do you remember? . . . Do you feel anything for me still? Because I loved you like no one else* – all these things echoed in her unspoken. There had been nothing she could read in his expression. She had had that one chance, in such a hopeless place with all those other people around them, and now he had gone. She had no idea where he lived. Of course, it was the best thing. What else could she have done? Yet ever since, she had been full of regret and longing.

All the way to Bessie's she sat staring through the window and ran the scene over and over in her mind, seeing not the streets they were passing through, but Roy Keillor's face.

Chapter Eighty-Two

Clarence was standing on the front step, peering anxiously along the road. He'd always been a bit short-sighted and still refused to wear glasses, despite the National Health Service. When he caught sight of her he waved agitatedly and took a few steps towards her with his stick.

'Took your blinking time!' he quavered at her. 'I've been waiting here . . .'

Violet didn't answer. No good getting cross: he was old and frightened. His hair was almost all gone now, barring a few wisps. You'd never think he was younger than Bessie, not even sixty yet.

'Go on up!' Clarence fretted behind her. 'Marigold's up with her, but she ain't no bloody good.'

Violet flung her coat on a chair on the way through and hurried up the stairs.

'Marigold? What's up – how is she?'

Marigold had lumbered to her feet from beside Bessie's big brass bedstead.

'She had a turn. This morning – before she ever came down.' Marigold's face was as blank as ever, yet Violet could sense something in her, a kind of suppressed excitement. Also, she stank of hard liquor of some sort. Poor old Mari, with all this going on.

She thought her mother was asleep. Her eyes were closed, hanks of grey hair on the pillow round her head, her face sunken. The left side of her mouth seemed tugged to one side, as if by an invisible thread. Violet could hardly believe her eyes. It was as if a huge tree had been felled. As she knelt down beside Bessie, though, her eyes opened and she gave a whimper of distress, nostrils flaring.

'It's all right – it's only me. What's up, Mom – you feeling bad?' There was no reply except for something Violet had never seen in her mother before: a look of utter terror in her eyes.

'Has the doctor been?' she asked Marigold.

Bessie made a loud, strangled sound.

'Can't she talk?'

Marigold shook her head. 'No. And she don't want the doctor. He'll make her go to the hospital.'

Looking at Bessie's frightened face, she knew Marigold was right.

'But Mari – Dr Cameron won't make her go. And we need to know what's wrong – how to look after her.'

Dr Cameron had known them all since they were children. He was about Bessie's age himself.

Marigold just stared at her sullenly.

'You've done everything right,' Violet reassured her. 'Only I think we need help. It's all right, Mom.' She squeezed Bessie's hand, struck by how cold it was. 'We won't let them take you away. But I'll get Dr Cameron to pop in and see you, all right?'

Violet walked down to the surgery to see old Dr Cameron. His rumbling Scottish voice had always been a comfort.

'I daresay she'll be averse to going near any hospitals,' he said jovially.

'She can't speak,' Violet said. She suddenly felt tearful.

'Can't *speak*? What, Bessie? Dear me – that does sound serious.'

Violet knew Dr Cameron was one of the people who had only ever seen the good side of Bessie, all the babies she'd fostered, pillar of the neighbourhood.

He came as soon as he could and stood looking down at her.

'Now, Bessie – what have you been up to? This won't do, will it?'

Bessie tried in vain to speak. Her eyes rolled with frustration and a sweat broke out on her forehead. All that came out were grunting, distorted sounds.

'You're worried I'm going to pack you off to the hospital, aren't you? You do know it's not the work-house any more? Things have changed, Bessie. You'd be better off there, you know.'

An agitated quiver was going on in Bessie's right hand and her face was working. Violet could see that every fibre of her was protesting. She took Bessie's good hand and was surprised how hard Bessie gripped it, face working.

'What, Mom? I can't make you out.'

Bessie was trying desperately hard to speak, but all that came out was, 'Arrr . . . arrr.'

'Clarence?' Violet guessed. 'You can't look after Clarence?'

She saw that she had guessed right.

'Don't you fret. We'll all look after him.'

Marigold's voice came from behind them. 'She wants to stay here.'

Dr Cameron turned to her. 'Yes. That's pretty clear. And I don't know that in terms of her health there's much to be gained from taking her in. But you're the one here, Marigold. D'you think you can manage?'

Marigold nodded, stolidly.

'We'll help you,' Violet hurried to say. 'All of us – I'll come over after work and Linda'll come sometimes ... And the neighbours'll help, of course.'

'Is that all right then, Bessie? Are you happy now?'

Violet thought how kind Dr Cameron was, his smiling eyes looking down at Bessie, who gave a relieved moan in reply.

'Violet – ' He spoke to her quietly, on the stairs, knowing Clarence was hovering about in the back room. 'You know, your mother may recover from this – but she may not. Another stroke and there's no knowing. If anything happens, we shall have to go against her wishes, I think. But we'll see for now – hm? She's not a well woman – that's all I'm saying. You'll all need to keep an eye on her.'

Chapter Eighty-Three

'Well, you sound cheerful this morning!' Mrs Richards said, smiling as Linda came humming through the bakery door, ready for work.

Linda nodded, pulling her hair back into a ponytail and putting on the little white hat. 'Cheerful' didn't feel a strong enough word for what she was feeling just now. In the weeks since she'd seen Rosina, she felt as if everything had changed, her whole outlook on life. She constantly bubbled inside with excitement. At her evening classes at the Commercial School she was learning shorthand and typing. She was very quick at shorthand. Her mind seemed to suck it in like a hungry sponge waiting for water. She practised at home, and Carol was fascinated by all the little Pitman squiggles and helped to test her. The teacher told her she was one of the best pupils she had ever had.

'If you carry on like this,' she said, 'you'll be faster than me! I'll be able to write you an excellent reference.'

She had no clear idea in her head about where she was going, only that she wanted to move on, to learn and make something of her life.

'I think you're marvellous,' Mrs Richards said, when she first heard what Linda was doing. 'Good for you, duck. Course, I could never have done it, not like you. And my Arthur wouldn't have liked it.'

Linda was so glad she'd found the courage to go and

look for her aunt. It was like finding a missing piece of a puzzle, a part of the family which she resembled, which could make sense of her feelings that no one else seemed to share. Even Carol, for all her clever liveliness, and all the love she felt for her, was not like her. She was a more settled sort, more like Mom.

Over those weeks she had thought a lot about things Rosina had told her – about Nana and her mother, and especially Marigold. The information that Marigold had had a baby, when she was only seventeen, had come as an absolute thunderbolt. She'd always felt sorry for Marigold, but now her heart ached for her. Her own baby and Nana had handed it over like a parcel! Hadn't the house in Aston always been full of babies? Always napkins and washing and a squalling bundle in Nana's arms. Always the neighbourhood hero, Bessie – *isn't she kind, what a big heart, isn't she marvellous?* – and yet her own grandchild! Her heart had not been big enough to take that one in. And there was Marigold, her pockets full of scraps of songs which she never sang.

She thought of how she'd felt when her monthly bleed arrived after that night with Alan, the tears of relief which showed her just how much worry she'd been carrying inside her. What if she'd caught for a baby then? It would have been the end of everything! It made her shiver even thinking about it. And Alan? It would have made no difference to him at all. She could have ruined her life for him, for nothing.

In all the weeks since the accident, she hadn't seen or heard from Alan.

At first, after getting home from Rosina's, amid all

the excitement that had raised in her, she felt ashamed of having written to him the way she did. Hadn't she been a bit of a coward? Shouldn't she have gone to see him instead, told him face to face? But when she heard nothing, she thought that was that. He had accepted it, maybe shrugged it off. She was free.

Of course she had had to explain to Mrs Richards what had happened.

'The thing is, I don't really see Alan any more.'

'Don't you?' Mrs Richards was astonished. 'Why's that then? He's such a nice boy, I thought.'

'Well, he is, but . . .' She shrugged.

'Well I never.' Mrs Richards looked deflated. 'That *is* a shame. I thought I was going to hear the sound of wedding bells before too long.'

Linda stared at her. 'I'm only sixteen, you know.'

'Well, I know, bab – but you don't want to go leaving it too long, do you?'

Once again Linda had that claustrophobic feeling. For a moment she wanted to scream. But she said nothing. Mrs Richards didn't mean anything by it. It was just what she was used to.

Late one afternoon though, at the time he used to appear before, Alan came to the shop.

'Ey-up,' Linda heard Mrs Richards say. 'Look who's here! How're you, dear? You have been in the wars, haven't you?'

He was on crutches, one leg still in plaster.

He pushed the door shut and came hopping over to the counter. Linda felt panic rising in her. What on earth were they going to say to each other? He looked very thin and frail, his dark hair quite long, collar-length and curling round his face.

'Hello,' he said to both of them.

Linda murmured a reply.

'I'll have a split tin and four doughnuts,' he said. It was strange to hear his voice again, quiet and well-spoken.

'Jam ones?' Mrs Richards said, sliding the bread into a bag.

'Yes please.'

'How're you going to manage, carrying them?'

He produced a cloth bag. 'I can use this with the crutches. It's all right. I'm used to it.'

Linda felt relieved. Alan talked only to Mrs Richards as she counted the doughnuts into a bag, and she thought perhaps he would not say anything to her, would just go. Perhaps he looked back on his time with her as some stupid mistake. But she knew how much this would hurt as well. It had hurt that he had not written back to her. And then he turned to her.

'Hello.'

She smiled, with her mouth, keeping her eyes neutral. 'When did you get out of hospital?'

'Only a couple of weeks ago. I've had a lot of trouble with this leg – ' He indicated his right leg, still in plaster. 'They've had to operate twice. I've got a metal pin in it now. They think it'll be all right, in the end.'

He looked up at her. 'Is your arm all right?'

'Yes.' She lifted it to show him, free of the plaster now. 'Thanks.'

'Go on, Linda.' Mrs Richards handed Alan his change and he awkwardly put it in his pocket. 'It's nearly closing-up time. You go along and help him carry the bag.'

'But . . .' Linda began.

'You'd like that, wouldn't you, Alan?'

Alan looked at her with injured eyes, and nodded.

Tersely, he said, 'I think a conversation might be in order, yes.'

He said it in such pettish tones that Linda felt immediately annoyed.

'Go on, Linda,' Mrs Richards urged.

'All right then,' she said, trying to sound indifferent. She didn't hurry putting her coat on.

Once they were outside, in the smoky winter afternoon, they started walking automatically in the usual direction they always used to.

'You could have visited. Just *once*, couldn't you?' His voice was full of hurt and rage. 'Wouldn't have killed you – instead of just writing that letter.'

Her own anger boiled up inside. 'You bloody nearly killed *me* – drinking and carrying on like that! Are you going to say sorry as well then? At least I wrote you a letter, which is more than you've bothered to do!'

'Well, I was having my legs smashed up and . . . and rebuilt, that's why. I wasn't in a fit state . . .'

'And I was worrying I might be having a baby – bet you never thought about that either, did you?'

There were tears in her voice, to her fury, and she choked the emotion down.

'After all we had – you just write to me like that . . .' They reached the corner of the street and he stopped, obviously tired from managing the crutches. They were close to the door of a corner shop.

Linda stood with her fists clenched in the pocket of her old duffel coat, the coat she had bought to look like him. 'You look like a real student in that,' one of the others had said to her at the Commercial School. She didn't want to let his emotion into her, to start feeling sorry for him.

'I had to. I can't stay with you. I don't think we're good for each other, Alan.'

'But I need you.' He sounded so pathetic now. He moved a little closer, as if he wanted her to put her arms round him. She kept them firmly by her sides.

'You don't.'

'I *do*. I've never loved anyone the way I love you, Linda.'

She pushed her chin down and looked at the ground. Their breath was white in the freezing air.

'How's your mom?' she asked abruptly. She didn't really want the answer.

'Bad.'

She nodded. 'Sorry.'

'Come back with me. I'm so . . .' He left her to fill in the words: sad, desperate, lonely. His eyes said everything without the words. 'I don't know what to do.'

Tenderness welled in her, and for a moment she imagined going back with him to the big, dark house, to the silence of a place from which his father was almost always absent and to which his mother might or might not ever return. And she would go up to his room, that brown space full of his Westerns and his fantasies of all he wanted to do and it would be just the two of them, the tight, enclosed world they had made together which needed no one else. And she would be with him and be stuck, rooted to the ground unable to get away. Her chest tightened and she had to take a deep breath.

'I can't.'

'Please . . .'

His face was distraught. He looked pathetic standing there with his crutches and his cloth bag of bread.

'If you needed me so much, why have you taken all this time to get here? Or not written?'

'I couldn't. I was upset.'

'I can't make things better. I can't. Even if I was with you, it wouldn't make any difference.'

'But it would! Remember – we were going to America together. I've been writing – while I've been in hospital. A script – I finished it. A new one.' He was speaking very intensely, leaning towards her, resting on the crutches. A woman came out of the shop and walked between them, giving them an odd look.

Linda looked at Alan. Would he ever go to America? Would he really?

'But it's not what I want,' she said. 'I don't want to go to America – not really. That's your dream, not mine.'

'I need you. I don't know what I might do if you don't stay with me . . .'

'I'm sorry Alan. I did love you, really I did. But everything's different now. I can't stay with you. I've got things I want to do.'

And she turned away and walked off, fast, along the road.

Chapter Eighty-Four

Violet closed the door of Rita's Salon behind her and locked up.

It was Rita's afternoon off and it hadn't been busy – Tuesday afternoon, and a freezing, late November day. She had had two ladies under the dryers until a few minutes before closing time.

'There – all done,' she said aloud, trying the door to make sure. She felt so proud, being able to take charge, to feel she could manage everything the day threw at her.

Rita, generous as ever, was talking about renaming the salon 'Rita and Vi's' – 'or d'you want it to be Violet? Vi sounds more catchy, don't you think?'

'Yes, it does. But there's no hurry – it'll cost us a bit doing that, won't it?'

She felt secure with Rita. Name or no name over the door, she was part of the business. Her life had a path now, and she had some say in it.

Walking along the road, past the shops and towards Bloomsbury Road, she felt contented. There was no need to feel ashamed of her house any more – even the front door was now a shiny green, thanks to help from Joe Kaminski. Linda seemed to have decided to take pride in herself – thanks, in some strange way that she didn't really understand, to Rosina – and Carol was well and thriving.

She pulled her scarf tighter round her neck. It really *was* cold. Must be snow on the way. She didn't want to think about Rosina. Not yet. Not that she ever had any falling-out with Rosina, but it had been so long with no contact, no knowing what bitterness or sadness might lie behind her silence. And Linda wasn't telling the whole story, that she was sure of. But she couldn't deal with that now. Not till a few other things were over. Not while she still had Mom to deal with . . .

Bessie would die. Sooner than they thought, by the look of her. She couldn't go on for long, not in that state. But it still seemed impossible that the huge, dominating woman who had ruled all their lives would not just get off her bed one day and take over again.

Violet'd told Marigold she wouldn't be over today, as she had to work on late, but Mari hadn't seemed bothered. She had to hand it to her, Violet thought. She was coping ever so well with Mom and Clarence. They always under-estimated Marigold, she realized – had done all her life.

Her mind ran over what she needed to do. Most days she did this on the way home: Linda should be back soon, Carol would be next door with the Kaminskis, where she went on the days when Violet wouldn't be home by the end of school. Get some tea on – mince tonight, the meat was in the fridge. Fridge! She was going up in the world! They'd get a television soon, she decided. Save up. It'd be nice to have a bit of chat in the house. She'd never thought she'd miss that when the girls were small, keeping on all the time, but it was surprising how quiet and lonely life could seem now. Mrs Smith down the road had hers on all day, even if there was nothing much on, just the test card. It was company, she said. Brightened the place up.

As she approached the house she met Mr Bottoms coming the other way, dressed in his neat little mac. It grieved him to speak to her, she could see, even after all these years. He still had them labelled as a 'problem family' even though they'd come through most of their problems. They didn't even have fights about the animals any more – Snowdrop and the dogs were too long in the tooth to cause any trouble. In any case, Reg's attention had shifted from next door to an anxiety about all the coloureds coming in. Sometimes he talked to her about it over the fence when she was hanging washing out. It wasn't like this before the war, he would say. Didn't she think it was wrong, things changing the way they were?

'They're letting too many in at once. We won't know where we are soon, if we're all mixed up together.'

Even now though, his whole bearing communicated fastidious disdain. As he came closer Violet found herself wondering what it must be like to go to bed with Reg Bottoms (still in his mac?), but the very notion made her want to laugh and she banished it fiercely from her thoughts.

Reg raised his cap with military precision.

'Aft'noon, Mrs Martin.'

'Afternoon, Mr Bottoms.'

No first names, even after all this time, no smile, even though her lips were curved upwards. She thought he was going to go straight past but he swung his arm back towards her house.

'Someone there for you.'

'Oh?' she frowned. 'Ta.'

She could feel there was someone else there, like a second sense, even from a distance. He was sitting, waiting for her, on the front step. She stopped at the gate, without going in, and they stared at each other.

Chapter Eighty-Five

Roy's brown eyes were fixed on her calmly, as if there was simply nothing else he could do but be here at this moment.

'I didn't know I was going to come.' He stood up, slowly. 'I was going home from work and I just had to.' He shrugged.

'How did you –' her throat had gone dry and she had to swallow – 'know where I live?'

'Rachel Miller told me. You know, little Bernice's mother. I've known her a while and she mentioned you.'

Violet walked towards him. Everything felt very strange, with an intensity that made it like a dream.

'No one's here. Not at the moment,' she said. 'You can come in.'

Automatically she led him through to the back, put the lights on, and the kettle, and felt pleased the room was newly painted and tidy.

'Sit down,' she urged him.

Roy sat on the edge of a chair, looking very ill at ease, far more so than the last time they met, as if there were things he had to say and didn't know where to begin, and seeing this calmed her. It wasn't just her then: there were things to say.

'Where's your daughter then? The little one?'

'Next door. My neighbours have her after school. I'll

have to get her soon. There's time for a cuppa first though. They're good to her – she likes it there.'

He looked at her in silence, really looked at her, as if drinking her in.

'How's the family?' she asked.

Roy nodded. 'All right. It's not easy, the wheelchair and that.'

'No. I know. It's a while since we've had that now. You still reading your poems?'

'Yes – well, if there's ever time. Actually, not much really.'

Violet carefully laid the pot and cups on the table, feeling the neatness of her own movements. She knew he was watching her and it gave her a powerful feeling, but she tried to keep herself calm.

Turning, she handed Roy his tea and he looked up into her eyes.

'Vi – she's mine, isn't she?'

They each had a thumb on the saucer.

'Your girl – Carol?'

Shakily she released the saucer and sat down, nodding.

'Yes. She is.'

'Did you know? Before I – before we left, I mean?'

Before Iris suspected anything, before he decided they had to move away, to do the right thing. He had to stick by Iris and the children, and she knew she would have to stick by Harry. She tried not to think of that last evening they had spent together, how she had cried and clung to him, trying to engrave the memory of his body on hers.

'No. I didn't know. And then, after, I didn't know where you were. Didn't think it would help if you knew anyway.'

'But your husband ... He must have guessed, worked it out?'

Violet looked down. For some reason, at the mention of Harry, a blush spread over her cheeks.

'He did. But he was in such a state, see. He said things happen in war, lots of things, and we have to go on and forget about it. It came out sometimes, now and then, and he'd have a go at me. But he was so poorly. He suffered a lot. He was in a Jap POW camp.'

'God ...'

'He was never right after. He passed away, last year.'

She sipped her tea, feeling like crying and trying not to. Roy watched her.

'You've had it bad. I'm so sorry I didn't know – about the baby, I mean.'

'Couldn't be helped. When I realized, I was frightened of course, upset. It's all passed now though, Roy. I'm just so glad to see her walking and happy after all she's gone through, in and out of St Gerard's and all that.'

'Yes, they're marvellous. Philip's going back soon.'

'How's Iris?'

Roy nodded. 'All right. It's not been easy, what with the polio and that, losing John, and then how Philip's been. She just ... well, as I say, it's not been easy.'

There was a silence. Even though they had been talking it was still impossible to say anything very much. Why exactly was he here? Violet wondered. He was still married to Iris, so it was not about her, he had not come back to revive what they had had. The only other reason he could be here, then, was to see Carol.

'Shall I go and get her?'

'Your daughter?'

She stood up. 'Yours, as well.'

'All right, baby?' Eva greeted her. 'Coming in for a drink of tea, or something stronger? She is fine, fine – she is playing cards.'

'Thanks, Eva, but I can't tonight. I've got a visitor and I need to pop back with her.'

'OK then. Carol! Your mother's here!'

Carol liked being at Eva's.

'She's teaching me Polish,' she had told Violet some time ago. 'I asked her. She said, "Why you want to learn Polish? No one speaks Polish except in Poland." But I said I wanted to.'

Violet had taken one look at some written Polish, which seemed to be all consonants and no vowels, and said, 'Oh, my word. I don't think I could do that.'

Eva said Carol had a good ear, and they parted from each other with a kiss and words in Polish.

'See you tomorrow,' Violet said. 'Sorry to rush off.'

'Why didn't you stay?' Carol said crossly. 'You normally do.'

'There's someone at home – an old friend from the war,' Violet said. 'I just wanted you to see him, that's all.'

'Oh,' Carol said, indifferently. 'Mom, when are we going to get a television?'

'When we can afford it.' Violet pushed open the front door.

Roy was standing in the back room and she could see he was nervous.

'Carol, this is Roy – we saw him at the garden party, d'you remember?'

Carol nodded, though she didn't seem very sure.

'I'm going up to my room. Isn't Linda back?'

'No – she'll be in any minute.'

She looked at Roy as Carol's feet were heard on the stairs. They smiled ruefully at each other.

'I s'pose I'd better be off,' he said.

She took him to the door, and as he was leaving he turned, as if about to say something more, then obviously thought the better of it.

'We might see you at one of the other parties,' she said. Then added, 'You can come again, if you want.'

Roy looked at her, and his eyes seemed full of sadness.

'Don't know if I should really. But thanks, anyway.'

Chapter Eighty-Six

Bessie lay drifting in and out of sleep, as she did most days now.

It was not a calm sleep but restless and full of memories. Sometimes they were of happier moments, of her marriage, when she felt light and lifted out of the prison of her body. When these visions faded she came back to the hard pillow under her head – her ears were sore now, chafed from lying there so long – and the burn of the mattress against her lower back. Sometimes when she was awake she lifted her good arm and peered at the hand which rose up in front of her face, wondering whose it was, that puffy thing with its cracked, yellow nails. How had she found her way into this old crone's body? Would someone come along and say a spell and let her out?

Faces came and went, Marigold's mostly. That it should come to this – being looked after by that sly, boozing half-wit! Violet came sometimes and asked questions. Was she all right? How was she feeling? Couldn't the girl see she couldn't answer? No bloody brains – never did have. Even that girl – one of the grandchildren – Linda, was it? Miss Hoity-Toity with her book learning. She'd been once or twice. Must be summat wrong if that lot were making an appearance . . . She would lie stewing in her thoughts until the dreamy, trance-like state came again.

There was one that was a real treat. If only it was like a machine, like one of those televisions and she could choose what to think about, she'd turn that on any time ... 1911, best year of her life. She'd had her job at the HP sauce factory then, one long whiff of vinegar, a big company, regular wages, and that was where she'd met Jack. They'd courted for a year, but it was 'let's get married' from the word go. Both nineteen they were, full of it. Worshipped her, he did, all their marriage – seven years when she was queen in her own house, with a man to feed and bed with and the babbies coming. And that day replayed in her mind. There she was, her hair long then, blue-black as a raven's and her still slender then, but strong as an ox. She was a sturdy mare, Jack said.

'I've had to be, you cheeky bugger,' she'd tell him.

'Well, you're my mare now ...'

She'd walked up to the altar in the prettiest lacy blouse, high collar, and a deep blue skirt. No father to give her away, no Mom. Her older half-sisters had scarpered by then and Mary'd died when she was fifteen. With that wheezing chest she'd never been built to last. There was only Clarence, sixteen and somehow old-mannish even then, to act as family and walk her up the aisle. And Jack stood there to greet her, beaming. This all played through her mind again like a beautiful, haunting piece of music, the spray of orange blossom she was carrying, the lace at her neck and her shoes, the smartest pair she'd ever had, in navy leather, and Jack's adoring smile. And then later, their first night. She'd saved herself for after the wedding. Not that it was her first time with a man ... But those thoughts weren't for this dream, this lovely memory. Shut that out, right out of all memory, back with all the other bad times, the dirt ... And she was back in Jack's arms, her man, her prize, with his lean, strong body and gruff, older-man ways even before he was twenty. He never cared that she couldn't read or write.

'That ain't no use to me,' he once teased her, running his hand along her thick thigh. 'There're other things much more important!'

God, he'd enjoyed her body – he'd revelled in it! He'd come home from work for weeks after they were married so hungry for her he'd let his tea go cold to have her first. And to crown it all, her first pregnancy had yielded two babbies! The midwife spotted it once she got big.

'You've got more than one in there, Bessie, I'd stake my life on it . . .'

'That's 'cause you're so flaming greedy,' she told Jack.

It all played in her mind, all those early days in Joseph Street, the little room with the range, their chairs close to the fire at night, the big brass bed she was lying in now – no, they bought that later on, but never mind. Then the babbies, Charlie and Marigold, twins safely delivered, wasn't she a miracle! Then Violet and Rosina, until there was a family, the house bursting at the seams . . . But of course before Rosina was born, Jack was dead. All those men killed out there in France and he gets Spanish flu. She sat that day she gave birth to Rosina and wept and wept. What a pretty one she was, right from the start, and just like Jack – and he'd never see her. She was no queen any more: her king had gone. All the bliss of the memories seeped away and once again she was back in the lumpy bed. Why did nothing good ever last? Everything was always spoilt. Always. And she was filled with hurt and bitterness, as if she might burst with it.

There was a beam of light in the room, dazzling as

she opened her eyes. Was it summer? Christmas, wasn't it, nearly, and cold? Where was Marigold? She wanted something, a cup of tea . . . And then she was gone again, slipping away into a doze.

This time it was different. Not these memories, no, for God's sake no! But there was no way out, as there had been no way out then. She was trapped in her vision of the past . . .

The accident happened in 1899, two days after Bessie turned seven.

April, what should have been the last days of the board school term, except that Bessie hardly ever went to school. She was Mom's skivvy. And she knew as soon as she came downstairs that her father hadn't come home again.

'You're not going nowhere!' her mother screamed at her. She was kneeling, sweeping ash out of the range, a grimy nightcap over her fading hair, which was scraped back severely from a face haggard from childbearing and disappointment. Her belly was heavy with the weight of another child, due any day now.

Bessie waited, in her ragged dress. It was brown and too short for her. Mary, her ten-year-old sister, sat hunched forwards on a stool by the door, each breath a wheezing agony.

'I don't know where that bastard is! No tea in the house, no milk, barely a crust.' Her mother reached out for the old coal pail. 'Nothing but a handful of slack and the cellar's scraped bare! You'll have to go and ask Mrs Preston if 'er'll borrow us some again . . . And go and get Agnes before she bawls the bloody house down and wakes William.'

Bessie climbed barefoot up the twisting staircase. She was a scrawny child with a wide face and thick black hair. Her mother only ever had eyes for William. At last, after seven girls, six surviving, the longed-for son had arrived.

The stair treads were bare, but so well worn that they were not splintery. The house was one of Birmingham's thousands of back-to-backs, one room downstairs, two up and an attic, and they were on the yard side, down an entry from the front houses on the street. The houses were crushed in round the vast array of factories and workshops, poorly built, no water, little air, over-crowded. If it rained hard they flooded, sometimes right up through the cellar to the ground floor, and water dripped in through the roof and left tide marks all down the walls, and the battle against infestations of bed bugs, roaches and mice was endless.

Agnes, snotty-nosed and hungry, was sitting up in the big, deep drawer in Mom and Dad's room where she slept. She was nearly a year old.

'Oh, shurrup, will you?' Bessie said, hoiking her out. The back of her clothes was all wet, as was the bedding. William, who was three, was still asleep in the double bed which took up most of the room, one tiny hand a fist in front of his face, his hair brown and smooth. Mom's little angel. With Agnes on her hip, Bessie thumped downstairs again.

'Oh, bloody shut up, will you!' their mother snarled at them both from the grate.

The older girls had already left for work. Bessie's mother, Ethel, had been married to a man who'd deserted her, leaving her with three daughters. In desperation she set up house with Thomas Harris, who wasn't her husband at all though she called herself

Harris for the look of it. With Harris she'd had four more daughters, one buried soon after birth, and William. Harris was a carter, a charmer and a boozer who drank away not only any money he managed, intermittently, to earn, but also the factory wages of Ada and Rachel, the two oldest girls by Harry Marston, who were sixteen and fourteen.

Bessie spent most of the day out in the yard, doing as she was told and minding the babbies. That was always her job, looking after everyone else. When Ada and Rachel got in from work they did nothing but boss her around. That was her life, skivvy to Mom, maid of all work to her elder sisters and mother to all the younger ones. There were other children out there, playing around mothers who were taking their turn doing their washing, steam from the heated copper billowing out through the brewhouse door, chats and quarrels over the mangle. By midday the sun got round and shed some warming light into the dank atmosphere, drying out the blue bricks, the washing strung on lines.

Throughout the morning she heard her mom's voice inside, raised in bitter complaint. Ethel, exhausted and heavy with the next child, fell asleep in the afternoon, face pasty white against her black dress. There was still no sign of her 'husband'. Bessie heard the other women's gossip about Mom, how she was 'at the end of her tether' and would soon be 'on the Parish', and their opinion about her father, none of which was complimentary. No family on the yard had more quarrels about where the next meal was coming from.

'No use to anyone that one . . . Er'd be better off on her own . . .'

When the older children came home from school, two of the raggedy lads played with William. Bessie was bored, and relieved to have him taken off her hands. She and some other girls were in a corner, beyond the brewhouse, with a handful of pebbles, playing 'jacks'. They often sat there, out of the way, and it was in the lee of the wall where the stink of the gasworks wasn't so bad.

'We're going down Sheppard's,' two of the boys said to Bessie. 'Willie can come with us.'

'Awright,' Bessie said indifferently. Mom let William go with them to the shop. They might buy him a stick of liquorice to keep him quiet and she was fed up with him. The girls went back to their game. Mary sat near them, very upright against the wall, lips tinged with blue. She was having a bad day, but they were too used to it to feel much pity for her, her rasping breaths as much the background to their game as was the sound of trains, chuffing along, or their brakes shrieking a few streets away.

But then the shouting started. One of the lads came tearing along the entry in his bare feet as if his hair was on fire. His face was smeared with smuts and he looked frightened out of his wits.

'Quick! Quick! It's Willie . . . He's . . .'

'What?' Bessie felt as if her heart was a stone.

'He got on the railway. We daint see 'im, honest! And we daint know where he'd gone. And a train came . . .' The boy, who was eleven years old, began sobbing, his face twisting with distress. 'We never saw it –'

Ethel was beside them, pushing Bessie out of the way.

'What're you saying?' Seizing hold of the boy's scrawny shoulders she screamed into his face. 'What're you saying? Where's William? Where's my boy?'

Bessie knew then that she'd heard it, the moment he meant, when the train screeched to a stop... She already understood that William was dead.

A policeman came to the house and told them they could not bring William's body home. Not possible, he said. They wouldn't want to see. Not the way it was. Neighbours came and went. The girls tried to comfort their mother but she pushed them away.

'You're no good!' she howled. 'I want my boy – my beautiful little boy! You – ' She clawed at Bessie. 'You were s'posed to be looking after him. If it wasn't for you he'd be here in my arms!'

Bessie lay in bed that night with her sisters. Their father had still not come home.

'I want William,' Sarah sobbed. She was only four.

Bessie wanted him too.

Distantly, from the railway, they heard the whistle of a train, like the wail of an unquiet soul, and the panting noise it made building up speed. 'You're no good...' it chugged out, 'you're no good...'

Within the week the house was full of the cries of her mother in her labour pains. Bessie's job was to keep the other children out of the way. Their dad was home that evening when Mom at last gave birth to a tiny boy. She announced that she was going to call him Clarence.

Thomas Harris looked at the tiny, screaming form with no emotion.

'Ah well, there yer go – got another lad now, Ethel – tek the place of the other one.'

Ethel glowered up at him. 'Nothing can take William's place.'

Bessie stared at the round, contorted face of Clarence, pressed against the blue-veined pillow of his mother's breast. She felt something untangle in her, a rush of relief that God had sent them another boy instead of William. It felt as if she was being given a second chance. She knew what she had to do now. With all her might she had to look after the babbies, and above all, she had to look after Clarence. Clarence was clean and new. That was what she must do. Then everything would be all right.

By the time she was eleven Bessie was left as mother and mainstay of the family. Thomas Harris was long gone. Ada, her oldest half-sister, was married, and Rachel came and went, didn't care for anything or anyone. Bessie was mother to Sarah, Agnes and Clarence, and to Susan, whom Mom had popped out, spawned by *him*. Arthur Seth Gibbins, his full name. It said so in the paper. One of the neighbours read it out to her after his trial.

'We're well rid of him now, Bessie. He's a madman. They'll lock him up and throw away the key.' He'd cut a woman's throat.

He might as well have cut Mom's throat. Did it for herself in the end, after Susan was born. Mom drank poison and left them all, and Susan only three months old.

It was by the grace of God he committed a murder or he would have been back, doing what he did to her that time. And she was there now, eleven years old, trapped under him on Mom's bed with Susan crying downstairs and his stink and him hurting her. He left her bleeding and she had to take an old blouse of Mom's and put it between her legs, lying curled up on her side, legs clamped together until it stopped. He had a beard with snuff trapped in it and sludgy grey eyes and ever after she never went near a man who wasn't cleanshaven. And while he was doing it to her his eyes were blind but it was her that felt invisible.

She was trying to get out of this vision of the past, but it paraded everything in front of her. Mom, that morning when she found her dead on the bed, body bent back, eyes and mouth open as if she'd had a terrible shock, her skirt rucked up, showing her white legs.

'Mom – Mom!' She had shaken and shaken her and then Clarence had come in. He stared and backed away, down the stairs again. She found him later in the brewhouse, curled up in the corner, his thumb in his mouth, and he was four then.

She woke, whimpering.

The sunlight was gone now and the room felt cool and grey. Her body was so heavy, like a mountain strapped to a bed, gross, impossibly big. She lay full of loathing and anger. Where was that blasted Marigold when you needed her? She couldn't even get up and sit on the po' by herself and she wanted that cup of tea. She wanted to kick and scream, like a helpless child.

It wasn't long before she heard footsteps on the stairs, Marigold's slow, cow-like tread.

Come on, come on, you great fat stupid trollop! Get yourself up here and give me my bloody tea. What's taking you so long?

There was a pause, and she heard Marigold catching her breath at the top of the stairs.

Bessie let out a shout of impatience which emerged only as a slurred groan.

Then Marigold hove into view, her square face appearing over the bedclothes. And no tea! *She hadn't even bothered to bring up the tea!* Was that the hard

512

stuff she could smell on her again – going about stinking like a distillery. *Filthy stinking trollop . . .*

Marigold stood, caught in her mother's glare of loathing. She looked down at her, hands on her broad hips, covered by her pond-green sack of a skirt. Her face was expressionless as it so often was, but there was a hardness in her eyes which even Bessie could see. *God, what's got into her . . . Help! Help me!*

Marigold's eyes narrowed. With a lightning move she snatched the pillow from under Bessie's head, which thumped down on to the mattress. Bessie gasped. What the hell was she playing at?

Marigold hoisted her skirt up with one hand to reveal the thick white thigh above her brown stocking, and half knelt on the bed.

She was holding the pillow up and her face was contorted.

'You think I'm going to keep on looking after you, don't you? Be your little slave for ever? Well, you're wrong. I'm not.'

Suddenly she lashed out and Bessie felt a sharp slap across her cheek. She moaned. The sight of Marigold's face was terrifying now, and she was trapped, trapped as she had been under Arthur Gibbins . . . She tried to move, to escape, but her body wouldn't work for her.

'All those babbies . . . You took in everyone else's babbies, but you wouldn't keep mine, my little Tommy.' She was howling. 'He was *mine*, not yours. *MINE!*'

Another slap, this time across the other cheek. Bessie heard herself mewling.

'You've had your life – and you've had all mine as well. Taken it away, and taken my babby away. And now you ain't going to take away any more . . .'

The pillow came down over her face with the force

of Marigold's whole body lying over it and Bessie managed to move her good arm, just for a second, but then there was no air, no breath, just the scream of a train whistle in her head coming closer, and closer, and after, all was dark.

Chapter Eighty-Seven

Linda was never sure, not absolutely, one hundred per cent.

'Can you go to our mom's this afternoon?' Violet had said. 'I need to work late.'

Going into Nana's house, Linda saw Clarence fast asleep by the fire in the back room, his mouth open.

She could hear Marigold upstairs, her voice, shouting, she thought. She'd have to go up, even though she was anything but looking forward to seeing her grandmother. Even in her depleted state there was something forbidding about Bessie.

On the stairs, she heard Marigold's voice again, saying something brief and emphatic, though she couldn't hear the words. As she went into the room she saw, or thought she saw, something. Did she? Was that how it was? Marigold holding Bessie's head up by her hair, as if she had a dog by the tail, and pushing the pillow roughly under her head. Marigold heard her and turned, straightening up, her face blank and guarded. And even after what happened next, Linda would wonder always, whether that was what she had seen in those seconds, or whether it had been a trick of her imagination. And yet she thought she knew, but didn't want to allow herself to know, what Marigold had done with that pillow in the moments before she got there.

Her aunt stood very straight by the bed, looking down, like a maid awaiting orders.

'How is she?' Linda said.

'I dunno.' Marigold seemed a bit stunned. 'Not too good.' There was a pause. 'Gone. I think she's gone.'

'Gone?' She started to feel shaky, like she had the morning she'd seen her dad lying there, dead. 'You mean . . . passed away?'

Linda went to the other side of the bed. She could see Bessie was dead. Her face was quite different. It was a bluish mauve, especially round the lips. She didn't look like herself any more.

She looked at Marigold and their eyes met. Linda remembered for ever what she saw in Marigold's eyes that afternoon. In that stolid, impassive face the eyes glowed, with defiance, and challenge and triumph. Linda met her stare. She thought of everything Rosina had told her. Her heart was beating terribly fast, but she spoke carefully to Marigold.

'Did she have another funny turn?'

Marigold nodded, still staring defiantly. They looked at each other in silent understanding.

Chapter Eighty-Eight

Violet walked through the gate of Witton Cemetery, holding her little bunch of flowers. It was the dead of winter after all, not a time for blooms.

'D'you want to come?' she'd asked Linda and Carol. Both of them shook their heads. They were playing Ludo, stretched out on the floor. Linda smiled up at her.

'I'll stay here with Carol – we could go and see Joyce.'

And Violet had been quite glad. It was the very last week of the year, the quiet, cold time before the new year of 1955 would break upon them. They'd buried Bessie before Christmas, after that final big stroke she'd had.

It was one of those still days when the sun never truly seems to rise. The path was edged with sodden leaves. Violet pulled her scarf further up, shivering as she walked between the rows of gravestones in the smoky light. She passed a middle-aged couple walking arm in arm, leaning into each other.

They had buried Bessie beside Jack, adding her name to the stone: 'BESSIE WILES – 1892–1954, A beloved wife and mother.' Charlie had insisted on organizing things, much to everyone's surprise, though it shouldn't have been surprising as he was the boy and the oldest. He suddenly came into his own.

Violet had brought a jam-jar of water, and put the little offering by the stone.

'Here you are, Mom.' Then as an afterthought added, '. . . Dad.' Not that she could remember Jack, or hardly. She had a dim memory of him being home, him being in bed, and sick, and then he was gone, like a shadow that had fallen on her life for only moments.

But Bessie going: it was going to take a long time to come to terms with that. She didn't feel sad exactly, not that. The state Mom had been in it was a blessing really that it came the way it did. *But I feel like an orphan*, she thought. *I'm lost.* Mom had been this big, dominating, endless presence in her life, inevitable, inescapable, at times cruel and unbearable but also comforting. And now it was like the roof being taken off. There was no counterweight above her, no one to look up to. She was top of the ladder now, and it felt a lonely place to be. There was Charlie of course, and Marigold, who was still looking after Clarence, but she'd never been close to either of them. Now, more than ever before, she wanted Rosina.

A card had come at Christmas. She knew Linda had written to Rosy after Mom died. Violet felt ashamed that she hadn't written it herself.

'Did you ask her to come?' Violet asked.

'Course I did.'

'Did you say we really want her to be here?'

'*Yes.*'

But come the day of the funeral, there was no sign of Rosina. In the card she sent, she had scrawled – she always had bad writing, Violet remembered –

Dear Vi – sorry, sorry, sorry I flunked it again. I want to come and I thought of you all and said a prayer on the day. Thought I could do it but when

it came I couldn't face it there with everyone. I will come, quietly and just see you one day. Promise.
Rosina. xx

PS Your Linda's a lovely girl.

'What's she doing down there?' she asked Linda. 'What's she so bothered about, coming back and everything? Anyone'd think she'd done a murder or something.'

But Linda just shrugged. (Why did she shrug all the time like that?) 'She'll have to tell you herself.'

'Well, she always was one to turn on the drama.'

But Violet kept thinking about her, and wondering.

Standing by the grave, she felt as if there was something else she was supposed to do. Were there some set words she should say? If so she didn't know what they were. No one had ever taught her anything like that. It seemed odd seeing Bessie's grave. It levelled her down to the same size as anyone else and seemed to have nothing to do with the mother she had known. She tidied the little jar of flowers and turned to leave, in the darkening afternoon.

Couldn't be bleaker if it tried, she thought, shivering. There seemed to be no one else around at all now, and she started to feel a bit uneasy. Why should the place give her the creeps? But it did, a bit.

Then she saw there was someone else up ahead, coming towards her, and felt somehow relieved. She squinted. Her heart began to beat harder. She was seeing things, surely?

The tall, thin figure came towards her. Even at that distance she could tell, somehow, that he was fixed on her, rather than anything else that was here. He had not come to tend a grave, he had come to find her.

'Hello,' she said, once he was near enough. She was surprised how calm and matter of fact she sounded. After all, she was used to pushing her feelings away. She mustn't let them surface, mustn't expect anything.

Roy smiled, nervously. 'The girls told me you'd come over here.'

'My girls?'

'I called at the house. I just ... Look, it's freezing out here. Let's walk a bit. They're not locking up quite yet.'

They turned back, along the main path of the cemetery, side by side, not touching. There was a silence which felt so full of feeling that Violet felt she must break it in case she was imagining it. She knew her feelings for him had not changed, that if she allowed herself to think about him and how they were together she was filled with such longing that it made her physically ache. But he was a married man ... She mustn't allow herself any thoughts like that. So, abruptly, she said, 'Why did you come to find me?'

Roy had his hands in his pockets. He gave a deep sigh.

'Seeing you again, seeing her – Carol, I mean ... I haven't been able to stop thinking about it, about you.'

She waited, watching her feet in their little black court shoes take one step after another, as he struggled to reach what he wanted to say. After a moment he stopped and turned to her.

'There's no point in me saying anything unless I say this.' Seeing her raise her eyes to look at him, and knowing that she could not hide the hunger in them for what he might say, he seemed encouraged. 'I've tried to do the right thing and got it wrong all the way along the line. I felt I had to stay with Iris ... Life doesn't

520

come easy for her. She's never been a very happy person. What I know now is that she never will be, whatever happens. And you were married then. It was a mess, I know. But if I'd known about the baby ... I can't even say how it felt seeing you again. It was like ... I don't know, like the sun coming out or something. So's I didn't know how I've got through these years and not been with you.'

'Roy ... Oh God, don't ...' As he spoke tears began to roll down her cheeks.

'I've got to, Vi.'

'D'you mean it? I can't believe this – that you're here, saying this to me ...'

'I had to come this afternoon. I don't know why. It was as if—' He reached out and put his hands on her shoulders. 'I've thought and thought and tried to hold back, tried to think I could stay with Iris, when all I want is to be with you. I thought if I waited long enough and did the right thing all that would fade. But there's never been anyone like you, not for me. I can't feel for anyone else the way I feel for you. And I've just made such a mess of it all ...'

'No, you haven't. I mean, it was just the way it was, back then. And Harry was so poorly ... If he'd come back and been all right it might have been different. But you'd gone by then anyway, and you were with Iris.'

He looked longingly down into her face.

'Poor Iris,' he said. 'It's been bad for her. I mean, I let her down first of all. And then the polio. She's convinced it was a punishment, a sort of curse – on me, I suppose. Sometimes I've felt it myself. And John died of it so quickly, within a few days. It was like being struck by lightning. We thought Philip would die as well, after that. It was terrible to watch – well, I don't need to tell you. And then the iron lung and everything . . .'

'I thought it was a punishment too, when Carol got it. I remember looking down at her in that thing and thinking, if only I hadn't felt anything for you, if I hadn't found out what it meant to feel that much for someone . . . Maybe we're not meant to feel so much? Maybe it pushes everything out of balance or something. As though, if there's too much love and happiness, something bad has to happen to make up for it.'

'It can't really be like that, can it? Don't you think we've had enough of the bad already, anyway? Vi, I love you. For what's left of our lives, after all this, I want to spend it with you – if you want it too.'

His sensitive face was full of earnestness. She reached up and gently stroked his cheek.

'But what about Iris?'

'Iris isn't happy with me. Ever since the polio, she's turned against me. She's like a closed book. We hardly speak to each other, but we've just kept on, for the boys. And because that was what we had to do. And I could manage it, going to work, looking after Philip, not thinking or feeling anything else or that anything might be better. And then I saw you again. And I couldn't go on like that. Not any more. If you still feel anything for me . . . I couldn't tell if you did, that was the worst of it . . .'

He stroked his thumbs across her cheeks, wiping away her tears.

'Do you?'

She nodded, half laughing, though the tears were still coming. 'Yes. Oh God, Roy, I can hardly believe this! Are you really here?'

'I'm here all right.' He took her in his arms and she

rested her cheek against his chest. 'I'm here, my love, and I never want to be anywhere else.'

She breathed him in, the loved, familiar smell of him, stroking his back. 'Oh, I remember you. I remember every inch of you.'

She pulled back to look into his eyes and he lowered his head, his lips searching for hers, and she knew she had found again what she needed.

They walked in the cemetery until it closed, arms round each other, talking, catching up on each other's lives, kissing, holding each other, not even aware any more of the cold and wind.

'I feel terrible about Iris,' she said as they went out through the gate.

'I'll see Iris all right, of course I will,' he told her. 'But she doesn't want me, not really. Sometimes I think she hates me. I've made her unhappy all the way along – well, me and the way things have gone with the kiddies.'

'Are you going home now?'

'I'd better. When can I see you?'

'As soon as you can.' She hugged him, squeezing him tight. 'Don't go away again for long, will you?'

He began to walk away, but strode back to kiss her again. 'I don't want to go. Don't want to leave you.'

She was laughing now, her heart lighter than it had been in years. 'Go on – don't worry, my love. I'll be waiting. I've waited this long, haven't I?'

Part Seven

1960

Chapter Eighty-Nine

They stood on the deck of the huge liner, all four of them in a line, waving to their wellwishers, who all looked so small down there on the quay. Linda couldn't see the exact expressions on Violet and Roy's faces but they had their arms round each other, like a little island together.

They'll be all right, she thought, blowing them yet another kiss. She knew now all the story about their love for one another, and about Carol. It brought tears to her eyes thinking about it, and about her own dad and how things had been. Mom was happy now, happier than she'd ever seen her. No Carol down there to see them off, of course: she wasn't allowed out. But the few times she'd visited her sister, she'd seen the joyful light in her eyes and knew she was in the right place for her. When they'd first told Rosina that Carol was going into the convent, she'd thought she'd be horrified. But instead, Rosina looked quite wistful.

'Wish I'd been like that,' she said. 'Done something with my life that was straight and pure.'

The ship let out a long, sonorous hoot.

'We're moving – my God, we're off!' Rosina cried. 'I can't believe we're really going! Oh, at last – I can't keep this up! I shan't have any tears left!'

As they finally pulled away from the dock a silence fell over them all. Their light coats were pulled round them in the strong breeze, eyes narrowed against the glare, a row of hopefuls in a long line of emigrants leaving Liverpool bound for the far side of the world – for Australia.

Bye, Mom, Roy . . . Linda said in her head. It was too far to shout now. *I'll give your love to Muriel and Dickie, soon as I see them.*

She glanced along at the others. Rosina, beside her, hair taken up in a neat French pleat, despite her protests, still had tears running down her cheeks. Irene, dry-eyed, was still bright blonde, but instead of the ponytail her hair was blowing back in waves from her face as she leaned over, shielding the flame to light up a cigarette. She'd been waving to her brother and to her son Kevin and his wife, who'd come to see her off, but now they had moved too far away. And next in line was Linda's cousin Vivianne, a wholesome, peachy-faced nineteen-year-old, her mop of honey-coloured curls blown all over the place, cheeks pink from the wind. She was staring into the distance at the fading coastline and the cranes and gantries of the dock with her dreamy blue eyes.

'She's so like Hump was,' Rosina always said. She was plump, pretty and half the time seemed in a beautiful dream. But Vivianne was going to be the most crucial part of the business.

'They may not have taught her much at that posh school I forked out for,' Rosina sometimes said. 'But they didn't half teach her to sew.'

Vivianne seemed able to master anything that involved shaping and sewing fabrics and Rosina also had a natural flair for clothes. She'd had to pick up her sewing skills from her daughter though! With Linda's commercial head and training and Irene's shrewd ways with money and people, they were going to make this embryo business of theirs work when they got to Sydney all right! *Glad-Rags*, they called themselves. After years Linda had spent learning the ropes, slogging away in other people's firms, they were going to make it happen for themselves. Be their own bosses. Rosina's ambition was to make costumes for the stage as well.

'They have theatres in Sydney, don't they? We could do that, I know we could. Us girls together – we can do anything!'

Linda breathed in the sea air and gave a final, symbolic wave, as she could no longer see them, to Violet and Roy, to her old home.

Irene stubbed out her cigarette under her heel and threw it over the side.

'Ooh, I hate goodbyes. I know we'll see them all before too long but it's bloody awful, isn't it? Thank God that's all over. Let's go in and get a coffee, eh?'

Once the voyage was under way, the day sunny and calm, the ship fell into a slow, rolling rhythm. That first day seemed to last for ever, as they'd embarked early.

Late in the afternoon they were all sitting in one of the lounges, out of the tiring wind on deck, drinking cups of tea. Irene, already feeling queasy, was dozing. Vivianne was reading *Harper's*, paying careful attention to all the dress designs.

Linda got her book out, a love story she had saved for the voyage, but it lay unopened on her lap. Her head was too full of real life to escape into a story! She could tell that Rosina, sitting opposite her, was restless as well. She smoked one cigarette after another.

'What're you thinking about?' Linda asked.

Rosina smiled. 'Just having to pinch myself. I was

thinking about you, love, to tell you the truth. I mean look at you – twenty-two and gorgeous, with it all in front of you. You look fantastic, Lin.'

Linda blushed. 'Well – ta! So do you.'

She had dressed up a bit to begin the journey – it was a special occasion, after all! She had a red and white scarf over her hair to keep the wind from blowing it wild, and round white clip-on earrings with little tan dots on that reminded her of toadstools in a fairy story. Her dress was white with a full skirt and big red spots – she'd watched Vivianne make it for her – and red shoes. All in all it looked very striking with her dark colouring and a splash of red lipstick. Rosina's outfit was similar – in shades of emerald green and navy.

'I mean it, though,' Rosina said. 'You've come out like a flower and it's lovely to see. I was just thinking about that scruffy little kid who came to find me in Soho!'

Linda smiled fondly. 'Seems like a lifetime ago now – but thank God I did!'

Rosina looked serious. 'Yes – things were at their worst with Richie then. I'm surprised you caught me on a day when I didn't have a shiner on one eye or the other. I was in control back then – but only just. Irene kept trying to get me to see sense. I can't pick men, you know that.'

'Your blind spot.'

Rosina put her head on one side. 'You can talk.'

'I know – I'm keeping right away from blokes for the moment. It's only seeing Mom and Roy gives me some hope. And Joyce and Danny – I s'pose they're OK.'

Over the past few years she'd had a number of brief, unhappy affairs. She always seemed to go for men who told her how much they needed her and then fell into possessive depressions and wouldn't let her go. But she did go. Although they were bad experiences at the time, none of them had touched her anything like as deeply as Alan had. It was as if he had scorched her capacity to love into something charred and shrivelled.

Four months after she'd left him, when she was still working at Wimbush's and going to night school, Mrs Richards greeted her with tragic eyes when she came into work.

'I've got terrible news, Linda. That Alan Bray – *your* Alan – he's in hospital. Tried to, you know, finish himself. He took a whole lot of pills . . .'

Linda always felt as if Mrs Richards was reproaching her over Alan, as if everything that happened to him was her fault for leaving him. What did she think was the right thing to do? Stay with him and be dragged down into hell as well?

Alan lived, and recovered, she heard, from a distance. She only saw him once more, years later, in 1958 in a pub. By then the Beat craze had reached Birmingham properly and there were groups of teenagers of varying degrees of education 'dropping out' or putting on a dropping-out pose, wearing the jeans and sloppy clothes she and Alan had worn early on, disapproved of by their parents, reading poems by Allen Ginsberg and dreaming of taking off on the road like Jack Kerouac. She and Alan had been Beats before Beats really arrived, she saw. They'd wanted out of their families, wanted to be different, to talk philosophy, tear down what they saw around them. *Howl* was the Beats' favoured Allen Ginsberg book. Yes – that was it. They'd both felt like howling against all that was in their lives. Thing was – she didn't any more, not by the time she saw him again. There was Alan, in the pub with a group of them, no one she recognized, and she hoped he'd found somewhere to be at home. He didn't see her, or pretended not to. But by then she was working for a big firm, had started to take more pride in herself.

Rosina knew the full story of Alan, as Linda knew her aunt's history, a pattern she now wanted to 'clean up', as she put it. They'd become very close over the years. Linda had finally got her to come home to the family.

She didn't make it to Bessie's funeral, but within two months Clarence went to bed one night and never woke up.

'I s'pose Mom was his life-blood,' Violet said. 'Poor old Clarence. She was like a mom and a wife to him all in one.'

Rosina had always been fond of Clarence as a child. She'd been able to get round him with her charms. And by then she had gained courage. She arrived the day before the funeral and Linda and Violet went to meet her at the station.

'I know it's ridiculous, but I'm shaking,' Violet said as they waited on the platform. 'I mean, she's only my little sister!'

Of course it was Linda who recognized Rosina and Vivianne. She'd been down to see them all several times by then. Clark was already away training for his pilot's licence. Rosina looked terrified, though she was dressed up to the nines, hat and all, with a brim that dipped down half covering her face.

'Come on –' Linda took her arm. 'Mom's more scared than you are.'

She watched the two sisters look each other up and down under the dim station lights. And then the tears came, and they were in each other's arms.

Chapter Ninety

She hadn't packed the album in her suitcase, because she wanted to keep it close to her.

That night, in the cabin, she sat on her berth and looked through it. Irene was already asleep in the other bed. She was not enjoying the voyage.

They'd bought the Brownie camera for the wedding, to have more photographs than the few professional ones. Linda had made sure of getting pictures of everyone, and arranged them, square white-edged images, carefully on black sugar-paper pages. Though she had not known, back in 1957, that she would be moving so far away, now the album was something very precious.

The main wedding picture was in pride of place on the first page.

'I'm not going to wear white or any of that carry-on,' Violet said. 'It's not right, not with how things are – and at my age!'

She wore a neat little suit in a soft cornflower blue, and in that picture, as she stood with her arm linked with Roy's, their smiles echoed each other's. Linda didn't think she'd ever seen two people look happier. There was such joy there, in her mother's eyes, in Roy's gentle smile. They'd been through such a lot to get there, what with waiting for Roy's divorce as well. Love hard won, Linda thought. Maybe that was the answer: you had to wait for it, long and slow.

Deep in her memory somewhere, like an old forgotten dream, she thought she did remember Roy. There was something familiar about him. When she found out that Carol was his, was only her half-sister, everything fell into place. It made sense of how Dad had been with her, how their mom had somehow withheld her affection, as if out of fear of how obvious it would be that she was favouring the child of the man she truly loved.

She and Mom got on so much better now anyway – understood each other better.

'I should never've let your nana talk me into taking you out of that school,' Violet said to her one day. 'I'm sorry, love. I was in such a state at the time, in a panic. I had no idea how much it meant to you.'

Linda turned the pages of the album, smiling. Pictures of herself and Rosina, of Clark and Vivianne. Clarkie was a handsome devil all right, though surprisingly shy. There were Charlie and Gladys, Gladys's mouth open in the picture, no doubt nagging as usual. And Joyce and Danny and the kids, three little faces all dark-haired and like Danny! They'd stopped at three – so far as Joyce was concerned anyway. Two boys and a girl.

'Danny'd have a whole nestful if I let him,' she said. 'But I've had quite enough of it, stuck here in the house all the flaming time.'

As soon as Charlie was at school, to the consternation of her friends she found someone to look after the children and went back to Bird's, on the Dream Topping. The firm were building a new site near Banbury, and Joyce and Danny were full of the idea of going, if they could. They could get a nicer house and Danny could have his own business, not just work with his dad. They were going up in the world, Joyce said.

Those kids'll be grown by the time I see them again, Linda thought, looking at Joyce's little brood. And she felt a pang of regret.

But turning the page again, a grin spread across her face. There was Marigold, her swarthy face beaming out from under the brim of a huge pink hat, and swathed in an equally huge pink dress. Marigold was having a whale of a time.

Now both Bessie and Clarence were gone, she had the house in Spring Street all to herself. She'd gone and got herself a job in one of the new launderettes that were opening up, paying her own rent and free to do as she pleased. She'd bought a little gramophone and some records. And what's more, she had Freddie nicely under her thumb. They went out and about together, to the pubs and clubs, the races or a show now and then. Freddie bet on the horses, winning quite regularly. Once he took them down to Rhyl with his winnings. They were, to all intents and purposes, a couple. Except, Marigold adamantly declared, 'I ain't marrying him and he ain't moving in here. I've had enough of all that carry-on, fetching and carrying for everyone else. He can keep his slippers in his own house.'

'Good for you, girl,' Linda said to the picture. These days the thought of Marigold made her feel very cheerful.

Carol had been at the wedding, of course. It was before she went into the convent. In fact she hadn't mentioned it to anyone by then. Linda realized it had always been on her mind though, beckoning. Her sweet, pretty face smiled out of the photo. The resemblance to Roy was so strong, seemed so very obvious, now they knew. It had been a hell of a shock to Carol, of course, when she first heard. It took time to come to terms with it and both of them had to work hard to get to know one another. And there was Roy's Philip, of course, who came sometimes. His operation had not been so successful as hers, and she was able to relate to him better than anyone because of having polio in common.

She entered the Selly Park Convent as soon as she was sixteen, to 'try her vocation' as the sisters called it. To her joy, soon after she arrived, Sister Cathleen was appointed Novice Mistress. Carol explained to them that for six months she would be there as a postulant, to try it out and see if the life was really for her. Then there would be a year in the novitiate before her first temporary vows. Perpetual vows came after five years.

It was then that Roy became her advocate. Violet was completely horrified by the whole thing. She cursed Sister Cathleen high and low, saying she had always wanted to get her claws into Carol and the Selly Park Convent was a horrible creepy place and Carol might as well be walling herself up in her own tomb. Roy talked her round.

'It's what she really wants, love. You can see it in her. No one's forcing her, are they?'

'But it seems such a terrible waste,' Violet sobbed. 'My little girl in one of those dark, dreary places, praying all day or whatever they do. And she's so pretty!'

'Are you really sure about this, sis?' Linda asked her the night before she left. They sat side by side on her bed. Carol reached out and squeezed her hand.

'I've been sure for ages. I just know it's where I'm supposed to be. I think God chose me, what with the polio and everything. He gives us all something we're supposed to do. That's why I can walk again.'

She wanted to be a nurse and work at St Gerard's.

Nearly a year ago, they'd been to her clothing ceremony after she'd been in the convent for six months. The nine novices of that year all filed into the high Gothic chapel dressed in white, as brides. That set Violet off before they'd even started. Some of the other mothers were crying too, seeing their girls all with their heads bowed in the white veils.

'You were given me as a surprise,' Carol had said to her, trying to offer comfort. 'Now you're offering me back.'

Midway through the ceremony they all filed out again and returned dressed in their black novices' habits, Sister Cathleen walking behind them. It would have been hard not to be affected by the solemnity of it all, and Linda found tears running down her cheeks as well. But at the celebration tea afterwards, Carol looked radiant. You could tell she knew she was in the right place.

Linda closed the album and lay back on the narrow bed with the book clasped to her chest. So the great adventure was beginning! It wasn't all uncertain – Muriel and Dickie would be there to greet them in Sydney. That was almost like finding another mom and dad.

Violet had told her that Harry had dreamed of going to Australia when he was young, but of course he'd never made it. The thought of her father's life, his broken dreams and shattered health, made her feel very sad.

I'm going for you, Dad, as well as for myself, she told him in her thoughts. *We're going to make it work, Rosina and me.*

Lulled by the motion of the ship, she fell asleep, holding the images of her family in her arms as they sailed the ocean to their new world, and a future of lives and loves of which she could now only dream.